HARLEY MERLIN AND THE DETECTOR FIX

Harley Merlin 7

BELLA FORREST

ONE

Harley

I couldn't stop laughing. I held my stomach and roared with hysterics, tears streaming down my face. Finch, Jacob, and Ryann were staring at me like I'd lost my mind. And, to be honest, I wasn't entirely sure I hadn't. Everything seemed so hilariously absurd.

We were in the Smiths' house, having dropped right into their Día de los Muertos celebrations through a portal. No amount of tequila could get that to make sense to a human.

"Harley?" Ryann said, her voice filled with concern. "Do you need some water? Should you be lying down?"

I brushed the tears from my eyes. "I'm sorry, Ryann. I'm so sorry. I know this looks bad."

"What are you sorry for? For appearing out of nowhere?"

"I guess you could say that." I struggled to regain my composure, the impulse to collapse into laughter still jolting through my veins. It was a weird sensation, but then, it had been a weird week. The Smiths' front room felt so ridiculously normal after being stuck on Eris Island, and arriving in the middle of a barbecue felt even more bizarre.

"So you're saying I didn't imagine that?" Ryann eyed me curiously, and I couldn't look away. She wasn't stupid. There was no way I could explain away the fact that we'd literally exploded out of thin air and landed in the backyard. Mrs. Smith hadn't been fooled either, though she'd made a show of ignoring what had just happened. Honestly, I had no idea where to start with all of this.

I took a deep breath, steadying myself. "No, you didn't imagine that."

"You really just appeared out of nowhere?"

"Yeah, pretty much." I eyed Jacob, who was trying to look anywhere else but at me. He'd put us in this situation, but I understood why. He associated the Smiths' house with safety, and it had been the first place he'd thought of when we'd found ourselves under threat in the Bestiary. Echidna was gone, already stolen by Katherine, and his panic had led us here. It was sweet, in a way, though that didn't make it any less tricky.

"You want to explain how? Because unless Mom laced those cookies with something, I can't understand how the heck you could've done that," Ryann replied. "This isn't some FBI stuff, is it? I know you've been working on security, but we didn't just see something top secret, did we?" She sounded genuinely worried, and I couldn't blame her. This was beyond human comprehension. A few months ago, I'd have been just as baffled as she was. I mean, I *had* been.

"If you really want to know what's going on here, I need to warn you— once I start telling you, there'll be no going back." I gave Ryann a serious look. "It's going to change everything you ever thought you knew, and that's not an understatement."

Ryann's eyes widened. "What do you mean?"

"It involves things you couldn't even imagine."

She paused, before nodding slowly. "I want to know. If it involves you, I need to. This is all too crazy to figure out by myself, and a little enlightenment never hurt anyone, right?"

"Oh, boy," Finch muttered.

"I mean, curiosity did kill the cat, but it's up to you." I cast her a small smile, wishing we were somewhere else right now. Telling Ryann the truth would only put her in danger, but I couldn't see a way out of this without coming clean. The Smiths cared about me. Surely they would find some way to understand what had happened to me, without it making their minds implode? Ryann was definitely the easier party to tell the truth to, while the jury was still out on Mr. and Mrs. Smith. Although, since they were still out in the backyard, I didn't have to think about that right now.

"I want to know," Ryann replied.

"Well, don't say I didn't warn you. It's not going to make much sense, but if you keep an open mind, you might not feel like you've walked into the twilight zone." I sighed with reluctance. "You remember that day I told Mrs. Smith I'd joined the security services?"

Ryann nodded. "Yeah."

"That wasn't entirely true. You see, I met this guy named Wade, who I told you about on the phone," I continued. "He turned out to be something called a 'magical,' and he happened to figure out that I was one of them, too. It's basically being human, but with a few added... uh, abilities. I can bend elements to my will, and I can feel emotions in people, plus a few others." I didn't exactly have time to run through the whole list.

She gaped at me. "Like a witch?"

"Sort of, yeah." I hesitated, not knowing how much to give away. "Anyway, we're in a bit of trouble. There's this woman, who happens to be my real aunt, and she's pretty much the devil incarnate. We've been trying to take her down, to stop her from doing some terrible things, but that ended up getting us in trouble, too. We came here because we were running from that trouble, and from the people who want to see us locked up for the things we've done."

"What have you done?" Ryann asked, holding her breath.

"Nothing too bad. We just took steps to try and stop this woman, and it didn't quite work out. So the authorities are after us, even though we were only trying to do some good. It's all gotten kind of complicated, as you can probably tell." I gave a wry smile, just as Mr. and Mrs. Smith walked into the room. *Great, a bigger audience is exactly what I need right now.*

"Harley? Is everything okay?" Mrs. Smith jumped in with the first question, while Mr. Smith stood at her side, still wearing his novelty apron showing a skeleton with tassels where its nipples should've been. I almost burst out laughing again, but I didn't want to freak anyone else out.

Ryann turned to them, a half-amused expression on her face. "She was just telling me that she isn't working for the security services. Instead, she's actually a witch, and she's been trying to stop some crazy woman from doing some bad stuff, which is why you saw her tumble out of the sky with these two at her side. She's running from people who want to see her locked up."

The Smiths stared at me. I should've been used to it by now, but I didn't like to see that look of fear and confusion in their eyes. They'd taken care of me and let me into their family, and I'd kept these secrets from them. That didn't make me feel good, no matter how I tried to swing it.

I thought about using a dose of my reverse Empathy to try and stop them from losing it, but it didn't look like I'd need to—they were surprisingly calm, if a little bewildered by what the heck was going on. Still, I could always use it if I had to. Humans were much easier to manipulate than magicals. *Careful, you're starting to sound like Aunt Katie.* I shuddered at the thought.

"A witch?" Mrs. Smith said, frowning deeply.

"Well, we prefer the term 'magical,' but that's about the crux of it," I replied. "I can do things that humans can't. So can these two—they're magicals, as well. They're friends of mine. Well, Finch is actually my half-brother. He's the son of this crazy woman and my real dad, but he's on our side."

As I said that, Finch gave a half-wave, a tight smile on his face. Our time on the island had confirmed that he was rooting for our team now, my suspicions surrounding him more or less dispelled. He'd been alone with Katherine in her office, and he hadn't switched sides. That proved to me that he wasn't going anywhere anytime soon. He cared enough, and had changed enough, to really be one of us. I was proud of him for that—not that I was going to say anything about it to Finch himself. His ego didn't need it.

"We should probably wipe their memories if we get the chance," Finch whispered, close to my ear. "We can just pretend we're guests for the weekend. I've got a couple of memory modifiers in the old arsenal of magic. I can get it done; just say the word."

I shook my head. "They need to be aware of the risks, Finch, before they decide to let us hide out here. We can't ask that of them and just wipe their memories." If anything happened to them because I'd withheld this kind of intel, I'd never forgive myself. I didn't want to lie to them anymore.

"What did you say, Harley?" Mr. Smith furrowed his brow, his eyes fixed on Finch.

"I was just saying you deserve to know what's really going on here," I replied. Until we decided it was safe enough to make our next move, we were pretty much stuck here. All three of us were fugitives now, and we had to take kindness and protection wherever we could find it.

"That you are all… magicals, as you call yourselves?" Mr. Smith seemed to be having trouble saying the word. They weren't freaking out as much as I'd expected them to, but shock could work in strange ways.

Ryann shook her head. "Are you sure you're not in some other kind of trouble?"

"What do you mean?" I arched an eyebrow at her.

"You know… *trouble* trouble. Stuff you shouldn't be mixed up in. FBI stuff, like I said. I know you're saying that we saw exactly what we saw, but you're talking about something that just isn't possible. Magic isn't real."

Mrs. Smith nodded slowly. "It does seem quite outlandish, Harley. You know you can tell us anything, and we'll support you, but this doesn't seem real."

"Yeah, I mean, if it were true, why wouldn't you have said something to us before?" A note of anger lingered in Ryann's voice, which took me by surprise. She was always the most chilled out of the Smith family, but now she was looking at me with disappointment. I'd broken our sisterly code of telling each other everything.

I dipped my head. "We're not allowed to make ourselves known to humans, even the ones we care about. It's forbidden in the magical code of conduct, and my hands were tied. Now we're in a lot of danger, and we need help. And if that means telling you everything, then so be it. I'm done bowing to the rules of the magicals, especially as they want to see us locked up, when all we've done is try to help."

My own bitterness was edging into my voice, but I wanted the Smiths to see how angry I was, and just how close to the edge of peril we were. They needed to see our predicament in order to make the decision to either help us or kick us out. I wouldn't have held it against them if they'd chosen the latter.

Mr. Smith scratched his stubble in contemplation. "Are you sure this isn't FBI related? This is too much for me to wrap my head around."

"But you saw us appear in your backyard," Jacob chimed in, finding his voice. I knew how hard it must have been for him, to speak to the people who had cared about him so much, and yet remembered nothing of him. The cleanup crew had made sure they had no recollection of Jacob after the awful incident with the Ryder twins and their torment of the Smiths.

"Yes, and we're asking if it was some scientific experiment," Mrs. Smith said, glancing awkwardly at her husband. This was proving harder to get them to understand than I'd first thought.

Finch rolled his eyes. "Nope, no science. This is all magic." A moment later, his body bristled with bronze light, his form shifting into that of Ryann. He had on her exact clothes, his changed eyes holding her gaze. She gave a startled squeak and ducked behind her dad. Mr. and Mrs. Smith stared in abject horror, their mouths dropping open.

"What the—how are you doing that?" Ryann gripped her dad's arm as she watched Finch parade around in her body. He had her motions down to a fine art, his soft giggle coming out as the identical imitation of Ryann's. It was creeping me out, too.

"Enough, Finch." I shot him a warning look. The last thing we needed was for the Smiths to run out of here in terror. If we didn't have their protection, then we would be vulnerable, looking for somewhere to hide away from Levi, the SDC, and every authority he'd told about us by now.

He morphed back into his own body. "Killjoy."

"We don't need anyone losing their dinner over your little tricks."

He shrugged. "I just figured the easiest way to get these folks to see what we're about is by showing them." He pointed at the trembling figure of Mrs. Smith, smirking as he did so. "See, it's already working."

You're a freaking liability, Bro.

"It's not all as creepy as that, I promise," I said, trying to get the Smiths back on our side. "For example, I can do this." I lifted my palms and forged a ball of fire between them, passing it from hand to hand like a slinky and then sputtering it out. I lifted my palms again and let Chaos run through my veins, building a lasso of Telekinesis. Aiming it at the TV remote, I snatched it up off the sofa and waggled it in the air for a moment, before setting it back down.

Finch gave me a slow clap. "Wow, real awe-inspiring stuff."

Ryann and the Smiths, on the other hand, were staring at me in shock. Mr. Smith looked like he was about to keel over, while Mrs. Smith's jaw was pretty much on the floor. Showing my abilities had done nothing to stop her from shaking. Only Ryann seemed to be dealing with it in a less freaked-out way, but then, she'd always been good at acting cool in high-pressure situations. She called it "training for her future as a lawyer." And, right now, I was glad I wasn't about to send all three of them to the hospital with cardiac arrests.

I ignored Finch and pressed on, wanting to prove it was more normal than they thought. "I know this is probably hard to take in, but I just want to show you that magic is very real, though we all have different abilities. It's luck of the draw with this magical stuff."

"And some of us get luckier than others," Finch muttered. I'd never experienced sibling rivalry before, as Ryann and I had always had a supportive relationship. But Finch was still sour about the list of abilities at my disposal, while he only had Shapeshifting, Telekinesis, and a very weak Air power.

"Did you say this guy was your half-brother?" Ryann glowered at Finch.

I nodded. "His dad is my dad, and his mom… well, she's the nutcase we're trying to stop. But he's okay, for the most part."

"Aww, shucks." Sarcasm dripped from Finch's words, making me smile despite the awkward situation.

"He was tortured by his mother and sent to prison for being her cult drone." I smiled at him, knowing how much he'd hate that. "His mother tried to have him killed, which led to a recent change of heart, and he's been helping us out ever since."

Mr. Smith nodded, understanding starting to dawn on his face. "And this woman is a danger to the magicals?"

"Magicals and humans," I replied. "She wants to change the world so that the magicals are on top, and the humans will be forced to do their bidding. She's pure evil, and that's putting it lightly."

"Is Jacob related to you, as well?" Mrs. Smith kept her eyes on him, looking confused. It pained me to see her struggling, her mind whirring to try and remember him. Emotions flooded away from her—confusion, curiosity, and a flicker of sadness that no doubt stemmed from some unconscious memory.

I glanced back at him. "Not by blood, but he's definitely family to me." A small, sad smile tugged at Jacob's lips. "He's been under the care of my other aunt—one who isn't evil and vindictive—for a long time, so he's pretty much related to me by this point."

"Well then," Mrs. Smith said quietly, "if these two are friends and relatives of yours, then they're welcome here in our house. You know that we would do anything for you, Harley, and if you're in some sort of trouble, then it's our duty to keep you safe. You can stay here as long as you need to. All of you. As long as you're safe, we've done our job. That didn't stop when you headed out on your own, and it never will."

Unexpected tears sprang into my eyes. "Thank you. Thank you so much." It was a relief, after so much turmoil.

Mr. Smith nodded. "And if there's… uh, magic involved, then so be it. We'll just keep on pretending everything is normal." He put his arm around his wife's shoulders and gave her a loving squeeze. I'd forgotten how much I loved seeing the easy romance and affection between these two, who still adored one another after so many years of marriage. Even Finch seemed pleasantly affected by the sight of them, since he wasn't wise-cracking or making any vomiting sounds like he normally would.

Ryann smiled. "Hey, I'm all for coming through for you and your friends, I just wish you'd told us about all this before."

"I wish I could've," I replied. "The truth is, I didn't really have a label for what I was until a few months ago, and I was afraid you'd put me in a mental asylum or something. I hope you can forgive me for keeping it a secret."

"I'll think about it, if you tell us everything," Ryann said, with a note of excitement in her voice. "You've got no idea how cool it is to have a sister who can make fire in her hands!"

"Why don't we sit down and talk about it?" Mrs. Smith said. "As you can imagine, this is a lot to take in, and I'm sure it'll make more sense once we've heard the full story."

I nodded. "I'll tell you as much as I can."

"Okay, well, while you all are having your little reunion, Jacob and I have some business to attend to." There was a hint of envy in Finch's voice. I understood where he was coming from—I'd had at least two good years while I was growing up, but he'd had nothing. I'd been taken care of by my dad and my aunt when I was little, while he'd been shipped off to a stranger.

And, at the end of it all, I had the Smiths to protect me and keep me safe, even now. All Finch had ever known was cruelty and torment.

"What business?" Ryann shot him a cold look. I wanted to reassure her that Finch was a decent guy, but that would have to wait until we sat down to talk.

"Magic business," he replied, turning to me. "We're going to ward the crap out of the house and the yard while you have your therapy sesh. Might as well put ourselves to some use, right?"

"Thank you, Finch." I meant it. We might have been hiding out here, where nobody would think to look for us—because, I mean, who'd be crazy or dumb enough to hide in a human home?—but, still, we needed to keep our wits about us. We needed to protect the Smiths as much as they were protecting us, and we had to be careful about how we moved forward. Echidna had been taken, and we still needed to find a way to seek out Katherine and stop her before she could complete the fourth ritual. Not only that, but we had to do it without the SDC's resources, and without the authorities catching us.

It was becoming clearer and clearer that we might have to start looking toward the worst-case scenario: Katherine completing all these rituals and becoming a new Child of Chaos. Eris, in the flesh. If she couldn't be stopped, then we'd all be plunged into a bigger battle—one in which no one in the entire magical or human world was prepared to fight.

I always win. Those had been her exact words. If she was right, then we weren't just woefully unprepared... we were all doomed.

TWO

Harley

"So, as you can see, Katherine Shipton is a class-A bitch." I glanced shyly at Mrs. Smith. "Pardon my French." Dawn had just risen beyond the kitchen windows, without me even realizing that a whole night had passed.

I'd left pretty much nothing out, telling them everything that had happened to me since I left my job at the casino. It didn't feel wrong to fill them in on the whole shebang, since there was always the option of wiping their memories after we headed away from here.

Mr. Smith gave a low whistle. "You've really been through the wringer, kiddo."

"And I think this is as apt a time as any to call someone a class-A bitch." Mrs. Smith looked at me with tears in her eyes, her hands clasped around a mug of now-cold coffee. I'd never heard any kind of expletive come out of Mrs. Smith's mouth, and I wasn't sure whether to laugh or cry along with her. When I actually stopped to put everything into words and explain it all to the people I cared about who hadn't been involved, it really hit home just how much we'd done, and how painful it was that we kept missing the mark.

The only part that I'd left out was their interaction with the Ryder twins. I didn't know if reminding them of it would somehow bring the memories back, and I wanted to spare them from that. It still haunted me, how close to death Mrs. Smith had been when the Death by a Thousand Cuts had been cast on her, and I didn't want her to have to suffer through it all again. It was one good thing that the cleanup crew had done, as hurtful as it was for Jacob.

Finch and Jacob had come back in after warding the heck out of the house and backyard and had joined us at the table to listen to my story. Now and again, they'd chipped in with anecdotes of their own, though I noticed that Ryann still looked at Finch with an air of suspicion. Jacob, on the other hand, had become an instant hit with the Smiths.

"She sounds like a total psychopath," Ryann agreed. "Who even decides to just set up a cult? Seriously, who just wakes up one morning and thinks, 'Oh, I know what I'll do today—I'll try and take over the world and create a new order and make everyone bow down to me. And I'll make myself the leader because I think I'm totally awesome.' That woman must have a doozy of an ego."

I laughed. "You have no idea."

"She asked me if she should get herself a crown," Finch said, rubbing his eyes. "I told her it wouldn't fit on her fat head. Let's just hope that psychosis doesn't run in the family, eh?" He cast me a knowing look as he popped a pill into his hand and drank it down with his own mug of cold coffee. He still thought she was responsible for the state of his mental health, but there was no Katherine-made hex, only the lasting genetic effects of the blood she shared with him.

"You know, you remind me of Harley," Mrs. Smith said unexpectedly. "It's taken me some time to put my finger on it, but you have a very similar sense of humor. She's always had a dry sort of humor, and you have it, too."

He dipped his head as though he was embarrassed. "I like to think I'm funnier."

"You wish." I nudged him in the shoulder. On the other side of him, Jacob was half asleep in his chair, lolling against the backrest.

With every inside-joke and nostalgic story about the time I'd spent in this house, I'd seen a flicker of longing in Finch's eyes. It was a stronger version of what I'd seen earlier, now palpable despite my inability to read his emotions. I knew he would've liked to have spent time with a family like this, surrounded by kindness and happy domesticity. He'd never known what it was like to be normal and had clung to anything he could, mistaking manipulation for love because it was all he could get from Katherine.

I've been lucky. Looking back, I could be truly grateful for everything the Smiths had done for me. During my two years here, I hadn't always been easy to deal with. And yet, they'd never expected me to change who I was for the sake of a simpler life.

"Well, I don't know about you, but I'm famished." Mrs. Smith stood up. "How does breakfast sound?"

I grinned. "Delicious."

"Seconded," Finch said.

Jacob nodded. "Thirded."

"I'll get some coffee going," Ryann added, getting up to join her mom in the kitchen. I listened to the music of their familiar rhythm—the clink of spoons and mugs, alongside the sucking sound of the fridge opening and closing, and Mrs. Smith's soft humming. Jacob yawned, staring around the room as if he was looking at it for the first time.

"You must be tired." Mr. Smith put his hand on Jacob's shoulder.

"A little," Jacob admitted.

"How about you and I have a chat while we're waiting for some coffee, eh? Decaf, of course. You're probably all in need of a good rest, and I wouldn't want you too hyper to sleep."

Jacob smiled so wide it damn near broke my heart. "Sounds good."

I suddenly remembered what my mom had told me when I'd said goodbye—I had to hold on to the little things that would bring me joy, like drinking coffee around the table with the Smiths, or listening to the comforting rhythm of them in the kitchen, or reflecting on just how much I cared for the two boys who sat with me in this weird situation.

"We need to talk," Finch whispered to me.

"Sure. I could use some fresh air." I nodded toward the back door at the far side of the kitchen, then told the others, "We're just going to stretch our legs. Be back in a minute."

Mrs. Smith smiled at me. "Of course, sweetheart." Ever since I'd told her about the encounter with my mom's spirit, she'd been looking at me differently, as though her own heart was breaking for me. I didn't quite know how to deal with it, especially as I still hadn't come to terms with the finality of that moment. I wanted to tell Mrs. Smith that my mom would've been proud of her and the way she'd taken care of me, but every time I tried to say the words out loud, my throat ended up blocked by an uncomfortable lump.

I cast a look back at Jacob as we headed out of the back door and into the dusky light of the yard, smiling at the way he was leaning into Mr. Smith, the two of them chattering animatedly about some old film I'd never seen. This was Jacob's chance to speak more closely with the people who'd been stolen from him. And I could see just how badly he needed to be with these people. He was scared and worried, with an undercurrent of loneliness drifting out of him, and it was for good reason. We were in dire straits, plain and simple.

"Nice folks," Finch said, the moment the door closed behind us. "I can see why you never fell in with the wrong crowd. Mrs. Smith is like Mother freaking Theresa in Old Navy. And Mr. Smith might as well be Mr. Rogers. Ryann's decent, too, though I get the feeling she doesn't like me much. First impressions have never been my jam."

I laughed. "They're good people, and Ryann's just protective of me, that's all."

"The foster system is a pain in the ass for anyone, but you landed on your feet, Sis. Maybe Katherine isn't the only one with nine lives." He paused, as if he wanted to say more about it.

I shot him a warning look. "Less of the parallels, okay?"

"Hey, she's just proof that you can have the best upbringing money can buy and still end up a colossal asshat. You've both got this way of making things turn out in your favor. I just wonder what happens when two people like that want a different outcome on the same thing. Does the bread land butter-side down, or butter-side up?"

I chuckled. "Am I a cat or toast, now?"

"I can mix my metaphors all I like, thank you very much."

"Then I hope it lands my side up," I replied. "I haven't been as lucky in other things, but it's nice to know the Smiths have got my back. I would've wanted the same thing for you—a family like them, to show you the good side of things. You deserved it as much as I did." This was getting too soppy for either of us. "Still, that didn't happen, so I guess we have to make do with what we've got now."

He snorted. "At least I'm still here, right?"

"An eternal thorn in my side." I flashed him a grin, and he smiled back.

"How's the brand holding up?"

I pulled a sour face. "It itches like crazy. I've got no idea how to hide this from the others. I keep tugging my sleeve down so Jacob doesn't see, but it's only a matter of time before someone spots it."

"You should get a wrist cuff. A fancy one. Lots of bells and whistles. Hella sparkly."

"Wouldn't the idea be to take the attention *away* from the brand?"

He shrugged. "Might as well make it pretty."

"I just hate the thought of even having it."

He sat down on the garden bench and swung his legs like a kid. "I'm not too happy about having two, if that makes you feel any better."

I smiled as I sat down beside him. "It does, a little."

"Should I get some wrist cuffs too? People will just think it's some sibling thing."

"Matching ones?"

"So long as they're sparkly."

As I sat back against the bench and drank in the cool morning air, squidging my bare feet into the dew-soaked grass, I could almost imagine we weren't in danger. If I closed my eyes, I could pretend that we were just here at the Smiths', visiting them for no particular reason at all. The only trouble was the nagging voice in the back of my head, reminding me of the massive mess we'd gotten ourselves into.

"Penny for your thoughts." Finch offered me a knowing look.

"I don't know where we go from here," I replied. "Levi will have undoubtedly made a bunch of arrests. I hate thinking about my friends locked up somewhere, trying to defend themselves when he just won't listen. Plus, I don't even know what state the SDC is in right now. Who knows how far they've gotten with cleaning up the Bestiary? Being here, so far away from them... I feel helpless. And I hate that. I can't even use my phone to find out how everyone is. Levi probably still has it traced, and I can't risk using a phone booth. Do they even exist anymore?"

"Yes, but only use one if you want to wind up getting stabbed or having some drunk dude piss on you."

"I'm serious, Finch."

"So am I."

I had to laugh to stop myself from boiling over with anger and frustration. "Right now, I just need to find out what's going on at the SDC, before I lose my mind."

"And then there's Katherine to think about," he added. "She'll be on her merry way to ritual numero four by now, and we need to find her and stop her before she can complete it. Déjà vu, right?"

"Yeah, it's like the worst version of *Groundhog Day*."

He smiled. "The island will have moved by now, but I've got a list of other locations she's moved it to before. By the time we've searched each one, though, she'll probably be knee-deep in Echidna's entrails. We could try going back through Salem, but I doubt the Strainer will still be there."

I nodded. "I've been thinking the same thing. Katherine isn't stupid. She'll have covered all tracks leading back to the cult, now that she knows what we were up to and how we got into the cult in the first place."

"If we thought our trials were bad, just think about what she's going to put the next wave through. I'm picturing scanners everywhere and all Shapeshifters put on constant watch," Finch said. "She'll be so pissed that Tess managed to trick her for so long. She hates being outsmarted. It reminds her that she's human—that she makes mistakes, just like the rest of us."

"I keep forgetting she's human."

"Well, she won't be for much longer if we don't get our asses in gear."

I sighed. "We literally have no resources here. All we can do is hide. What good is that going to do us, in the long run? As long as we're here and she's out there, we're wasting valuable time. I doubt the members of the National Council have any more insight than we do. Nobody seems to know what to do about her, and that's pretty friggin' terrifying."

"It's a head-scratcher, I'll give you that."

"I'm not one for throwing in the towel, but I just don't know what to do. The only thing I'm certain of is that we have to stick together," I said.

"Careful, Harley. I might hurl into your foster parents' nice flowerbeds."

I smiled. "I mean it. We need to stick together. Not just you, me, and Jacob, but us and the rest of the Rag Team, too. We can't let Levi stick his oar in and stop us from getting to Katherine."

"So what's your plan? 'Cause I'm stumped."

"First, we need to find a way to get Wade's help." I'd been thinking about him nonstop ever since abandoning him in the SDC. He'd be one of the first on Levi's hit list. I needed to get him out of there and back by my side.

"Why am I not surprised? Wonderboy strikes again!"

I shot him a withering look. "Listen, Levi won't stop until you and I are in Purgatory for the rest of our lives, but I'm not about to let that moron win. He cares more about keeping up appearances and controlling me than stopping Katherine. Wade is our way back into the SDC."

Finch chuckled. "There she is—the firecracker of doom. Levi's problem is that he's stubborn enough to think that the National Council will just handle Katherine. But you're right, they're not doing enough to stop her. It's the blind leading the blind, the stupid leading the stupid."

I sat up straighter. "It's not going to be easy, but we can do this if we break it down into simple steps first. From there, we work through each task, one at a time."

Finch's eyes widened. "And here I was, thinking you never listened to a word I said."

"I do when you have something useful to say," I replied. His words to me on the island had made perfect sense—if you just focused on one thing at a time and moved through every mission in bite-sized chunks, anything was possible, even if it seemed like a mammoth task on the face of it.

"Okay, Captain, what's our first order of business?"

I smiled. "Find out what's going on at the SDC and figure out a way to reach Wade, if he isn't stuck in a cell somewhere. All of the comms will be heavily monitored, so we'll have to be sly about it."

Finch grinned like the devil he was. "You know me. Sly is my middle name. And I might know just the person who can help us with this. But, to get to them, we'll have to go outside, into the city."

Well, it wasn't as if we could hide here forever, right?

THREE

Jacob

The Smiths were the best. I had really missed this, just sitting around, drinking coffee, chatting and stuff. And Mrs. Smith's breakfasts... damn, they were good. I'd gotten so chubby last time. Her pesto sandwiches were killer.

"Is there a school at this coven you've been at?" Ryann asked. She looked dead tired. I probably did, too.

I took a massive bite of my sandwich. "Yeah."

"Do you like it? I know school can be a pain sometimes, but it's worth it in the end. I don't really know how the system works for magicals, but presumably you can go on to study somewhere else? Is that right?"

I shrugged. "I think so. And yeah, it's not too bad. I've got some friends and stuff, so it's okay."

"I bet you do." Mrs. Smith set another sandwich down for me. She rested her hand on my shoulder for a minute, and I nearly flinched. Touchy-feely stuff wasn't normal in the foster system. I was still getting used to it from the Rag Team, but I'd forgotten how easy it came to Mrs. Smith. She liked to fuss. And I didn't mind her fussing. The last place I'd been at, before the Smiths', there'd been none of this. It was dog eat dog. I was lucky to get a couple of Cheerios and a bit of spoiled milk before I got booted out to get on the bus for school.

"And what about girls, hm?" Mr. Smith smiled at me. That was taking me a while to get used to, too—people looking at me and not shouting. Isadora had been working on it with me. She called it my "recovery." I was glad Harley had turned up and all, but the days with Isadora had been cool. I wondered what a shrink would make of that. Momma's boy with no momma, probably. All twisted up inside, same as the rest of the kids like me.

Not Harley, though. She confused me. Like, I didn't get how she'd come through the same system and turned out the way she had. She should've been totally messed up. But she wasn't. She had her crap together, though she was always gearing up for a fight. That definitely came from the foster system. Fight or die—the foster motto.

"A few of my friends are girls," I replied. "They're cool."

"Nice boy like you, I'm surprised they aren't all swooning over you." Mrs. Smith chuckled.

"You're embarrassing the poor boy!" Mr. Smith put his arm around Mrs. Smith's waist. "Take no notice of her. If you've got yourself a girlfriend, then good for you. You don't have to tell us old farts about it. We probably wouldn't have a clue how you even date these days. Tinder, is it? Or Fumble?"

I snorted into my sandwich. "It's Bumble, I think. I don't use those things. I'm only sixteen."

"Fumble? My goodness!" Mrs. Smith howled with laughter. "You need to get your mind out of the gutter before you put Jacob off his breakfast."

"At least I don't know what it's called. You'd be worried if I did." Mr. Smith grinned. "See, when I met this delicious morsel, she was waiting at the bus stop on the corner of 41st Street. I was driving by in my new Mustang, and she caught my eye right away. I knew I had to speak to her, but the moment I pulled up to ask her if I could give her a ride, she hopped right onto the bus and disappeared. I kept going back to that bus stop every day, until I spotted her again. Two weeks, it was! But it was worth it. The moment I started talking to her, I knew she was the woman I was going to marry. We had our first date at the beach, and I won this little stuffed rabbit for her from a stall. We've still got it somewhere, don't we?"

Mrs. Smith nodded. "It's in our room, right by my vanity." She smiled playfully. "Shows how much attention you pay to the things in this house. I look at it every morning and remember that day. I can still smell the buttered popcorn and the cotton candy if I think about it. And what song was playing? Do you remember?"

"'Unchained Melody.'" He pulled her closer and started to sing it.

Ryann gave me an apologetic look. "You'll have to excuse them. They've been married twenty-five years, and they're still as sickeningly in love as the day they met."

"I don't mind it." I sipped my coffee. I'd heard the story before, but it was nice to get to know the Smiths all over again. The Ryder twins had taken this from me. It wasn't fair. None of it was. At least Mrs. Smith couldn't remember what had happened to her. I didn't like the idea of her having to deal with that.

"So, what can you do?" Ryann asked. "Harley and that boyband wannabe showed us what they can do. What's your trick?"

I smirked. "Boyband wannabe?"

"I haven't seen frosted tips since the Backstreet Boys."

"Sorry, I don't know who they are."

Ryann chuckled. "Ah, the youth of today." She took a sip of her coffee, while Mr. Smith provided the accompaniment with the rest of "Unchained Melody." Ryann looked like she might die of embarrassment, focusing on me to distract herself. "So, do you have any skills?"

I nodded. "Yeah, but I can't exactly show them to you. I mean, you've already kind of seen one of them."

"I have?"

"That portal outside... that was me. That's what I do." I stared into the mug. "I can sense out other magicals, too. I have an Earth ability to go with it, but it's not very strong."

Her jaw dropped. "*You* made that portal?"

"Yeah."

"That's insanely cool. Does that mean you can travel around wherever you want?"

I smiled. "In theory. I haven't had much chance lately, but I'd like to."

"Can you sense any magicalness in me?"

I put out my feelers, but nothing came back. "Afraid not. You're totally human."

"Ah well, can't blame a person for being curious." She offered me an encouraging look. "Can you do some of this Earth stuff? I'd like to see that."

"Uh… I guess so." Shyly, I reached out for a small herb box that sat on the breakfast bar. Putting my hands around it, I gathered Chaos into my palms. Feeding it into the soil, I watched as a thin stem spiraled up. It unfurled to reveal a violet daisy. I had to admit, it was some of my best work.

"That's super cool." She touched the petals, as if she didn't believe they were real.

"Not very practical, though." I shot her a shy grin.

She shrugged. "Not everything has to be. Plus, you can make freaking portals. I'd say that covers the practical side of things."

"I guess so."

As she continued to examine the flower, I tried to put myself back in this domestic picture. Could I ever come back to live here? I didn't even know if that'd be possible. Besides, I already had a new family, in a way. I belonged with Harley, Isadora, and the others. I belonged in the magical world, not this one, as nice as it was. Plus, there were a lot of wrongs that I wanted to right. Wrongs that my parents had committed, when they'd been in the cult. I owed it to their victims to make it right. I owed it to myself, too.

We'd already come a pretty long way. Harley was getting stronger. We were getting closer to stopping Katherine each time we tried. And even though I'd messed up here and there, I'd learned a lot, too. There was a lot about Portal-Opening that I still had to discover. It was a complicated ability, and I'd just scratched the surface. Isadora could do things I couldn't.

Yeah, I loved and missed the Smiths, but they had each other. They had their family already. I was better off with Harley and Isadora, folks who got me. Folks who understood where I was coming from.

Finch and Harley walked back in, looking excited.

"Thank God we missed the singing," Finch muttered. I shot him a dirty look. I knew Harley thought Finch was okay now, but I had to be wary.

Harley ignored him and looked at me. "Jacob, we need to go somewhere."

"Now?"

She nodded. "Yep, pick up a sandwich to go. We've got places to be."

Something was going on. Something big. Harley had that glint in her eye. She'd gotten her fighting spirit back, and I couldn't wait to see where it was going to lead.

FOUR

Harley

I balled my hands into fists at my sides, keeping my Chaos ready in case we needed it. After calling Dicky—my personal cab driver—to come and pick us up, and leaving the Smiths' house forty-five minutes ago, in pursuit of this mystery person who'd suddenly revved up Finch's enthusiasm engine, we'd entered sketchy territory. It was a world away from the pleasant, tree-lined streets and modern houses where the Smiths lived. Finch hadn't told us exactly where he was taking us, but I recognized the streets of Oak Park almost immediately.

Dicky's cab had dropped us off twelve blocks ago, and we'd been walking ever since, with Finch leading the way. San Diego had been my home for as long as I could remember, and I'd seen my fair share of its shadier underbellies. I'd spent six months in a house around here when I was twelve, and that had been long enough to know this neighborhood wasn't good news.

Then again, there were always good people, no matter where you went or where you came from. Just because a place had a bad reputation didn't mean that the folks who lived there were bad, and I'd learned a long time ago that it didn't serve anyone to judge a book by its cover. How Finch had come to know this place was slightly more unsettling, as I didn't like to think about Katherine having dealings with anyone in this neighborhood—readymade followers who didn't care about maiming or killing others, as long as it served them.

"I still don't get why we couldn't have just portaled to this place," Jacob muttered, as we walked along. I could feel his anxiety, his head snapping at the slightest sound. I didn't know a huge amount about Jacob's foster history, but I was pretty sure he'd endured his fair share of dodgy neighborhoods, too. He had that look in his eyes—that fight-or-flight flicker.

Finch rolled his eyes. "Because you'd blab, that's why."

"I wouldn't!"

"You can say that till you're blue in the face, but it won't change the facts. When people know about things, those things stop being secret. It's not that I want to keep this from you, since I'm *actively* taking you to this place, but it's happening on my terms. I want my contact to be safe, no matter what. And that means we're doing this the old-fashioned way." He flashed Jacob a grin. "Besides, it'll be good for your legs. With all that portaling, you'll start to forget how to walk."

"It's not like I'd tell anyone where I'd portaled to," Jacob said, clearly frustrated. To be honest, so was I, but if it gave us results, I'd follow Finch through every neighborhood on the West Coast.

"This way." Finch gestured down an alleyway, which veered off from a street filled with the melted husks of burnt-out cars and the jagged scars of smashed-in windows. On the farthest corner from where we stood, a cluster of dark-clothed figures gathered in a shop doorway, the glowing ember of a cigarette flashing every couple seconds like a warning beacon. Bluish smoke coiled in the air, and sharp laughter barked across the empty street toward us. This was one of the first signs of an infected neighborhood—the snickering gangs grouping together like diseased cells, ready to spread across the streets and houses and inhabitants until they engulfed everything.

I listened for the sound of anyone following us as we made our way down the alleyway, coming out into the street on the opposite side. Here, the houses looked like hollow shells of their former glory. The paint peeled from every exterior, the windows covered in panels of cardboard and duct tape, some of the front doors riddled with bullet holes.

"You want to tell us who this person is, since we're putting our lives on the line right now?" I whispered, as Finch got his bearings.

"She can help us. That's all you need to know."

"How can she help us? Who is she?" I pressed.

"She's an old friend."

I frowned at him. "She an old flame or something? Tell me it didn't end badly, and things aren't going to get thrown at your head."

"Men and women *can* just be friends, you know. As far as I know, nothing will get thrown at my head, but you can never really tell with this pal of mine. She's a law unto herself. Sucks when you don't know everything that's going on, doesn't it?" He flashed me a wry smile, before unleashing a dramatic sigh. "Fine, have another tidbit if you want to ruin your appetite for mystery and wonder. She's a rare magical. And she can help us peek inside the SDC—let us know what's going on in there, now that we're on the run. Happy now?"

"Ecstatic."

"I can't promise she'll be able to help us get in touch with Wonderboy, but she's got some tricks up her sleeve that surpass even my devious prowess." He grinned, clearly pleased that it was his plan that had gotten us out of our dead end. "She might be able to give us some pointers, at the very least."

"If she's rare, this friend of yours, how come she isn't working for Katherine in the cult?" Jacob asked.

Finch smiled. "This might blow your mind right out of your skull, but I didn't ship everyone I met off to Katherine's cult. Garrett, for example."

"Yeah, but Garrett isn't a rare magical," I said.

He faltered, his eyes widening. "You got me there."

"So, why *didn't* you give this rare magical up to Katherine?"

Finch shrugged. "I felt sorry for her, I guess. She's got this sick magical mother to take care of, and a little human half-sister she's crazy about. There's a lot to respect about her." He paused in thought. "I didn't want her mom and her little sister to get lost in the healthcare and foster systems if I told Katherine." He flashed me a look. "So, you see, I've had a conscience for a lot longer than you think."

"And what's her rare ability?" I pressed. It was crazy to think that barely a week ago the thought of Finch even having a conscience had been an abstract idea. But, now that I'd seen other sides of him, I could well believe that he'd protect someone because of his tenuous sense of morality.

"Kenzie is a Morph," Finch replied, his tone sullen.

"A Morph?" I remembered hearing about those—rare magicals who could put their consciousness into the mind of another creature and use it in whatever way they wanted to. "I guess, if your friend can find a creature small enough, that might give us a pretty good shot at peeking inside the SDC without being detected."

Finch nodded. "That's exactly what I was thinking. Great minds, Sis. Great minds."

"Yeah, I don't buy it," Jacob interjected.

"Don't buy what?" I glanced at him.

"That you didn't give this Kenzie girl up to Katherine because you 'felt sorry for her.' That doesn't sound like you at all. And you were totally under Katherine's spell before they sent you to prison. You'd have given her up. So what's the real reason?"

I smiled at Jacob. "He's got a point. This Finch is way different from the Finch you were before."

Finch lifted his hand to his heart. "You wound me."

"Spill, Finch." I folded my arms across my chest as we came to a halt outside a gated garden that led up to a dilapidated building. The grass in the garden had grown almost as tall as my waist, interspersed with broken bottles and about a thousand rusting soda cans. A feral cat peered at us from the top of a moldy, abandoned sofa, its yellow eyes flashing as its tail lashed to and fro.

Finch shrugged. "Morphs aren't as rare as other rare magicals. We had other potential profiles to fill the Morph spot. So Kenzie wasn't needed, not really. I let her slip through the cracks. I knew that, if she was taken, her mother and sister would be left alone. I really did feel sorry for her, and her family, so I kept her off the radar because I could."

I stared at him in disbelief. We weren't talking about more recent times here, after Adley's death had caused his change of heart. No, this was an evil, evil time in Finch's life. A time when he'd had no issue with leading missions that would get people killed, and he'd done whatever Katherine asked him to do, the moment she asked him to do it. The knowledge that he'd done something genuinely good, and pretty freaking empathetic, during those dark days was a total shock to the system.

"Well, well, well, looks like Jiminy Cricket was in the building *long* before you joined us, huh?" I nudged him in the shoulder.

"Yeah, because I was a totally soulless monster before Princess Harley came down from her shiny castle and gave me the gift of a conscience, right? You'd love it if that was true, wouldn't you?" he retorted. "Hero complex much?"

"I mean, it's not far off."

Jacob chuckled. "But, if he already had a conscience, then that means you weren't the one who brought that out of him."

"Way to take my crown, Jake." I offered him a playful smile, though Finch didn't seem amused at all.

"In case you've forgotten, *I* was the one who decided to change, and it hasn't all been halos and freaking cupcakes!" he snapped. "You've got no idea what I've given up, just so I can live with myself a bit easier. And I don't care what anyone else says, morality is overrated. End of story." His voice caught in his throat for a split second.

I frowned at him. "What have you given up?"

"Nothing… nothing. Forget I said anything." He dipped his head and pushed through the rusted, overgrown gate before I could press the subject. Still, it stuck with me. I thought back to his encounter with Katherine in her office, just him and her, and wondered if something had happened in there that might explain this weird behavior. Had she made him an offer, back there, that he'd refused for our sakes?

Jacob and I followed Finch toward the abandoned building, ducking through an iron door that was hanging half off its hinges. Inside, everything was pitch black. Putting up my palms, I forged a small ball of fire that could easily be mistaken for a match or a lighter, if anyone was secretly watching. Using its glow to see by, we crossed an empty concrete hall toward a narrow stairwell on the opposite side of the debris-ridden room. Everything was covered in graffiti tags, and the dank scent of pee and decay lingered around every corner as we mounted the stairs.

Finch stayed ahead of us, climbing the stairwell until he reached the very top floor. A long landing stretched out in front of us, and Finch headed straight for the nearest doorway. It was one of the only places in this building that still *had* a door, with the number "1" painted on the wall beside it. Finch knocked, the sound echoing through the empty structure like a gunshot, setting my teeth on edge. Beside me, I could feel Jacob shivering, his emotions slipping into terror.

A moment later, the door creaked open and something emerged from the shadows beyond. There was no face, no figure, only an object being pushed out into the hall. My heart leapt into my throat as a glint of dark metal reflected the glow of my fire. Two dark hollows of a double-barreled shotgun stared me right in the face.

FIVE

Harley

"Guess you never did learn any manners, huh?" Finch said dryly. "That any way to welcome an old friend?"

"Depends on the friend," a voice rasped out of the darkness. I tried to make out her face, but it was more or less impossible. Kenzie could see us, but we couldn't see her.

"I'd call the shotgun overkill."

The voice chuckled quietly. "I'd call it the right amount of kill, if this thing goes off in your face."

"Not thinking of squeezing the trigger on your old pal Finch, are you? I've gotten used to this mug, and I don't fancy having it rearranged."

"You haven't changed, have you?"

A figure stepped into the faint light cast by a blinking emergency bulb down the hall. Kenzie was younger than she sounded, with mocha-brown hair that had been scooped into a messy bun. Countless piercings sparkled in the gloom, from her earlobe to the top of her cartilage. She wore a cropped hoodie with an expletive emblazoned across the chest, a small tattoo of a pawprint appearing just above the waistline of her black jeans, which had so many rips in them that there was almost more skin than denim.

Finch smiled. "You sound disappointed."

"Not really. Leopards don't change their spots, and neither do assholes who promise to help a girl out and then leave without a word. Shame on me, right?" She flashed him a menacing grin. "Who're your buddies, anyway?" Kenzie eyed Jacob closely, the barrel of her shotgun swinging between my head and Finch's. It wasn't exactly the hopeful encounter I'd been expecting.

"How about you put down the shotgun, then we talk?" Finch replied.

"How about you make your intros before I really need to scratch this itchy trigger finger? It's driving me crazy, man." She held his gaze, with the shotgun pointed at me. I doubted she'd miss.

Finch put up his hands. "This is my half-sister, Harley. And this is Jacob, who's... well, it's a long story. He's pretty much Harley's family, which makes him almost my family."

Kenzie looked me dead in the eyes, which was preferable to a shotgun barrel. "You never said you had a sister. How do I know she's who you say she is? Trusting you has always been a game of chance with pretty low odds, Finch."

"I'm definitely his half-sister. Believe me, it's not something I'd lie about, no matter how much I might want to sometimes," I replied, trying to win her over. "His dad is my dad. Different moms. Which, if you know who Finch's mom is, is a huge relief for me. Even having that woman as my aunt is bad enough."

A small smile tugged at her lips. "She's the one who's been causing all this trouble on the magical world TV, right? I never knew why you never wanted me to get involved in her business. Funny what cats can hear when you think nobody's listening."

Finch stared at her. "That was you on the sofa?"

"Who else would it have been? I needed to stretch my legs, and I didn't feel like walking past those punks at the top of the street. At least if they throw stuff at me as a cat, I can sprint away. It's not as fun trapped in a human body." She grinned at him, her eyes flashing with amusement.

"Does this mean you'll put the gun down and let us in?" Finch paused. "And that, maybe, you forgive me for up and leaving?"

Kenzie laughed. "I'll put the gun down. Not sure about the forgiveness yet. You all should have some coffee. No offense, but the three of you look like crap. You only get bags like those two ways—panic or partying, sometimes both. Since none of you are smiling, I guess we can rule out partying." She turned and went inside, motioning for us to follow. "You in some sort of trouble?"

"You could say that," I muttered.

With the shotgun over her shoulder, Kenzie led us into the living room of what could loosely be described as an "apartment." A bed was pushed against the far side of the main room, with an anemic bulb flickering to reveal the sleeping, catatonic figure of an older woman. Meanwhile, in the center of the room, perched on a lawn chair that had seen better days, was a little girl with the same mocha-brown hair as Kenzie, scooping cereal from a cracked bowl. Her eyes were fixed on the TV, which was stacked on top of two dirty beer crates. A rerun of *SpongeBob* was playing on the screen. The picture got fuzzy whenever I took a step in the wrong direction, the kid flashing me an irritated look when it sputtered out for a second or two.

"I thought you said you were getting out of here?" Finch said, surveying the room. The wallpaper was peeling away from the damp walls, and patches of mold had taken over most of the corners in the apartment. How this place even had electricity and running water was beyond me.

Kenzie snorted. "With what dough, Finch? You see it growing on those shrubs in the garden out front?"

"Couldn't you have… borrowed some?"

"I was trying to keep myself *out* of trouble, remember? It hasn't been that long, has it? You losing your mind in your advancing years, buddy?" Kenzie stepped into the kitchen, which was nothing more than a tiny annex through a door to the left. I heard the clank of cups being yanked out of cupboards.

"So, you never made it out of here?" Finch seemed sad about it.

"Nope. Couldn't afford anywhere new, not with Mom's bills stacking up and having to keep Inez in food and clothes and stuff. Plus, this place is out of the way, it has no rent, and nobody comes knocking for anything after the dog attack a few months back."

I arched an eyebrow. "Dog attack?"

"Some guys were snooping, so I had to do something about 'em. Ten minutes locked in this building with a German Shepherd the size of a small bear, and they never came back again. They were just desperate to get out with everything intact."

"You did that?"

She nodded. "I borrowed a dog from one of the upscale neighborhoods near this job I was doing. Made sure those morons didn't get a good look at the poor thing when I Morphed for the attack, and then I took the dog back as if nothing had happened. The owners did ask why there were bits of leather jacket stuck in the dog's teeth, but I told them he'd gotten hold of a chew toy. Which, in a way, I guess he had."

"How's your mom doing?" Finch nodded to the older woman in the bed.

"She's getting worse," Kenzie said simply. "You know Alzheimer's. It's not really one of those things that gets better, dumbass."

"Hey, I was only trying to be polite."

My heart sank for this poor girl, who seemed to be barely scraping by. And, on top of it all, she had to watch her mom slowly lose her grasp on the world and everything in it.

"Isn't there some magical cure for Alzheimer's?" Jacob asked innocently.

Kenzie gave a cold laugh. "What, just wave a magic wand and it'll all go away? 'Fraid not. Even if it wasn't at an advanced stage, I wouldn't be able to fix it for her. Alzheimer's is a human disease with no magical cure. It sucks, but it's true."

"I thought she was making improvements, last time I saw you?" Finch chimed in.

"Nah, that was just a blip to give me hope. A nasty little trick that the mind plays, apparently, with Alzheimer's patients. Sometimes, they have total clarity for weeks, and then *bam!* They can't even lift their heads off their pillows. It's been more of the last one recently. Mom can't do much for herself anymore, so I take care of her."

"Couldn't you ask one of the covens to help so you don't have to do this by yourself?" I asked, realizing it was probably a stupid question. If Kenzie could have done anything to help her family, she would've. She seemed like that kind of girl.

Kenzie barked out a sour laugh. "I'd rather see all three of us die than reach out to one of those sick places," she snapped. "They shunned my mom for being a Mediocre. They forced her into being a Neutral, when she didn't want to be. She wanted to belong—she didn't want to be out on her own, without a coven to help her. They blocked her from all the support she could have used, and they didn't give a crap about any of it. They're snobs and idiots and bastards, and I hate every single one of them."

Finch gave a low whistle. "Looks like I'm not the only one who hasn't changed much. Sounds like you hate the covens even more than you did before."

"Damn straight."

"How come the covens haven't asked you to join them?" I asked, a light-bulb of curiosity going off in my head. "If you've got a rare ability, then it's pretty unlikely you're a Mediocre. The covens must have been falling over themselves to get at you."

Kenzie smiled victoriously. "They don't even know I exist. I got my Morph ability from my dad, but he died before he even knew my mom was pregnant, so he couldn't exactly pass the message on. And my mom... well, she was so upset about being shunned by those assholes that she didn't tell them I'd been born. She had me at a human hospital instead of a magical one and kept me hidden whenever anyone came calling for the twice-yearly 'Neutral checks.' It wasn't too hard. When I was really little, Mom would give me to one of the neighbors to look after for an hour, and when I got older, I just went for a walk when the inspectors were due and came back when it was safe. Piece of cake. Suckers. Bet they wish they could get their hands on an ability like this."

"I'm sorry about your dad," Jacob murmured. With his chin dipped to his chest, he scuffed his shoe against the floor. I could tell how uncomfortable he was, as a wave of sorrow washed over him. He was probably thinking about his own dad, and how they'd never met either.

"He was a hero," Kenzie replied, her chest swelling with pride. "I never met him, but Mom used to tell me stories about him all the time. She still does, but she doesn't exactly know she's telling stories. Sometimes, she thinks she's still living through those days, which makes it a bit weird, but... anyway, yeah, my dad was a hero."

"How so?" I scoured the room to find some sort of memory of him. A moment later, my eyes fixed on a photograph that had been put up high on a shelf on the back wall. It showed a man in military uniform, a beret tilted on the side of his head, a wide, toothy smile on his lips.

"He worked for the UM Peacekeepers. The White Berets. He died in a magical intervention in Iraq, got hit by a stray bullet, right through the heart," she explained, her voice never wavering. "Not even the strongest magical can dodge a sneaky bullet, not if it hits them there."

I frowned. "The UN Peacekeepers? United Nations?"

Kenzie shook her head. "UM Peacekeepers. United Magicals. They help out in warzones."

"I'm sorry to hear that."

Finch nodded. "Looks like we're all in the dead dad club. Fun times for everyone."

"You don't always have to say the first thing that comes into your head, you know," Jacob shot back. Finch looked at him in surprise. It wasn't very often that Jacob raised his voice to anyone, but I knew it would only spur Finch on to wind up Jacob even more. That was my half-brother to a T.

"No, but I *want* to." Finch grinned. "It keeps things fresh, since you never know what's going to come out. Keeps you on your toes."

"Was your dad part of a coven?" I ignored Finch, keeping my focus on Kenzie.

She nodded. "Yeah, he was a member of the SDC. Had been for years. He was one of their golden boys, and they'd accepted my mom, too, because of him. But when he died, they cast her out and made her become a Neutral instead of a coven member. That was almost worse, because they'd taken her in and then chucked her out like yesterday's trash."

"Alton Waterhouse wasn't in charge when that happened, was he?"

"Nah, it was some Halifax dude. Asshole, apparently. Colossal, gigantic asshole."

Finch opened his mouth.

"Not a word, Finch!" I snapped, and his face fell. "So, you've been living here with your mom and your sister ever since?"

"Yeah, I'd rather live under the radar than owe the SDC in any kind of way."

"What if we needed your help, but it involved the SDC?" I broached the subject, feeling increasingly dubious about Kenzie being an asset to us.

"I'd tell you to shove it up your—"

"What if I said I could give you something to help your mom if you do us a favor?" Finch cut in, grinning. I had no idea what he was talking about. We had no script to begin with, but he was probably improvising now.

"What kind of favor?" Her interest was definitely piqued, her eyes widening.

"Well, you asked us if we were in some kind of trouble, and that goes without saying—we're in a crapload of trouble," Finch went on. "You might be the only person who can help us. And, if you do, I can give you a rare talisman that'll help your mom. It won't fix her, but it'll improve her condition. I'm talking mental clarity, increased function, regained memory— enough so that you don't have to be by her side twenty-four seven. This thing is custom-made. It was meant as a gift, but its former owner died and the talisman got lost. And then along I came and snatched it up at a very reasonable price. I had no idea what I was going to do with it, but now I know."

What was Finch talking about? He hadn't mentioned any of this to me on the way over here, and while I understood his reluctance to reveal much about Kenzie, I couldn't get why he wouldn't have at least mentioned this rare artifact. Did it even exist? Was that why he hadn't said anything, because he knew I'd argue with him over the morality of lying about something like that? We couldn't offer Kenzie hope, if there was no talisman. That wasn't just immoral, it was downright cruel.

"What talisman?" Jacob said the words I wanted to.

Finch grinned. "I've got me a nice little stash of scrolls and thingamabobs in one of my secret hidey-holes. I'm something of a connoisseur when it comes to black market goods. I've collected stuff for years, most of it illegal, or forbidden, or NSFW. But I've picked up some awesome items in my time." He paused and looked back at Kenzie. "And you can have that talisman, if you help us. As soon as I get to my secret stash, it's yours. Only trouble is... it's inside the SDC. And we can't go there until we know what the fallout is like, and I can't go there until hell freezes over and elephants start talking Latin.

But… if you get us a glimpse of the SDC, then that talisman is yours, even if I have to get one of my minions to fetch it."

"Who're you calling a minion?" I asked.

"Not you—I mean the *other* minions. Wonderboy, et al." He smirked. "Speaking of which, we could also use your help getting in contact with a guy named Wade. Harley will give you all the details. She's obsessed with him."

For a long time, Kenzie said nothing. Instead, she just looked at Finch. "Why didn't you give me this talisman before, if you knew it would help my mom?" Her voice was thick with emotion when she finally broke the silence, her eyes glinting with anger and frustration. I felt for her. Even knowing that Finch had changed didn't alter some of the terrible decisions he'd made in the past. If he'd kept this talisman from her, then he'd have to add that to the list of things he needed to repent for.

Finch sighed. "Because I wasn't a very good person when I knew you before. I'm trying to change that." He paused, clearing his throat. "Back then, I thought that keeping you off Katherine's radar was courtesy enough. I was an ass. I'm sorry for that. But, right now, I need your help, and I'm more than happy to give you the talisman once I get to it. Back-scratching, and so forth. Tit for tat, in a purely PG-13 kinda way."

"Trying to change doesn't mean you have changed," Kenzie said.

I offered her an encouraging glance. "He's come a long way, I promise you."

"That doesn't mean I can trust him. I know you better than you think I do, Finch. You were ruthless back then. Who's to say you won't screw me out of that talisman after I've done what you want?" Her eyes burned, her tone cutting.

"That's the beauty of this plan," Finch replied, his confidence surprising me. "You'll be able to see for yourself. That talisman is in the SDC, and we want you to help us spy on the SDC. It's a win-win. I tell you where to find the talisman, and you help us out. Job's a good'un."

Kenzie paused. "I doubt I'll have time to find the talisman for myself, but I expect delivery of it as soon as possible."

"Does that mean what I think it means?" Finch waggled his eyebrows.

She sighed. "I swear to everything I have that I will put this shotgun square between your eyes and blow your brains out if you screw me over. Capiche?"

Finch chuckled. "Capiche."

"And you know I mean it. I'll Morph into a snake, find you, and make your life miserable." She narrowed her eyes at him and lashed out her tongue. "You don't stiff a Morph, Finch. You know that."

"Noted. Snaky surprise if I screw you over." He gave a mock salute, but at least she was smiling again. I wondered what sort of friendship these two had had, back in the days before he got hauled off to Purgatory. They didn't seem like the most obvious acquaintances, but it was clear that he cared about what happened to her and her family. Yet another surprising entry to add to Finch's lengthening list of good deeds.

"How does being a Morph work?" I wondered aloud. I'd heard about it a couple of times, but it'd never made absolute sense to me.

"Why don't you try piggybacking, see for yourself?" Finch replied.

I frowned. "Eh?"

"Since you're Miss Uber-Empath, why don't you try taking your power to the next level?" he explained. "I've got a nifty little spell you could use to see through Kenzie's eyes while she's out of her body. If you cling to her emotions, you should be able to hold on pretty tight and keep up some sort of bond while she's away."

"When did you turn into a cave of wonders for cool spells?" I hadn't forgotten the memory trick he'd pulled back at Eris Island, the spell he'd used to trap Tess by replaying her own words. It had scared and amazed me in equal measure, since I didn't know what else Finch had up his seemingly lengthy sleeves.

"You want to do this now?" Kenzie watched me curiously. No doubt she was as intrigued to find out what this spell of Finch's would do as I was.

I shrugged. "No time like the present."

"And we're on a pretty tight deadline," Jacob said, with a nervous smile.

"Fair enough. The sooner we do this, the sooner I get my talisman—right, Finch?" Kenzie gave him a pointed stare.

"Couldn't have put it better myself."

With that, Kenzie sat down on a rickety stool in the middle of the dingy kitchen. I stood behind her and put my palms on her temples, as per Finch's instructions about this piggybacking spell, with my fingers covering her eyes.

"What do I say?" I whispered to Finch.

"*Video in Oculis Vestris*," he replied. "It means, 'I see through your eyes.'"

Taking a deep breath, I repeated the words. "*Video in Oculis Vestris.*"

My vision went white, even though my eyes were still technically open. My body stiffened as if someone had lashed bungee cords around me and was pulling them tight. It was impossible to move. I had no choice but to stand right there, like a statue, and endure whatever came my way.

SIX

Harley

My vision exploded back into my head, massive objects appearing out of the hazy white of my former blindness. I tried to gasp as something wooden shot up in front of me, towering above like a skyscraper, but my voice wasn't attached to my body anymore. I couldn't make a sound.

I guess I'm just along for the ride, right?

Focusing on the weird landscape ahead of me, everything enormous and terrifying, I realized I wasn't in my body at all anymore. I was watching through the eyes of something scuttling across the filthy kitchen floor at an alarming speed, super close to the ground. Or rather, watching through Kenzie's eyes, who was, in turn, watching through the eyes of the creature whose body she'd Morphed into.

The creature hurried under the massive wooden structure, which I quickly realized was a chair leg, as we zipped past a pair of huge, human legs. *Kenzie...* Behind her, I saw myself, Finch, and Jacob, though they were all so high up that it was hard to make out any expression. I could only hear the rumble of their subtle movements as they fidgeted awkwardly, Jacob scuffing his foot against the cracked, ancient linoleum. The sound boomed in my ears like I was by the speakers at a rock concert, making me feel sorry for whatever this tiny creature was. Humans made a *lot* of noise. I guessed the creature Kenzie had Morphed into had to be a mouse, judging by the size and the speed. A rat would've been bigger.

The mouse rushed out of a hole in the wall, darting right through the cement and stone, before emerging into the dark hallway beyond. It barreled down the stairs without hesitation and leapt through a gap in the metal door of the main entrance, scurrying out onto the streets. Its head turned left and right to check that the cat was nowhere to be found, then sped away down the sidewalk.

Sticking to the shadows of the wall, it whizzed past the cluster of thugs who stood at the top of the street. The gang members were too busy laughing and talking to pay much attention to a single mouse, which gave me some hope that it might have the same effect inside the SDC. Although, in all my time inside the coven, I'd never actually seen a single creature that didn't belong to either the Bestiary or the Aquarium.

As the mouse sped onward, I started to feel a bit weird, like I was stuck in a mega-fast slideshow, with everything rushing past me at breakneck speed. At this height, nothing looked the way it did to a human. Even discarded soda cans were bigger than this mouse, which made the roaring rumble of car tires totally panic-inducing. They were like giant machines, growling past at a deafening volume.

It didn't actually feel like I was *in* the body of the mouse. That was Kenzie's territory. I was just piggybacking on her view, with everything flashing past me like a movie on fast-forward. Now and again, a sneaker or a boot came way too close for comfort. If I really focused, I could hear the ocean in the distance, the waves crashing against the coastline. For all of the world's frightening hugeness, there was something pretty freaking amazing about being mouse-sized.

The mouse sprinted past endless streets and packed markets. It twisted through town squares and wide boulevards, before it finally reached an expanse of towering greenery. I had no concept of how much time had passed, or how far we'd traveled, but it felt like I'd been on a lengthy journey.

The mouse bolted through the grass toward a huge building. The Fleet Science Center gleamed in the near distance. I couldn't wait to see what state the SDC was in, my heart hoping that it wouldn't be too bad, after the near miss of the Bestiary almost failing. Not being able to see my friends, or even speak to them, had been unbearable, especially knowing that Levi would be making their lives miserable.

About ten minutes later, we perched for a moment on the drop between the sidewalk and the road. Across the way, I could see the glass doors of the Fleet Science Center, with a steady stream of visitors coming in and out.

This is the part where you show me how to get in, Harley. Kenzie's mental voice bellowed into my mind, scaring the living daylights out of me. I could only imagine how my real body was reacting to the fright, back at the dingy apartment. *I'm guessing I can't just walk right in, even as a mouse. I mean, I'm all for trying everything once, but I'm not convinced I can chew my way through an interdimensional bubble.*

I wondered if Kenzie could hear what I was thinking, thanks to this attachment spell that Finch had given me. I focused on my thoughts, hoping it'd somehow increase the volume enough.

Head through the revolving doors and go across the entrance hall, I replied to her.

You should really be doing this in a GPS voice. Make it more authentic.

At the reception desk, take a right, and then make a left toward Kid City. Once you have reached your destination, you must go straight through Kid City, toward the service door at the back of the area. I tried to think in a more robotic voice. *That any better?*

She laughed in my head. *Perfect.*

Kenzie led us quickly across the slippery floor of the main foyer, the mouse's miniature claws clacking on the hard surface as it skittered toward the right-hand doors. The mouse darted between a narrow gap made by a kid on his way out and hurtled toward Kid City.

Even now, this route reminded me of my first visit to this place. Had I known how things would turn out, back then, I wondered if I'd have made the same decision to stay at the SDC. *Yeah, probably.* After all, Wade and my friends were here. My home was here, even if Levi was intent on kicking me out of the only place where I'd ever belonged. I wasn't about to lose everything I'd gained without a fight.

Reaching the service door at the back of Kid City, the mouse lingered in the short tunnel where the fire exit stood. Clambering up the doorframe, it clung to the door handle. I whispered the usual *Aperi Portam* spell, but nothing happened. In mouse form, it looked like we couldn't get into the SDC until someone from the coven opened this door. And there was no telling how long we'd be waiting here for that to happen.

Is there a time limit on your Morph ability? I asked Kenzie.

It's a stamina thing. I can hold out as long as I want to, or until I get really tired and can't hold the mental link anymore. Don't worry, I've got a good few hours in me.

The idea of waiting a couple of hours for someone to come by wasn't exactly comforting. If things were really bad inside the SDC, then Levi could well have introduced some kind of curfew or ban on leaving, which would mean that this was a totally wasted trip. But could he really hold an entire coven hostage? I hoped not.

After twenty minutes or so of anxious waiting, the mouse turned its head at the sound of footsteps approaching. To my huge relief, a familiar face was heading directly toward us, through the service tunnel. *Dylan... you beauty!*

Say what? Kenzie's voice echoed in my head.

This guy. He's a friend. Stay close to him, if you can.

Will do, she replied. As Dylan used the *Aperi Portam* spell on the fire exit door, the mouse sprinted after him in a burst of speed, keeping close to his heels as we entered the SDC. The sharp teeth of the bronzed dragon statues glinted down at us in the hallways of the SDC as we hurried along the marble floors. I knew the SDC was massive, but this was on a different scale entirely.

We following this dude? Kenzie asked.

Yeah, let's see where he goes.

The mouse kept to Dylan's heels, darting into the shadows whenever he looked down. Kenzie was good at this. It was almost like she had the mouse's senses too, prompting her to flit elsewhere if she thought she'd been spotted.

This place ain't too shabby, huh? I love me a dragon statue, she said. *It must've cost a fortune. Seriously, look at all the gold and bronze! I swear those eyes are rubies or something. Are they?*

I have no idea. Probably.

She gave a low whistle that ricocheted through my mind as we passed a set of windows that looked out on Balboa Park. *And those are some snazzy-ass curtains, man! The view ain't too bad, either.*

As we ran after Dylan, following him through hallway after hallway, I realized that not everything was back the way it had been. The destruction and devastation that the near failure of the Bestiary had caused was still pretty obvious, with a lot of the corridors still under reconstruction. Men and women were hard at work, letting Chaos flow from their palms as they rebuilt broken walls and windows. Everything that had been lost had to be replaced, though the same couldn't be said for the lives that had been stolen that day.

Before long, Dylan stopped outside one of the doors in the living quarters. I knew this door; I'd visited Tatyana here often enough, though probably not as much as I should've. Between breaking the Suppressor, fighting Katherine, making out with Wade, and trying not to get kicked out of the SDC, I hadn't paid as much attention to my friends as I'd wanted to. We were always pursuing some dangerous mission, which meant that spending any time just talking or hanging out had been almost impossible. I hoped that'd change, once we'd taken Katherine out.

Dylan knocked, and Tatyana answered a moment later. She glanced up and down the walkway that looked down on the magnolia trees below, before pulling Dylan inside, the mouse following after.

These two dating or what? Kenzie asked.

Yeah, they are.

Well, no offense, but I don't want to see anything I shouldn't be seeing, if you catch my drift. You sure this is a good idea?

I'm sure. I wasn't, but she didn't need to know that. Besides, there were plenty of places to hide if anything… odd happened.

The mouse edged closer to the plush cream loveseat at the far side of Tatyana's room, where my two friends had just sat down. Everything about Tatyana's living space was chic and sleek, just like her—the epitome of modernist, minimalist interior design. It made a stark contrast whenever I went to Santana's room, which was as vibrant and messy and colorful as she was, but they both had their charm, just like the women who lived there.

"Any luck with Henrietta?" Tatyana asked. *Henrietta who?*

Dylan shook his head. "She's got no idea where Imogene might be, or how to drop her a line. She was asking after Astrid, though—didn't know why she couldn't leave the SDC and come and speak with her, herself. She's worried, really worried. I tried explaining about Levi and stuff, but she didn't seem to know about any of it. I think Astrid's been trying to keep it quiet, but how much longer can we really keep quiet about it? He's got Alton in custody, for crying out loud. I'm just surprised nobody else has come along to deal with it, you know?"

I realized that this Henrietta person had to have something to do with Astrid, though I wasn't sure what. Were they related somehow? Astrid had always kept her family situation pretty hushed up, until we'd discovered that Alton was her dad. Whoever Henrietta was, it looked as though Astrid had been banned from leaving the SDC to go see her, which was why Dylan had gone instead.

Tatyana nodded. "He won't release Santana, either. Or Isadora. I tried to go and speak with him while you were out at Waterfront Park, but he wouldn't even see me. I've been putting together a case for why he should free them, but if he won't speak to me, what can I do about it? He is, quite possibly, the most stubborn individual I have ever encountered, which is made all the more annoying by the fact that he is a prize idiot."

Dylan smirked. "Did you at least make it to his office this time?"

"Almost. I was about halfway down the hallway before I was marched back to the living quarters." She shook her head. "That imbecile just won't listen to reason, from anyone. I know he would *have* to listen to Imogene, if she persuaded him to free the others. I'm certain we could convince her that we did what we did for the right reasons, and that she would demand that Levi change his mind. But if we can't reach her, then we're stuck. Levi simply shuts down the moment he hears anyone speaking in their favor."

"Tell me about it," Dylan muttered. "Where's everyone else?"

"They said something about meeting in the infirmary, but I don't know if they'll still be there. I wanted to wait until you got back."

"How does a walk sound?" Dylan smiled at Tatyana, whose face lit up. Dylan was just about the only person who could make Tatyana smile when everything around her was falling to pieces. They were so different, as people, and yet so very, very sweet as a couple. I wondered if that was what people saw when they looked at Wade and me. Or were we more similar than either of us would have admitted?

"Lead the way, handsome," Tatyana replied. They got up off the seat and headed for the door. The mouse scuttled after them, following them back down the stairs and past the magnolia trees, walking toward the infirmary.

SEVEN

Harley

Own these hallways, things were in a terrible state—worse than anywhere else in the coven. The interdimensional bubble shimmered, so it was still operational, but here it covered enormous stretches of blank, black nothingness. There were no walls, no windows, no furniture, no features, only impenetrable darkness to the right-hand side of the corridor we hurried down. I supposed nobody had fixed this section yet, but it was an eerie reminder of the fragility of this place. It was all fabricated from Chaos, and it could all be taken away again if the right nutjob decided to take down the Bestiary.

Trailing Tatyana and Dylan, we passed through the swinging doors of the infirmary. For the first time in a long time, the number of occupied beds outnumbered the empty beds, with patients languishing in various stages of recovery. I couldn't see them properly from the mouse's tiny height, but most of them had bandages and gauze covering unseen wounds. Tatyana and Dylan strode toward Krieger's office, the mouse hurtling in through the gap in the door before it swung shut behind them.

Inside, Wade, Astrid, Raffe, and Louella were already around Krieger's table. I was pretty surprised to see Raffe there too, since his dad was terrified of him and his djinn, but I guessed the djinn could be very persuasive when it wanted to be. It'd probably made a deal of some kind—"keep me out of a cell and I won't cause any trouble." That sort of thing.

Can we get a better view? I asked Kenzie.

Give me a minute. The mouse scurried toward the far workbench and scrambled up the leg, before skidding to a halt beside a brown glass jar filled with cotton balls. It gave a decent view of the others, my focus fixing on Wade for a moment. I'd missed that face of his. I wished I could jump across that instant and kiss him so hard, but I doubted he'd appreciate a smooch from a rodent, no matter how cute.

"Any news from my mom?" Astrid looked up eagerly, as Tatyana and Dylan took their seats. *Ah, so that's who Henrietta is.*

Dylan shook his head. "She doesn't know where Imogene might be. Doesn't know how to get hold of her, either. My guess is she's knee-deep in this Katherine stuff for the Cali Mage Council. I mean, it's not like Levi's going to go out of his way to help, is it? He's happy enough here, out of the way, where he doesn't actually have to do anything."

Wade scowled. "This place should be swarming with security magicals by now, though. The National Council should've sent people to investigate, but there's been nothing."

"You think he's deliberately keeping a lid on Echidna going missing?" Raffe's eyes glinted red.

Krieger nodded. "I would not be surprised. I've been baffled by the absence of National Council security. Even in our recent coven meeting, Levi didn't say anything about Echidna. It's as though he's pretending it never happened. O'Halloran and the rest of the security magicals have been strangely obedient in the face of so much devastation. They haven't asked a single question about Echidna either. I would have expected O'Halloran to say something, even if nobody else did."

I had to agree—O'Halloran wasn't a sheep. He did his duty, but he didn't follow blindly.

Wade pulled a sour face. "Something weird is going on here."

Great minds...

"Plus, Levi has all comms in and out of the coven monitored, so it's not like we can send word to anyone," Astrid added. "And you heard what Levi said—if any of us are caught discussing it, it's a one-way ticket to the same cells as Alton, Santana, and Isadora. Bellmore has already taken a leave of absence because of the stress of his reign, and I wouldn't be surprised if more follow suit. Though he'll probably threaten them again to make them stay."

This Levi guy sounds like a pain in the ass, Kenzie's voice echoed in my head.

Understatement of the century, I replied. If he was making threats like that, then he was running scared. Those weren't the actions of a man who wanted to help; they were the actions of a man who wanted to cover himself.

"Bellmore took a leave of absence?" Wade replied, surprised.

Astrid nodded. "She said it was due to personal health, but I'm pretty sure it has more to do with Levi. She left yesterday. Levi wasn't too happy about it, but she'd have filed a complaint against him if he'd denied her. Which I'm guessing he doesn't want. He doesn't seem to want any outsiders coming in."

"Good for her," Dylan muttered. "Wish I'd thought of that."

"I wouldn't be surprised if he promotes those threats to Purgatory, if people start working against him," Tatyana said. "He can't risk word getting out, but the question is—why? Why is he so intent on keeping this information about Echidna inside the SDC, and why doesn't he want outsiders coming in? Does he think he can resolve this himself?"

Wade snorted. "Not freaking likely."

"He said he's working covertly with the National Council and the new president," Raffe replied coldly. "I heard him talking with O'Halloran and the others this morning. He seems to think that revealing Echidna's disappearance to the public would just throw the magical world into unnecessary panic. I might even agree, if it wasn't my father spouting it. Most of what he says is BS, and I'm worried this might be, too."

Leonidas Levi, the king of bullcrap. The more I heard, the surer I was that he didn't care about anyone but himself, so it didn't seem likely that he was keeping quiet for the sake of the public.

"Katherine is too powerful now," Krieger added. "I suppose, while the higher-ups are figuring out a way to stop her, they don't want magicals losing their minds because Echidna is missing. But I assumed the public has been largely unaware of the rituals. They wouldn't understand the importance of Echidna being missing."

"Unless that's been leaked," Louella said. "Or they're worried it might be leaked. All it would take would be one post on social media, and that'd be it.

Mass panic. Even if news of Echidna being missing didn't get out, the news that the Bestiary nearly failed might. That'd be enough to freak people out."

Raffe nodded. "And you say you don't think it's likely that my father is trying to resolve the issue by himself, but you don't know him the way I do. He might be trying to get to Echidna first, using a small team of his own handpicked security personnel so he can get all the praise when it's all done and dusted. Right now, he really needs a win, or he's going to lose this position, as well as any respect he's managed to gain over the years. The Cali Mage Council would throw him to the wolves if it got out that Echidna was taken on his watch, so maybe that's why he's keeping quiet about it."

There seemed to be a number of reasons for Levi keeping quiet about Echidna, and it was hard to tell which one might be the real reason. It could well have been a mixture, with the most self-serving options probably being the closest to the truth.

"That sounds plausible, knowing Levi," Tatyana said. "He was supposed to be getting this place in order, but instead it'll look like he was responsible for the magical world's biggest catastrophe in recent history. He'd probably lose his seat on the Mage Council, too."

Dylan frowned. "So he stands to lose a ton if people know Echidna is gone. They'll know it means Katherine's on ritual number four and gaining ground. They'll be looking for a scapegoat, and he'd make the perfect one."

"That doesn't mean we have to just accept the rules that Levi is laying down. When have we ever done that before?" Wade eyed the present members of the Rag Team. "If we let him cover this up for his own benefit, then we're accessories to his stupidity. There's got to be something we can do about Katherine, even without access to unmonitored comms."

That's my boy.

Krieger smiled. "I can think of one way we might be useful."

"Go on..."

"Well, I'm very close to completing the magical detector to an operational degree. Once I've made a few final tweaks, we can use the bloodied rag that Finch left and find Katherine with it." He paused, his brow furrowing. "The only trouble is, I fear I may need Jacob's help in order to use it. I took a sample of his Chaos, yes, but more will certainly be required for such a task."

Dylan groaned. "We don't know where he is, Doc."

"All we know is that he's with Harley and Finch, but there's been no sign of any of them," Tatyana added.

Astrid nodded reluctantly. "I've been listening out as much as I can, and I know for sure that Levi has sent security magicals to search for them, but they haven't come up with anything so far. It's radio silence, as far as they're concerned. So, either they're really, really, really, far away by now, or they've found a good hiding place and are keeping their heads down."

I'm right here! Obviously, I couldn't make myself known to them, but it felt weird to be so close and not be able to say a word.

"Do you think they might be at the Smiths'?" Louella asked. "Jacob talks about them a bunch. If he was in a panic, he might have gone to the first place he could think of."

Astrid smiled. "I thought about that and changed the address in the coven system. If they go looking, they won't find the right house. Since we've had a new influx of security magicals, they shouldn't be able to tell the difference. Even if they can, it'll give me time to come up with something else. So far, no details have been sent there. I guess they don't think there's any way that Harley would go straight to people she cares about."

I hoped it would be enough to deter the security magicals from bothering the Smiths, though they'd already promised to cover for us if anyone came knocking. Ryann was a tough nut to crack, especially when she went into future-lawyer mode. She'd throw the book at them... literally, if they tried to push their luck.

"Do you think it might be possible to get Jacob back?" Krieger didn't sound too hopeful.

Louella's eyes widened. "If you went to Levi and explained what you need Jacob for, he might be able to arrange some kind of amnesty for him. You know, maybe say that he can be off the hook if he works exclusively for you on the magical detector. Then, Levi could get the word out, somehow, and that might be enough to bring Jacob home."

As I listened to them discuss what they could do to get Jacob back, Wade's gaze darted toward the mouse. We were tucked behind the glass jar, but I got the feeling he was looking straight at me. His stare didn't shift. Before I could say a word to Kenzie, to get her to stay put, she made the mouse scurry out from its hiding place and go behind a metal box that provided more cover.

As the mouse peered out from behind it, we saw that Wade's gaze had followed. His brow furrowed slowly. I wished I could've transferred some of my feelings over to him, to let him know I was right there, but my abilities didn't work here. I was just a passenger—a distant visitor, able to observe and nothing more.

He mean something to you? Kenzie asked.

Yeah, was all I replied.

I can get the mouse to wave, if you want?

I chuckled. *I don't want to freak him out.*

Suit yourself.

"So, is that our next order of business?" Tatyana asked. "Finding Jacob?"

Raffe nodded. "That and helping O'Halloran get Isadora and Alton out of jail. He might not be saying anything about Echidna going missing, but O'Halloran is being pretty vocal about them being locked up. He wants Santana out, too, same as the rest of us, but the chances of her being released are slimmer than ever."

"Levi thinks he has the upper hand by keeping her behind bars, the idiot," Tatyana said.

A grimace twisted up the corners of Raffe's mouth, his eyes flickering red. "Yeah, he doesn't seem to get that me and the djinn can be a team when we want to be. And neither of us is going to stop until Santana is out."

Wade sighed, drawing my attention back to him. "I'm going to head over to Waterfront Park for a little bit, see if anyone's talking about Imogene. Even with this level of urgency, Levi might not be willing to offer amnesty to Jacob. But Imogene would, for sure."

Astrid nodded enthusiastically. "She might be just the ally we need right now."

Wade stood and cast a subtle glance at the mouse. "Plus, I could do with a couple of hours away from this place. The espresso at Shiloh's Café will help. Just don't tell Levi—or anyone else—where I've gone, okay? I don't want to have to deal with anyone right now."

To my surprise, he left his phone on the table, walking away before anyone could stop him. I supposed, with me MIA, the rest of the Rag Team could understand the need for a few hours of privacy. I realized that this was my chance to reach out to him safely, without being caught by Levi's new monitoring systems. *I need to get to Shiloh's Café ASAP!*

"Do you think it's a good idea for him to be out on his own, at a time like this?" Louella asked quietly.

Raffe shrugged. "Levi's too busy interrogating Santana, Isadora, and Alton to bother with him right now. Or any of us, for that matter. My father won't even notice he's gone, and if he does, I'm sure Wade will tell him where he can stuff it."

"But what about security?" Louella sounded worried.

"Wade will be able to give security the slip and head into Waterfront Park, no problem," Dylan replied.

Tatyana nodded. "There are benefits to this kind of disarray, even if they don't benefit everyone."

I wondered if maybe Wade really had sensed me here. Was that why he'd headed to Shiloh's Café in such a hurry, or was it purely coincidence? I couldn't tell. Anyway, it didn't matter, because the outcome was the same: I knew where I had to go to speak to him, face-to-face. Plus, I'd need to get Jacob back into the coven, with Wade's help, so he could get started on the magical detector tweaks and we could get a move on finding Katherine.

Can we snap out of it? I asked Kenzie.

No problem. This mouse is going to be so confused when I Morph out. She'd barely replied when I came rushing back into the dingy kitchen in a blinding flash of white. I blinked a couple of times to clear my vision of the milky haze, only to find Jacob and Finch eyeing me curiously.

"Everything okay? You getting a craving for cheese?" Finch broke the silence.

I smiled at them both. "No craving for cheese, but we need to talk. Now."

EIGHT

Jacob

fter recapping the conversations they'd overheard during their mousecapades, with Kenzie giving us a moment alone in the kitchen, Harley looked at me. She had that sad expression on her face, the one that said, *"Please, Jacob."* But how could I do what she was asking? Like, seriously? It was suicide. Or stupidity. One trip in a mouse and her brain had shrunk to the size of a pea. She had to be off her rocker to even suggest I go back to the SDC.

"Krieger needs you," she said again, quietly. "He'll protect you from Levi, I know he will. And the thing is... well, the magical detector won't work without you, and we've got to find Katherine before she can get ritual four done. I know it's a lot to ask, and I know you probably don't want to go back, but it may be our only chance of getting to Echidna before the clock runs out on her."

"Are you crazy?" I stared at her.

"I wish I was, but I'm deadly serious."

Finch smirked. "You sure sound insane to me, Sis. I'll fetch my spare straitjacket if you'd like."

"Jake is needed there," Harley insisted. "It's the only way to put that rag you snatched to good use, Finch. I know it sounds bonkers, believe me, I do, but they really want to have him back so he can help them progress with the detector. Without him, they're treading water, trying to figure out what else they can do. And they don't have any other options right now. End of." She turned back to me. "I wouldn't ask if it wasn't completely necessary, Jake. You know I wouldn't."

"Levi will have my head on a stake," I shot back. I'd been under his nose as Tarver for ages, and he hadn't noticed. He didn't like being made to look stupid. I wasn't sure he'd gotten over it, or if he ever would.

"No, he won't," Harley replied. "Do you really think Levi won't be frothing at the mouth to have that thing working? He'd happily keep your head off any pikes if you can help get it operational. Then, he can be 'the director responsible for bringing the magical detector into existence.' He can bathe in applause to his heart's content, and soak up all the congratulations, even though he didn't do anything toward it. Plus, you can be our eyes and ears in the SDC while we tackle the Katherine problem from a different angle. This way, we're covering all bases. Plus, if we do this with Levi knowing you're there, we're not putting anyone else at risk of being an accessory and ending up in a cell."

"This some sort of math lesson?" Finch muttered.

Harley flashed him a smug look. "Divide and conquer. Simple as."

You sound more like him each day. People had quirks. Harley and Finch weren't any different. Finch had started to say stuff like "end of" or "period" or "simple as," and Harley had started using similar endings in her sentences, around the same time. It wasn't something most folks would notice, but I'd always picked up on little things like that. It was like a person's signature, almost. They mimicked people they were close to, almost out of habit.

"So, you and me are working together again?" Finch arched an eyebrow.

"Afraid so," she replied.

"Great. That worked out so well the last time." He pulled a face. I knew he was secretly pleased. Harley was ace. It didn't hurt to be on her team. Yeah, she was headstrong, but she had confidence because of it. That was a cool thing to follow.

"We need to work like this, on different teams." She folded her arms across her chest.

Finch grinned. "What, so we've got the Goody-Two-Shoes Gang and Double Trouble?"

"Or the Rag Team and Sub-Team One." She shook her head.

"Why do we have to be 'sub' team?"

"Does it really matter what we're called?" she asked.

He shrugged. "It might, since we'll probably be using codenames from now on."

"How about you pick names from King Arthur's legends or something?" I suggested. I expected a sour look from Finch, but he and Harley seemed pleased by the idea. "You know, since you're both technically Merlins."

"Let's have Gwen and Percy," Harley said. "Guinevere for me. Percival for you, Finch."

"Wasn't he the useless one?"

Harley grinned. "No, but he was the one who wanted to search for the Holy Grail all by himself, thinking he didn't need anyone else's help."

"My kind of knight. He was probably right," Finch murmured. "If we're using codenames, we'll probably need to use burner cellphones—that might be our only way to communicate with Wade and the others, from here on out. If there's one thing humans are *really* good at, it's staying under the radar. We'll need to get down to a human level to stand a chance of keeping in touch with the GTSG."

Harley frowned. "GTSG?"

"Goody-Two-Shoes Gang," I replied, with a chuckle.

"See, he gets it!" Finch smacked me hard on the back. I almost staggered forward. It was the closest thing to a hug he'd ever given me. Did this mean he was warming to me? Doubtful.

"So, I can't stay here with you?" I looked to Harley. She had the final say here.

She shook her head and smiled. She and Isadora both had this way of staring at you that made you feel like you were the only person in the room. Not in a weird way but in a nice, calming way. The way a sister or a mother might look at you.

"How am I supposed to convince Levi not to lock me up?" I tried not to sound as worried as I felt. Years in the foster system had toughened me up, but I still had some softer bits left—bits that weren't as tough. One of those bits was doing things totally alone. I reacted the same way when I had to speak to someone on the phone. I didn't like it. It put me on edge.

Harley gave me a reassuring smile. She probably sensed my unease with her Empathy. "It'll be okay, Jake. You head back to the SDC in a total frazzle, like you've just escaped. You play the victim like a pro, and say you were coerced into helping us. Make sure Krieger is in the room when you speak to Levi."

"How do I do that— how do I play the victim?" I asked. To be honest, I wasn't that great of a liar.

"Say we threatened you or something. Make it good, but believable. As in, don't go *too* big. And then, plead forgiveness like your life depends on it. While you're doing that, Krieger will most likely intervene on your behalf and make Levi see why he needs you at the SDC. From there, you keep us in the loop as often as you can—safely—using a burner cell. We need to know what Levi is up to, and what's going on at the SDC. And how you and the others are, of course. We need eyes in the coven, and all the help we can get while we're on the outside."

I frowned. "What if Levi asks me to spill the beans about where you are?"

"Give him a fake location." Finch's tone made me feel like a dumbass. "Tell him whatever. He'll send dudes out to find us and find nothing. He'll get bored of asking, eventually. And he won't be able to do anything to you, torture-wise, because you're the sacrificial lamb for this magical detector. You're untouchable, my friend. You might just be the only kid who can lie to him without getting sent to Purgatory."

"And what about you?" I looked back at Harley. "What will you do? Will you lie low for a bit?"

She shook her head. "While you head back to the SDC, I'm going to go see Wade at Waterfront Park. Finch is coming, too."

"I am? Since when?" Finch shot her a look. It was all for show. Now that they were closer, I knew Finch would never let Harley go anywhere on her own. He cared too much. I almost said so out loud, then remembered his last few threats. I probably didn't have too many lives left.

"Since now," she replied. "I need backup, in case anyone followed Wade. You can Shapeshift into someone else, and I'll keep myself covered up, incognito-style. Black hood, shades, that sort of thing."

"Oh yeah, *real* inconspicuous. Because the people creeping around in shades and hoodies never look like they're up to something sketchy." Finch chuckled coldly.

"I haven't made my final outfit choice, Finch, but you get the gist. Anyway, this is for Jake's benefit, not yours," she said. "Krieger is still worried that the magical detector might not work, so we'll need as much help as we can get, since we're the only two constantly out in the field. Essentially, we have to be the contingency plan. We need a backup."

"I thought I was your backup?" Finch smirked.

She sighed dramatically. "We need a backup in case the magical detector doesn't work, even with your help." She glanced at me. "Finch and I are going to come up with a way to find Katherine without the detector, so we're not completely sitting ducks if it doesn't work. The only way to stop Katherine right now is to rescue Echidna, and we can't get to the Mother of Monsters without finding Katherine. Chances are, they're in the same place. We can't fight that bitch head on, but we can get in her way."

"How are we going to find Katherine, though?" I was curious. If the National Council couldn't find her, why did she think she could? I didn't mean it in a horrible way. I was genuinely intrigued. Harley always had unusual ideas. I got the feeling this was going to be the same. Another one of her strange, yet useful plans.

"I was thinking my parents' Grimoire might help find her," she replied. She didn't disappoint. "There was this 'finding hidden things' spell inside, the last time I looked. It was probably called something cooler than that, but that was the essence of it. It found missing things. Not like an ordinary tracker spell, but something more powerful. It being more powerful probably means it's more precise, too, which will be useful when it comes to Katherine."

Finch scowled. "You love your tracker spells, don't you?"

"Does it still sting, Bro?" She smiled back at him.

"Right in the pride, Sis. Right in the pride."

"I don't get it." I looked between them.

Harley laughed. "Finch got caught after a tracking spell flagged him down. He'd have gotten away with it, too, if it wasn't for that pesky Rag Team."

"Lap it up, Sis. We all make mistakes. At least I'm repenting now." He paused. "And how's this for a slice of forgiveness—it'll save me a couple of

Hail Marys at least. I remember, ages ago, Katherine being so pissed off that she couldn't get her hands on her sister's Grimoire. She was desperate for it, for some reason. I don't know if she wanted to destroy it, or what, but she wanted that thing like it was a Furby in the nineties, with Christmas a couple days away. She could never get into the New York Coven to retrieve it, and it's since been the one thing she hasn't been able to swipe, though I'm guessing her desire for it hasn't gone away."

"Did she mention anything in it that she might have wanted, specifically?" Harley's eyes had widened.

Finch shook his head. "She just wanted the whole thing. She wanted to look through it. I don't know if there was something in particular she was after."

Harley tapped her chin. "Does Katherine have the same ability as me? Can she read unfinished Grimoires?"

"Not that I know of, and I doubt she'd have kept that secret from me. You know how she loves to brag."

"Well, if there's something in that Grimoire I might've missed that Katherine wants, then it might be something that can be used against her. She's got to have a weakness, right? Nobody is invincible. Not even Children of Chaos are, since they can be challenged." Harley nodded, as if to herself. "Yeah, I need to get that Grimoire. But, for that, we'll need some serious manpower."

"Let me guess… Wonderboy?" Finch rolled his eyes. But there was a quiet fondness in his voice. Wade was important to Harley. So Wade was important to Finch by association.

"You think he'll be able to help?" I asked. "He might not want to cause any trouble, with all this Levi stuff going on."

She smiled. "He'll help, no matter what."

"You're probably right." I'd seen Wade and Harley together. He'd have done anything for her. Danger and trouble weren't obstacles. He helped her whenever she needed it, and she did the same for him. That was why they worked as a couple, even though they were shy about it. They didn't need to be, since everyone knew. They were super obvious.

"So, are you really okay with this?" Harley held my gaze. She was giving me one more chance to back out, if I wanted.

"Yeah, I'll go." To be honest, I didn't have a good feeling about this. But I understood there wasn't another way. Not a better one, at least. "You'll be careful, right? You won't do anything too risky for this Grimoire?"

"We'll do what we have to," she said. That didn't answer my question, but I knew it was the best answer I was going to get. Giving me the details would only have worried me. She was trying to spare me that.

"Ooh, actually, I've got one more task for you, pal." Finch clamped his hand on my shoulder.

"What?" Harley and I replied together.

"Find out why Levi is keeping a lid on this Echidna thingy, like Harley said he was." Finch's eyes lit up with curiosity. "And find out what the National Council members are doing about the mega-bitch. They keep messing up, or worse, not even showing up to the party. The Muppet Babies have gathered more information than the Council up to now, and that's pretty terrifying. A bunch of rogues being in a better position than the most powerful people in the country. Alarm bells are *clanging* in my head. And Levi keeping things quiet about Mamma Monster is like one huge, annoying air-raid siren going off on repeat in my noggin. Seriously, it is HOWLING right now. There be a fuzzy little knot in here somewhere, Jakey-boy, and you need to untangle it. How're your nails?"

I frowned at him. "Why?"

"Are they good at unpicking knots, Jakey?"

"Oh… uh, yeah, I guess."

"That's what I like to hear." Finch clapped me on the back again, knocking the air out of my lungs. I knew he only did this to assert his dominance. I didn't fight back because there wasn't much point. Still, it was getting pretty tired. Shaking it off, I turned toward Kenzie, who'd just walked in through the kitchen door.

"Are you going to help us?" I asked her. She'd been very useful up to now, and the Morph trick was pretty neat. It could come in handy, in the future.

Kenzie shook her head. "I ain't part of any coven, and I don't plan to be. There are only two people in this world I care about—no offense, Finch—and they're my mom and my kid sister. Nobody else matters. Even if this psycho witch manages to do her thing and get all powerful and zappy, I'll be looking out for my own. I'll get us out, without no coven helping us neither."

She shot Finch a warning look. "And I'll be expecting that talisman soon, Finch."

"Sure thing, Power Ranger."

Kenzie frowned. "What?"

"You know—Mighty Morphin'…? Never mind. My humor is wasted on all of you." Finch pouted. "You'll get your talisman, don't worry."

"There is one way I can help you." Kenzie walked over to the kitchen cupboard and reached up to the top shelf. She dragged a plastic storage box out of the dirty hole. My eyes flew wide as she lifted the lid. It was full to the brim with burner cells, SIM cards, and chargers. "You guys talk way too loud. You need to be more careful about that. Not around me, but around others. Folks don't always come bearing gifts, if you know what I mean."

Finch grinned. "You're a gem, Kenzie."

"Ah, save your soppiness for someone with a heart." A smile twitched her lips. A real one. I could tell she was secretly pleased by Finch's nice words. I doubted a girl like her heard a lot of kindness.

"And the coven won't be able to trace these?" Harley asked, as Kenzie passed her a cell. She gave one to me and one to Finch, too. I turned it over in my hands. I had no idea where she'd managed to get all these phones and stuff from. Harley, on the other hand, didn't seem massively shocked by the sight.

Kenzie shook her head. "Nope, they're way outside any dumb coven system."

"You've got quite the collection." Harley smiled. "You get these fresh off the corner trucks?"

Kenzie chuckled. "Yeah, as a matter of fact. These, too." She reached out and opened the narrow pantry door. Inside, there were more cells stored in plastic boxes. Hundreds of them. "How d'you know about corner trucks, huh? You look way too smart to be a hood rat."

"I was never one myself, but I knew enough of them," Harley replied.

"Best way. Once you're one, there ain't no turning back."

"Is this how you can take care of your mom's bills?" I nodded in the direction of the living room, where another rerun of *SpongeBob* was about to start.

Kenzie nodded. "It makes me what we need to get by. Hopefully, I'll be able to save a little, once I have that talisman Finch is going to send. Might even start a college fund for my kid sister. Get her out of this place." A flicker of sadness passed across her eyes, and it hurt me to see. She really wanted to make a change for her mom and sister. And she had to do it solo, with no help. That had to suck.

"Why can't you just set up a PI agency or something? Spy on cheating husbands with your Morph powers? Who'd know, right?" Finch said. "It'd be way easier than all of this."

"What I did today is as close as I'm gonna get to a coven. If they find me using my Morph abilities, they'll drag me into one of those places by my earrings. With Mom the way she is, I'm not risking it. You think they'd let her in with me? No chance. They'd probably put her down, like a dog or something, just to get her out the way. Playing the human game is easier, believe me."

Harley looked sad. I understood that. It would've been awesome to have Kenzie with us, either with the Rag Team or with the Merlin squad, but it didn't look like that was going to happen. I got it from Kenzie's side, too. She needed to look out for her family, and they were the only thing that mattered. I'd never had a family, not really, so I was only just starting to learn what that felt like. What caring for folks did to your brain. How it changed things.

"It's a shame you can't get more involved, given what's at stake with Katherine Shipton." Harley's tone was odd. These were persuasion tactics. Harley was usually pretty good at them, but Finch was better, since he was ruthless.

Kenzie smirked. "It ain't my fight. I know you get that. I look after my own, that's all."

"It's everybody's fight now, Kenzie." Harley pushed back. "If Katherine wins and becomes a Child of Chaos, the first thing she'll do is decide who gets to have magic and who doesn't. Nobody will be safe. There won't be anywhere to hide, not for you or your family. She won't care. You won't be any safer, and there won't be a single hood rat who can protect you from her, because they'll either be dead by then, or they'll be working for her."

Kenzie looked like she was about to reply, but Harley cut her off, her expression softer.

"You can take your time thinking about it. If you need to get in touch, you know how to get ahold of us with the burner phones. I've got your number, and you've got mine. Use it whenever you need to," she said. "Katherine is coming for everyone. Keep that in mind, especially as she's got an eye for rare magicals, like you. I'm not saying this to scare you or try to guilt you into joining. I just want you to know what you're going to be up against— what we're all going to be up against."

She frowned. "I'll think about it."

"Glad to hear it." Pocketing her new cellphone, Harley walked out of the kitchen with Finch and me following. We couldn't waste time on someone who might not join us. I hoped she would, but while the fight was everyone's fight, it was also every man for himself.

There was only one clear thing to take away from that—Harley's persuasion skills were definitely getting better. Even I would've followed her after that, if I weren't already.

NINE

Jacob

I burst out of a portal into the infirmary. Everyone's heads snapped up. They stared at me in shock, eyes bugging out of their faces. I guessed it was a pretty dramatic entrance for me. I wasn't normally the kind of guy who went for that sort of thing. But this was necessary.

Nobody was expecting it, a mix of confusion and happiness on their faces. That was nicer than disappointment, though. They were probably desperate to get Harley back, but they looked pleased to see me anyway. Second prize, so to speak.

"Jacob!" Louella cried. She leapt at me like a spider monkey and threw her arms around me. My cheeks went fiery hot. Not in a flirty way—in an embarrassed way. Louella had never hugged me like this before. I didn't even have a chance to hug her back. My arms were sort of frozen, hanging limp at my sides.

"What the heck are you doing here, man?" Dylan barged past Louella and clapped me on the back. It hurt. A lot. I could've sworn he kept forgetting how strong he was. One friendly pat from him was like a hammer between my shoulder blades.

"You not pleased to see me?" I flashed a nervous smile.

"Of course we are." Tatyana put her arms around me, and I damn near died. She smelled like heaven. Actual heaven. Vanilla and chocolate and all the good smells. My throat closed up as I put my hands gingerly on her back. I didn't dare squeeze her, not with Dylan watching. And not with my cheeks on actual fire. "We just weren't expecting you. We've been worried sick!"

Raffe nodded and edged closer. "Yeah, Levi's going to have a freaking field day when he sees you. No Harley or Finch?" He patted me on the back. I was still trying to get my breath back after Tatyana. That woman… I couldn't even remember why I was here. It'd gone kind of foggy in my head.

"Are you okay? Are they okay?" Krieger chimed in from the other side of his desk. His familiar voice cleared my head. I was glad to see these guys again. Still, the fact that Santana and Isadora weren't here was weird. Astrid and Garrett were absent, too, but at least they weren't locked up. Garrett was probably still in LA, and Astrid was probably busy elsewhere. Wade wasn't here either, but Harley had said he might not be, since he'd gone to Waterfront Park. I hated seeing the Rag Team in pieces. It was always better when the gang was all here.

I dragged in a breath. "I managed to get away from them, yeah. They made me help them because they needed my portal stuff. I don't even know where we came from. Finch blindfolded me and they took me somewhere, but I got away and came here."

The silence stretched. I could've heard a pin drop.

The next moment, they exploded into laughter. Big, hearty laughs. Even Krieger was grinning.

Tatyana put her hand on my shoulder. "So that's the story they told you to go with, is it?"

I glanced at them. "I know I'm not the most convincing actor, but… yeah. That's the cover story I've got to tell Levi."

"Don't worry, I'll help you with Levi," Krieger replied. "I have a use for you that he will be eager to hear, and I'm hopeful it will keep you out of harm's way. Will you accompany me to the director's office?"

I shrugged. "Might as well."

I hadn't expected O'Halloran to be here. He seemed to have been promoted to Levi's bodyguard. Not that a position like that was much of a promotion.

But I supposed Levi had a growing list of enemies, so it was probably a good idea for him to have some beefy security.

I stood close to Krieger. If O'Halloran was Levi's protector, Krieger was mine. He might not have had the muscle, but he had the brains. He'd get me out of this. Harley had been sure about it, so that gave me some confidence. Enough to not crumple under the pressure, anyway. Levi was a total worm, but he was still kind of scary.

"Explain yourself," Levi said. "I'm running short on patience right now, so I suggest you don't test it."

I kept my cool. "Finch forced me to portal him and Harley out of here. They want to help with the Katherine situation. They just don't want to end up behind bars. I'm not involved in what they're doing, though. I was just the getaway driver—the *unwilling* getaway driver."

Sticking to this act was hard. I'd never been a good actor. In kindergarten, I'd been demoted from the donkey in the annual nativity because I wasn't convincing enough. And this was way harder than being a donkey.

"But you're saying you condone what they're doing?" Levi stared at me.

"I'm just saying that they're trying to do something pretty important. I'm not saying they're doing it the right way… I guess I just want you to be a little lenient, since their goal is the same as yours."

Levi snorted like the pig he was. "Those two vile excuses for magicals are both criminals. They are self-serving, reckless, and dangerous. They would likely murder me in my sleep if they had the chance, the way their father would've done. It would be better for all of us if Katherine executed them, though that would deny me the pleasure of watching them rot in a cell for the rest of their lives."

Anger burned in my lungs, surging through me faster than I could stop it. How dare he say that about them? Harley had done everything for the sake of the bigger picture. She'd done everything for the SDC, and for magicals everywhere. She'd gone to hell and back to be powerful enough to match Katherine. And all Levi could do was throw stones. I wasn't exactly Finch's cheerleader, but he was a better man than Levi. He wasn't a coward. He owned up to his mistakes, mostly, and was trying to make things better. But all Levi was doing was serving himself.

"At least they're not running scared." I spat the words out. They wouldn't stay in my mouth. "You're only acting like this because you're panicking. If you could open your eyes, you might see that they're trying to help. This is about more than you."

Levi's face reddened. He was mega angry now. I didn't care. I probably should've, but I didn't. He needed to be told. I was the youngest person in this room, but Levi was the only one spitting his pacifier out of the stroller.

Krieger put his hand on my arm and stepped in front of me. "Director Levi, I require Jacob's assistance in completing the magical detector. I need to utilize his Sensate abilities in order to get it to work. He is invaluable to the operation, and he must stay here in the SDC, with me, if we are to stand any chance of finishing it."

Levi scowled. "Will that take long?"

"I have several tweaks to make, and then, in theory, it will be fully operational." He paused for breath. He'd been rattling the words off like a machine gun.

"I don't see why Jacob has to help with the practicality of it," Levi replied coolly.

"With Echidna missing, I'm sure you understand how vital it is that we find Katherine before she can complete the next ritual. The magical detector is our best option at this present moment. It may be our only way to discover her whereabouts. She has already infiltrated magical society on a huge scale, and we simply can't find her without extra means. We need the magical detector, and that means we need Jacob. It can't be done without him."

O'Halloran raised his hand. "Director Levi, you and I spoke about how we might find Katherine after the incident in the... uh, after we..." His eyes glazed over. "Anyway, I think the doctor's right. It'd be a useful weapon to have, to find that woman. No one else seems to have any idea where to look for her. She's like a needle in a haystack. If the doc thinks Jacob can add the right whatever to this detector, then we've got to take the shot. It'd put us ahead of anyone else, for sure, and it'd be useful for the authorities to have, too."

I didn't like him calling it a weapon, but he was a security man. He thought of everything in terms of fighting talk. Still, I hadn't expected him to back us. Although, he'd gotten kind of weird back there. Like, he'd gone fuzzy when he'd tried to talk about Echidna. But I guessed these dudes had been through a fair bit since I'd been gone. Maybe he was still trying to process the incident.

Levi gave another piggy snort. "I'm already working closely with the National Council to find Katherine. I don't need to run the risk of letting you two loose on some untested magical device in order to discover her. Your assistance is not necessary anymore."

"You say that, but you don't seem to be making much progress," Krieger said. "We must spread the word to as many covens as possible, so that they can—"

"That won't happen, for reasons I have already expressed to you," Levi snapped. "Those who need to know already know, and that is where it ends. We are handling this, and more people do not need to get involved. It will only cause mass panic, and that is not what we need at a time like this."

Bull. I wasn't buying a word. I couldn't say that, since I was trying not to get arrested here, but I wanted to call him out. His body language was all over the place. His eyes kept flitting—a sure sign of lying. I could read most people like a book, and Levi was telling a pretty weird tale right now. He seemed nervous and cocky and stubborn. Not a book with any kind of happy ending.

"And the detector?" Krieger prompted. All business, all the time. "This is a global issue now, Director Levi, with or without the Echidna issue being released to the public. We need to focus on the detector, or all is lost. That's our way to finding Echidna and getting her back."

Levi rolled his eyes. "Fine, you can keep the turncoat. However, as long as he remains here, working with you, he is not permitted to leave the grounds of the Fleet Science Center." Levi walked up to me and put his fingers against my neck. "*Oculi tibi*," he murmured. I flinched as a white-hot pain seared my skin.

"What did you do to me?" I growled, putting my hand over my neck. I felt the raised edges of a circle, and it stung when I pressed too hard.

"It's a ward that will allow me to know where you are, at all times." He smirked. I wanted to punch him. "It's something I was forced to come up with after Harley and Santana's duplicate shenanigans. I won't be falling for *that* again."

"And you'll leave Harley alone, until this is all over?" I glared at him.

He laughed coldly. "Not a chance, boy. The order is still out for their capture. I have specified that Harley is to be taken alive. Finch... I couldn't care less what they do with him. Dead or alive is fine by me."

My burner cell was currently burning a hole in my boot. I wanted to speak with Harley, but I'd have to wait until it was safe.

"You can go." Levi stared at me. It wasn't a request. I was only too happy to leave his stupid office. Who did he think he was? The Prince of Persia? This dude boiled my blood. It made me feel sorry for Raffe. Having this asshat as a dad couldn't have been easy. I'd rather have had no dad than this doofus.

Krieger led me out of the office and paused for a second. "Meet me in the infirmary in an hour. Don't get into any trouble. Have a shower, grab a bite to eat, and get yourself in a better mindset for this detector work. Just keep to the appropriate areas of the coven and you'll be fine."

I nodded. "Sure. What will you be doing?"

"I need to have a word with O'Halloran to cement some more details. We still need to get Isadora and Alton out of their cells, and Levi is proving to be one hard-headed... well, it wouldn't be polite of me to say, so close to his office."

I smiled at the thought of what insults Harley would've used. She'd have had some way stronger words for Levi. And the feeling was probably mutual.

TEN

Harley

F inch and I speed-walked through the familiar glass-walled arcades of
Waterfront Park, the sunlight glancing in from the outside world as we
tried to keep a low profile. Plenty of people were around, and we were more
or less blending into the crowd. Finch had it easy, thanks to his Shifting ability. He'd transformed into some magical I didn't know, with long hair tied
back in a ponytail and a beard to match. It wasn't exactly the super subtle
approach I'd been looking for, but nobody seemed to be batting an eyelid
at him.

Without an Ephemera to help me out, I was pretty much stuck with the
old-school style of stealth, with a hoodie under my leather jacket. I had the
hood low over my face, but not so low as to scream, "I'm not supposed to be
here."

"Yo, Hell's Angels, we need to head over there." I gestured to a narrow
side-alley that cut between a collectibles store and the magical equivalent of
a Pottery Barn. Shiloh's Café was on the other side, stretching out onto a
pretty terrace that overlooked the human Waterfront Park.

The café was one of the hidden gems of this place and was secluded
enough to allow someone to have a conversation without worrying about
security magicals eavesdropping. It was gussied up as a sleek, hipster-esque
establishment, serving avocado in any one of a hundred ways. I passed a

pretty wall made of flowers at the entrance to the café and rolled my eyes. One for the Instagram crowd. As if to prove my point, there was a trio of teenagers in front of it taking about a million selfies.

"I might look like I belong on a motorcycle, but you're the one who's not exactly blending in," Finch whispered. "We should have stuck some Ray-Bans and a flower crown on you. Then you'd have looked right at home."

"Over my dead body."

"If you get caught, it might be."

I shot him a look. "Do you see him anywhere?" We'd just stepped through the stained-glass doors of Shiloh's. A few customers sat around with laptops, sipping matcha lattes and absently scanning through their phones, but I couldn't see Wade.

"Wonderboy, twelve o'clock." Finch nodded toward a pane of glass on the far side of the café, tucked between a wall of old, obscure movie posters and another flower wall. Through it, I could see the terrace that Shiloh's was famous for. It was a small veranda, really, but it gave an incredible view over the park and was distant enough from the café itself to give some privacy. Wade sat at one of the white metal tables, the kind you found rusting away in old gardens. He lifted a cup of coffee to his lips, while his gaze flicked across a folded-up newspaper.

Avoiding the overly chirpy servers at the edge of the bar, Finch and I headed for the back door that led out onto the terrace. Wade was the only occupant. He looked up as we approached, but he didn't seem remotely surprised. Instead, he smiled… a small smile that spread into a wide grin. It was the smile I'd been missing since we parted ways. He leapt up from his seat and wrapped his arms around me, pulling me close. I relaxed immediately, letting my arms slide around him as I sank into his embrace. This was all I'd wanted—to be back in his arms, breathing in the spicy scent of him.

"You have no idea how happy I am to see you," he murmured against my shoulder, placing little kisses along it.

"I think I can see how happy you are from here," Finch replied, rolling his eyes.

I ignored him and held Wade tighter. "I've missed this. I've missed you so, so much."

"I've missed you, too. Man, it's so good to just hold you again." He pulled away and gazed into my eyes. "I knew it was a long shot, but I was hoping so much that I'd find you here." Then, he turned his gaze to my Hell's Angels pal and arched an eyebrow. "You, not so much. Where'd you find that magical to add to your repertoire, or do I not want to know?"

Finch pouted. "Hey, this is one of the best ones I've got. Show some respect to your elders."

"Maybe if they stop putting my girlfriend in danger, I might."

"In danger?" Finch snorted. "I got her out of the hornet's nest, thank you very much. You should be kissing my vintage boots."

"Not likely." Wade smiled back at me, a hint of something strange in his eyes. It was like he was trying to read me but couldn't. "I'm just glad you're okay. I haven't stopped thinking about you since you left. I've being going out of my mind, worrying about you... and missing you."

Still buzzing off being able to see him and hold him again, I sat down, and Wade and Finch joined me. I reached out to put my hand on Wade's, but he moved it away and lifted his cup instead, taking a sip of his coffee. It was a bit odd, but I guessed he hadn't seen me try and reach out for him. Embarrassing, yeah, but nothing I couldn't shake off. I was about to dive into my line of questioning, when I felt a curious emotion drifting toward me, from Wade. There was a wave of relief and happiness, but there was a hint of something else—an emotion I couldn't figure out. It was somewhere between disappointment and annoyance, but it was too small to properly home in on. Subtly, I sent out a more powerful wave of Empathy, to try and get a better read on his emotions. Fine tendrils of hurt, disappointment, and annoyance came flooding back, those feelings almost lost in the larger current of relief and happiness. Clearly, he was peeved that we'd up and left the way we had, back at the SDC, but he was trying really hard not to show it.

"Is something wrong?" I decided to give him the opportunity to get his grievances out in the open.

He shrugged. "Not at all."

"Did you forget that I can read your emotions?"

He looked sheepish. "Ah... yeah, I suppose I did for a minute there."

"What's up?"

"Nothing." He shook his head slowly. "I'm just being stupid. I guess I was a little irked by the way you guys just left us, that's all."

"And avoided Levi's wrath," Finch pointed out.

"I know, I know. Don't get me wrong, I'm glad you got out when you did, but I just... I wish I could've gone with you. It's been crap without you." Wade sighed, visibly shrugging off his sullen mood. "Like I said, I'm being stupid. I know you didn't have a choice, or you'd just be in the same situation as Santana, Isadora, and Alton. How did you get the Atomic Cuffs off, anyway?" He glanced down at my wrists in surprise, as if he still expected them to be there, like two vastly inconvenient bracelets.

I smiled anxiously. "I can break them with my Chaos if I concentrate hard enough."

Wade gave a low whistle. "Impressive. Not that you weren't *already* impressive." He paused. "Let's just hope Levi doesn't find out about that, or he might skip protocol and lock you in a Bestiary box, and I don't want that to happen."

"I'd like to clap some on him, believe me." I grimaced at the thought of Emperor Levi on his golden throne at the SDC.

"We going to get on with this, or what?" Finch cast a glance back at the café door.

I sat down opposite Wade and fixed my gaze on him. "How did you know we'd be here?"

He chuckled. "A little mouse told me."

"You knew it was me?! I mean, it wasn't *me*. Finch has a Morph friend, and I saw through her eyes."

"Ah, I was wondering how you did it." He smiled, and finally reached out to take my hand. "It's pretty rare for an outside creature to get into the SDC. I figured that, if it was somehow you, you'd hear me say I was coming here and you'd show up. It's a relief to see you alive. It really, really is." He finally took my hand gently and lifted it to his lips. My body flushed at his touch, to the point where I wished Finch wasn't here, eyeballing us both like a mother hen.

"It's good to see you alive, too, with Levi running wild. Speaking of which, what's been going on at the SDC?" I jumped straight into it, knowing we didn't have much time to waste. Finch had been right about that. "I heard a couple of things, but I'm still hazy on the details."

Wade quickly brought Finch and me up to speed on what had been happening inside the SDC, and how they were still trying to get Santana, Isadora, and Alton out of the cells. He explained all of Levi's new crackdowns, and how he was intent on finding us, but they had no leads as of yet. That was good to hear, as I didn't want the Smiths getting dragged into this, nor did I want Kenzie and her family getting trapped in our web. I wanted her on board, but not at the expense of her family's safety. When he was finished telling us about the latest goings-on at Levi HQ, I told him about where we'd been, and our plan to go after my parents' Grimoire, to get the "find hidden things" spell and use it to seek out Katherine and rescue Echidna.

"That's why we need your help, and that's why I was hoping you'd be here," I said, coming to the end of my recap.

Wade smiled. "What do you need me for? You've got Finch, haven't you?" He was teasing me, and I probably deserved it.

I chuckled. "Please don't be mad at me about leaving the way I did. I didn't exactly have a choice."

"I know, but you literally vanished into thin air without a word." There was a note of genuine hurt in his voice. "We've all been worried sick, especially with Levi's security team on your tail. I had no idea where you were, or if you were even alive. None of us did."

"It was a snap decision," I replied. "Like, as fast as it takes to open a portal and drag someone through it fast. It was the only way we could keep things going with our Katherine mission, given Levi's obsession with keeping me under lock and key. He's made it clear he doesn't want us involved, but if we don't stay on track, we'll lose any advantage we might have." I softened my defensive tone. "I would've taken you with me, if I'd known I was going somewhere."

Wade nodded. "I'd probably have pushed you through the portal if we had to do it again. I just… was worried." He squeezed my hand. "And, of course, I'll absolutely help you. No way on earth I wouldn't."

"Hate to throw a wrench in this sweet little therapy session, but it can't just be the three of us," Finch chimed in. "We need someone with National Council links. Someone who can help us get the good stuff—the actual intel on how to get into the New York Coven without setting off a bunch of alarms, so we can snatch dear old Papa's Grimoire."

Wade tapped his chin. "I hate to agree, but Finch is right. We're sort of working with a skeleton crew now that Levi is watching everyone, and Santana is locked up, so we can't use her Orishas for duplicates. Plus, security is heightened all over the magical world now that Katherine has advanced past the third ritual. All the defenses that the covens are already using have been magnified, even without them knowing about Echidna, which makes things even harder, since we'll need eyes and ears in every important organization in the magical world. And, right now, we just don't have the manpower to do that."

"Do you know what the National Council is actually doing about Katherine?" I asked.

Wade shook his head. "No idea. Everything's a bit weird where that's concerned."

"Weird how?"

"Well, Levi is keeping a lid on the whole Echidna incident, which you probably already know from your mousey infiltration. Apparently, the whole issue is being resolved internally, with the National Council and the president, but I'm finding it hard to believe that they wouldn't have sent *someone* to investigate the Bestiary."

"There haven't been any new arrivals since then?"

"None at all. I asked Tobe, and he corroborated. Tobe was told to write an official report, stating that what happened in the Bestiary was just a glitch. I know that's partially true, but it's leaving out a huge piece of the action. That's what's being fed to the covens worldwide, to try and placate them, and Tobe didn't feel as if he could go against Levi again."

I frowned. "Why would he do that? Why would Levi keep a lid on something like that?"

"Because the magical world is already crapping their pants over Katherine. If they found out she'd nicked the Mother of Monsters, even if they didn't know about the rituals, that'd be enough to get everyone's panties in a bunch. There'd be mass panic," Finch replied, as if I was a dumbass.

"You agree with Levi, then?" I replied.

Finch smiled. "Nah, I'm just guessing that's the sort of bull he's feeding everyone. There are already rumors that magicals are jumping ship from covens everywhere, from here to Timbuktu. Whether that's to hide or join

Katherine, who knows, but it's getting the covens' asses in gear. Meanwhile, Levi gets to be the one in the know and in control."

"And if the National Council members are *actually* doing something to find Katherine, then they're probably wasting a lot of resources," Wade said. "They need to be rallying people, but if their focus is on Katherine, plus everything else, then they're going to wind up spreading themselves way too thin and get nothing done at all. Least of all find Katherine."

Finch nodded. "Exactly, they're half-assing a bunch of things instead of whole-assing one thing."

"Which is why we need to get this Grimoire," I replied. The more I thought about it, the more convinced I was that this was the only way to go, especially since my Suppressor broke. My instincts kept drawing my mind back to it, and that had to mean something. "It might just help us do what the National Council has failed to do up till now. Not that I think they're incompetent tools, as you like to say, Finch, but Katherine is more powerful than they know how to handle. We've got abilities and knowledge that they don't. That gives us an edge, and we really need one of those if we're going to bring Katherine down."

"Yeah, so incompetent tools." Finch chuckled to himself.

"I'm sick of Katherine getting away with everything, and the rest of us constantly stumbling at the last hurdle." I paused uncertainly. "And I've got this funny feeling that I'm supposed to go to my parents' Grimoire. It's something Katherine can't touch. Finch told me that she wanted it so badly, ages ago, but she couldn't get her grimy little hands on it. That pull I feel *has* to mean something. I'm bound to that Grimoire by Chaos itself, and I have this weird sense that it's pointing me in that direction for a reason."

"Chaos is talking to you now?" Finch smirked.

"No, that's not what I mean, but it's maybe *driving* me."

Wade nodded. "I think you might be right. If Katherine wanted the Grimoire, as you say, then maybe she wanted it so nobody else could have it. We need to ask why she didn't want anyone else to have it. I'm not saying it might be her weakness, because I don't think she actually has one, but we need to explore every avenue we've got."

Her weakness... I didn't feel the same as Wade. I knew she had to have a weakness somewhere inside her. Nobody was invincible. Not even Katherine pain-in-my-neck Shipton. And even if her Kryptonite had nothing to do with my parents' Grimoire, I'd sure as heck find it. Maybe with that "finding hidden things" spell. Maybe it didn't just work on physical objects—maybe it worked on intangible things, too. I wouldn't know for sure until I held that book in my hands again.

"Even if we go after the Grimoire, we've still got the issue of boots on the ground," Wade added. "We need someone with National Council ties who can help us navigate the new security measures and keep us up to date with what the National Council is actually doing."

Finch grinned. "Who's behind door number four?"

"Eh?" I stared at him.

"Oh come on, you don't know who Wonderboy is referring to?"

"No idea."

"Wonderboy?" Wade muttered.

"Garrett Kyteler. The one. The only." Finch smirked. "He's helped you Muppet Babies before, and he'll help you again."

"Hey, don't forget that you're a Muppet Baby now." I nudged Finch in the arm, getting a scowl in return. Still, it didn't quite reach his eyes, which looked pretty pleased. He liked being part of a team, I could tell.

"The good news is that Garrett isn't at the LA Coven today," Wade said. "He swung by the SDC to speak with Astrid, and she told us that he had a meeting with Remington Knightshade. It could be useful for us to go and speak with Remington, too, to ask what he thinks about the secrecy surrounding Echidna. Maybe he'll have the real reason for us."

I nodded. "Good idea. Then, once we have Garrett's help, we can start planning our way in and out of the New York Coven. It's going to need to be airtight, or we'll end up spending the rest of our lives rotting in Purgatory. Who knows, they might even bring back the death penalty as a special treat."

"They're not touching you." Wade squeezed my hand again, making me smile despite the terror in my veins. "I mean it. No matter what happens, you're not going to Purgatory. And we'll make sure we have a clear entry and exit strategy in place for New York, so you can get that Grimoire and prove to the magical world that you've got the strength to take Katherine down, in a way that nobody else has. That'll shut Levi up, for sure. And I'll be by your side the whole way."

"I wouldn't do it without you."

He lifted my hand to his lips and kissed it, sending a jolt of lightning through me. "You never have to. We're in this together. We have been from the start, from the moment you agreed to come into the SDC."

And now we're so much more... He wasn't just my friend and work partner anymore; he was the man I loved. That might have weakened some people or made them foggy about what needed to be done, but that wasn't the case for us. Yeah, we wanted each other to be safe and did some stupid stuff to make sure that happened, but we were better together. We *worked* better together, and we complemented each other. He had more experience and insight, which I needed right now, and I had the means to get this Grimoire and use it to track down that evil witch to whatever rock she was hiding under. It was a perfect match.

And, to be honest, I needed him now more than ever. I needed that support to lean on for encouragement and logical critique, since I'd—hopefully temporarily—lost the stability of the coven that had taken me in. I was going against them by carrying on with the mission, and they'd turned against me for refusing to back down. Then again, without Alton at the helm, it wasn't the same coven anymore.

In that moment, a sudden thought struck me: What if I could never go back?

ELEVEN

Harley

I leaned against Daisy's hood, fanning my face with an old magazine I'd found in the footwell. Finch and I had driven the eight hours from San Diego without pausing, right up the coast, while Wade was coming via the more conventional route of having Jacob portal him here from the SDC. Jacob couldn't come with him, but he could at least open the portal for Wade. We were supposed to meet him in a circular expanse of ground in front of the manmade lake beside the Palace of Fine Arts, as per Finch's strange instructions, but we still had twenty minutes before he was due to arrive. Wade couldn't be gone for too long at a time, with Levi watching everyone so closely.

"I could eat a walrus," Finch said.

"You ate an hour ago."

"Half a pack of ancient gumdrops doesn't count, and neither does a greasy sandwich six hours ago, before you say anything about that."

I smiled. "At least you've had something."

"I still don't get why you wouldn't let me drive half the way. This thing is a beauty." He smoothed his hand across Daisy's chassis with quiet appreciation. He'd taken her from the Fleet Science Center parking lot, having shifted into an impound official from San Diego Parking Enforcement, but as soon as he'd brought her to me, I'd taken over in the driver's seat. Nobody got to drive Daisy but me.

"Come on, we should head out." I flashed him a look. "Let's hope this goes well."

He grinned. "Have I ever let you down before? Pre-gargoyle, naturally."

"Jury's still out." I grinned too, clapping him on the back.

Locking Daisy up, we headed across the parking lot and skirted around the side of the more modern part of the Palace of Fine Arts, before entering the beautiful gardens. I'd never been here before, and the sight took my breath away. The architecture was forged from stunning sandstone, with reddish tinged pillars that featured friezes of warriors and beasts carved into the plinths above. They were like ruins from a time that had never existed in continental America, a piece of European history dragged right over the ocean and plonked in the middle of San Francisco. Lush greenery surrounded the ancient-looking structures, with a large lake set in front of its main feature—a domed building with an open interior.

Fountains burst upward like geysers in the otherwise still lake, genuinely making me feel like we'd come to someplace other than San Francisco. I had no idea why Finch had made us drive all this way. We needed to get to Remington, at the San Francisco Coven beneath Alcatraz, but that island was all the way in the center of the bay, a long way from where we were currently standing in the shade of the pretty, domed structure. Unable to help myself, I walked right to the edge of the lakeside and leaned up against what looked like a twisted cypress tree.

"Pretty cool, right?" Finch came to stand beside me.

"I had no idea this place was here."

"There's a lot you don't know, Harley. I'd be shocked if you even knew there was a world outside of San Diego."

"Hey, I've been to New Orleans, and Paris, and I've been to Eris Island. Anyway, I've met more legends than you could even dream of—Papa Legba, Marie Laveau, Echidna, Gaia… my mom. And if we ever get through this, I'm seeing everything. I'm going to travel this whole world."

"I keep forgetting about your Suppressor stuff. You went through a lot to break that, right?"

I nodded. "More than you'd believe."

"Is it getting better?"

I shrugged. "Yes and no. I have more control, but things are never going to be completely in balance." I remembered what my mom had told me about feeding my Darkness when it asked to be fed. That still worried me, since I didn't know just how hungry that side of me might end up getting.

"That sucks."

"Yeah... I suppose it does."

"The Spiderman paradox."

I frowned at him. "Huh?"

"With great power comes great responsibility."

"Ah yes, I forgot you were a massive comic book nerd."

He grinned. "They have some good lessons to live by. Lex Luthor, for example: 'Some people can read *War and Peace* and come away thinking it's a simple adventure story; others can read the ingredients on a chewing gum wrapper and unlock the secrets of the universe.' Comics are pure literature, but snobs like you just think they're dumb stories with pictures."

"What does that even mean? You're not going to unlock anything with aspartame or whatever."

"Maybe that's because you're not one of the chosen ones who can read the secrets of the universe." Finch chuckled to himself. "Your mind isn't open enough."

"My mind is plenty open, thank you very much."

A rush of air made us both turn toward the domed building. Wade stumbled out of a portal, blinking in the San Francisco sunlight. Fortunately, there were no ordinary folks around to see a great big hole tear open in space and time. It snapped shut behind him as he spotted us and walked over. Unlike us, he looked fresh as a daisy, his hair clean, his clothes neat and ironed. Meanwhile, Finch and I stank of eight hours in a car and the fast food we'd wolfed down on the way.

I closed the distance and put my arms around Wade in a way I hadn't been able to do back at Shiloh's. He smiled and buried his face in my neck, gripping me tight. This was the reunion I'd craved. I drank in the spiced, dark scent of his cologne and held him closer, as if he might suddenly disappear again. As he pulled away, he leaned down and kissed me tenderly on the lips, my mouth responding in kind, regardless of the fact that Finch was watching us. I didn't care. I needed to kiss Wade before I went crazy.

Finch cleared his throat. "Deadlines, guys. Deadlines."

I laughed and broke away from Wade. "Seriously, you can't give us a minute?"

"You've had it."

Wade put his hand in mine as we walked back over to Finch, who still stood at the water's edge. "So, you want to tell us why you chose this place, Finch?" he asked. "I'm not too happy about you making Harley drive eight hours up the coast for this, even if we do have to see Remington."

"What, you'd rather we'd swanned into the SDC, used the mirrors, and gotten ourselves caught?" Finch shot back. He had a point. Either way, we would've had to make this drive. I wasn't exactly looking forward to the return journey. Finch's taste in music was awful, and if I had to listen to one more Blake Shelton song, I was going to rip my hair out. He had no concept of driver comfort.

"I guess not."

Finch smirked and gestured to the lake. "This is how we get into the San Francisco Coven without being seen."

"This is a lake, Finch." Wade didn't sound convinced.

"Very perceptive." Sarcasm dripped from his words. "Yes, it's a lake, but it's a lake with hidden passageways underneath it. This is the secret way into the SFC. Not that any of you would know about it. It's not exactly common knowledge. Hence the 'secret' part."

Wade gave a cool laugh. "You seem to know a lot of things about other places, and their secret entrances."

"It was part of my responsibility as a cult member. And, what can I say, I took my job seriously." He puffed out his chest. "I was the king of recon and espionage."

"Did they give you a crown for that?" I replied.

"I asked for one, but the budget wasn't what it could've been." He smirked. "See, there are a lot of hidden details in this world, and you just have to know where to look. There are magical secrets on this planet that you wouldn't even know existed, even if you walked right past one."

I smiled. "That's why you've been wasting your potential with the cult. The good, non-psychotic magical world could use a secret sniffer dog."

"King, not sniffer dog. A little respect, please."

I chuckled. "Sorry."

"And anyway, it's because of the cult that I learned all this stuff. I guess it's like learning how to be a really good sniper because you're about to go into a war and kill people. It's not ideal, but it brings some useful things with it. Doesn't make me want to go back and do it again, but at least I've got the know-how now."

"How very poetic," I murmured.

"That's life, Sis. It's not all puppies and rose petals. Sometimes, we have to do bad stuff to get some good out of it."

Wade raised an eyebrow at me. "It really bugs me when he starts making sense."

"Now, watch this." Finch turned away and stepped right into the water, disappearing under the surface with a faint ripple. A couple of minutes passed, and he still hadn't reappeared. Wade and I exchanged a worried look.

"Do you think he's okay?" I peered at the water, but I couldn't see any movement underneath it.

"I'm not sure." Wade looked about ready to go in after Finch, when the water churned, exposing a swirling hole in the surface of the lake. A shimmering bubble rose up over it, shrouding us and the opening in some sort of time-lapse or concealment shield. Finch emerged from it a couple of seconds later, dripping wet and grinning like a maniac.

"What the—?" I gaped at him.

"Neat, right?" He brushed a hand through his soaked hair, slicking it back. "This is how we get to Alcatraz."

"But what is it?"

He smiled. "During the Salem witch trials, magical communities got so freaked out about getting arrested, beaten up, and executed that they created an entire interdimensional tunnel system underneath the United States. This one wasn't always under a lake, but additions have been made over the years. Additions that have since been forgotten, because people are idiots."

"I've never heard of any tunnels like this," Wade said.

"Like I said, they've been mostly forgotten about because people are stupid and don't read the history books as often as they should. The authorities know about some of them, and there are entrances all over the place, if you know where to look."

"So they're basically emergency escape routes?" I asked.

"Yeah, pretty much. Back when they were built, the Bestiary was still in its early days and it wasn't powerful enough to protect all the covens at the time, so the magicals had to put their own security measures in place." Finch fluffed out his t-shirt, which was sticking to him. "Not all the tunnels are still standing. Not the last time I checked, anyhow. Some are really old and dangerous, crumbling to pieces, so we'll have to be careful. This one isn't in the best state it could be, but I've seen way worse."

I frowned. "And this tunnel leads directly to the San Francisco Coven?"

"Why would I suffer through an eight-hour car journey with you if it didn't?" Finch shot me a look. "I hate to say it, but someone needs to introduce you to the power of deodorant."

"Says you. Someone needs to introduce you to the power of modern music."

"Heathen."

"Lover of dad music."

Wade stepped in. "How come nobody knows about this entrance?"

"It's an unregistered location," Finch replied. "It leads right into the coven's interdimensional pocket, using the *Aperi Portis* spell."

"*Aperi Portam*," I corrected.

"No, *Aperi Portis*. It's a modification of the other spell. It's how we're going to get inside undetected."

"This is insane," I said, half to myself.

Wade nodded. "If these are all across America, and the authorities don't know about the majority of them, that's bad news. How many does Katherine know about?"

Finch shrugged. "Not as many as me. I'm a sucker for a loophole, and I know my fair share—things I never told Katherine. If you help me stay out of Purgatory, maybe I'll tell you more of my sordid secrets."

I shook my head. "You can keep the sordid ones to yourself. We just want the useful ones."

"I knew it was only a matter of time before you started to bargain," Wade muttered.

"Then why do you sound so surprised?" Finch laughed. "You know there's no way I'm going back to Purgatory. You probably knew it the moment you agreed to let me out so you could get me involved in your Muppet games."

"You're going back, Finch," Wade replied.

"Nope, I don't think I am."

I glanced at Finch. "He has done a lot of good for us."

"Are you out of your mind?" Wade gaped at me.

"I'm just saying that, despite all the harm that Finch has caused, to me as well as everyone else, that's starting to fade a bit compared to what Katherine did and will continue to do." I could tell I wasn't going to convince Wade on this subject, but I couldn't stay quiet about it. "I guess I'm looking at this as his probation. If he does enough good to counteract the bad, then maybe he doesn't deserve to live out the rest of his life behind bars."

Finch grinned. "I'm touched."

"I know you are." I shot him an amused look. "In the head."

"You're so predictable," he retorted, but I could tell he was pleased he was sort of winning me over. The truth was, I still hadn't been convinced about his true loyalty until his private encounter with Katherine in her office. He could have gone back to her then, and it probably would've been the easiest route for him to take, but he hadn't. He'd defied her and put himself at further risk for our sake.

"Then we're going to have to agree to disagree on this," Wade said. "As far as I'm concerned, he's going back to Purgatory one of these days."

"Just say you'll rethink things." I wanted him to be on Finch's side. "He's kept me alive so far. That's got to count for something, right?"

"Never thought I'd see you two lovebirds on opposite sides," Finch said.

"We're not on opposite sides, we're just having a healthy debate about you," I replied with a smile.

Finch chuckled. "Like I said, I'm touched."

"I can't promise I'll change my mind about you going to Purgatory, Finch, but… I suppose I can give it some more thought," Wade said unexpectedly. "But now's probably not the time."

"Look what a little bat of those lashes can do, Sis." Finch grinned. He drew his fingertips across his lips, zipping them. "Well, if we're not hashing this out now, and Wade has promised to think about it, how about we get on with breaking into the SFC?"

"That's the most sensible thing you've ever said," Wade replied. A hint of tension lingered between us as we approached the swirling vortex of water and headed into the tunnel. I didn't know how I could make Wade truly see just how much Finch had changed, or how I could get him to see things in a different light. I'd thought the whole cult thing might've changed his perspective, but I still had a ways to go, by the looks of it. But I was determined to try, especially as he seemed to be teetering on the edge of coming around to the idea. Everyone deserved the chance to clear their name and make amends for the bad things they'd done. I still had to do that for my father, and though Finch hadn't quite been cursed in the same way as Hiram, I knew he'd never have ended up doing those terrible things if he hadn't been raised by Katherine's cruel hand. He'd earned the same courtesy by joining us, and by staying true to his new position.

I had no clue what they'd talked about in that office, or what temptations she may have offered him, but I knew he'd cast her aside for good in the pursuit of being a better person. If we didn't set an example and allow him to be forgiven, after all the good he'd done, then we were no better than Levi. And I would rather have kept Finch out of prison myself than see us put in the same category as that bitter, twisted troll.

TWELVE

Harley

W ater whorled all around us as we walked through the interdimensional tunnel. The stretch of tunnel we'd entered had swept back into a solid mass of water at our backs. The passageway through the lake was beautiful, showing clear water surrounding us. Fish swam casually along, without a care in the world.

However, as the water disappeared and gave way to the underbelly of San Francisco, the closing of the tunnel behind us became more worrying. Where there had been water, there was now solid earth and pipes and foundations, everything that made up the core of the city. I stayed close to Wade as we pressed on, my heart pounding in my chest with every step we took. Waves of rippling terror, combined with an undercurrent of despair, bombarded my senses, though it wasn't coming from me, and it wasn't coming from Wade, either.

It took me a few minutes to realize that it was coming from the tunnel itself, which had once saved so many witches from the humans' paranoia and pursuit. I had to stop and cling to Wade as a particularly volatile explosion of emotion went off inside me.

"Are you okay?" He sounded worried.

I nodded, dragging in a breath. "It's this place."

"What do you mean?"

"I… I can't explain it." I closed my eyes, but that only made things worse. It was almost like I was back in the passageway of Eris Island with a horde of spirits floating around me, their emotions fierce and deeply personal. Only, I couldn't see the ghosts of the people who'd fled through these tunnels. I could only sense their residual energy pulsating in the narrow passage. I clamped my hand to my chest, feeling an overwhelming sense of panic. My breath came in sharp gasps as I prayed for it to pass.

"Harley?" Finch appeared at my side. "Is something up?"

I nodded. "I can feel them all around me."

"Feel who?"

"The people who came through here." A burst of stomach-churning terror held me frozen in the passageway, unable to put one foot in front of the other. I could almost hear footsteps running behind us, but there was nothing but solid earth. These people had been running, breathless from their escape, and it had made me breathless too. Sweat poured off my brow and dripped down my back, my hands clammy and shaking as I gripped Wade's arm tighter.

"Is it your Empathy?" Wade said. "Is it acting up?"

I gritted my teeth as pain hit me in the gut. "Someone died here… more than one person." I was feeling the moment it had happened, a blade cutting right through my abdomen. Anguish and fear overwhelmed my senses in a relentless tide.

"Can you walk?" Wade glanced down at me, but I could barely see him. My eyes were full of tears—falling for people I'd never known, but whose emotions I could feel as keenly as my own. I began to understand that this was some new facet of my Empathy, one I'd only experienced a few times before, like when I'd held Marjorie's photograph and felt the emotions of the people in it. I'd also experienced a version of it when I'd touched my parents' Grimoire, but I didn't know if that was the same thing, or if that was just a Merlin thing.

"I can walk," I replied. I had to. Gathering my Chaos into me, I put up a blockade against the onslaught of emotions, shutting them all out so I didn't lose my mind. I didn't want to block them all out like this or push away the importance of their pain and fear, but there was no other way I could continue.

Feeling a dull ache as the emotions kept trying to get in, I let Wade put his arm around my waist to keep me from stumbling, and we set off down the tunnel. As we reached the water again, making our way to the island of Alcatraz, I tried to focus on the eerie scenery that surrounded us. This was a once-in-a-lifetime view, to be within the heart of the water, but there was something scary about it, too. It wasn't clear and welcoming, like the lake had been. Instead, it was dark and gloomy, the swirling shadows stretching away into the distance.

After what felt like an hour of walking, with the ghosts of so many tortured souls hounding me, the tunnel came to an end. A shimmering shield lay up ahead, swirling in the same way the entrance to the passage had. Only, here, there was a door behind it. Finch approached it first and whispered, *"Aperi Portis"* as he gripped the handle. The door opened outward, and Wade and I followed Finch through it as the rest of the passage collapsed behind us, leaving only the shield between us and the water. I was relieved when Wade closed the door behind us, glad to have my feet on more solid ground.

"What did I tell you?" Finch whispered with a grin. We stood in a corridor, deep below Alcatraz, within the walls of the SFC. I could tell from the grotto-like glow of the lights in the stone recesses and the cozy vibe of the place.

"Okay, you pulled through for us," I replied, flashing him a smile. "I'd give you a round of applause, but it might blow our cover."

I was about to suggest we get a move on and head to Remington's office, when two magicals came around the corner of the hallway. We froze and they froze, their eyes narrowing in suspicion.

"You there! What are you doing here?" The first magical approached us, with the second following close behind.

"This is a restricted area. You shouldn't be here," the second said. They were dressed in black, similar to the security uniforms at the SDC. I guessed it was true that all of the covens were upping their security measures, thanks to Levi's half-truths about the state of things with Katherine.

"We're not causing any trouble," Finch replied.

"Then why are you here? How did you even get in? There haven't been any arrivals through the mirrors, and I haven't seen any of you around here."

The first magical eyed us closely. I felt Finch stiffen at my side, sparking concern that he was about to do something stupid.

Fortunately, Wade stepped in front of him. "I arrived late last night. I was transferred from the Houston Coven, and these are my research colleagues." He gestured back to us as he took a step closer to the two magicals.

"Last night? We'll have to check the mirror entries." The second magical glanced at the first, their expressions curious.

"Absolutely." Wade got even closer to them. "I'd be happy to come with you."

"You'll have to. All of you." The first magical was about to turn away when Wade closed the gap and pressed a thumb to the foreheads of both security officers.

"*Efferant universa animo sopor,*" he whispered. The two magicals fell backward, collapsing to the ground, their eyes turning white as they lay there on the floor. They still seemed to be breathing, which was good, but I had no clue what he'd just done to them. I'd never seen him use a spell like that before.

"I guess everyone's got tricks up their sleeve that I don't know anything about." I smiled at Wade. "Impressive, Wade. *Very* impressive."

"Believe me, I can do a whole lot more." He chuckled, his eyes sparkling with mischief.

"It wasn't that impressive," Finch muttered. "And I swear, if you two keep flirting, I'm going to throw myself out of that door and right into the San Francisco Bay."

I laughed. "We'll save it for later. Right, Wade?"

"Definitely." He flashed me a wink.

"I mean it. I'll drown myself." Finch pretended to barf, which only made me laugh harder. After coming out of that tunnel, it felt like a weight had been lifted from my shoulders. I knew we had a lot of serious stuff to do, but it felt nice to be able to laugh like this, if only for a couple of minutes.

"Come on, let's find Remington before we get into more trouble." I nodded to the security magicals, who snored softly. Hopefully, we'd be in and out before they even woke up, and if this was a restricted area, it was unlikely anyone was going to come across them. Still, I'd learned that it was a bad idea to leave knocked-out security people in the open.

Taking one of them by his arms, I dragged him into the nearest nook—a carved hole in the stone wall, which would cast enough shadow to keep him hidden for a while. Finch and Wade followed with the second guard, until the two magicals were safely stowed away in the recess, tucked behind a weird decorative statue of a satyr playing panpipes. It had amber eyes that seemed to watch us as we worked, a twisted grimace on its carved face. *Ugh, this is giving me the heebie jeebies.*

We walked away from the smirking satyr, which reminded me a little too much of Finch, and headed up the corridor toward the main part of the coven. However, before we could even step out into a new hallway, Finch called us to a halt.

"It's somewhere around here," Finch whispered.

"What is?" I asked.

"Patience, Sis. Patience." Finch smoothed his hands across the raw rock wall, until his fingertips hovered over an oval-shaped amber stone that was embedded so deep you'd have missed it if you didn't know it was there. Which, evidently, Finch did. He pressed down on it with his index finger, prompting a narrow door to open with a shudder, tiny fragments of rubble falling to the floor.

"Voila!" he announced.

"I wish I could crack open that skull of yours and see what's going on in there." I shook my head in disbelief.

Finch grinned. "All you'd get is a handful of goop. My secrets are my secrets."

He clambered into the narrow passageway, with Wade and me scrambling in afterward. The door slid shut behind us, but the corridor beyond was lit with the same glowing firefly lamps that were all over this coven, giving it that grotto vibe that I liked so much. At least here there were no ghosts or spirits trying to attack me with their emotions.

We walked along the passageway single-file for ten minutes before we reached another door. There'd been other doorways branching off from the narrow passage, but Finch had ignored them all, making a beeline for this one. He put his hand on the doorknob and whispered the same *Aperi Portis* spell that he'd used to get the interdimensional tunnels to open. A soft click echoed through the corridor, and then Finch turned the handle and opened the door wide. I gasped in surprise when I saw the room beyond. I'd been here before. In fact, this was exactly where we'd been planning on heading.

Remington Knightshade sat at his desk, his head turned over his shoulder in complete shock, while Garrett stared at us from the opposite chair. Clearly, they hadn't been expecting any interruptions. Especially not the three of us creeping out of a secret door in the back of Remington's office. I wondered if Remington had even known this door was here. From the look on his face, it seemed like he hadn't.

"Harley? Wade?" Remington eyed us both, before his gaze stopped at Finch. "*You.*"

Finch rolled his eyes. "Why does everyone say that?"

"What are you doing here?" Remington pushed his hand across his desk, his fingertips reaching for his phone. *No... No, don't do that!*

"We need to talk," I said. "And I need you to listen."

His fingertips gripped his phone, but he made no move to pick it up. Instead, he just kept staring at me, as if he didn't quite know what to do. After all, Finch and I were wanted criminals, and Wade had just made himself an accessory, guilty by association. I had no clue if Remington would be willing to put himself in that same rocky boat.

THIRTEEN

Jacob

I'd decided to make myself scarce for a bit. Not too scarce, since I wasn't allowed to leave the Fleet Science Center, but there was some pretty cool stuff here to keep me busy. I found myself by the space station exhibit. Checking it out. Reading some things. I'd always been interested in astronauts and stuff. It was neat to look up at the sky and know there were people out there, up in a tin can above Earth.

Reading a new part of the exhibit about Tim Peake and a couple other astronauts, I smiled to myself. Like, what if I could portal from here to the ISS? Would I even be able to do that? I didn't know how far my portal abilities stretched. Could they go beyond the stratosphere? I was still learning about Chaos and its limits, and beaming up to the International Space Station would probably end one of two ways: I would be arrested and questioned by the US government, followed by a cell in Area 51, or I'd miss and end up in space, where I'd explode or something.

I just wanted to clear my head. It didn't feel right, being here without Harley. I'd texted her about Levi's compromise to let me stay and told her about Levi's whole secrecy jam—how he wasn't saying anything about Echidna, but he was apparently working with the National Council. He kept threatening me with Purgatory about keeping the Echidna thing quiet. It was like a broken record.

At least I knew she was okay. I'd sent Wade on his way a while ago, to meet her in San Francisco, although I didn't fully know why they were there. Something to do with Garrett.

Everyone at the SDC was hella wary of Levi. Nobody could go against him. He had the security magicals and O'Halloran jumping to every order he barked. They weren't saying a word about Echidna either, even though it was their job to keep tabs on the Bestiary. I'd spoken to Tobe, and he thought it was mega weird, too. Something smelled fishy. And while Levi was messing around, Katherine was getting closer to completing the next ritual.

I kept thinking about O'Halloran and the way he'd just blanked out about Echidna. It'd been more than a brain fart. It'd been like a full-on block in his head. He seemed normal, other than that. Krieger had said he'd speak to O'Halloran again, on his own, to see if it was something we needed to worry about.

I patted my pocket to make sure my burner cell was where it should be. Then, I kept reading about the ISS. It was like some crazy therapy. I could read the boards, look at the pics, and put my thoughts in some sort of order. My brain was like a ball of yarn that was in bad shape. Unpicking and unknotting it was taking ages.

"Hey, not so fast. Everyone's going to get a sticker."

I got distracted by a voice nearby. Some group of little schoolkids had swarmed this girl, who was dressed in the Fleet Science Center's tour guide uniform. She looked stressed. They were all reaching up like octopuses, trying to snatch stickers out of her hand. The teachers weren't doing anything to help.

Her head was bent as she tried to fend off their sticky little hands. She had short, dark hair that was getting in her eyes. When she stood up, she swept her hair back and took my freaking breath away. She had to be the cutest thing I'd ever seen. Freckled, pale skin. Petite, if that was the right word for small. An elfish face. Big, dark blue eyes. She looked like she'd popped out of an anime I used to watch. *Kiki's Delivery Service*, Studio Ghibli vibes.

Damn...

My palms were already sweaty. Great. I didn't know whether to help her or not. I mean, this was her job. She'd probably think I was butting in if I tried to do something. But those little brats were swarming her, literally. They were clawing at her silver waistcoat and tugging on her pants.

"Make a line, kids," she urged. "Everyone gets a sticker. I have enough, so just make a neat line and then you'll all get one."

"But I want the rocket ship!" one little twerp complained. He looked privileged. Puffy cheeks, slicked back hair, the kind of clothes that hadn't been cool since the 1920s.

"You can't pick and choose," the girl replied, super flustered.

"But I WANT the rocket ship!" the kid wailed. *Ugh.* Even if I hadn't been a foster kid with a big old chip on my shoulder, I'd have hated brats like this anyway.

"Well, you'll have to wait and see what's left when it's your turn."

I made a choice. Pushing down my anxiety, I stepped toward the group of kids. "Hey, did you guys know that Pluto has a heart made of ice on it?"

They looked at me, blinking like feral rabbits. "No, it doesn't," one kid said.

"It does too. See?" I pointed to a nearby picture of Pluto. Sure enough, on its surface was a stretch of ice that looked like a heart. It captured the little girls' attention first. They rushed up to the picture and cooed over it.

"Look, it loves us!" one girl said, clapping her hands together.

"Did you know that Pluto isn't a planet anymore?" another kid replied.

"Yes, it is!" a third insisted.

"No, it's not. They stopped it being a planet. They made a law to say it couldn't be one." The second kid nodded his head as if he knew everything. It was hard not to laugh.

"Actually, it's called a 'dwarf planet' now." I looked at the kids, holding their attention. "It means it's too small to be a real planet, but it's still sort of one. It's just a dwarf one."

"Like a gnome?" one kid said.

"Uh… kind of, but it's more about the size. Gnomes are more for gardens. Dwarf just means 'small.'"

A little girl shook her head. "No, dwarves are people."

My cheeks flushed. This wasn't the conversation I'd expected. "Well, yes, they're a type of people, but it can also mean something small." *Awkward.* I wasn't impressing anyone with this. And I didn't know how to talk my way out of it. I hadn't meant to imply anything against dwarves.

"No, they're not real people. They're in *The Hobbit*. My dad reads it to me."

I sighed with relief. "Yes, but in *The Hobbit* they're called dwarves because they're smaller than other people. And they are real people, too, in the real world. Not the characters."

"Is that true?" The little girl eyed me suspiciously.

"Yes. It's why people who are born smaller than other people have something called 'dwarfism,' because of their size. But they're not the same as the characters in *The Hobbit*. You shouldn't get them confused."

"*You're* confusing me," the girl complained.

Another kid nudged her in the arm. "He's just saying it's called a dwarf planet because it's smaller than the others, stupid. It's not rocket science."

"Well, actually, it is!" A little boy giggled, clearly hyped by his joke.

I looked over at the tour guide to see what she was making of this. She smiled at me, her eyes twinkling. I smiled back, hoping she couldn't see how red my cheeks were. They had to be burning like beacons right now.

As the rest of the kids gathered around the Pluto picture, all of them stroking the ice heart, the girl finally had the chance to hand out the rest of the stickers without having to deal with a mini-sized uprising. Even the twerp who'd wanted the rocket ship barely looked at his sticker. He was too fixed on the Pluto picture. She really was a beauty. Pluto, I mean. For years, the Hubble telescope had done her dirty. She'd been a fuzzy speck. Now, we could see her in all her glory, and she'd shown us love in return. No idea why I thought she was a she, but it seemed to fit.

"You want a sticker?" I looked up to find the tour guide beside me. She had a sticker on the end of her fingertip. The rocket ship. "You've earned one. I thought they might eat me alive." Her voice was soft and sweet, like a marshmallow. And her face. Not that her face reminded me of a marshmallow. It just looked soft and smooth, her cheeks plump in a nice way.

"Uh... sure." I took the sticker and put it awkwardly on my t-shirt.

She chuckled, and it was the best sound I'd ever heard. "Only the best kids get the rocket ship."

"Not like that spoiled twerp?"

"No, he got an amoeba. I save those for the kids I don't like."

"Harsh."

"Too harsh?" She eyed me.

"Not at all."

Her smile returned. "Good. I was starting to wonder if I should even be in this job for a moment there."

"Are you here a lot?"

"Are you asking if I come here often?"

I almost died of shame. "No, no, not at all. I just meant… uh, have you worked here long?"

"A few months. Trying to save some cash for a car and college, the usual sort of thing. The only reason anyone does this kind of job, right?"

"I guess so."

"Nah, it's not that bad, actually. I usually like it, but this group of kids is particularly… feisty. And the teachers don't seem to be paying much attention to them." The girl shot an annoyed look at the group of adults standing nearby, who were chatting amongst themselves. "It's a shame, because this is usually the best part of the tour. The space station stuff is my favorite."

"Mine, too," I blurted out.

"I guessed. Good call on the Pluto thing." She smiled, and my heart felt like it was going to explode. "I've got a picture of it up on my wall at home. We never gave her the respect she deserved, and then she went and had a complete glow-up when the satellite did its fly-by, showing off her heart and everything."

She thinks Pluto is a she, too. I knew I had a goofy look on my face, but I couldn't wipe it off. This girl was super cool. Pretty, nerdy, funny… perfect.

"Are you going to college soon?" I couldn't figure out her age just by looking at her.

"I've got another year of high school."

So she's a year older than me. Cool. Harley said I had a problem because I liked a more mature woman. Tatyana, for example. Yeah, she was way out of my league, and age bracket. This girl was probably out of my league, too. But at least I wasn't a kid to her. I thought about Harley and felt my cheeks burn again. She'd have teased me mercilessly if she'd been here right now. I missed her, but for the moment I was glad she wasn't here.

"I've got a year and a half," I replied, even though she hadn't asked.

"Cool." She smiled shyly. "What's your name, hero?"

"Uh... Jacob."

"Well, Uh Jacob, I'm—"

"Suri, we need you in the gift shop. Are you finished with the tour?" A member of staff rudely interrupted us. He looked frazzled. His name badge read "Eli—Sales Manager." I'd seen him a couple of times. He always looked frazzled. I wondered if he'd been born that way.

She nodded. "Yeah, I just finished. Do you need me right now?"

"I wouldn't be over here if I didn't."

I didn't like the way he was talking to her, but she seemed to take it in stride.

"Okay, I'll be right there." She glanced at me as Eli stormed off. "Well then, I guess I'll see you around, Uh Jacob. I've got stuffed toys to sell at a hugely inflated price."

"Yeah, see you around. Enjoy your... uh, toys." With that, she walked away. I couldn't have felt more stupid if I'd tried. *Enjoy your toys?* She probably thought I was an idiot.

Suri... I rolled the name around in my mouth. It felt nice. It sounded nice. And it suited her. It really did. And she'd called me her hero. I couldn't stop grinning. I wasn't anyone's hero. Their mess-up or their liability, sure, but never their hero.

I had things to do, but I figured it wouldn't hurt to hang around the exhibit a while longer. I covered my rocket ship sticker with my palm and smiled wider. Who else were the kids going to get their useless facts from?

FOURTEEN

Jacob

An hour later, I'd moved on to bugs. The schoolkids had vamoosed, but there were plenty of other people about. Visitors were taking pictures beside the oversized sculptures of bumblebees and dragonflies. The real reason I'd chosen this exhibit was because it was opposite the gift shop. From here, I had a good view of Suri. She was on the cash register, selling over-priced toys, just like she'd said. I couldn't fault her customer service. She had a grin for every person she served.

I was in the middle of sneaking a sly look, when I froze. She was staring right back, her whole face lighting up in a smile. Man, I could've looked at that smile all day, every day. She had to turn back to her next customer, eventually, but it'd been enough to get my heart going.

From then on, it became a game. I'd look, and she'd catch me, and vice versa. I probably looked like a total weirdo, standing beside a four-foot wasp, gazing at some girl, with a rocket ship sticker on my shirt. I didn't care. She was worth being labeled a weirdo for. Plus, it was an awesome distraction from the coven. When she looked at me, I wasn't thinking about Levi or Katherine or the end of the world. Playing this glancing game, I just felt… well, normal. And what made it even better was that she was normal, too. Like, actually normal. When she'd stood next to me, I hadn't sensed any magic in her whatsoever with my Sensate ability.

Santana and Raffe make it work, and he's a djinn. That was way more complicated than a human and a magical, right? Tatyana and Dylan had made it work, and they were different, too—a Herculean and a Kolduny. Heck, even Harley and Wade were making it look easy—a scrappy foster kid and a classy dude in head-to-toe Armani. Why wouldn't I be able to make it work with Suri? Yeah, she was human, but there were harder things to overcome.

You're living in la-la land, pal. I turned my gaze away from her. She couldn't know what I was. She wouldn't know what to make of me. Plus, I'd be getting her into this mess with Levi, and the coven, and Katherine, and all that bad stuff. It would be too dangerous for her. She was too damn nice to put in the middle of that, and I wasn't worth the risk.

But what if we just got smoothies together? That wasn't a commitment. It would just be smoothies. Smoothies weren't dangerous. Not unless you got too close to the blender. But where could we go for that kind of thing? I wasn't allowed outside this building. It had a café, yeah, but I would never have subjected Suri to the drinks here. She probably wouldn't have subjected herself to them, either.

I couldn't exactly invite her back to my place, smack bang in the middle of the coven. *Oh, by the way, there's this huge interdimensional world inside the place you've been working for months, where magicals live—yeah, magicals. Like witches and wizards, that sort of thing. Don't freak out.* That wouldn't fly. But I was desperate to have some kind of date with her. Girls like this didn't come along too often. Especially not ones who willingly spoke to me.

"Penny for your thoughts, Uh Jacob." I looked up to find Suri standing in front of me. I'd been so wrapped up in my thoughts that I hadn't noticed her walk over.

"I was just… uh, thinking about the life cycle of a leaf-cutter ant." *Idiot!* She'd caught me off guard. My tongue was all tied, my body paralyzed. But, surely, I could've come up with *something* else? Anything else!

She laughed. "I thought maybe you were trying to play it cool. You know, aloof, James Dean type of thing. The life cycle of a leaf-cutter ant is way more interesting, though."

"I'm not sure I'm the James Dean type."

"I don't know about that. If I put a trench coat on you and turned up the collar, maybe swooshed your hair back a bit, you'd fit the part to a T. No cigarette, though. It's bad for you."

I couldn't tell if she was teasing me or not. "Swooshed my hair? Is that a technical term?"

"For sure." She swept her own hair back to show me. "See?"

"Ah, now I get it. The swooshed look suits you."

She smiled. "Does it?"

"Yeah, though anything would probably suit you." That was smoother. At least, I hoped it was.

"Even a Fleet Science Center uniform?" She smoothed down the suit jacket of her uniform. "I hear Dior is very into silvers this season, especially the really cheap, polyester kind."

I chuckled. "Like I said, anything suits you. Even silver polyester."

"So, is this what you do all day, when you're not in school? Just hang around the bugs and space exhibits?" She paused. "I only ask because I haven't seen you around here before, and I'm usually the first to spot cute guys."

My heart lurched. *She thinks I'm cute!* "I come here now and then, when I need a distraction."

"Did you find one?"

"One what?"

"A distraction." Her eyes sparkled with mischief.

I was about to answer when I felt a familiar tingle in my heart. It was exactly what I hadn't felt when I'd stood next to Suri before. She'd made my heart thunder like a runaway herd of cattle, but this was different. This was the subtle twinge of a nearby magical. My Sensate ability, in action. I put my hand over my heart as the sensation began to build, getting a bit uncomfortable. Was it just the coven? There were loads of magicals there, in its little parallel dimension. Maybe someone had come out for a walk, like I had.

The only problem was, this tingle felt way stranger than an ordinary magical. It felt different. Raw. Cruel, somehow. It gripped at my heart.

"Hey, you okay there?" Suri put her hand on my shoulder. "You look pale. Are you sick? Do you need to sit down? I can get you some water."

I shook my head. "No, I'm—"

A crystal marble the size of a ping-pong ball rolled across the floor between us. I couldn't even move to kick it away as it erupted in a pillar of white light. A time-lapse bubble exploded out of it. The glittering glow spread out in a way I'd never seen before. It shot out in four strands, from the central pillar, making a cross. That cross spun, and the bubble rose from the ground up. It met in the middle, forming a dome over our heads.

Who's doing this? I tried to look around, but I couldn't see anyone suspicious. Only visitors, who hadn't noticed what was going on, thanks to this weird version of a time-lapse bubble.

Suri's grip on my shoulder tightened. I looked into her eyes and saw terror, her mouth wide in shock. I opened my own mouth to speak, just as the bubble lit up in a pulse of blue and cut us off from the rest of the world. To any onlookers, we'd probably vanished. Not that they mattered. Suri was what mattered.

"What's going on, Jacob?" she whispered, her face turning white.

"It's okay. It's going to be okay." I had no idea if it was. I just needed to say something to calm her down.

"What the hell is happening?" Panic shivered from her every word, and she stared frantically at the visitors who happily cruised past. They were oblivious. I put out my hands to steady her. She grasped at my forearms, taking shaky breaths. All I knew was that this was magical, and it was coming from a dark place. A cruel magical, somewhere near.

"Breathe, Suri."

She shook her head. "I can't! I can't breathe!"

On instinct, I pulled her to me. She buried her face in my chest, her whole body shaking violently. No sooner had I put my arms around her than a rush of air blew me forward. I staggered with her, holding tight. I wouldn't let her go. Glancing over my shoulder, I saw a portal tearing through the fabric of space and time. But this was nothing like my portals, or Isadora's. Instead of gaping darkness surrounded by a crackle of bronze energy, there was nothing but blinding white light and edges that burned red. Every particle sparked and fizzed, thrumming as if it had a life of its own.

What the... I froze in horror as Naima emerged from the swirling white vortex. *No... no, you died! You were dead! I saw you get crushed.* I couldn't get the words to come out of my mouth. My throat had pretty much closed up.

The beast bared her fangs and lunged forward. With her claws out, she snatched Suri right out of my arms and dragged her into the portal. It happened so fast I could barely think.

"NO!" I leapt into the portal after them, just as it began to close.

I landed on my stomach a second later, on a patch of wet grass. The wind had been knocked out of me. My ribs ached as the initial pain of landing subsided. With a groan, I dragged myself to my feet.

Blinking away the white light that had seared the backs of my eyes, I looked around. Naima and Suri were nowhere to be found. I didn't know whether to be more shocked or terrified. If anything happened to Suri, it'd be my fault. I should've known better than to be out in the open like that. Of course Katherine had eyes on me. Of course something like this was going to happen. Any kind of attachment spelled weakness, and she'd pounced on mine. Literally.

How did she bring that beast back to life? I'd watched Erebus crush Naima to death. I'd seen the blood spray out of her mouth and heard the crack of her bones. What ungodly, freakish thing had Katherine done this time? I should've known that, too—Katherine would never have let her sidekick die. But that wasn't important now. I needed to find Suri. She was an innocent in this. A terrified bystander. I should've gone back to the coven when I'd had the chance and left things as they were—a nice encounter with a pretty girl, nothing more.

Naima had clearly been waiting for an opportunity to strike. She couldn't have gotten to me while I was in the coven. *Levi was right.* That pained me to admit. He'd told me to stay close to the coven. I should never have gone outside it. *See, you are a liability. You're no hero.* I'd been an idiot, and now Suri's life was on the line.

Rubbing my eyes, I noticed the strangeness of wherever I'd landed. It'd looked normal through blurred vision. But now, I realized it was anything but. I was standing on a tiny island, surrounded on all sides by water. But not normal water. No, this was more like... well, liquid light was the only way I could describe it. It shifted and glinted, the iridescence moving like ripples in a pond. It was incredibly weird, but sort of beautiful. Like melted pearls. Millions and millions of ponds like this stretched away to the horizon of bright, white sky. It was hard to tell if the sky was reflecting in the ponds or the ponds were reflecting back at the sky. Either way, it hurt my eyes.

The ponds each had a small island in the center and were connected by grassy pathways. This stuff was white, with a diamond sheen that made it look like glass. There were rose-like flowers growing, too, each one pure white, down to the stems and the leaves. The Queen of Hearts would've had a field day. This place was pretty peaceful, in the eeriest way. Totally silent.

I peered across the odd landscape, hoping for a sign of Suri or Naima, but they didn't seem to be here. *They have to be.* Even if I couldn't see them, I had to find them. I'd traipse across every single pond if I had to.

I lifted my hand to my neck. The scar that Levi had left on me was burning. He was bound to figure out I wasn't in their dimension anymore. But it wasn't like he could send a rescue team. He probably wouldn't, even if he could, just to spite me. He'd wait until I came back instead and lock me up the moment I appeared. I didn't so much care about that, as long as I could find Suri. I needed to get her out of here before Katherine did something to her.

I was about to set off across the nearest grassy path, when I noticed a man standing nearby. I hadn't seen him at first because he wasn't exactly solid. He seemed to be semi-transparent, getting more or less opaque depending on how the light hit him. He was staring right at me with an unsettling look in his eyes. He didn't look angry or anything, but there was a fondness in his smile that set me on edge.

"Jacob… I didn't expect to see you here," the strange man said, approaching.

"Do I know you?" I couldn't wrap my head around any of this.

The man looked like I'd smashed my fist through him. "Yes, you know me."

"I do?" I couldn't place him, for the life of me.

"My name is Elan."

My heart jolted. The name was so painfully familiar that it hit me right in the gut. Sucker Punch 101. Everything I'd ever been told about my parents came flooding back.

Elan had been my father's name.

FIFTEEN

Jacob

I'd never met my dad, but I knew he'd gone portal-opening for Katherine on a cult mission. Then, he'd vanished, and nobody had known what had happened to him. He'd never come back. Most people thought he'd gotten stuck somewhere between dimensions.

"Are you… are you my dad?" I asked.

The man nodded. "Yes, Jacob. Yes, I am."

I wanted to believe him. I really did. But there was something off about him. He moved in a weird way, as if there was a time lag or something. And that transparent thing was strange. Was this what happened when someone got stuck between dimensions? Did they turn see-through?

"What's up with you? Why are you all… transparent?"

He smiled. "It's a long story. There will be time, in due course."

I'd wanted this moment all my life. And now that it had arrived, for some reason I wanted to run away from it. There was something weird about him. Plus, given his past, I didn't know if I could trust him. What if he was still working for Katherine? He'd done it before.

"Are you… Are you still on Katherine's side?"

"No."

I frowned. "You might be lying."

"I might be, but I'm not," he replied. "I was done with her a long time ago."

"How can I believe that?"

"Are you worried I'm going to hurt you?" He looked concerned but still ambiguous.

I shrugged. "Maybe. I don't know. Last thing I heard, you were Katherine's minion. How do I know that has changed?"

"Trust me," he said simply.

"Yeah, people have said that before, and it hasn't gone well."

"I realize you must have heard some terrible things." He paused. "But, as an assurance that I mean you no harm—watch." He stepped forward and put his hand out, but it passed straight through me. He couldn't touch me, even if he wanted to. I didn't know whether to be glad or disappointed. Especially as I still didn't know if I could trust him.

"Look, I'd really love to talk and figure this out—whatever *this* is—but there's something pretty urgent I need to do first. If you're really not on Katherine's side, then maybe you can help," I managed.

He nodded. "Anything for you." He sounded legit, but that didn't mean he was.

"Did you see any other people come through here, not long before me?" Suri needed me. And with every second I wasted, I was putting her in more danger than I already had. Even so, a thousand questions raced through my head. Questions that had to wait.

Elan frowned. "Should I have?"

"Maybe. I don't know." I bit my lip, frustrated. "All I know is, Katherine Shipton stole a girl from the coven I've been staying at. She snatched her because of me, and I have to get her back. She's also kidnapped Echidna, the Mother of Monsters, so if you know anything about that, that might be useful, too. I don't know if Suri is part of that, or what. Or if I'm supposed to be part of that. But I need to get Suri back before Katherine does something horrible to her."

Elan nodded slowly. "That would explain all of the unusual sounds I've been hearing in Lethe, lately." His voice sounded strangely faraway, as if it wasn't quite attached to him.

"Lethe?"

"Where you are now," he explained. "This is the Land of Light, otherwise known as Lethe, and if what you're saying about Echidna is true, this is likely where Katherine plans to kill her."

I frowned. "But what do you mean about unusual sounds? Why would there be weird sounds?" I was having flashbacks about those freaking Purge beasts in Tartarus. I didn't want to have to fight my way through a horde of them again.

Elan smiled. "You don't know who Echidna really is, huh?"

"She's the Mother of Monsters, right?" I figured he had more insight into her than I did.

"And what do mothers normally do?"

I frowned. "Give birth."

"Do you think she'd do that quietly?" Elan chuckled.

"Oh." It hit me. Unusual sounds. Giving birth. Monsters coming out of Echidna. She'd definitely make some weird-ass sounds if she was shooting out creature babies all over the place. If I hadn't been worried before, I was terrified now. Suri was here, somewhere, and those baby monsters could be after her. Katherine definitely wouldn't hesitate to feed her to them.

"Where are these sounds coming from? Do you know?"

Elan shook his head. "I only hear the noises in short bursts. If Katherine is holding Echidna here, then she must have control over the situation. She's likely bottling up the babies as soon as they come out, to use for her own ends. I get the feeling Katherine has changed very little since the last time I encountered her." Yeah, my dad definitely had more insight into Echidna than I did. Although, from what Harley had told us about Eris Island, this wouldn't be the first time Katherine had used Purge beasts to benefit herself. In the cult, she used them for power. Maybe she was getting what she could out of Echidna now, Purge beast power-wise, before she completed the fourth ritual.

"How come the Child of Chaos here hasn't kicked her out? I'm guessing it's Lux, right?" I asked.

"It's hard to say. Children of Chaos are fickle. Lux might be biding her time so she can keep an eye on Katherine, or Katherine might be keeping under the radar due to the strange behavior of Lethe, as a place."

"What do you mean?"

"Well, you must have arrived here right after this girl you're looking for, yes?"

I nodded. "Yeah, I jumped through the portal a couple of seconds after them."

"Portaling into this place doesn't work the same as it does in other places, otherworlds included," he said. "The ponds and the landscape continue to shift in a constant cycle. Unless your feet are firmly on the ground, the world beneath you will move without you. It almost killed me when I first arrived here." He glanced at me with sad eyes. "Can I ask you something?"

"Uh... I guess."

"Are you like me?"

"How do you mean?" I could see a resemblance between his face and mine, but it was hard to tell with the transparent thing.

"Are you a Portal Opener?"

I gave a small smile. "Yeah."

"I always wondered if you might be." That stabbed at my heart. He'd thought about me. All this time, he'd been thinking about me.

"Can you help me get to the source of these noises?" I forced my emotions down. I couldn't be vulnerable right now. If Echidna was making these sounds, then that was probably where Naima was, with Suri. And, maybe, if I got really lucky, Katherine would be somewhere else.

"I can, but you'll need to be careful," he replied. He seemed hurt, but I couldn't fix that yet. Soon, I hoped, but not yet. "These ponds are treacherous. They have a hypnotic quality that can draw a person in and drag you down in a second. I would have suggested you try to portal your way around here, but if you miss a single step, or land in one of these ponds by accident, there'll be no way to rescue you. They're deadly, and they won't ever let you out."

"What are they made of?" I glanced down at the nearest pond, watching the shimmering ripples of the pearlescent light-liquid. It was pretty hypnotic. I could've stared at it for hours.

"Lethe is an otherworld with peculiar rules. It doesn't abide by any physical laws, and it is rife with snares intended to keep you here," he said. "We'll have to work our way across the grass pathways. It'll be a long trek, but it'll be safer than the alternative. Plus, it'll give us a little bit of time to talk, if you want to?" He cleared his throat and turned away. "I understand your urgency, but this is the only way to ensure you get there without getting caught or killed. No matter what your task is, you have to keep yourself safe first."

I nodded reluctantly. "Then lead the way." I still wasn't sure if I was ready to talk. This was all a bit much. Rescuing Suri was stressful enough. Adding years and years of abandonment issues and therapy to the mix was a recipe for disaster. But what if I didn't get this chance again? I couldn't let fear stop me. I couldn't let those years of pain win, not if I could get some answers here. Even if they weren't the ones I wanted to hear, it'd be something.

We walked across the diamond-grass pathways, though my dad moved strangely. It was somewhere between floating and walking, making me feel like a heavy elephant next to him. After a couple of minutes, my first question appeared. It was a simple one. One that hopefully wouldn't involve too much deep digging into my emotional psyche.

"How is this even possible?" I asked.

Elan looked at me. "Lethe?"

"No, you being here. If you got stuck here, why didn't you just portal back out again? Everyone thought you'd gotten stuck between dimensions, but if this is an otherworld, then that can't be true."

He sighed. "Because... Because I'm dead, Jacob."

I almost toppled into one of the ponds. Even with him being all see-through, it'd never occurred to me that he might not be alive anymore. I'd gone through a bunch of weird, Portal-Opener-related scenarios, and death hadn't been one. That was the trouble with loved ones—even if someone told you, point blank, that they were dead, it was hard to believe it.

Even now, I was having trouble. That couldn't be right. I knew my mom had died, but I'd always clung to the hope that my dad was alive out there, somewhere. I'd always dreamed of being reunited one day. I'd pictured rescuing him a thousand different ways. And now, to hear that chance had been stolen from me... I couldn't come to grips with it. It wouldn't sit right in my brain.

"What do you mean?" was all I could say.

"I died, Jacob." His eyes filled with pain.

"How?" I wasn't even sure I wanted to know. That would've killed the last flicker of hope inside me, that he'd gotten it wrong.

"To tell you that, I have to start at the beginning." He turned his face away from me. Like it was too painful to say while he was looking me in the eyes. "You see, your mother and I were seduced by the picture Katherine had painted of an idyllic world, where magic ruled and those who were unworthy were denied their magic, while those who needed it the most were given more power."

He glanced at me, as if to gauge my reaction, and I tried not to make a face. "It sounds insane now, to think we were sucked in by her words, but if you know anything about her, then you know how charismatic she can be," he continued. "She preyed on us, because we came from difficult back-grounds—ones that made us easy to manipulate. Being Native American, I'd become disenchanted with the state of our nation and the way they treated my people—magical and human alike. Katherine promised to change that. She promised to give power back to those whose blood and life were bound to this soil. She said those of Native blood would be the first to be gifted with more power.

"And then, with your mother, who was a Latina, smuggled into the country as a baby and dragged around by the cartels all of her life— Katherine promised her a better future, where nobody was judged by where they had come from or how legitimate they were. She said that when she became the leader of her brave new world, her citizens would transcend being 'American' or belonging to any one country. She said we'd be citizens of Eris instead."

"Why would you believe her?" I'd never been sucked into Katherine's "charisma," so I couldn't understand how anyone could be. Even my own parents.

"Because we were wronged by everyone we'd ever met, even magicals. When your mother first discovered her abilities and sought out a coven, they treated her like dirt. Katherine offered unity and belonging that we'd never experienced before," he said. "Even now, I think, why *should* magicals be the ones who live in hiding, afraid of how humans might react? I don't agree with Katherine's way anymore, but I still wonder if there might be a chance for humans and magicals to live together with everything out in the open. But maybe that's just wishful thinking. Anyway, back then, I felt that there was no balance and no justice, and Katherine made herself seem like the only solution to that imbalance."

I was starting to understand a little better. Being half Native American and half Latino, I'd experienced my fair share of judgment and discrimination. I'd been called a lot of names in my life. And I wasn't as old as my dad had been when he joined the cult. Maybe, after a few more years of that constant grind, I might have felt similarly. Words stung like barbs and clung on long after they'd been hurled at you. Plus, I'd never had to face the mistreatment of my people head on. My mother and father likely had, considering where they'd come from and the time in which they'd been born.

"In the end, we joined the Cult of Eris. We were some of its earliest members," my dad went on. "I met her there—your mom. The moment I laid eyes on her, I knew she was the woman for me. I'll never forget that laugh, or that long, dark hair, and those brown eyes. She could hold the attention of a room simply by being there. And I felt like the luckiest bastard alive, to have her love me, and to love her in return."

I smiled, but his tone turned sad.

"We were married on Eris Island, on a beach in the middle of summer. She was wearing this flowing white dress with a red sash across the waist, and she had flowers in her hair. I can still smell them, if I close my eyes. Your mom always smelled good, like vanilla and cinnamon and cloves. I loved her, Jacob. We loved each other very much, beyond all sense and reason. Some days, I loved your mother so much that it actually hurt, right here." He touched his chest, his hand passing through. "And you were born from that love."

I dipped my head. "Did it change for you? I know it did for Mom, but I haven't been able to find out as much about you."

"My love for your mom?"

"No, your feelings toward the cult."

He smiled. "I thought you were trying to say that you'd heard that your mom stopped loving me. That would have killed me all over again."

My heart wrenched. I was still trying to come to terms with the fact that he was dead. Being here, speaking with him, it seemed ten times as impossible.

"As for the cult, both of our feelings toward it changed when you were born. Katherine kept demanding more and more from us, and the missions started to change in nature. Before, we'd been recruiting or gathering intel, but then she started to expect violence and subversion. Evil things, which went against the cult's official purpose—the very reason we'd joined. We started to worry that we'd gotten ourselves into a bad situation. As soon as we started to refuse to do certain things, the threats came. Most of them were aimed against you."

I struggled to fight back tears. I already knew this part, more or less. My mother had tried to protect me, and she'd died doing it. I was the reason my parents weren't around anymore, and that would stick in my gut for as long as I lived. No matter how many times I heard what had happened, it never got any easier to swallow.

"We then realized that, not only was what we were doing wrong, it could also get you killed. Our son. Our boy. Our sole purpose." My dad seemed to be struggling, too. "However, we were in too deep. We could never have gotten away without you being taken from us, not if we'd just up and left, anyway. So we came up with a plan. We agreed to perform a series of Katherine's most dangerous missions, in the hopes of regaining her trust. During one of them, we planned to use the time to give your mom the chance to get away with you. I gave her an Ephemera with my power inside it. The idea was to get you as far away from Katherine as possible with the help of an old friend of your mom's."

"What did you do for Katherine?" I forced the words past the lump in my throat. At least I was more or less certain I could trust him now. The sadness on his face wasn't a lie. I didn't need Empathy to read that. He really had tried to break away from Katherine, but it clearly hadn't worked out the way he might've hoped.

"We were sent to steal the Merlins' Grimoire, but that failed. We couldn't take it from New York because of their forces, and the death toll kept rising as we tried to get to it," he replied. "I realized that we were getting ourselves in more trouble. We were in New York, standing in Central Park, and I told your mother to leave, right there and then. She refused at first, but I said she had to, for your sake. I said I'd tell Katherine she'd died, and you'd been killed. I knew, even then, that Katherine wouldn't buy it, but I needed to give your mom a head start. I kissed her, and I kissed you, and I left. That was the last time I ever saw her alive. And, honestly, I never thought I'd get to see you again, but I was always content in the knowledge that you were alive somewhere."

I frowned, trying to ignore the creeping agony in my chest. I couldn't think about my parents' last moment right now. If I did, that'd be it. One of these ponds might as well have dragged me down. "The Merlins' Grimoire? Why did Katherine want it?"

"She's scared of it."

"But why? How come Katherine couldn't get near it?"

My dad smiled. "Getting near it isn't the problem, unless you're Katherine. The Grimoire itself is warded against her. She didn't know it at the time. Hester and Hiram charmed it, in the event that Katherine tried to get her hands on it. That was a dead end for Katherine. She couldn't get close to it. She couldn't destroy it. No one could destroy it, and we tried—well, we pretended to, but others really tried—to no avail. Then, she tried to make it disappear. She relied on us for that. That was our mission, just before we parted ways. We were supposed to snatch it, at all costs, but we secretly bailed and told the New York Coven about Katherine's attempts. That was why I had to tell your mom to go that day, in case Katherine caught on to what we'd done. It was too dangerous to bring you back to the cult again. Anyway, ever since then, it's been under special care."

"That doesn't explain why Harley had access to it," I replied, still pushing down my feelings. "Two other friends of mine touched it, too. If it's warded, then surely nobody should be allowed to touch it."

He held my gaze. "Harley? Harley who?"

"Harley Merlin. Daughter of Hester and Hiram."

He looked surprised. "They had a child?"

"Yeah, before Katherine murdered them both."

"She must have had a difficult life," my dad murmured, before giving a small shrug. "It's a Merlin Grimoire. It would make complete sense that their daughter could touch it. Anyone can touch it, in theory, aside from Katherine, as long as it wants to be touched by them. And anyone can feel its influence, but nobody can perform the magic within it, because it's unfinished and the Merlins were very sneaky. That's why Katherine is scared of it."

"What do you mean?"

"Turns out, there's something in the Grimoire—something nobody knows about, but it's dangerous enough to get Katherine worried. It's hidden, by all accounts. She told us herself that she thought there were entire pages hidden in it, according to what she knew of her sister's wily ways, and I'm pretty sure that there's something in those hidden pages that might be able to end her. That's the only reason she would be so frightened by it that I can think of." He paused. "The only comfort she took in our failure was that nobody would be able to find those invisible pages, and nobody would be able to read the Grimoire because it remains unfinished. Anyone who browses through it wouldn't know those secret spells are there; they'd only see what the Merlins wanted them to see. Even then, it'd be useless to them."

A sudden thought dawned on me. "What if there was someone out there who could read unfinished Grimoires?"

My dad tapped his transparent chin. "Even if such a magical existed, they wouldn't know where to find those pages."

"What if that person was Harley Merlin?"

"If Harley could perform such a feat of magic, she may be a different story. Her Merlin blood might allow her deeper into the Grimoire, providing Katherine didn't find out that she had the book. Katherine might not be able to touch it, but she could still get someone else close enough to take it from Harley."

Fear gripped my chest. Harley was already on a mission to get the Grimoire. Under no circumstances could Katherine find out about that. Only a few people knew about it, which reduced the risk of a leak. I just hoped that'd be enough. Harley needed to stay under the radar. Way under it. And I had no way of telling her. Not while I was in the Land of Burning Retinas. One other thing was bugging me, but I didn't know if my dad would have the answer.

"What if Katherine found out that Harley could read the Grimoire and cast spells from it?" I felt like I was missing an important piece of information.

My dad shook his head. "I don't know. I can only hope that, if Harley goes after that book, Katherine doesn't get in the way or find out what she's doing."

"Hopefully, she's too busy with sacrificing Echidna and completing her next ritual to be worrying about Harley." I had to convince myself that was true. Katherine couldn't be in every place at once. And right now, her focus wasn't on Harley. That worked in our favor. In fact, Harley's timing probably couldn't have been better.

I glanced up at my dad. The light caught him in a way that made him look completely solid. I'd pushed down my emotions for long enough, for the sake of Harley and Suri and Katherine. But I couldn't do it anymore. I couldn't walk next to my dad and not wonder why, and how, he was dead. I couldn't be cold anymore. He didn't deserve that, after everything he'd been through. My parents had made bad choices, and they'd paid the ultimate price. And, to be honest, I'd forgiven them a long time ago. If this was the last chance I might ever have to speak with my dad, I needed to make the most of it. I needed to hear him out. And, more than that, I needed to know…

"How did it happen?" I murmured, my throat tight.

My dad dropped his chin to his chest. "After I told your mom to go, I returned to the cult and told Katherine that you'd both died in a firefight with the New York security magicals. For a while, she let me think that she believed me. And then she hauled me into her office one day and told me she knew I was lying because she'd just had your mom killed, though they hadn't been able to find you. I collapsed. I thought my world had ended. I'd been so sure that I'd convinced Katherine, and then she took it away from me. My one consolation was that you were okay, but I was broken into pieces that day." He paused, crystal tears falling onto his cheeks. "She had her security force me into opening a portal to an otherworld. This one. She was preparing the groundwork for the rituals and needed to know if a Portal Opener could take her there. I didn't want to lift a finger to help her, but she forced me to open the portal nonetheless."

"And you got stuck here?" My heart thudded with hope. If he was trapped somehow, maybe he wasn't quite dead. I'd seen Alton bring Astrid back from the brink of death. Maybe he could do the same for my dad.

He shook his head. "I was so desperate to escape her, and to stop her from performing the rituals, that once I portaled through to this place with Katherine, I… I threw myself into one of the pools. I felt its hypnotic pull and I went with it. Deep down, I knew what it would do to me, but I did it anyway. I knew I'd die in there, but it was better than the alternative of being Katherine's personal gateway to the otherworlds."

He killed himself... That was even harder to stomach. The tears finally came as I heard the agony in my dad's voice. I couldn't even imagine the pain he'd been in, to do something like that. And yet, I understood why, in a way. He'd wanted to stop Katherine, same as us. And he'd done everything possible to do that. He'd taken his own life to thwart her. My dad was braver than I'd ever be. In his position, I didn't know if I'd have been able to do the same thing.

"It worked, for a while." I wanted to comfort him.

"The look on Katherine's face was almost worth it," he replied. "She was so shocked and angry, she had no choice but to slip back through to the real world before the portal closed. She couldn't risk getting trapped here, not without a living Portal Opener. I'm guessing she found another one? Tell me it wasn't you... Tell me she didn't force you to do that."

I shook my head. "She used Isadora Merlin instead, Hiram's sister."

"I suppose I knew she'd find someone."

"Although, now she can do it by herself," I admitted bitterly. "I'm guessing that's how she pulled me in here, though she sent her lieutenant to do the dirty work."

"She has increased in power." It wasn't a question.

"Yeah... but how come you're stuck here? Why haven't you moved on?" I wiped the tears from my eyes. Harley had told me a little bit about her encounter with her mom's spirit. She'd told me how hard it was. Now, I understood. This was painful beyond words. To have him near, and not be able to hug him. That was torture. All I wanted was for him to be reunited with my mom. He deserved to be with her again. So they could be happy together.

He cast me a sad smile. "I'm a spirit, Jacob—not alive, and not a ghost. I could never move on because I died here in an otherworld. Chaos doesn't like that, for some reason. So, I've been here, lost and waiting, ever since. There's nothing I can do about it."

I thought of the underworld myths Louella had read to us. In Tartarus, people who'd done bad things in their life were made to endure hard tasks for eternity, to pay for that. Was this my father's version in Lethe? Was this

his punishment? I hated the idea of it. I didn't want him to have to suffer through this lonely existence for the rest of eternity. But, then, he had killed and stolen and betrayed an entire community of magicals for the sake of the Cult of Eris. That had to come at a price. And my dad was evidently paying it. But he wasn't the one who should be paying... Katherine was.

Anger sparked in my chest. I had to stop Katherine, like my dad had tried to. If she was here, right now, then I needed to find a way to portal Echidna out of this place, to stop Katherine in her tracks. That, and get Suri out. Katherine wasn't getting any more pawns in her sick game of chess.

"What's the matter?" My dad peered at me with concern.

"I need to get to Echidna. Now."

He nodded. "At least there's one thing I can do for you. It may be the only thing."

"I'm alive because of you," I said. "I'm alive because you and Mom sacrificed yourselves. You've already done enough. More than enough."

"She would be so proud of you, Jacob. As proud as I am, to see the young man you've become." His voice sounded choked. "It's not every young man who'd risk everything to save an innocent. Nor would any person go after Katherine the way you are, trying to hit her where it'll hurt. Not only that, but I can tell that you're surrounding yourself with good people—people who will guide you through life, the right way. You have no idea how much comfort that brings me. You're brave, and kind, and strong. Just as we'd hoped you would be. And maybe you'll make better choices than we ever did."

I wished I could've shared in my dad's hopefulness. Instead, all I could think about was the massive danger I was walking into. I was about to go and save Suri and make a last-ditch attempt to steal Echidna away from Katherine. One man's brave was another man's stupid. I didn't know which side I was leaning toward. Stealing Echidna was a long shot, but if I didn't do it now, I knew I might never get another chance. Levi would be all over me the second I got back, and he probably wouldn't listen to a word I said. Plus, doing this came with a huge risk of death. And I didn't want to die here.

But if I did die here, at least I'd have gone out making a noble sacrifice, like my parents had.

SIXTEEN

Harley

———————

"Give me one good reason why I shouldn't call security on you right now." Remington scraped back his chair and got up, his eyes narrowed. Garrett, on the other hand, was still sitting down, looking totally confused. We'd literally appeared out of nowhere, and he had no clue what was happening, but at least he didn't look as angry as Remington did right now.

"We wanted to speak to you about Echidna being stolen, to see what the National Council is actually doing about this huge mess." I held my ground. He was way taller than me, with those tats running up his neck giving him a hard edge, but I wasn't about to let him intimidate me.

He froze. "What did you just say?"

"We want to talk to you about Echidna being taken."

"What do you mean? When did this happen?" He frowned. "Did this just happen—is that why you're here?"

I shook my head. "No, it happened a couple of days ago."

"What?" The sound came out as a gasp.

I stared at Remington, my shock reflected in his face. Was he trying to say that he had no idea about any of this? That couldn't be right. How could a member of the California Mage Council, one of Levi's own people, not know about Echidna being taken? I was surely getting my wires crossed somehow… but then, this was Levi we were talking about. All bets were off when it came to him.

"Did nobody tell you?" Wade stepped into the room, with Finch closing the door behind us. The door itself was camouflaged into the rock walls, and as soon as he'd closed it, there was no sign of it even being there. I could see how Remington might have gone all this time without knowing it existed. I couldn't see it, and I was standing right in front of it, more or less.

"No… No, they didn't." Remington's mouth curled up in a grimace. "And you're sure she was stolen, not just moved to a more secure facility?"

"Yep, Katherine Shipton definitely took her," I replied.

"Who else?" Finch said. "She almost took the Bestiary down while she was at it."

Remington visibly recoiled. "So you're saying Katherine Shipton almost destroyed the Bestiary and took Echidna while everyone was distracted? This really happened? I'm sorry to keep asking, but I'm trying to wrap my head around this. We heard there'd been some sort of glitch caused by a cult attack, and we felt the ripples of it here for a short while, but I had no idea that Echidna had been stolen. We were told it'd all been resolved, and the perpetrators had all run off."

I sighed. "Nope. Katherine took Echidna. I saw the empty box with my own eyes."

"That son of a bitch." Remington slammed his fist onto a nearby shelf, almost knocking it off its perch.

"You going to tell *him* not to swear, too?" Finch cast me a wry look.

"You really didn't know?" I was more concerned about that, right now.

"I really didn't," Remington replied. "Like I said, we were told there'd been some kind of glitch, but that it'd been fixed and there was nothing to worry about. I should've known that worm was up to something. You can't trust a single word that comes out of his mouth!"

Wade frowned. "Why would he be trying to keep a lid on this, though—the part about Echidna being taken?"

Remington gave a bitter laugh. "If only you knew him the way I do." He shook his head in disbelief. "Levi will be keeping this theft a secret because it happened on his watch. Even people who don't know why Katherine needs Echidna, which isn't that many beyond the authorities, would be running scared. There's a reason she's been kept on ice, all these years. Just the idea of her being on the loose would cause mass hysteria, and Levi would instantly be fired for his incompetence."

"But Levi said he'd told the National Council and the president about it." Garrett spoke for the first time, seemingly finding his voice.

Finch snorted. "And if you believe that, I'm Bruce Wayne."

"I'm inclined to agree with the fugitive," Remington replied. "If he's told the National Council and the president, then why the heck hasn't he told the California Mage Council? We should be working this out together, not being kept in the dark. No, this stinks of something rotten. There's got to be more to it—something we're not seeing. Levi is proud to a fault; if he's gone to these lengths to keep the covens, and us, from knowing, then maybe he's not quite being honest about who he's actually told. He'd almost certainly have been shoved out if the president knew about this. She wouldn't have some useless, lying, pathetic weasel in charge of the SDC if she knew this had happened. I can't believe it."

"Glad someone said it," Finch said. "If he *has* told the president and the National Council, then things are way worse than we think."

"What do you mean?" I eyed him curiously.

"Well, it means that they're not only keeping secrets, but they're playing favorites. And covering their asses without thinking about everyone else. It's been bugging me since we found out that Levi was keeping it quiet." He paused. "They should at least be letting the coven directors and the other Mage Councils around the world know what's happened. But they haven't. That's weird. Really weird."

"Do you think Katherine might have something to do with keeping it quiet?" Wade asked.

"I was just about to say the same thing." Remington huffed out an exasperated sigh.

"How, though? Her influence is pretty far-reaching, but how would she be able to manipulate that many people?" I couldn't fathom it. And I didn't really want to, because the idea that she might somehow have a stranglehold on the biggest powerhouses across the globe was terrifying. We already knew she was sending her cult members out to countries in Europe, and that they were pretty much everywhere in the US, but surely she hadn't managed to gain a foothold that strong.

Remington shook his head. "I don't know, exactly, but I'd stake a lot on assuming her influence has already spread farther and faster than we're aware of. Maybe her cultists have gone deeper into the upper echelons of the magical world. Maybe they're doing something to the president, or to the National Council, or maybe even to Levi. This is Katherine we're talking about. Nothing and nobody are out of bounds, and if they're all willing to keep this kind of intel away from the Mage Councils and the coven directors, then there's something wrong. Very wrong."

"That's the beauty of what she does." Finch's expression had darkened into a bitter scowl. "She does the crazy stuff because nobody would believe it."

"Lex Luthor?" I cast him a reassuring look.

"She makes him look like a kitten."

Remington sat back down, rubbing the tattoos above his collar. "Finch is right. He's probably learned a thing or two from his mother. And, since he's with you two, I'm guessing he hasn't broken ranks yet?"

Finch smiled. "Don't plan to."

"I should definitely be reporting you to Purgatory right now, but since we've got bigger fish to fry, I'll let it slide for the moment. You seem to be useful here, and we need all the insider help we can get." He seemed torn about the idea of letting Finch go, but he wasn't alone in that. "I'll have to be smart about gaining information, until I have concrete evidence of what's going on. I do agree it's best to keep this from the public, though, for fear of mass hysteria. Like I said, if people found out the Mother of Monsters had been broken out of the Bestiary, there'd be an exodus from the US and a bunch of people trying to gain citizenship in freaking Greenland. It's bad enough that people are already abandoning their covens because they're running scared of what Katherine might do."

"Or worse, they're going to join her out of desperation," I said. "But we can't have the entire magical population freaking out over Echidna."

Remington glanced at me. "Which brings me back to the question of what you want. Why did you come here, to me? You said it was to find out what I knew about Echidna and what the National Council members were doing, but I know you better than that. That can't be the only reason. So, spit it out, while I'm still feeling generous in the helping department. I'm already putting my career on the line, just by listening to you and not getting security in here, so take that as a sign of my willingness to assist. We're not exactly drowning in options, are we?"

I shook my head. "No, we're not, but I have one option. One that might be the best shot we have at getting rid of Katherine for good and fixing all of this in one fell swoop."

"Sounds like wishful thinking, but go on."

"I need to get to my parents' Grimoire in the New York Coven without getting caught." I doubted Finch's secret network knowledge would be enough to get us past heightened magical security.

"What good will that do you?" Remington replied.

I took a deep breath. "Well, the thing is, I have the ability to read from unfinished Grimoires. Last time I visited the book, I lost control while I was reading from it, and the spell just sort of came to life. It poured out of me, as if I was on autopilot or something. I tested the theory with another unfinished Grimoire, and I could read from that, too. The only difference with my parents' book is that I can still read it, even without the book being in front of me. The spells have this way of... I don't know, transferring or something. It's how I summoned Erebus when we were in Tartarus, trying to stop Katherine." *And it's how Shinsuke Nomura got killed.*

"It would've worked, too, if Katherine hadn't used some rare-ass spell to turn it around," Finch added.

"That's impossible." Remington was staring at me now, like he was scared of me. "There hasn't been a magical who can do that in hundreds of years."

Garrett shook his head. "She's telling the truth. I've seen her do it, too. She did it in the Luis Paoletti Room one time when I was with her. She almost read out the Dragon's Kiss curse, even though the book wasn't finished. She probably would've, if I hadn't stopped her. Grimoires have a weird effect on her, weirder than with normal people."

Normal people? Thanks, Garrett.

"I'm hoping there's a spell in there that can help us with Katherine. At the very least, I'm pretty sure there's one that can help us find her, whenever we need to. That'd be beyond useful, since the hardest part is tracking her down to stop her from doing all of this stuff." I felt Wade's eyes on me and turned to find him smiling. He put his hand on the small of my back, offering me reassurance.

It was a risky move, getting my rarest ability out in the open with someone with such close links to Levi, but I knew we could trust Remington. He hated Levi more than we did, especially now.

Remington nodded slowly. "Well then, if that's the case—and I'm having trouble absorbing that, by the way—then you should know that the Grimoire is now protected. I'm guessing they've upped security of the book since the last time you were here, as they have on everything. The Grimoire isn't exhibited in Special Collections anymore."

"Seriously?" I said, my face falling. As if we needed yet *another* obstacle in our path.

"I don't know if that has to do with you, or if it's just coincidence, or if it's tied to Katherine being back on the scene, but the coven decided that a glass casing wasn't enough," Remington continued. "The New York Mage Council had it moved to a secret room in their coven—where it used to be, actually, before they thought Katherine had dropped off the face of the earth and exhibited it in Special Collections. We get reports on these things, but obviously not ones on powerful Purge beasts going missing."

"Yeah, I've heard that she wanted the book, but I didn't know she'd tried to steal it." That perturbed me, to know she'd actually made moves to swipe it. Then again, if it was still in New York, that meant she hadn't been able to, which was a small comfort. Plus, it was good to hear that it hadn't been shipped off to some covert facility in the middle of the Atlantic Ocean or something. If it was still in the New York Coven, then it could be reached.

Remington was still looking at me in that strange, alarmed way. "I should've realized you might be the kind of magical who could read unfinished Grimoires, given your bloodline. It's not all that often that someone has two lines from the Primus Anglicus in them."

"I'm starting to think I should feel insulted that people keep forgetting me." Finch folded his arms across his chest.

"Can you do what Harley can?" Remington shot back.

"No, but—"

"Then stop with the sulking. So what if the spotlight isn't on you? Suck it up. You've got no idea what your half-sister is, do you?" Remington's angry tone took us all by surprise, especially Finch. "She's more or less a direct imitation of the Primus Anglicus themselves, who were all born with the four elemental powers at their disposal and tended to have two or more other abilities in their arsenal. They walked the line between Light and Dark, having both inside them, like Harley does. Her like hasn't been seen in the magical world for, as I said, hundreds of years. There's some ancient stuff at play here, and it'd do you some good to show the appropriate respect."

Finch gaped at him. For once, he was speechless.

"Most magicals have forgotten that there were even people who could read unfinished Grimoires, the way the Primus could. They forget that there was a time when everything was new and you couldn't just go to a spell book and find what you wanted." Remington's tone softened. "And to see someone like you appear in our time, is… well, it's remarkable. By all rights, you shouldn't exist."

Comforting. "Now that my Suppressor has broken, I'm hoping I'll be able to read the spells a little easier, without losing control."

He nodded. "I have to say, I'm fascinated to know what you found. Odette told me there were only a few full pages, before she took on the role of Librarian. She'd obsessed over powerful Grimoires, and your parents' book had been one of her favorite topics."

His voice sounded choked as he spoke of her. He quickly turned his face away, a muscle twitching in his jaw. In that moment, I felt awful. I'd completely forgotten about the relationship between the two of them and the pain he must still be feeling after Odette was brutally murdered.

"I promised her I'd stop Katherine." The words came out before I could stop them. I'd also promised her I wouldn't let anyone hurt her, but I'd failed on that one. I wasn't going to let her down again, even though she wasn't here anymore. I owed her that much.

"That's why I'm helping you," he replied quietly. "If you think you have a way to stop Katherine, then I want you to do it… for her. For Odette. I couldn't keep her safe, and that will haunt me for the rest of my life, but I can try and stop the same thing from happening to magicals and humans across the world. It's the only reason I'm still breathing, to be honest. If it wasn't for the fact that Katherine was still alive, posing a threat to everyone, I'm not sure I'd even be here."

I hadn't expected that much honesty from Remington. The agony in his voice stung deep, my Empathy bearing the brunt of his overwhelming grief as it flooded away from him. I felt it as if it were my own. It was mixed with anger and hatred, and the bright spark of a love that still burned inside him that hadn't been extinguished, even though Odette had been.

"Did Odette tell you anything else about the Grimoire?" I asked.

"There were rumors about hidden pages, but I don't know how true they are. Nobody was able to verify it, not even her." I could see how much of a struggle it was for him to actually say or hear her name out loud. He'd likely said it the first time without thinking.

"Hidden pages?" My heart lurched excitedly. I'd have been happy enough with the spell to find hidden things, but if there were secret pages, then maybe there was even more to my parents' Grimoire than met the eye. I glanced back at Wade, whose eyes were wide. Even Finch looked eager, an expression of dawning realization drifting across his face. *Is this why Katherine wanted that book so badly? Is there something in there that can stop her?*

Remington nodded. "It's a bit of a conspiracy theory, and the covens have never verified it. I think they're worried about people finding out that the Merlins got the better of them. It doesn't look too good for them, to have two insanely powerful people make a book that nobody can perform the spells from, which also has secret spells in it that even those who can read from it might have trouble finding. It's embarrassing, frankly."

I smiled at the thought of the covens stressing out about this book, desperate to know what was in it without giving away the fact that they had no idea. My mom and dad were feared and respected, and clearly admired… until Katherine got involved and destroyed them. Well, she wasn't going to do the same with their legacy. All I could think about was how deliciously ironic it would be if I found a way to end her with the very book that she couldn't get her grubby mitts on. It would be my mom and dad's last brave act, implemented by the person with their blood still running in her veins.

"One of their spells definitely came out the last time, when I read it," I said, thinking back.

Remington smiled. "Then you're more precious than you know, as that means you are the only person on this planet who can perform the spells from an impossible book. One that has outfoxed magicals across this globe for years, since your parents died. That's why it has to be you... you have to be the one to get it. I can see that now. There isn't another like you anywhere. You're an ancient anomaly."

"Hey, I'm not *that* ancient."

He chuckled. "I mean that your bond with Chaos is ancient. Take Finch and the giant chip on his shoulder. He has the same blood in his veins, but he didn't turn out the way you did. You are, to put it politely, a total fluke. Only you can do this."

"Lucky you," Finch muttered. "I wouldn't want the responsibility anyway."

He was trying to be funny, but I could see the concern in his eyes. He was worried about me and the path we were headed down. So was I. I hadn't quite realized just how much rested on my shoulders, if I was the only one who could make any sense of the Grimoire. Even Wade seemed on edge about it, his former smile disappearing, replaced with what almost looked like a scowl. He probably hated the idea of me being put in more danger, especially if Katherine found out that I was on my way to get the Grimoire.

"So, how do you suggest we do this?" I focused back on Remington.

"You should sit down, all of you. We've got a lot to talk about." Remington gestured to the random array of chairs in his office.

I walked over to the armchair beside Garrett, while Finch grabbed a stool and perched on it, thug-style, his hands between his thighs. Wade was the only one who didn't sit down. Instead, he stood to one side, his arms folded across his chest. A pulse of anger ebbed away from him, and I really wanted to ask him what was up. Before I could, Remington started talking again, bringing my attention back to him.

"You'll need to put some measures in place before you can get into the New York Coven." He paused, a note of reluctance in his voice. "As you've probably guessed, I can't be directly involved in any of this, given the massive illegality of you even being here. But that doesn't mean I won't help you do this. I have to, for Odette's sake."

So do I... and for everyone else Katherine might butcher if I don't.

SEVENTEEN

Harley

"You say you've heard something about Katherine's desire for the Grimoire, yes?" Remington held Finch's gaze. My half-brother's words of wisdom from Eris Island came rushing back—I had to break things down into bitesize pieces and not get distracted.

"Katherine always talked about how she wanted it. It made her crazy—well, crazier than she already is." Finch smirked, but he was putting on a front. I could nearly always tell when he was pretending.

Remington nodded. "Did you know she'd tried to steal it?"

"No. I didn't know it'd gotten that far."

"Well then, I should probably start by going over her past attempts," Remington replied. "New York covered it up as best they could, but Odette told me a lot of things she wasn't supposed to. And then there are the Mage Council archives, which detail some of the attempted thefts."

"I'm guessing that got covered up?" I said.

He nodded. "It's not very well known amongst the general public, for obvious reasons, but it might make you understand why they've increased the magical security surrounding the Grimoire now that Katherine is back in action. To be honest, I'm amazed you were even able to get close to it, Harley. I know it was being exhibited in Special Collections, but even then, it was supposed to have this dulling shield around it to prevent people from getting too near."

"It did? I didn't feel that." All I remembered was being drawn to that glass case like my life depended on it, as if I had metal in my veins and that book was the magnet, pulling me in.

"It should've. That was why it was placed where it was, so it was out of the way of potential treasure hunters and what we term 'dark tourists.'"

"Dark what?" Garrett arched an eyebrow.

"Dark tourists. They're people, in this case magicals, who track down items and places and landmarks that relate to great tragedies or dark moments in our heritage. If you've ever been to Salem, you'll understand what I mean," he explained. I kept my head down, not wanting my face to give away that we *had* been to Salem. "Anyway, the Grimoire had this dulling shield put on it, not to mention a bunch of wards, to try and divert people away from it. Although, it seems like it didn't work on you. I get the feeling that the Grimoire *wants* you to read it and perform the spells. If that's the case, then I'm worried that there might be some nasty side effects to it, too."

"Like what?" Garrett chimed in.

"I don't know. But if it wants to be read, then it might have some unexpected hold over you, Harley. You've already said that you felt like you lost control when you read it."

My stomach gripped with old guilt. "The very first time, I almost summoned Erebus and got my friend killed."

"That's the type of thing I'm talking about." Remington released a nervous sigh.

Eager to change the subject, I shook off my residual feelings about that day. They still haunted me, when I thought of what might have happened to Santana if she hadn't saved my ass with her Orishas. "So, with all the security measures and the secret stuff my mom and dad wove into the Grimoire, you're telling me that nobody knows what's really in that book, aside from my parents? And, partially, me?"

"Precisely."

I couldn't ignore the nagging feeling that there was something important in there that might change the rules of the game against Katherine. Our ace, so to speak. There was no other reason, as far as I could tell, for them to go to the trouble of hiding pages.

A gut-wrenching realization hit me. I'd always thought that they'd expected to finish the Grimoire, but now I wasn't so sure. What if they'd put all of those measures in place as a contingency in case they couldn't? Had they known Katherine might kill them?

"What if they put it in there and made it so Katherine wouldn't be able to read it? That way, she'd have no idea what sort of weapon could be used against her," I said.

Remington smiled. "You've got good instincts, Harley."

"Yeah, because putting two and two together to make four is super hard." Finch rolled his eyes. "All of this is really interesting and everything, but there's no point in making assumptions. I think you're right, just for the record, but we need to start planning our approach instead of worrying about why Katherine wants it. We get the book, we find out why. And that's the way the cookie's going to crumble. But Katherine can't find out about this. The Grimoire freaks her out. Any hint that we're after it, and she'll skewer us."

Garrett nodded. "I agree. If you're going after that thing, then discretion is key."

"Yeah, what he said." Finch flashed a shy smile at his friend, but Garrett didn't return it. "We need to be smart and subtle. No alarms. No alerts. No suspicion."

"There's a spell that Odette told me about once," Remington said, his voice thick. "I don't even remember why she told me about it. We'd been out for dinner, I think, and we'd come back home, and she was flipping through some book. She did that a lot. I'd gone to the kitchen to get a drink, and I came back in, and she had this huge smile on her face. She made me sit on the floor next to her, and she showed me this page from a dusty tome."

His brow furrowed at the memory, like it was both bitter and sweet to remember. I could feel frustration coming off him, too, like he was struggling to get the details right. She hadn't been gone long, but that was the heart-breaking truth of loss—memories and faces began to fade, becoming blurry and unclear over time. The more you fought to hold onto them, the more they slipped away.

"What was the spell?" I prompted, noticing that he'd retreated into himself.

He looked at me as if he'd just remembered we were in the room. "The spell? Yes, the spell. It's a perversion of *Aperi Portam,* called *Aperi Si Ostium.* It allows you to open any door, anywhere, at any time, no matter how warded it might be."

"Cool," I murmured. "I'm guessing not too many people know about it?"

"No, exactly. You can see why it's not a very well-known spell. In the wrong hands, it'd be a disaster. Anyway, she was so excited when she found it. At the time, we were still hiding our relationship, since she wasn't really meant to be getting into any kind of relationship while she was making her case to become the next Librarian. The rules were stricter, back then, about having visitors in the Mage Council headquarters."

I felt awkward, knowing what he was getting at. "That must've sucked."

He nodded. "I was still in training, and she said it'd be useful for us so we could see each other whenever we wanted to, without worrying about mirrors and that sort of thing—she said we could use it to meet in secret."

"So, it's a portal spell?" Finch said.

"Not quite. It doesn't go to otherworlds, and the range isn't as impressive. You couldn't use it to travel to Berlin, for example. We tried, hoping for a romantic weekend, and ended up in Virginia." He smiled privately, and my heart went out to him. Katherine had not only murdered the woman he loved, but she'd stolen the happiness from his memories, too.

"I'm guessing it's illegal, then?" Wade cut in, his expression irritated. *What's up with you all of a sudden?*

"Very illegal, so don't go sharing it with anyone," Remington warned. "And there are repercussions you should know about, too. Some doors are best kept closed. Only use it when you absolutely have to."

"How does it work?" I pressed. Time was of the essence, after all.

"All you need is a piece of charmed chalk to draw the door you want."

Finch snorted. "Charmed chalk? What is this, Nickelodeon?"

"You find some chalk, you charm it with the *Aperi Si Ostium* spell. Call it something else if it makes you feel better." Remington evidently had no time for Finch's sass. "Now that you know the spell, you can get into the New York Coven without being discovered. All you have to do is draw the door, think of where you want to go, say the words, and then you go through it."

"Are these doors permanent?" I asked.

Remington shook his head. "No, they seal shut the moment you've walked through them. Something to do with keeping the fabric of time and space in order. If a door is ever left open, then the fabric of reality starts to crumble around it, and you really don't want that to happen. If it ever did, the world itself would start to leak through it to who knows where. So it has a failsafe already built in to stop that from happening."

Panic jolted through me. "Wait, can that happen with portals, too?"

"If one was left open, I imagine so. Although, that ability tends to have the same failsafe built in."

"Okay, so that gets us in, but what about the security when we actually get there?" Wade scuffed his shoe against the floor as he spoke. The angry streak seemed to be fading, which meant it had to have stemmed from all this chat about Katherine. That was a relief.

"I'll have to look into a few more details about their heightened security system before you can head there," Remington replied. "Give me a couple of hours, and I'll get what I can for you."

I frowned. "A couple of hours? You realize we're on a bit of a tight schedule, right?"

"It's better than the alternative." He gave me a cool look.

"I guess…" My stress levels were already through the roof, and waiting to hear some intel about New York wasn't going to do anything to bring them down again.

"There's another thing you should know that Odette told me." Remington hesitated, as if he wasn't sure whether to continue.

"Cat got your tongue?" Finch narrowed his eyes.

"I hate to say it, but stopping Katherine may not be possible, as far as the rituals go. Odette always said there was a chance that someone who was determined enough could get through them, as long as they managed to outrun and outsmart the authorities. Katherine is already on her fourth, and we've got no idea how far along she is with that one. So we may have to start prepping for what comes after she kills Echidna. After that, there'll only be one ritual left."

"You make it sound as though Echidna is already dead." I leaned forward in my chair. Did he know something we didn't?

Remington sighed. "She may well be. The truth is, the Mother of Monsters was lost the moment she was taken. We might have stood a chance at stopping her completing the fourth ritual if we'd kept Echidna out of her hands, but that didn't happen. That's probably why Levi is keeping quiet about the situation. Arrogant prick. He likely knows it's already too late to avoid the fourth ritual being completed."

"Then why isn't everyone freaking out?" Finch replied.

"I don't know." Remington tapped his fingertips against the desk. "I can't understand why the National Council and the president, of all people, would agree to this secrecy. It doesn't make sense. But I'm going to see if I can change that. I'll discuss things with the Mage Council first, sans Levi, then take appropriate action. The others will be as outraged as I am, but we'll be able to come up with a better solution, working together."

Garrett nodded. "Taking extra security measures against Katherine isn't going to be enough for the covens, if we're saying what I think we're saying about Katherine. The higher-ups in every coven around the world should know how close Katherine is to becoming a Child of Chaos. It isn't right that they're being kept in the dark."

"Has LA been told the same thing about the so-called 'glitch'?" I peered at him curiously.

"Yeah, as far as I know," Garrett said.

Remington sucked air through his teeth. "I'll get to the bottom of this, don't worry. Levi won't get away with it."

"So, what do we do until then?" The idea of staying here for a couple of hours didn't sit too well with me. Finch seemed agitated, too.

"Not hang around here, for starters. I'd still like to have my job at the end of the day," Remington replied dryly. "You're still fugitives, remember? There's nothing I can do about that, not at the moment, anyway. Imogene and I are pretty much the only ones on the California Mage Council who don't want you to be in this situation."

"What, so you've taken a vote or something?" I asked.

"Not exactly. We've been trying to sway the rest of the Council to stop chasing after you both, but it's proving tricky. Imogene has almost managed to convince them that you should be left alone, Harley, but the same can't be said for you, Finch. Still, we'll keep trying. And even if we get them to stop chasing one of you, that's better than nothing, right?"

Nice to know someone has my back. I would've given anything to be able to have a chat with Imogene right now. She'd know what to do and how to get us out of this mess. I mean, she'd probably be pissed that I'd lied about going to Anchorage, but she was one of the few people who'd be willing to understand my reasons. It sounded like she already did, to a certain extent.

It was a huge relief to know there were still a few magicals in this world who didn't want me stuck in Purgatory with Finch. I had to cling to that. One day, I might be able to salvage my reputation from the ashes that Levi and Katherine had created.

EIGHTEEN

Jacob

With my dad at my side, I crossed the glinting pools. As far as the eye could see, there were more and more. But it was hard to know if we'd already passed some of them. If this place shifted constantly, like my dad said, then maybe it was turning around us. That would definitely make reaching our destination harder. My dad seemed to know where he was going, though. And I figured he'd been stuck here long enough to have his bearings.

We were getting closer to those weird noises. The sounds didn't fit the peaceful vibe of this place. Pained shrieks and scary howls. Somewhere between a wolf and a whale sound. I guessed the piercing screams were coming from Echidna. I'd never been near a woman giving birth, but these sounds lined up with what I imagined that'd sound like.

The more we walked, the louder the sounds grew. And the closer we got, the more dread I felt. I was sweating, even though there was no visible sun to make it hot. My palms were clammy. Clammier than when I'd first set eyes on Suri.

"We're almost there," my dad said. Another scream filled the air. It sounded like a wounded animal who'd been skewered with a knife. I shuddered, but I had to be brave now, the way Harley and the rest of the Rag Team would've been. I'd been alone for a lot of my life, but since meeting them, I'd pretty much forgotten how to be a lone wolf. I'd started to rely on the pack, and now I didn't have them to help me. It felt wrong.

We paused at a valley with a long, shimmering river running through the center. Smaller streams branched off, filling the pools. A narrow island lay in the middle of the river. On it, I spotted Naima. She was dangling Suri over the river, holding her under the arms with a nasty smirk.

"Help me! Somebody help me!" Suri screamed. The sound was like a block of ice in my chest. "Please, somebody! Please, stop this! I'll give you anything you want, just let me go. You can have all my money, whatever you want, just let me go!" Tears ran down her cheeks. She thrashed wildly, but Naima wouldn't release her.

Naima chuckled. "As soon as I drop you in the water, you will forget everything. It will drag you down and give you eternal peace. What is there to cry about?"

"Let me go! I don't know what I've done, just let me go!" Suri sobbed, her cheeks red.

This was all my fault. I should never have gone into the Fleet Science Center. I should've known that Naima and Katherine were watching the SDC. For a collector of rare abilities, I was a double threat—Portal Opener and Sensate. And why this girl? Why Suri? Was it because they needed a human sacrifice, and she'd happened to be closest to me at the time? Or because they'd watched me take an interest in her and knew I'd try to save her?

They'd probably seen the perfect opportunity. Me trying to flirt. Me openly crushing on Suri. Me laughing with her. This way, they'd have known I wouldn't leave without her. They'd have known I wouldn't try and portal away, abandoning her here. After all, they'd seen me with the Smiths. They knew I'd never leave a human behind, especially if I was the one who'd gotten them into trouble in the first place.

Farther up the island stood a tent made of red silk. It looked like one of those old kinds they used in sword-and-sandals movies. It even had a golden spire at the top, with a flag waving in the breeze, a golden apple on it.

Katherine...

Was she here? I could only see Naima, Suri, and a white plinth with a crumpled-up figure on top of it. It reminded me of the other sacrificial altars we'd seen in the other otherworlds.

The creature on top of it suddenly unfurled. Limbs shot out, the creature arching its back and unleashing another ungodly scream. A coiling, snaky tail spilled out over the edge of the altar, but her top half was human. Echidna.

Glowing green stones surrounded the altar. I'd seen stones like that before. They were entrapment stones, the kind used to catch Purge beasts. Or, in this case, keep them restrained. Echidna had cuffs on her wrists, too, though they seemed to give her more movement than normal Atomic Cuffs. Her hands weren't bound together, but a gleaming blue line wavered between the cuffs, like an electrical current.

I ducked, lying flat on the white grass as a bright flash of light erupted from the tent. A few seconds later, a figure stepped out and walked toward a chair beside the altar. Well, "chair" was sort of an understatement. It was more of a throne. She plopped herself down and hoisted her legs over the gilded arm. The long, emerald-green dress she was wearing draped over it.

"Do you have to make that racket?" Katherine rolled her eyes. "You're not the first creature to give birth, you know. I did it myself once. Never again. I've never been the same, if you catch my drift. But I don't remember making such a fuss over it. You'd think you'd be used to it by now, after pushing out hundreds of ghastly brats."

"You'll burn for this, Katherine," Echidna hissed.

"No, I don't think I will." She smirked. "I'm more likely to rule over any kind of hell. When will you catch on? I'm going to be a Child of Chaos."

"They'll stop you!"

Katherine laughed. "Who? I don't see anyone coming to your rescue, do you?"

"You might kill me, but you won't make it to the end of this."

"Ugh, change the freaking record. If I had a dime for every time someone has said that to me... well, I wouldn't have as much money as I do now, but it'd be a nice little nest egg."

"Release me, while you still have the chance." Echidna bucked against her restraints, but they held her fast.

"You know, it's a good thing those entrapment stones are keeping her small. Otherwise she'd be popping out monster ankle-biters every minute."

Katherine kicked her feet happily. "Every hour is bad enough. I'm running out of jars."

Naima flashed Katherine a fanged grin. "Another of your excellent ideas, Eris."

"One of my finer moments, for sure."

I noticed a pile of Mason jars on the floor beside the altar. About twenty of them. They were filled with black smoke. Empty ones lay on the other side, ready to be used. Why hadn't Katherine killed Echidna yet? What was she waiting for? I glanced up to ask my dad about it, but he'd vanished. My chest almost exploded. He'd abandoned me. He'd just... gone. Now, I was on my own here. With Katherine and Naima and a hyper-fertile Purge beast in the valley below. *Well, this can't be good.*

"Would you put that thing down, Naima?" Katherine tapped her fingertips on the golden armrest. "All this screaming is giving me a migraine, and that little portal imp clearly isn't in any rush to play the dashing prince. I don't see any white knights on the horizon, do you?"

"There has been no sign of the boy, no."

"Look, I'm always game for a dramatic entrance, but that relentless wailing gives me a headache. Humans are so tiresome." Katherine sneered. "They get snatched by one magical and they lose their minds. Just knock her out or something, and wake her up when lover-boy finally shows. Kudos for your quick thinking, by the way. This is precisely why I brought you back. I would've been so mad if I'd had to start over with a new lieutenant."

"It is my duty and my pleasure to serve you, Eris."

"And always so gracious." Katherine sighed. "What would I do without you, Naima? On second thought, don't answer that. My ego needs stroking, not bringing down. How are your ribs?"

Naima grimaced. "Getting better, Eris."

"I guess that's to be expected. Not everyone can just bounce back from being almost crushed to death. If you could do that, you'd be me."

Naima reluctantly pulled Suri in. She collapsed on the ground as Naima let her go, sobbing into her hands. I realized that Naima must have improvised when she'd taken Suri. Would they have taken someone else, if they'd been there? Had Naima picked Suri out because I'd shown interest—because she happened to be in the wrong place at the wrong time? I had way too many questions that'd probably never be answered. But it was clear that Katherine wanted me for something. To get me on her side, maybe? To bargain? This was her trap, and Suri was the unwilling piece of cheese. *Does that mean I've walked right into it?*

Anger bubbled inside me. How dare she do this. How dare she use an innocent human as her pawn to get to me.

Without my dad at my side for moral support, I had to admit things had gotten a bit scary. I was totally on my own. But I couldn't back out now. I couldn't just portal away and leave Suri. If I didn't show, Katherine would just kill her because she wasn't useful anymore. I couldn't let her suffer because of me. Plus, there was Echidna to think of. I was too close to her not to try something. There was too much at stake.

The trouble was, Katherine was literally expecting me.

I glanced at Suri to give myself strength. Naima was prowling behind her, and Suri was shaking violently. It was like she didn't dare look up at her attacker, out of sheer terror. I could hear her whimpering from here. She looked so lost and small, and I was the one who'd put her in this position. I was the one who'd put her in danger, when all she'd done was be kind to me. I was still wearing the rocket ship sticker.

"Incoming." Katherine got out of her throne and paused beside the altar. Echidna was thrashing, a scream rising in her throat. Another monster baby was on its way. "At least you'll leave a decent legacy, Echidna. These jars alone will power the island for months. Won't that be nice, knowing you haven't died in vain? So many people do, and it's tragic, really. At least you're being useful before I sacrifice you."

Echidna was too far into giving birth to reply. I couldn't take my eyes off her as she let out a terrible scream. And, all the while, Katherine just stood there and watched her, with an amused smirk on her face. How could I get Suri and Echidna out of here without Katherine catching me? It seemed impossible. They were close, but not close enough.

Before I could think about it anymore, a huge black pearl erupted out of Echidna. My stomach churned. This wasn't like a normal Purge. The pearl hovered in the air for a moment, then popped like a bubble. Black smoke billowed out. It started to take shape, looking like a gargoyle. Leaving Suri on the ground, Naima lunged over to the altar and plucked up a Mason jar. She caught the monster baby in it like she was pouring juice.

This is it. This is my shot.

Gathering Chaos into my palms, I opened a portal and slipped through, focusing intently on the island. It was a big enough target to land on without accidentally hitting the shiny water. Anywhere else, and I'd have been screwed. I jumped out, right next to Suri. But Katherine wasn't standing by the altar anymore. Instead, she was right there, in front of my face. And she was smiling like she'd already won.

"Silly boy," she purred. "Did you think I hadn't seen you? Teenage boys are so predictable. Give them a damsel to save, and they come running."

You idiot. The "taking his time" thing was yet another ruse. And I'd walked right into it.

"I was wondering how long it would take you to get here, actually," Katherine went on. "You're even more punctual than I'd hoped." Naima moved to capture me, her claws out. "Not yet, Naima. We don't have to rush this, and I don't want you accidentally slashing the merchandise."

Naima stepped back obediently. My mind raced. I had to outsmart this cow. She'd just played me for a fool, but I wasn't giving up yet. Lethe was a tricky place. I could make that work to my advantage. I was close enough now, to both Echidna and Suri, to portal them out of here. I just had to be fast. Really fast.

"It's literally like taking candy from a baby, only your human friend here is the lollipop." Katherine chuckled. "Do you want to see that, Jacob? Do you want to see me take your candy from you? I could drop her in one of these pools, and she'd be lost forever. Or maybe a bit of good old-fashioned blunt trauma would work better? A slash across the throat? The red would look so very striking against all this white. Or, you could agree to join me, and this little human can walk free."

So Suri is *a bargaining chip?* That was why they hadn't just snatched me. Plus, they would've had to deal with me trying to portal away, at any opportunity. This way, Katherine clearly thought she'd found a reason for me to agree to join her.

I glanced at Echidna, who was recovering from her latest birth. I felt like I was back in the Asphodel Meadows, about to make the wrong decision again. It had been worth it that time, even though it had cost Quetzi his life. Isadora had lived. And I wanted Suri to live, too. That same impulse pushed through me.

I moved to open a portal, the bronze energy already in my hands.

"*Pluma quasi lumen, quod in tabula rigida,*" Katherine said, calm as anything.

My body seized up and I fell backward like a plank of wood, hitting the ground hard. Suri gasped, and tears trickled down her cheeks. She looked so afraid. At first, I was freaked out that Katherine might have used the same hex she'd used on Isadora, but I didn't feel particularly bound to Katherine. Plus, I knew it couldn't be that. Isadora had made Bellmore put the same anti-hex on me, after that incident. I guessed Katherine must have known that the jig would be up on that, because she'd definitely used something else. This just felt like a way of immobilizing me.

"Jacob? Jacob, what's going on?" Suri whimpered. "I just want to go home. I don't want to die. I don't want to die."

"You're not going to," I promised.

Katherine snorted. "Big words, Jacob."

"She has nothing to do with this. Just send her back. You don't need her," I shot back.

"I will, if you agree to join me. It's a very simple exchange, Jakey." Katherine leered down at me. "If you don't, then she's dying today. And you're going to watch. Just so you know that you had every chance to save her, by saying those little words: 'I agree, Eris.' I might even let you hold her in your arms when I'm done, so you can feel the weight of your decision. Literally. Oh, it's going to be so heartbreaking, like a Shakespearean tragedy. Romeo and Juliet, in the flesh. I can hardly wait. Only, you can change the story, if you want, but that's up to you. Maybe Juliet doesn't have to die. I always thought she was an idiot for stabbing herself anyway. Who does that over some boy? Why not change the ending, Jake? Come on, I know you want to."

"Why are you doing this? Do you really want me to join you that bad?" I narrowed my eyes at her. "What's the point? You don't need a Portal Opener anymore. And why bring an innocent human into this?"

Katherine smiled. "Don't you remember what I said in Tartarus?"

"You wouldn't shut up, so it's hard to pinpoint one thing."

She chuckled darkly. "I told Harley that she was going to watch everyone she loved die. I told her she'd suffer. And I want you to be here, with me, to witness you and your friends' greatest failure to date. And, perhaps, if you choose right, she'll hear of how you joined me. That'll sting her more than if I just killed you outright. Not that I don't have that in mind, if need be. I want you to see, with your own two eyes, that you failed... again. But it doesn't have to be a total loss, if you decide to switch sides. You can turn that failure into a victory by joining the winning team, and you can save this creature in the same breath. What's not to love?"

I knew what was coming next. I knew what she wanted me to see.

"Speaking of which, the girl," Katherine added, "was just a stroke of serendipity. The perfect bait to lure a stupid teenage boy to me. So I'd have you right where I wanted you. Front row for the fourth ritual showdown."

NINETEEN

Jacob

K atherine's spell had me stuck. I couldn't move. Suri couldn't, either.
"Bring them closer." Katherine flashed Naima a wink. "But not too close."

As she sauntered back to the altar, Naima did her bidding. She started with me, picking me up like I weighed nothing and carrying me over. She laid me down on the ground, giving me an up close and personal view of Echidna. I fought to turn my head as she went back for Suri, before placing her down next to me. She was close enough that my hand brushed hers. It wasn't much, but it was the best I could do to bring her comfort.

"Jacob? What's happening?" Suri whispered, her eyes wide with panic. "Do you know these people? What are they?"

"It's a long story, but I'll get you out. I promise."

"I can't die in this nightmare, Jacob. Please don't let me die."

"I won't. I swear I won't."

Tears started to fall down her face again, her lip trembling. She squeezed her eyes shut as if she could make all of this disappear. I wanted to get her out right then and there, but this spell was doing a number on me. I could turn my head left to right, but the rest of me was like a block of concrete.

"Now then, what do you say we get this party started?" Katherine grinned. "It wouldn't be right to have you die without an audience. Personally, I'd prefer an obedient crowd of admirers, but these two will have to do. And who knows, maybe our Portal Opening friend here will bow to me when all of this is over. Silver linings all around."

Echidna writhed under her restraints. "You can't kill me. I am more ancient than anything you've ever encountered."

"You don't have much of a choice, sweetheart." Katherine rubbed her hands together and closed her eyes. She ignored Echidna's howls as the Mother of Monsters fought to break out of the green ropes. Her voice deepened as she began the ritual. *"Veniam ad vos bestias Matris sacrificare. Aemulator stare coram me sicut tu. Hic est donum Quarto requiritur ad cæremonias istas. Vide eius chaos meae tenetur, nisi qui in summa egestate huius meam."*

I had no idea what she was saying, but it didn't sound good.

"You can't even speak Latin properly," Echidna sniped. "You're more likely to turn me into a shrimp than complete your ritual."

Katherine smiled. "My Latin is fine. Don't worry, Chaos will understand."

"Of course you would butcher an ancient tongue. You can barely speak in your own."

"At least you're keeping things entertaining. Most of my victims just cry and beg for their lives, the usual boring rigmarole."

Echidna fought against her restraints. "You won't see me beg for my life. You forget that my life is already running in the veins of every Purge beast I've ever birthed. Even if you kill me, I'll be avenged."

Katherine snickered. "I'm shaking in my Jimmy Choos. You think I can't handle a couple of pesky Purge beasts? I handled you, didn't I?"

"You got lucky."

"Luck shouldn't be sniffed at." Katherine tutted. "And you're clearly forgetting that I birthed my own Purge beast, one far stronger than anything you've come up with. Do your children have souls? No, they don't. Mine does. So what does that say about you?"

"I think it says more about you, that you had to Purge your only companion."

Katherine sucked air through her teeth. "Oof, low blow, Echidna."

"You must have been a lonely child. I bet your parents despaired of you."

"They did when I killed them." Katherine grinned like the devil herself.

"The shock was the best part. They really didn't see it coming, even when I split them apart from the cells outward."

"Parents always see the best in their children, even when they're obvious psychopaths."

"See, who needs therapy when I have you?" Katherine replied. "I bet you look at your big, ugly babies and think they're the cutest damned things you've ever seen."

"Ah, and some of my children became your only friends, too."

That made Katherine pause. "Gargoyles are not friends, Echidna. They're pets. Tools to be used."

"But I bet they made you feel less alone, didn't they?" Echidna was giving her best here. She wasn't going to let Katherine kill her without making her feel like crap first.

"You're starting to annoy me." Katherine glared down at the Mother of Monsters.

Echidna smirked. "I wouldn't want to make this easy." She seemed resigned to her fate, but she wasn't going down easily. She was older and wiser, by far. And, weirdly, she didn't seem as evil as Katherine. That was something I never thought I'd say.

"At least you'll be quiet soon." Katherine reached into the folds of her gown and took a ceremonial knife out of... well, somewhere. *Ego autem dedi sanguinem vertuntur, industria sit fluxus in me.* As she lifted the blade above Echidna's chest, the Mother of Monsters gave me a sideways glance.

"Tell Harley that our deal still stands," she said. "Only, it'll be my firstborn, Leviathan, who will collect what is owed. Naming Harley's firstborn. Tell her that."

Katherine sneered. "Don't waste your breath. Once I'm done with Harley, there won't be a speck of her left, let alone a viable womb. The only thing Leviathan will be doing is bowing to me, the new Child of Chaos. Eris herself."

"You love talking about yourself in the third person, don't—" Echidna never got to finish her witty retort. The blade came down, plunging into her heart. Black, oily blood oozed out of the wound and spread across her chest. She choked on it, splatters of the same substance bursting out of her mouth. As her eyes widened, her body flaked away in black strips. Each one turned to smoke as it hit the air, until there was nothing left of Echidna.

"What did you do to her?" The words tumbled out before I could stop them. I knew Purge beasts turned into smoke when they were killed, but I hadn't expected the same thing to happen to Echidna. For some reason, I'd thought she'd be immune, or that she'd just keep her form.

Katherine smiled. "Impressive, right? It's the blade. This baby is forged from alchemist fire and silver. One of the rarest blades in existence. Perfect for killing powerful monsters, and a steal at six easy installments."

Seconds later, a bright tornado of silver light shot up from the altar. It tore open the blinding white sky, and tendrils came shivering back down. They crept outward like liquid hands and sank right into Katherine's body. She threw her head back, and her eyes turned silver. Her whole body lit up as the energy filled her. I could see her actual veins beneath her skin, pulsing with pure Chaos. A few moments afterward, the gaping hole in the sky closed, and the last of the tornado pummeled into Katherine. Her body glowed with an internal light, her eyes flashing like mirrors. I knew what it meant. Katherine had completed the fourth ritual. Nobody had tried to stop her.

She staggered forward, into the altar. Hunched over, she dragged in air. Her fingers raked at the marble, the knife clattering onto the surface. Clearly, the effects of the ritual were getting harder for her to swallow. The energy must have been immense. No matter how strong she was becoming, Chaos would always be that little bit stronger. Until she completed the rituals, at least.

"Oh, that feels good." She stood back up and shivered.

"Are you well, Eris?" Naima made to step forward, but Katherine stopped her.

"I'm just peachy. More than peachy." A smile stretched across her lips. She lifted her hands and watched, transfixed, as silver strands twisted around her fingers. "I wonder what I could do with this? Maybe all I have to do is snap my fingers, and you two will just—*poof*—evaporate." She looked down at me. "What do you think? Should I kill you and your human pet with this if you don't agree to join me, or should I keep you both around regardless, so you can witness my completion of the final ritual? Your abilities would still be useful, for sure, so I can be sure I have your power at hand for my future regime, to flow into others. I'm so close now. Can't you smell it?"

"What?" I asked.

"The death of a Child of Chaos." She licked her lips. "It's like cinnamon sugar on hot cocoa. It's like marshmallows on a campfire. It's so sweet... and so addictive, and I can almost taste it on the tip of my tongue." She swept her hands across me and Suri, releasing us from the paralyzing spell.

I sat up immediately and grasped for Suri, helping her to her feet before Katherine put another hex on us. She leaned into me, burying her face in my shoulder. I put my arm around her protectively. Her chest heaved as she sobbed, panic-stricken.

Katherine stepped toward us. "Now, what to do with you both? I've been procrastinating. It's a bad habit I'm trying to kick. Maybe I'll keep you as an unwilling assistant, portal boy. I'm strong enough now to take that power right out of you. Although, I'd prefer you to be willing. What do you say? One last chance to join me and save your girlfriend? Tick-tock, tick-tock..."

"As long as you leave Suri out of this. Let her go home," I said in a low voice.

"Not a chance." She paused. "Does that mean you're agreeing?"

I sneered. "Over my dead body."

"Ugh, so cliché. But fair enough, have it your way." She lifted her palms. But before she could conjure a single strand, a portal tore open right behind me. Katherine's eyes flew wide, and a roar of surprise slipped out of Naima's mouth.

Elan appeared beside me, Lethe's strange light making him phase in and out of a solid body. He hadn't come out of the portal, but he was enough to distract Katherine and Naima.

"You!" Katherine narrowed her eyes at him. "I was wondering if you'd make an appearance, you slimy son of a—" The words died on her lips as Isadora stepped out of the portal with Louella, the two of them sprinting at Suri and me. They dragged us into the portal, just as my dad sent out a bright white light. It hurtled straight for Katherine and Naima, knocking the latter back. Katherine stayed standing.

As the portal began to close, my dad turned and smiled at me. One last time. He hadn't abandoned me. He'd been watching this whole time, looking out for me.

Katherine rolled her eyes. "You were never one for theatrics, Elan. What changed?"

"Necessity," he replied.

"This won't stop me, you realize."

"No, it won't." My dad grinned wider. "But it'll get my son away from you."

The portal closed before I could hear any more. As we stumbled back into the SDC, I was relieved to see Suri in Louella's grasp. But that was about the only relief I was going to get from this. Katherine had completed the fourth ritual. She'd done it so easily that it seemed ridiculous. We were supposed to be making it harder for her, not easier.

And then there was my dad... I'd never see him again. Even if I went back to Lethe, he might not be there anymore. Katherine had gotten stronger, and I didn't know the limits to her newly absorbed power. Could she kill a spirit all over again? Would she? Or would she lock him in a jar, the way she'd done with Harley's mom? I couldn't see a single outcome where I'd get to speak with him again. That stung. Right in my heart. I'd spent so many years wanting to see my parents again, and now that road had come to an end. There were no loopholes.

I'd had a lot of hopes in Lethe, and they'd all been dashed. I hadn't saved Echidna. I hadn't stopped Katherine. And I wouldn't have gotten Suri out if it hadn't been for Isadora. And now, Katherine would be on to the fifth ritual before we could even blink.

TWENTY

Jacob

"I don't understand what happened. What *was* that place? And what were they doing? There was all this glowing stuff and sparks and... what did I see back there? Seriously, what did I see?" Suri glanced up at Louella, while Krieger prepared a syringe. She was clinging to Louella like a life raft while she rocked backward and forward on a chair in the infirmary.

"You're safe now," Krieger replied. He took the syringe off a silver tray and injected its contents into her arm. Slowly, she relaxed into the chair. Her eyes closed. Soon, she looked like she was asleep. I realized he must have given her a mild sedative, which was probably for the best. She hadn't stopped murmuring since we'd come back through the portal. I kept trying to talk to her, but she kept turning her face away, like she didn't want to see me. I couldn't blame her for that. Not after what I'd just put her through.

"Don't do anything else to her," I said. Krieger looked like he was preparing something else. "Don't wipe her memory, please. Not yet."

"I couldn't even if I wanted to," Krieger replied. "She needs to be calmer before we can wipe her memory. Otherwise, there's a chance the spell will not stick as it should. That is usually the case with younger humans. They have surprisingly resilient minds."

Isadora nodded. "We probably shouldn't overwhelm her until she comes around again." She looked to me. "How are you doing?"

I swallowed the lump in my throat. "Not great."

"You did a brave thing back there."

"No, I did a stupid thing." I balled my hands into fists to keep the tears away. "I should've known Katherine would be watching the SDC. I put Suri in danger. There wasn't anything brave about it."

"You went after her. That was brave. You could've left her, but you didn't," Louella chimed in. "And I know you, Jake. I know you were probably trying to think of a way to get Echidna out, too."

I shrugged. "What does it matter what I wanted to do? I couldn't do any of it. Suri probably would've been mulch if you hadn't arrived when you did."

"What happened?" Krieger sat on the stool opposite me.

"Katherine… she completed the fourth ritual. Echidna is dead, and she sucked up all that energy." Tears welled in my eyes. "I couldn't stop her. I couldn't do a damn thing. I tried portaling, but she was one step ahead of me. It was a trap, and I walked into it. Katherine wanted me to join her and used Suri as leverage. I was never going to agree, but Suri was bait."

"You couldn't have known that," Isadora said.

"No, but I should've."

"Don't beat yourself up about it, Jake. Katherine has probably been planning something like this for a while. It's not your fault." Louella held my gaze. I could tell she meant well, but disappointment colored her tone. They were all disappointed. And scared, probably, for the same reasons I was.

Katherine was one step closer to her goal. I had so much grief and disappointment and frustration and anger running through me that it was hard to string a simple sentence together. I'd tried to do something good, and I'd failed miserably. I'd tried to be the hero, and I'd almost gotten Suri killed.

"Wait…" I looked to Isadora. "How can you be here? Aren't you supposed to be in the cells? How did you know where to find me?"

She walked over and hugged me. I didn't resist. "We can talk about that later. I just want you to know that you did your best under impossible circumstances. Suri is alive because of you. I saw Katherine—she was brimming with power. The fact that you were still alive is a testament to how well you coped."

I clung to her. I tried to take her words and make myself feel better, but it wasn't working. I just kept thinking about Echidna and Katherine, and how we were in an even worse position. I kept trying to think of what else I could've done. Would I have changed the outcome if I hadn't gone into the Fleet Science Center this morning? Would Echidna still be alive if I hadn't? Or would it only have been a delay of the inevitable?

"Seriously, how are you here?" I pulled away from Isadora. I could at least get an answer to that question.

"Turns out, that tracker Levi put on your neck works. It alerted him to the fact that you'd gone missing, but he couldn't locate you with any of his own magic. Being in an otherworld skews conventional trackers. He came to me in the hopes that I'd have an idea of how to find you." She paused. "I told Levi I could help if he released me back into the coven, for good. He did, given the stakes of you being missing. It was actually the info Finch gave us that helped. Now that we know you can use a personal item to open a portal to someone, I used one of your t-shirts—sorry if it was one of your favorites. But it led me right to you."

I frowned. "Why would Levi have come to you?"

"Actually, O'Halloran suggested it. He was talking with Krieger when the news broke and convinced Levi to ask me for help. The portal took me to Lethe, but I wasn't expecting to find you the way I did. Katherine is clearly moving way faster than any of us anticipated."

"Who's the girl?" Louella nodded to the slumped figure of Suri.

"I'm Suri," she mumbled, half asleep. "And you've got some seriously good drugs in this place…" She passed out again, her arms going limp.

Krieger chuckled. "She's been through a lot, especially for a human."

"Does Levi know she's here?" I looked up at the CCTV camera in the corner of the room.

Isadora shook her head. "He knows you're back, and you're recovering, but he doesn't know about Suri here. I called Astrid to tell her to tamper with the security footage. We don't want him knowing there's a human in the building. Me and Astrid have got a decent code going. It's necessary, given Levi's latest wave of doom and gloom."

"I guess that's good." I dipped my chin to my chest. "I just wish I could've stopped Katherine."

Louella came to sit beside me. "You can't think like that. We need to look forward now."

I sighed. "She still has one ritual, I guess. That's one more chance to stop her."

Isadora nodded. "The LA Coven head honchos already have the recovered, rare magical children in protective custody. With reinforced security."

"That's good to know." It gave me a little bit of relief.

"You've been gone longer than you think," Krieger explained. "Time seems to work strangely in this Lethe place."

"How long have I been gone?"

"Eight hours."

I gaped at him. "What?"

"Who was the guy with the light show?" Louella asked.

The tears came flooding back. "He was my dad."

"Elan?" Isadora looked suddenly sad.

"Yeah. I found him when I landed in Lethe. He died there. His spirit is trapped there. I don't really want to talk about it." My voice croaked.

"Then tell us more about the girl," Isadora urged, putting her hand on my shoulder. I hated pity. And it was coming off all of them. I didn't need to be an Empath to feel it.

"She was just some girl I met in the Science Center. We got to talking after I saved her from a group of schoolkids. She's one of the tour guides." I pushed down my sad thoughts.

Louella nodded. "Yeah, I think I've seen her a couple times, when I've been passing through. She works in the gift shop too, right?"

"Yeah." My mouth twisted into a grimace. "But she was just an opportunity for Naima to pounce, according to Katherine. They were waiting for me to slip up. Katherine wanted me in Lethe, one way or another—she wanted me to see what she did to Echidna, and she wanted me to switch to her side. I think she wanted to send some kind of message, to back me into a corner. Her usual 'look how powerful I am' bullcrap."

"So, she's on the last ritual?" Louella dragged in a nervous breath. "Do you think she has enough rare magicals to perform it?"

Isadora shrugged. "Honestly, I don't know. And, without Finch here, we can't exactly ask."

"Plus, she may be saving her own rare magicals for her future army so she doesn't run out of specific abilities. From what I understand, if a particular power goes out of existence, she may not be able to resurrect that ability when she gives abilities as a Child of Chaos. I may be wrong, but that's the theory," Krieger added. "She may wish to use magicals who are, for lack of a better word, expendable. Those children would fit that description."

"Either way, we can be sure Katherine's got a backup plan for her backup plan. Harley said that, remember?" I gritted my teeth. I hated Katherine so much that it actually burned in my chest. "If she has to use her own magicals, she will. To her, everyone is expendable."

"Seems like there's a pattern in Katherine's behavior." Isadora leaned forward in her chair. "She may have tried to have you and Harley killed, but the majority of her interactions with you two have revealed a certain level of... obsession. She wants to break you down until you've got nothing left to give. My guess is she's doing it so that, when she becomes Eris, she can be there to pick up the pieces. So she can use you and give you no choice but to bow to her."

Krieger nodded. "Katherine is no fool. She can appreciate the value of natural talent and rare ability. And she would probably like to nurture it, given the chance. There's a reason she has so many loyal followers, and while that has something to do with her power, it likely has more to do with her charisma. That's why people are running from their covens to join her—because they may feel they ought to be on the winning side, and the side that is offering more."

"I've known Katherine for a long time, and I think you're right," Isadora replied. "She has a way of persuading people to do things. It's the same trait that can be found in many influential leaders across history—the most evil ones."

"We should tell Harley about what happened," I said.

"I was just about to suggest that. Do you have a way of getting in touch with her?" Isadora glanced at me.

"I've got a burner phone." I patted my pockets, feeling the outline of it. "Yeah, I still have it."

"Good, because right now, she might be the only hope we have left."

TWENTY-ONE

Harley

W e were back in the Palace of Fine Arts, and Wade and I were sitting by the lake, watching the fountains erupt. The sun was high in the sky and warm on my face, the earthy scent of the cypress trees drifting on the breeze. If I closed my eyes, I could pretend that nothing bad was going on, and we were just sitting here in the pretty afternoon, admiring the beauty of this place.

A small smile turned up the corners of my lips as I wondered if Wade and I would ever get the chance to have a vacation together. Maybe he'd be able to come on the Smiths' next family holiday, if we lived that long. My smile evaporated. That was the trouble with this Katherine stuff—it infiltrated everything else, making it impossible to keep my thoughts light and happy.

Finch and Garrett were getting snacks and drinks from a stand at the far side of the gardens, laughing at something. The former frostiness that had existed between them seemed to be thawing a bit. Finch looked happier, leaning up against the stand, making a rude gesture with the ketchup bottle. *Ah, Finch... ever the joker.* And the fact that Garrett was laughing back only spread Finch's smile wider. I'd almost forgotten how close they'd been, once upon a time.

Still, even with the Queen of Evil permeating all my waking thoughts, it was kind of nice to have a moment to gather myself before we went, full steam ahead, into the mission to snatch the Grimoire. Moments like this didn't come along too often, these days. Plus, it was nice to be alone with Wade. The problem was, even though he was sitting right next to me, he couldn't have been further away. We'd already been sitting for a good five minutes, and he hadn't said a word apart from, "Yeah, I want sauce on my fries." Not exactly thrilling conversation.

Fiddling with my pendant to try and push away the anxiety rising through my stomach, I leaned into his shoulder. He stiffened slightly, but he didn't move away. Maybe I was just imagining things. Maybe this was his stress showing through, manifesting as distance instead of fear.

"You okay? You've been kind of quiet," I said, knowing it was a dumb observation but not sure how else to start.

He looked down at me. "I've just got a lot on my mind."

"New York stuff?"

He nodded. "Yeah... it's a lot, right?"

"You could say that." I focused on the fountain as it sprang upward. "You sure that's all?"

"I promise."

"You've been quiet a lot today. Is it something I've done? Or something someone's said?"

He kissed my forehead. "No, it's not you. It's just this mission. It's a massive risk."

"But it'll be worth it, if we can do it." I had to keep convincing myself of that, in case I suddenly lost my nerve.

"Maybe..." He kept his gaze on me and tilted my chin up. He had that intense look in his eyes that I loved, and his stare flickered to my mouth. I knew what came next, and I was only too happy to get involved.

Slowly, he leaned in and kissed me gently on the lips. As soon as his mouth touched mine, I melted into him, letting all my fears and concerns drift away, leaving only him and me, and the soothing sound of the fountain cascading back into the lake. I looped my arms around his neck and felt his hands slide around my waist as he kissed me deeper, telling me without words that nothing had changed between us. It was a huge comfort, especially considering the danger we were about to head into. For that, I needed all the support and extra strength I could get.

As I pulled away, a goofy grin on my face, he kept his arm around my waist. Satisfied, I nestled closer into his chest, listening for the steady beat of his heart. It would have been bliss, had it not been for the wave of unsettling emotions coming off him. I didn't want to shut them out, because it gave me some idea as to what he was thinking. I knew it was borderline prying, but he'd been acting so odd that I needed a bit of extra insight. Right now, I could feel contentment, a ripple of desire, and a flurry of love, but it was somewhat tainted by the undercurrent of anger and bitterness that bristled alongside.

"You've gone quiet on me again," I murmured.

"Have I?"

I nodded. "Are you sure there's not something else on your mind?"

He sighed heavily. "It's… no, it doesn't matter."

"Come on, tell me. You can tell me anything."

He kissed my hair. "It's Finch."

"Finch?"

"Yeah."

"What about him?"

Wade shrugged. "I'm worried about his influence on you. He ruined your reputation. He made you run from the SDC. He took away your chance to clear your name. It's not right. You deserve a future for everything you've done, and are doing, not a lifetime in Purgatory."

Wow, someone's been harboring some resentment. The spike in his bitterness hit me like a slap to the cheek. All this time, I'd thought he was just angry about Katherine, but it was Finch he was mad at. I couldn't exactly disagree with the points he'd made, but I didn't want to be going into the New York Coven with a fractured team.

"If Katherine wins, my future won't exist. None of ours will." I held his face in my hands. "But, if we defeat her, then I might have enough brownie points to buy my way out of Purgatory."

"But why should you have to buy your way out of Purgatory? You shouldn't be in this position in the first place," he said sharply.

"What's up with you, Wade? What's with the attitude?" I had to put it bluntly. Beating around the bush wasn't going to get us anywhere.

He turned his face away. "I'm pissed because I'm putting myself at risk here, while you're making friends with your murderous psychopath of a half-brother. The guy who, newsflash, tried to kill you not that long ago. How can you even think of him as trustworthy? As far as I'm concerned, he hasn't proven jack. He looks like the same old Finch from where I'm standing, and I'm not too eager to charge into New York with someone like him. If he screws us over, then we're not just looking at a life sentence in Purgatory, we're looking at Katherine coming down on us and taking the one thing that might stop her. Have you even thought about that? Have you even thought that Finch might be a huge, elaborate ploy to get close to her one weakness?"

I stared at him, my blood pounding. I knew he was in a foul mood, but I hadn't expected a tirade. He had every right to be conflicted about Finch, given his history, but he didn't have the right to come at me like that. Despite appearances, I still had my concerns about Finch. Not just him, but all of this. Wade was supposed to be helping me, not making me feel about the size of a gnat. And yeah, maybe he didn't mean everything he was saying, but that didn't stop his words from hurting.

"I—" A loud buzzing cut me off. Tearing my eyes away from Wade's angry face, I reached into my pocket and took out my burner cell. Jacob's name flashed up. Sliding the answer button, I put it to my ear. "Jake? What's up?"

In the space of a five-minute phone call, Wade's harsh words paled into insignificance. Somehow, Katherine had managed to move the goal posts again, without us even realizing.

TWENTY-TWO

Harley

"Everything okay?" Finch stared at me with ketchup smeared across his mouth, like a dime-store Joker. The smile on Garrett's face died the moment he saw me. Evidently, my own face was giving just about everything away, and I didn't care. Anger shot through me like a thousand pinpricks, and I couldn't do anything to push it down. *Way to ruin the mood, Merlin.*

I put the phone back in my pocket and tried not to lose control. "Nope."

"What's going on?" Wade peered at me with concerned eyes, his previous anger gone.

"Echidna is dead. Katherine completed the fourth ritual." I sucked in a furious breath. "Naima laid a trap for Jacob, and he ended up in Lux's otherworld by himself. He followed some human girl that Naima snatched to lure him there. Isadora had to portal in and save him, so it must have been a pretty near miss with Katherine. Anyway, said *human* girl is now in the SDC's infirmary, just to make things extra freaking messy. One bit of good news, though—it means Isadora is out of jail. Turns out, Levi needed her to get Jacob back, and they brokered some kind of deal. So there's that." I balled my hands into fists and fought to calm my racing mind, using some of the Euphoria techniques to clear my thoughts of all the bad, violent, punchy stuff.

Garrett snorted. "Levi's brain is going to fall out of his head when he finds out there's a human in the SDC."

"What, like your girlfriend?" Finch snapped back. Man, that boy just couldn't help himself. Even when he was trying to build bridges with his old friend, he just had to go and say something like that.

"She's different." Garrett took such a violent bite of his sandwich that I could've sworn he was picturing it as Finch's head. The two of them had a long way to go, to get back to some sort of friendship. Not that it mattered right now what state their relationship was in. This news had put us at about one minute to midnight on Katherine's doomsday clock. If I'd thought we were running out of time before, this had made things a million times worse.

"It's not like we weren't expecting something like that to happen," Wade said, taking me by surprise. I'd thought his attitude had gone away, but here it was again, rearing its ugly head. I sensed the same angry agitation that had been there before. *Where is this coming from, Crowley?*

"Hello? Earth calling Wade. Katherine has just completed the fourth ritual, which means there's only *one* to go before she becomes a Child of freaking Chaos." I tried to rein in my anger. It wasn't entirely directed at him, and I hated that I was unleashing it all at him. I guessed I was still harboring a little bitterness about the things he'd said.

"We had a feeling she might get the fourth ritual over with before we could do anything to stop her," Finch cut in. "So, right now, we just need to focus on mambo number five. She might not even get that far if we get the Grimoire and find something juicy inside. A tantalizing tidbit, if you will."

"Did they say anything else?" Garrett asked. "What are the others doing while we're out here risking our asses?"

"Krieger and Jacob are getting back to work on the magical detector, though I think Jacob's a little shaken up. He just faced Katherine on his own, so of course he is." I took a steady breath. *Happy thoughts, happy thoughts, happy thoughts.* "Anyway, they're getting some of the preceptors involved to speed things up. Krieger's also eager to figure out what's going on with O'Halloran and the security magicals—they're still acting weird. So he's going to look into that. They shouldn't be blindly following Levi in all this Echidna secrecy. Not that her being stolen matters now. We missed that friggin' boat."

"We just need to focus on *our* mission." Finch wiped the ketchup from his mouth. "Bitesize chunks, remember?"

I nodded slowly. "We need a good entry strategy into New York, so let's hope Remington has something for us. I'm not wasting any more time standing around here eating while Katherine is on her way to completing the last ritual. You think she's resting on her laurels? No, she isn't."

As if beckoned by my fury, my phone suddenly buzzed in my pocket. Plucking it out, I caught sight of the caller ID and swiped the answer button. Remington had put his number into the phone before we left so he could call us back to his office as quickly as possible.

I stared out at the fountain, but I couldn't find any peace in it anymore. Once again, Katherine had ruined it. "Tell me you've got good news."

We crept back through the secret doorway into Remington's office, only to find a full house sitting and standing around his desk. Isadora, Louella, Dylan, and Tatyana looked up at us in surprise as we entered, but Remington simply took it in stride. I wouldn't have been surprised if he put a really heavy bookshelf in front of that doorway, once we were gone.

"What… What are you doing here?" I was already a chaotic mass of emotions, and seeing them had me teetering over the edge of a full-blown meltdown. They had to be fuming with me, after I'd abandoned them in the coven. Wade had made his feelings about it pretty clear, so they had to be feeling the same. However, they weren't looking at me with any anger, and I couldn't feel any animosity coming off them. Instead, I sensed only relief, and anxiety, and happiness.

"We wanted to come and see you." Tatyana smiled at me. A rare enough sight as it was, and a welcome one.

Dylan nodded. "We couldn't let you go off without a farewell party. No balloons, sadly. They would've made us stand out a bit."

I laughed. "But how did you get out of the SDC?"

"We're not under coven arrest." Louella beamed.

"So you really are out for good?" I glanced at Isadora, unbelievably happy that she was here.

Isadora nodded. "It was part of my deal with Levi. I told him I wouldn't be caged in the coven like an animal, and he was so desperate that he agreed."

"Plus, Isadora and I go way back, so I thought she might be useful in this meeting," Remington added.

"You called them?" I didn't quite know what else to say.

"I did. I thought we could use some fresh eyes on this." He gestured for the four of us newcomers to sit before continuing. "With the stakes as high as they are, now that Katherine is way ahead of the curve, you'll need all the help you can get to sneak into the New York Coven. Hence, I called for the cavalry."

I sank down into one of the armchairs. "Does this mean you couldn't find us a way around security?"

"Not exactly." Remington rubbed his tattooed neck. "You have the door-opening spell, but you'll need a full, updated plan of the building itself to navigate it without running into trouble. The layout of the New York Coven used to change every month, but they've altered it, so it now changes every week, as an extra security measure."

Finch grunted. "Extra annoying, you mean."

"It is annoying, but it's the facts," Remington replied. "Plus, as of this morning, it's been warded against Portal Openers, too. New York somehow found out about Jacob and Isadora being on the scene, and they know of their connection to you, Harley. So, they've decided to kick it up a notch, old-school, with magic that is hardly ever used, given the rarity of that particular ability."

"Does that mean they know we're planning to steal the Grimoire?" My stomach sank like a rock.

Remington shook his head. "Not necessarily. It just means they're taking precautions, with you being a fugitive and all. They're covering all bases."

"That stuff actually exists?" Garrett chimed in. "Anti-Portal-Opening stuff? I wouldn't have thought anyone would bother, since there aren't many of them around."

Dylan nodded. "Yeah, that's pretty niche, right?"

"I've never heard of anything like it," Wade added, his tone still sour. "You sure they're not just spouting this crap to put Harley off?"

Remington and Isadora exchanged a knowing glance. "Isadora, do you want to take this one?"

"I might as well, since I was the one who created the damn thing." She paced the floor in front of Remington's fireplace. "Years ago, I wrote a spell, for security purposes, which would help keep out Portal Openers. It wasn't clear, back then, how many of us were still in existence, and I knew that not all magicals, even Portal Openers, were necessarily good. Elan, for example—Jacob's dad. At that time, he was working for Katherine, and he was one of the ones who tried to steal the Merlin Grimoire. New York secretly asked for my help and, naturally, I obliged. I never thought they'd use it against me, though I suppose I should've expected it. Covens don't change. They look out for themselves above anything else."

I guessed, after everything that had gone on at the SDC recently, she wasn't about to change her mind about covens. She hated them, as a rule. And now, she probably hated them even more. The SDC had turned against her, with Levi locking her up. And the leaders at New York were now using Isadora's own spell against her. I had to admit, she'd kind of had a point about them.

"So, how do we get in if we can't portal in?" Wade pressed.

"You'll have to go in the old-fashioned way," Remington replied.

"What, through the front door?" Finch gaped at Remington as if he'd lost his marbles.

"No, not through the front door. Through a back door, which you'll have to locate." Remington took some papers off his desk and handed them over to me, not that I had a clue what to do with them. Geography had never been my strong suit. I couldn't tell my Idaho from my Utah.

Finch glanced at Tatyana and Dylan, a mischievous smile on his lips. "How come djinn boy didn't come with you? He's never one to miss out on a party. Did Levi finally have the guts to lock that dog up?"

"Watch who you're calling a dog," Dylan shot back.

"Is that what happened? Did Levi lock Raffe up?" I hated to think of any of my friends in one of those cells. The memory of how Adley ended up was still pretty raw in my mind.

Dylan shook his head. "Nah, he wouldn't dare. But Raffe's not doing too good, man. He's losing it. You can see him fighting this thing he's got in him, but nobody knows if he's winning or losing anymore. Everyone's worried he's just going to go full beast mode, where the djinn takes over and does something to Raffe that he won't be able to fix."

"Like what?" I didn't want to think about the horrible possibilities.

Dylan shrugged. "That's the problem. We don't know."

"What about Santana? Can't she help him?"

Tatyana pursed her lips. "Levi still has her in the cells. Alton, too. Pending yet another 'review.' I think Levi is just using it as a way to torment them some more."

Louella nodded. "Astrid is spending half of her time with them, to keep them company, but the rest of the time, she's monitoring the internet and CCTV for signs of the cult in action. I've been helping her as best I can, but technology isn't really my thing. I'm more of a books and essays type of girl."

We were in a stressful limbo right now, while Katherine was gaining ground as if she was taking a walk in the freaking park. It didn't seem fair that we were struggling at every hurdle, while she was breezing from ritual to ritual. But bitching about it wasn't going to get me anywhere. Life wasn't fair. And good didn't always triumph over evil. Those were the stark, bitter-to-swallow facts.

I glanced down at the New York Coven plans, trying to make sense of them. "So, if we follow these, we'll be able to reach the Grimoire without being detected?"

"That's about the size of it, yes," Remington replied. "Stick to this, and you hopefully can't go wrong in terms of getting to the book. As for the Grimoire itself, I doubt you'll have any trouble reading it, given your bloodline and what you told me about your abilities. You just need to make sure you aren't spotted or caught when you actually reach the book. I can't factor that in and put it on those plans for you, I'm afraid. It's something you'll have to deal with when you're there, and you can see the security for yourself. There may be guards and wards—we just don't know."

Isadora cast me a sad look. "There's nothing else we can do, given the circumstances. Levi won't be reasoned with. He's too scared. He won't relinquish any extra information, and he sure as heck won't lift a finger to help you do this."

You don't say. Levi was a dangerous liability, and he was fast becoming a thorn in everyone's side. He could have done so much more to stop Katherine from completing the fourth ritual, but he'd just tried to save his own ass instead. In my head, he was the lowest of the low.

"Speaking of the devil, I'm going to make one last effort regarding Levi, as I promised," Remington said. "I've already set the ball rolling on taking the secrecy issue up with the California Mage Council. I'm due to meet with them shortly, to discuss everything. They need to know that Echidna is gone, and Katherine has completed the fourth ritual, and they need to know that Levi has kept it quiet. We might've been able to do something if more people had known, and he took that chance away from us. Now, we need all the covens involved. Levi doesn't get to dictate that, and he's going to know about it."

"He's blinded by his stupid pride," Isadora added. "He wants the SDC to bring down Katherine, exclusively, for nothing more than glory and fame. He doesn't care about the consequences of his actions."

"But what about this stuff with the National Council and the president?" Wade asked, his tone less frosty. He made a good point. If they knew about all of this, and they were keeping quiet too, then it wasn't just Levi acting like a prize idiot.

Remington frowned. "I keep wondering about that, and it still doesn't make a single scrap of sense. If the National Council and the president know about Echidna and have agreed to keep the Mage Councils and the directors in the dark, then there's something really fishy going on here. I said it before, I'll say it again."

"Can you make some headway with that?" Isadora asked.

"I'll do what I can."

"You're the only one who can," I reminded him. "Isadora and the rest of the SDC keep getting threatened with Purgatory if they go against Levi. He won't stop droning on about it, according to Jacob. Which means that none of these guys can say a word about it. Only you can." It was a massive cause for concern. I'd have liked to have dealt with it myself, but I was too busy with Katherine to be able to bring that asshat down. "And someone needs to stop him from getting in our way."

Isadora smiled. "Don't worry, I'll handle the stuck-up jerk. I'll make sure he stays out of your way, at the very least."

"Then it's in good hands." I smiled back at her, feeling pride flow away from her in comforting waves. She believed in me, and that was exactly what I needed.

"There's one more thing," Remington interjected.

I struggled not to roll my eyes. "What now? A troll? A dragon? A floor made of molten lava?"

He chuckled. "No need to be facetious. It's not actually about New York on this occasion." I offered him an apologetic look, and he continued. "We know some people are fleeing the covens already. If the entire magical world finds out about Echidna, it may give some magicals a reason to join Katherine, to make sure they're on what they believe is the winning side, if or when she ascends as a Child of Chaos. Again, not many people know about the rituals, but they may fear that Katherine intends to release a horde of Purge beasts or unleash a Purge plague that she's sucked out of Echidna, or something equally terrifying. They'll put two and two together and make twenty. Magicals aren't perfect. They're still mostly human creatures, and their instincts are to survive, at all costs. Some might see survival as a retention of magic, by staying by Katherine's side."

"Darwin's got a lot to answer for." Finch tutted. I could almost have commended him for trying to bring some levity to what was otherwise a hugely depressing situation.

"As I was saying." Remington shot him a cold look. "The covens have been fighting a losing battle up to now, and so has the National Council. With that in mind, you need to be careful whom you trust. Nobody is impervious to Katherine's influence, not even the higher-ups of magical society. The cult has clearly infiltrated pretty much everywhere, at this point, and no security measure is foolproof. Katherine prides herself on her discretion and sneakiness when it comes to her operatives. She saves the amateur dramatics for herself, since she's the lead in her own vision."

"What's your point?" Wade had gone back into stern mode. Even Remington seemed taken aback by his abruptness. I kept trying to convince myself that it was just nerves and stress, but I'd never seen him like this before.

"I was getting to it," Remington replied. "I will do what I can to get the word out about Echidna, to the others on the Mage Council and the coven directors, at least. Meanwhile, we have to hope that the National Council members really are starting their secret recruitment of an army."

Isadora frowned. "Although, in light of recent developments, an army might not do much."

"Sis and the Grimoire, on the other hand… Am I right?" Finch grinned at me.

"Yes, you're right." Isadora held my gaze. "Harley may well be the only one, now, who can find a way to stop Katherine before she ascends."

No pressure…

TWENTY-THREE

Jacob

I sat at Krieger's workbench. I was supposed to be focusing on the magical detector, but I kept looking at Suri instead. She was still a bit dopey from the meds. But at least she wasn't crying anymore. I didn't want her to feel sad or scared. Even if we had just been to an interdimensional world and faced a psycho with an overgrown cat for a sidekick.

Krieger was tinkering away with the device, which looked like a big block of metal pieces that had been thrown together, straight out of a steampunk world. Cogs. Wires. Bronze panels. Little buttons and levers. And a thing in the middle that looked like a metal eggcup. It had a glass orb for the egg. Inside, that little scrap of my ability swirled around, like someone had dropped a paintbrush in water.

Isadora examined the pieces. "It won't be much use if it's not portable. How far does this reach from here?"

Krieger frowned. "It has some range, but I understand what you're saying. I've been thinking about the size of it for some time, trying to think of ways I could make it smaller. Most of the device is simply there to power up the detector. It requires a vast quantity of energy, and I can't quite decipher a way to make it smaller without compromising on the power aspect. It simply won't work if it's not suitably fueled."

I didn't have much of a clue, either. If it needed a power supply that big, then it needed a power supply that big. There was no way around that. Not that I knew of, anyway. But Isadora had a glint in her eye. An idea seemed to be forming. She was good at that. And she always got a little hyper when she had a good idea.

"How about speaking to an alchemist? It's their job to make powerful things in small sizes, right? I know Bellmore consulted Jacintha when she made the pouches for me, so I'd have something small enough to wear." She tugged at the one around her throat. It was there to deal with the lasting effects of the hex that Katherine had put on her after she'd been captured. Remembering Jacintha took the smile off Isadora's face. The coven hadn't forgotten her.

Krieger nodded. "I hadn't thought of that. I suppose, with this being so practical, I'd neglected to consider alternative methods." He tapped his chin in thought. "Yes, perhaps it might be a good idea to get Rita Bonnello's advice on this. She is a highly gifted alchemist, with many accolades to her name. And there is a great deal of energy to be found in alchemical procedures. Perhaps Rita may know of a suitable substitute for... well, all of this." He waved his hand across the bulky device.

"Can I come?" I asked. I didn't want to leave Suri, but I had to get out of here for a bit. The walls were closing in slightly. I called it the "foster kid effect." Too long in one room, and we got antsy.

"Of course." Krieger smiled at me. "I was just about to suggest that, especially as Levi has asked that you don't leave my side. With sleep and meals being the obvious exceptions."

Suri blinked at me. "Do you have to go?"

"Isadora will keep you company." I grinned at Isadora. "She's not as bad as she looks."

"Cheeky."

Suri nodded slowly. "Okay then."

"I won't be gone long, I promise." I offered her a reassuring smile.

"I'll keep her safe, Jake." Isadora put her hand on my shoulder. "I can't promise I'll be very entertaining, but you're in good hands, Suri."

I left the infirmary with Krieger and headed for Rita Bonnello's office. I kept thinking about Suri the whole way. I couldn't help it. She was fixed in my mind. Honestly, I didn't know if it was what had happened in Lethe, or if

I would've been like this anyway. She'd appeared in my life, and I didn't want her to go anywhere. Even though I knew, eventually, Krieger or someone would have to wipe her memory, for her own sake. It was probably a little selfish, but I didn't want her to forget me.

Krieger knocked on Rita's door.

"Come in." A silky, Mediterranean voice echoed back. I hadn't been around the new preceptor much. Things had gotten crazy after she'd been introduced, after all. She was probably wishing she'd never accepted the position here.

I followed Krieger into the room. It smelled crazy good. Candles burned everywhere. They filled the place with this sugary, spicy scent that made my mouth water. Rita sat at an elegant black desk on the far side of the room. Everything had been stamped with her vibrant flavor. There was a red velvet couch in front of the fireplace. And a fluffy rug that had likely been torn off the back of some bear. The wallpaper was a deep red, with golden designs on it. And there were fancy statuettes everywhere. I'd never seen so many boobs in one place. Not that I was complaining.

"Ah, Dr. Krieger, what a pleasant surprise." She lifted the tiniest cup I'd ever seen to her red lips and sipped it like she was in a coffee commercial. I realized my mouth was hanging open and quickly stared at something else. Only to find boobs. *Dammit!* This room was a minefield.

"I was hoping you might help me with something," Krieger replied. He went to sit opposite her, but I stayed where I was, trying to find a safe spot to look at.

"Oh?" There was a hint of a laugh in her voice. Not mean, or anything. It was just part of the way she sounded. Like everything was a little bit funny. She effortlessly fixed a flyaway strand of her long, dark hair as she spoke.

"As you know, Jacob and I have been working on a magical detector to help us trace magicals. More specifically, at this point, Katherine. However, we've been having some difficulties with the size of the device. It's too large."

"Can there ever be such a thing?" She chuckled. However, it didn't sound like a genuine laugh to me. It sounded like she was covering a different feeling, like she was forcing it, though I didn't know what that feeling might be. Discomfort, maybe?

Krieger fumbled in his chair. "Uh... in this case, yes." I was embarrassed for him. Rita was a force of nature. Smart, sexy, sassy. Formidable. This was her power play. My gift for reading people was coming in handy. This was how she asserted herself, by making others feel uncomfortable. Men, I guessed, mostly. So they knew who was boss. But it was subtle enough that it wasn't obvious.

"Well, what seems to be the problem?" She sipped her espresso like she hadn't said anything rude.

"The power supply is much too... uh, excessive." Krieger stumbled over his words. "And we need to make it much, much smaller if the detector is going to be viable. It has to be made more portable to extend the range."

Rita set her cup down. "I'm not sure that I'm your woman, Dr. Krieger."

"You don't know of any alchemical way in which this could be achieved?"

"It's not that. It's more of a question of morality." Rita glanced at me, making me look away. "While I agree with the principle of the device and the practical benefits, I worry that such a machine might end up in the wrong hands and be used for the wrong purposes. I'm not suggesting that your intentions are skewed, Doctor, but there would be countless individuals who might lust after such a device."

I cleared my throat. "I've already spoken to Krieger about that. I thought the same way you did, but he changed my mind. If it's regulated, and it's protected at all times, then nobody can get it. We'd make that happen, for sure. Plus, with everything going on with Katherine, this is pretty much the only way to identify her. Nobody can track her down. This device is the only way to get ahead of her." I squirmed as she stared at me. "I don't need to tell you how important that is right now. She's on the final sprint. We don't want her crossing the finish line. The device gives us a shot—one we really need."

Rita kept her gaze on me. A small smile crept onto her lips. She let her fingertips trail around the rim of her espresso cup. I could see the faint smudge of her lipstick on the white ceramic. She was trying to gauge me. Figure me out. Beautiful people were always the trickiest to read. They bamboozled you with their looks, male or female. But I looked back at her, just so she'd know I meant business.

She sat back in her chair. "I need some time to think about it. As I said, there are many ethical implications to contemplate. You say you will protect the device, and that you will regulate its use, but such things are not assurances. You don't have the ability to promise that."

"Perhaps we could add a failsafe of some kind, if that would give you peace of mind?" Krieger asked.

She paused, glancing over him. "Alchemy is complex, and it offers many solutions—but it does not offer all solutions. Once I have had the chance to think, I will speak with you again. Then, and only then, will I conscientiously be able to give you my answer. I understand the time restraints involved, so I will do what I can to give you your reply before any deadline has passed."

I wanted to say more to convince her. But what could I say? I understood where she was coming from. And she made a bunch of good points. Plus, Rita didn't seem like the type who did anything she didn't want to. Me pushing her, or begging, wouldn't change anything. Krieger seemed resigned, too. His shoulders were slumped.

"Well, I hope you'll make the right choice," I said. That was all I could do for now.

Back in the infirmary, we told Isadora what Rita had said. She didn't seem too surprised.

"I suppose it's understandable, but I wish she could've given us a clearer answer. Does she know that we're running out of time to do this?" She looked up at me. It wasn't an accusation about our ability to persuade Rita. She just wanted all the facts. That was her style.

I nodded. "She said she did."

"I don't like all this uncertainty," Isadora said. "It's not like she's the only one with concerns, but we're all finding a way to look past them, to see the bigger picture. We could go to Levi and get him to make her help us, but I get the feeling she wouldn't take too kindly to that. I wouldn't, either. If I know one thing, it's that you don't want to piss off an alchemist, or you might end up with a nasty surprise. One that makes a cherry bomb look like a party popper." I got the sense she had some firsthand experience of pissing off an alchemist.

"So, what? We wait?" I looked between Krieger and Isadora.

Krieger shrugged wearily. "What else can we do?"

"Suri's in the quarantine room, if you want to go and talk to her. She looked tired, so I told her to go and lie down. It's the only place with no windows." Isadora gestured to the ward outside. "Astrid's got the CCTV covered, so we shouldn't be getting any unscheduled Levi visits anytime soon."

I nodded. "What are you guys going to do?"

They exchanged a look. "Figure out if this can be done without alchemy, I guess," Isadora replied.

"I might be able to detach some of the power cells, but it'll require a great deal of testing." Krieger looked pale and sweaty. I guessed he'd had his hopes set on Rita. And now everyone was back at square zero. After all, a magical detector with limited range was as good as useless. Especially for catching Katherine.

TWENTY-FOUR

Jacob

"Knock, knock." I tapped on the metal door of the quarantine room and peered around it. Suri lay curled up in the farthest bed of four. I'd never seen anyone use this room. Then again, there hadn't been a disease outbreak since I'd been here. A Bestiary near-collapse, sure, but nothing as human as a contagious sickness.

Suri didn't move, but I knew she wasn't sleeping. Her body language was too tense. I didn't know what to do. Did she want me to leave her alone? She hadn't said so. Taking that as a good sign, I stepped into the room and walked over to the bed. With her back still to me, I sat down on the bed next to her.

"Hey, you okay?" It was a totally stupid question. Of course she wasn't. But I didn't know what else to say.

She snuffled into her pillow. "Mm-hmm."

"I just wanted to come and talk to you about everything. You're probably wondering what's going on and who we are. Maybe even *what* we are, in case Isadora didn't cover that when she was taking care of you. You probably think we're aliens or something, but we're not. We're human... mostly."

"Mostly?" Her lip trembled as she slowly turned over. She wiped her eyes. She'd been crying again. Her face was a little puffy, her eyes red-rimmed. But she was still cute as heck. After what she'd seen, I guessed the last thing she wanted was to have to deal with another unknown entity. Naima and Echidna had been enough, probably. And a glowy, superpowered Katherine wasn't likely to have been a comfort either.

I smiled. "I am, but I have some… extra stuff. Magic is the easiest way to put it."

"You're a wizard?" Her eyes widened.

"Not quite. I'm a magical."

"That isn't the same thing?"

"Magical is the word we prefer. Wizards and witches sound a little too… cutesy."

She pulled her blanket up to her mouth. "Is that how you opened that thing—that big hole?"

I nodded. "Yeah, that's one of my abilities. I'm what's known as a Portal Opener."

"What about that crazy woman?" She looked panicked.

"She's another magical, but she's one of the most evil ones you'll ever see."

"Where were we?" Her hands were shaking on the blanket, making it quiver.

"When I came to get you?"

She nodded.

"It was a place called Lethe—an 'otherworld.' It isn't exactly part of Earth, but it's joined to it. It's like an interdimensional place that exists beyond the normal rules of nature and stuff. Normally, nobody goes there, but Katherine and Naima—that cat-like creature you saw—were hiding out there, with that scaly monster woman. She was their captive. She was part of something important, and Katherine used her to gain more magic. Basically." I knew I wasn't explaining very well, but I was doing my best. Anyway, she didn't seem to want to run off screaming. That had to be a good thing.

"And where are we now?" She glanced nervously around the quarantine room. "Your friend said this was a hospital, basically."

"This is the infirmary in what's known as a coven."

She reeled back. "Like *American Horror Story*?"

"No, stuff like that gives us a bad rap in the human world. It's why we keep ourselves secret. I mean, could you imagine if humans knew about us?" I chuckled. One look at Suri's startled face and I quickly changed the subject.

"This coven is more like a community center, I guess, for magicals. People live here, people learn here, and it's a place where magicals can belong. Most magicals join a place like this. Even if they don't, covens keep tabs on them. It's for safety and security, really."

"That sounds kind of cool," she said, taking me by surprise.

"It is."

"Are we still in San Diego?"

I nodded. "Covens are usually hidden inside these interdimensional bubbles, so humans can't see them. This one is hidden inside the Fleet Science Center."

She gaped at me. "You're kidding."

"Nope. That's why I was in the Science Center when I first saw you. I was taking a walk outside the coven, to clear my head. I do it to calm myself down if something's getting to be a bit too much in here. Some of the magicals here even work in the Science Center, as a cover."

Her eyes twinkled with awe. "Seriously?"

"Seriously."

"So I might have met one of you before?"

I shrugged. "If you've been working in the Science Center for a couple of months, it's pretty likely. Although, most magicals who work there prefer to take roles behind the scenes. Archives, admin, that kind of thing."

"What else can magicals do? Can everyone open portals, like you can?"

I shook my head. "No, it's actually pretty rare. Isadora can do it, too, but we're the only ones we know about—who are still alive, anyway." I thought of my dad and swallowed the thought. Otherwise, there'd be two crying teenagers in this room. "The most common ones are Elemental abilities— Fire, Water, Air, Earth. Every magical has at least one of those. Some have more than one ability, some don't. It's luck of the draw. One of my friends has about a million."

She gasped. "That's insane."

"It takes some getting used to, for sure."

"Did you always know what you were?"

I smiled. "I knew I was different, but if you're not surrounded by magicals from birth, you end up having to be told, same as you are now."

She frowned. "You weren't?"

"No." A lump clogged my throat. "I was abandoned as a kid, after my parents died. I lived most of my life in the foster system. I didn't find out about all this stuff until much later than most people. But I always knew I could do certain things. It's just way weirder, because you have no idea what's going on and no one to tell you that it's normal."

"I'm sorry." Suri gripped her blanket tighter. "That must have been awful."

I turned away to fight back tears. "It's taken some getting used to. All of it."

"Did you know your parents at all?"

Get it together, Jacob. "I met my dad in that place we were in. He got trapped there because of that evil woman, Katherine. Although, he was still dead, the way I'd always thought. Aside from that, I never had the chance to know my parents. My mom died soon after I was born, and I don't think her spirit is hanging around anywhere, so that's about it where they're concerned."

Suri shuffled closer to the edge of the bed. "I'm so sorry, Jacob."

I shrugged. "Like with the magical stuff, it's just luck of the draw. What about your parents?"

"My mom works all the time, so I don't see a lot of her, but she tries to be around as much as she can. She separated from my dad when I was young, and he moved away to Georgia to start a new family with the woman he left us for. I haven't heard from him since I was about ten."

"I'm sorry."

She gave me a small smile. "Luck of the draw, right?"

I chuckled. "Right."

"Any siblings?"

"Not that I know of. You?"

"Two half-sisters, but I've never met them. Other than that, it's just me and my mom." She shuffled closer and stuck her hand out of the blanket. Turning her palm up, she looked at me. Did she want me to hold her hand? Gulping, I reached out. Her hand was small and soft and smooth. I didn't even mind that it was kind of clammy. Mine was, too.

We stayed like that for a couple of minutes, in silence. I looked at her; she looked at me. And I had to wonder what was going on. It seemed as if she liked me. But how could she, after what I'd put her through? Weirdly, I felt closer to her because of it. Maybe, just maybe, she did too. After all, she still wasn't running. Maybe she liked "different." Maybe she liked "unusual."

Trouble was, this was breaking so many coven rules. Even if I liked her, and I *really* did, it wouldn't change the future. Her mind had to be wiped. That was protocol. I couldn't change that. And yet, I wanted the chance to have something with her. Or, at the very least, see what there might be between us. Those eyes were hard to look away from. And my heart was pounding. We weren't saying anything, but we were also saying a lot.

"What were you and the doctor talking about?" Suri broke the silence.

"You heard that? I thought you were out cold."

She shook her head. "Not quite."

"It might not make much sense."

"It's pretty interesting."

I smiled at her. "Well, we're building this machine, but we need help. I went to speak to the alchemist. She was kind of reluctant, but I hope she'll decide to give us a hand."

Suri blinked up at me. "An alchemist?"

"Yeah, it's like a person who can change one thing into another, with chemicals and that kind of thing. Rita is one of the best. That's what Krieger said, anyway."

"I didn't know they existed anymore. Aren't they a medieval thing?" She looked puzzled.

My head snapped toward the door as a voice echoed through the infirmary, disturbing our conversation. Rita Bonnello's exotic voice. I glanced back at Suri and lifted a finger to my lips. She suddenly looked worried again.

"Stay here and stay quiet. Nobody can know you're here," I whispered. "If they find out, they'll make you leave."

She nodded, frightened. "Okay. I'll stay quiet as a mouse. I don't want to leave yet."

"I don't want you to, either." Reluctantly letting go of her hand, I hurried to the door and slipped out, closing it behind me. Rita was up ahead, about to walk into Krieger's office. I ducked back to give her a chance to step inside without seeing me, before I followed. I hadn't expected her to come to us so soon. And I hoped she had good news for us.

I walked into Krieger's office a minute later. Rita sat beside Isadora, with Krieger opposite. She looked pleased, crossing her elegant legs as she perched on the workbench stool. She smiled at me as I took up one of the spare seats.

"You made your decision?" I jumped right in.

She chuckled. "It took less time than I thought, though I assure you I was thorough in my examination of all the facts. I understand the circumstances and the urgency of this matter, but you must realize that I had to be at complete peace with whatever decision I came to." She spoke as powerfully as she dressed. "I've made a habit of never immediately saying yes or no to anything that might alter the lives of many. However, you'll be pleased to know that I've decided to assist you."

I reined in a massive sigh of relief. "That's good to hear."

"I thought you might say that." She glanced over at Krieger. "Does this version of the device currently work?"

He looked sheepish. "I have tested it time and time again, but there seems to be something amiss with the mechanics. It's a matter I haven't yet resolved. I can't quite tell if it's to do with the power-up of the initial charge, or if there's something else inside the device that's causing it to short out prior to the main surge. Whatever it is, the device begins to power up, only to sputter out before it can fully get going."

"We've tried everything," Isadora added. "We've rewired it countless times and checked every panel and circuit to see if there's a glitch or a crack, but we haven't found anything yet that should cause it to keep sputtering out the way it's been doing."

"And I don't think it's the Chaos, right? You can see it in the glass orb." I pointed to the glass egg in the middle of the detector. The swirl of my Chaos still twisted inside.

Rita smiled. "If I were to make an assertion, I would say you're lacking the correct type of energy. It can't be purely electrical. I don't wish to step on your toes, Dr. Krieger, but electrical power is rarely compatible with Chaos-based contraptions, even if you trap the energy inside a thermal globe, as you have done." I could have listened to her all day. "I see what you've tried to do to accommodate for the Chaos element, but you would need to have even more power cells to get a single spark of what you want out of this. As you want it smaller, I don't think that's the solution you're looking for."

"No... you're right about that," Krieger replied. He looked slightly disappointed that he'd missed something like that. I wanted to reassure him. After all, he was a physician by trade, not a magical engineer. No amount of personal interest and research could make up for years of training in that field. Krieger had done a killer job already, considering his knowledge on the subject.

"What would you suggest?" Isadora interjected.

"As with many objects like this, I would suggest utilizing some chemical reactions inside the device, to power it up efficiently, while compensating for the Chaos. That should make it run without a hitch and allow you to downsize considerably. You may be able to run it from a single battery, if we can create the right quantity of energy from chemical fission." She rearranged her bracelets, looking satisfied but not smug. I could tell she genuinely wanted to help. She was simply giving her expertise, unapologetically.

"I've spoken with several other preceptors about this, but none of them have suggested a chemical reaction." Krieger stared at the device intensely.

"That's because none of them are familiar with the field," she replied.

"Oh, I wasn't trying to discredit your theory. I was simply speaking out loud." Krieger flushed. "I happen to agree with you. I'm just sorry I didn't think of it first. I thought it might be too volatile, considering the Chaos we're using, so I neglected the idea."

"The thermal globe should protect the Chaos, keeping it separate from the energy surge," Rita said. They were tossing around words I vaguely knew, but I would've believed anything she said. She hadn't become so renowned in her field of expertise for nothing.

"So how do we go about this?" Isadora replied. She looked just as enamored with Rita as the rest of us. Girl crush central.

Rita looked over the magical detector. "I believe it could be resolved with a modified alchemy spell. As you've pointed out, Chaos can become volatile when combined with chemical reactions, so we'll have to be careful with the levels and the chemicals used alongside the spell, but it's something I'm very familiar with. I was the project manager on forging backup cells for coven generation. You can see my work in the SDC's Aquarium, for one. I also happen to be one of the main researchers and alchemists on the Tesla project, though that has taken something of a back seat with all of this Katherine business."

"The Tesla project?" My eyes were bugging out of my head. Tesla was my jam. I'd even had a poster of him on my wall at one point.

Rita smiled at me. "It's a global initiative to provide free, renewable energy for the human and magical population, named after our most treasured, magical, scientific mind. It utilizes the fragments of Chaos that get trapped in the atmosphere, but we're still a long way from completion." She chuckled. "But enough about my accolades. I hate pride, even in myself. I will set to work on preparing a special battery and fuse for you, Dr. Krieger—one that can accommodate and utilize a more intense, efficient current, by using raw energy to power a smaller version of this device. In the meantime, I suggest you dismantle this ugly block, until it's reassembled with only its necessary components that don't relate to power."

"I can help with that." I raised my hand to volunteer.

"As will I," Isadora added. "Although, I may not have as much time as I'd like. I have a few other things to look into." I knew what she meant. She still had some inquiries to make about Levi, O'Halloran, and the security zombies.

Rita stayed focused on the detector. "You must make sure that every single wire and circuit in the new device works flawlessly. If I put this new battery in there and the machine isn't perfectly assembled, it'll cause an explosion so powerful that it'll take down half of the coven. Chemical fission, combined with a strong alchemy spell, is not to be taken lightly. It must be perfect."

Krieger paled. "We'll work on it until it is."

"Good, then I'll see you all soon." Rita edged off the stool and crossed the room. Her black dress looked like it cost more than I'd make in a lifetime. But if she was involved in projects like the one she'd mentioned, I guessed she was making a fair bit of dough.

"Should we get started now?" I eyed the device. It really did look like an ugly block.

Krieger nodded. "As they say, there's no time like the present." He paused. "However, there is one thing I wanted to talk to you about first."

"Oh?"

Isadora cast me an apologetic glance that I didn't like. "It's time, Jake."

"Time for what?"

Krieger cleared his throat. "It's time for us to wipe Suri's memory and send her back into the human world. She likely has parents who are worrying about her, and we can't have anyone sniffing around the Science Center. There's too much at stake."

Panic lurched in my chest. "Not yet. Please, not yet. Just give her a couple more days."

"There's no use in waiting, Jacob."

"Why not? She isn't running off screaming, is she? And she can just send a message to her mom, let her know she's okay. She can use her cell and say she's staying at a friend's house. Her mom won't worry—she works a lot, so she's never home anyway." I knew I sounded desperate, but I didn't care. I wasn't ready to let Suri go.

Isadora smiled sadly. "Sounds like the two of you have been getting on like a house on fire."

"Please, guys. She's calm now, and she's not causing any trouble."

"Her being here is trouble," Krieger replied.

"Come on, just a couple more days. She's been through a lot. What if she has some kind of PTSD when she's out in the human world? Shouldn't you keep an eye on her for a bit longer, make sure she's really okay? It's probably safer if you keep her here for another few days, just to be sure her mind will hold the memory wipe."

Isadora glanced at Krieger. "Perhaps a few more days wouldn't hurt?"

Krieger stared at her in disbelief, before shaking his head with a laugh. "Very well, a few more days. I can't argue with your logic, though I think it may come from a more personal place than you would have us believe." He smiled. "Just be careful, do you understand? You can't take her into any of the coven's public spaces, and you can't let anyone see her. Otherwise, it will be all of our necks."

"What about the dragon garden?" I blurted out.

Krieger's frown deepened. "I'm not sure that's—"

"It might be safe after midnight," Isadora suggested. I grinned at her. This woman always had my back, even in this. I loved her for that.

"I suppose it is safer after midnight, when everyone is asleep." Krieger was backed into a corner with Isadora on my side. "Although, you'll have to use your portal abilities. *No* wandering in the halls. I will give you an infirmary pass that will allow you to be out of the living quarters at night, in case anyone should happen upon you, what with there being heightened security all over the place. It's fortunate your tracking chip was destroyed when you went to Lethe, but it took a lot of convincing to make sure Levi didn't implant another one. I told him your body might reject it, due to the residual otherworld energies. Complete nonsense, of course, but he bought it. At least for now. Essentially, this infirmary pass will make me the one responsible for you and your whereabouts, at all times, so do *not* abuse it. I'm doing you a favor here, and I expect you to act accordingly."

Isadora flashed me a subtle wink. "You just need to make sure nobody sees Suri, isn't that right?"

"Yes, that's correct," Krieger replied. He sounded tense. "If Levi gets wind that there's a new face around the coven, then you, Isadora, and I will all be permanently screwed. And you know I hate to use such coarse language, but I feel it's important you understand the risks."

"I understand. I promise I understand. I just want to show her some of this place before she has to go," I explained. "She's excited about it. And, up until now, she's only seen the scary side of magic. It'd be nice to show her some of the good stuff, too, even if she's not going to remember any of it."

At that moment, Louella came into the office. She had a face like thunder. "Where is she?"

"Sorry?" I frowned at her.

"The girl. Where is she?"

"She's safe. Why?" Isadora interjected, looking worried. "Has something happened?"

"The human needs to go, now. Jacob, you need to get rid of her." Louella wasn't playing around.

"Louella, what's happened?" Isadora pressed.

"Levi's on the warpath. If he finds her, he'll have you all strung up for it," she replied. "Plus, it's not safe for her here, not with things as weird as they are. Levi's got total control of the security magicals and O'Halloran. I thought I'd test the theory that something was wrong with them and see if I could figure anything out."

"Was it the same pattern I noticed?" Isadora asked, her brow creasing.

Louella nodded. "They blank out whenever anyone mentions notifying the covens about Echidna. And they clam up at the mere mention of Echidna being taken. It's like they're buffering, and then they change the subject, repeating the same damn thing about Levi handling it and that nobody can know. The usual Purgatory threats tend to follow."

"That doesn't sound good," I mumbled.

"We're dealing with enough without having to worry about Levi finding a human." Louella crossed her arms. "Because then he *will* send you to Purgatory. Wipe her mind and send her packing, before Levi comes looking for trouble."

I gaped at her like a beached fish, trying to find a reply.

"Even O'Halloran hasn't improved, then?" Isadora said before I could speak.

Louella shook her head. "I mean, he acts normal until someone mentions Echidna. He got you out, and he's still trying to get Santana and Alton out, which shows he's still hanging on to some of his senses, but this Echidna stuff is eerie." She turned back to me. "Suri being here is just putting us in more danger, since Levi is clearly doing something batty to the SDC. I'm sorry, Jacob, but she has to go, for all our sakes."

She was mad, I could see that. But Suri didn't deserve to be booted out. I'd made the whole PTSD thing up as an excuse, but that didn't mean it couldn't happen. And I didn't want her feeling messed up while she was back out in the human world, with nobody to turn to.

Krieger intervened on my behalf. "I've already agreed to let Suri stay for another day or two so I can check for any lasting effects of what she's been through. The memory wipe won't work if she isn't in a good state of mind. And that presents a far greater risk. She's seen and heard things about Katherine. If the memory wipe doesn't stick, she may well leak those things to the human world. We can't afford to have that level of panic and exposure, if they were to believe her."

Couldn't have said it better myself!

"Can't you just use a more powerful memory wipe?" Louella replied.

"Not without turning her brain to mush." Krieger smiled at her kindly. "I will be keeping an eye on her, so she is no harm to anyone. Besides, just because the world may be ending doesn't mean we can't appreciate good company. That is all Jacob is asking for, and I happen to think it may be a good idea."

Louella rolled her eyes. "Has everyone gone mad here? Seriously, where's the tea party and the Cheshire Cat?"

"The decision has been made, Louella," Krieger said softly.

She turned to me. "Well, if you're intent on being a fruit loop, just... just be careful, okay? As long as Katherine is out there, you're not safe. You witnessed that for yourself. And neither are the people close to you. I'm not saying this to be mean, I just don't want you, or Suri, getting into something you can't get out of. Lethe was a near miss. I don't want you to be in that kind of situation again." She drew in a shaky breath. "We were so worried, Jacob. We were so worried that you'd... just, be careful."

My initial anger toward her subsided. She didn't mean any harm. She was just concerned for me and for the rest of us. I understood that. But she had to understand that I wanted a few days with Suri to remind myself why we were doing this. Because it wasn't just magicals who stood to lose their lives if Katherine succeeded. It was humans, too. Suri would strengthen my resolve to fight for what was good in the world.

"I was about to start looking more into this weird behavior from O'Halloran and the others, Louella. You've done some good work, getting the ball rolling." Isadora defused the tension. "I'll take it from here and see what I can find out."

"You will?" She sounded relieved.

"Of course. There's some kind of voodoo at work here, for sure, and I'm not going to stop until I get to the bottom of it. Having an egomaniac as a leader is one thing, but if he's using magic to influence the minds of the security team in some way, that's a direct violation of the magical Geneva Convention." Isadora took a breath. "And I need to find out if we're dealing with a simple narcissist or an actual criminal."

TWENTY-FIVE

Jacob

A few hours later, I sat at Krieger's workbench, elbow-deep in metal bits and pieces. Krieger and I were taking the magical detector apart, as promised. It was proving to be trickier work than I'd anticipated. Not that I wasn't enjoying it. I liked using my hands for something useful. But I was sort of distracted. Suri sat beside me, up close and personal. Watching us work.

"Thank you for sticking up for me," she said. I almost dropped the cog I was working on.

"Sorry?"

She smiled. "I overheard some of your conversation with... uh, Louella, is it? I'm terrible with names."

I nodded.

"She was talking pretty loud, so I couldn't help hearing some of it... and I was sort of listening to what you were saying. I wouldn't say eavesdropping, but pretty close. Anyway, I just wanted to thank you for sticking up for me and letting me stay. I appreciate it." She glanced down at the screwdriver in her hands. She was acting as surgical assistant to our disassembly of the detector. "Things aren't great at home. I'm always out at work or school and my mom is working about a billion shifts at the care home. She probably won't know I'm missing; we're always like ships passing. Sometimes, I can go a whole week without seeing her. This place is a pretty neat distraction. It's amazing, honestly. And it was right next door to where I work, this whole time."

"It's nothing." I tried not to look into her big eyes. "It's for your safety, really. But I'm glad you like it here."

Krieger smiled to himself. He said nothing, just carried on with his work instead. I was grateful for that. He'd had my back when Louella had come in. I knew he'd put his neck on the line, when he didn't have to. I respected that massively. He'd given me the chance to get to know Suri better, and that was worth a hell of a lot. Even if Krieger had insisted she had to go, I probably would've crept back into the Science Center and watched her from afar. *Too creepy?* Maybe. But I'd just have been waiting for an opportunity to speak to her again, even if she didn't know who I was. That came with its own set of flashbacks. It was hard enough with the Smiths. I couldn't imagine how hard it would've been with Suri. Or would be. We hadn't crossed that bridge yet.

"What is this thing?" Suri pointed to the remains of the detector. It was pretty much in pieces by now. It was going to take ages to reassemble properly. The most important set of Legos I'd ever worked on.

"It's a magical detector," I replied.

She chuckled. "A who-said-what now? Human here, remember? You've got to dumb these things down. I'm still getting used to the fact that there are witches and wizards and cat-beasts, and big, evil glowing people in this world."

"Sorry." My cheeks were hot. "It's basically a device that finds people who have magic in them. Well, Chaos. Chaos is the name for that magic. It's in everything, but only magicals can use it."

"That doesn't seem fair." Suri smiled at me, letting me know she was teasing. "Why do you get to have all the fun?"

"It's not always fun, believe me." I picked up the thermal globe and held it in my palms. "This strand in here is a captured piece of Chaos. Mine, to be exact. See, I also have the ability to sense magicals, so I'm a Sensate and a Portal Opener. And we're going to use this device, with my Chaos inside, to track down that big, evil glowing person you were talking about."

Suri gave a low whistle. "This stuff is so cool. It's like something out of a book, but then it's completely real. My mind is being blown right now, Jacob.

Dr. Krieger here might have to piece my brain back together when he's done with this."

Krieger laughed. "I would find that far easier, at this point."

"Is it hard to fix?"

Jacob shrugged. "Yes and no. It's just time consuming."

"I guess you must like this sort of thing, huh?" She passed me a handful of bolts.

"I've always loved taking things apart and putting them back together. I used to always be in the workshop at school, building things. I wanted to be an engineer, but then... well, this happened." I gestured around me.

"You can't do both?"

I pulled a doubtful face. "That depends on how this stuff with Katherine goes."

"That sucks. You should be allowed to do both, regardless of what this crazy lady does."

If only it were that simple. "Who knows? Maybe I will. But right now, I'm focusing on this. I have to, for everyone's sake."

"Is it this Katherine woman who's affecting the security magicals? I heard Louella mention that something was up with them." Suri glanced up at me, worried. There was still a lot about this world that troubled her. I could see it in her eyes, despite her enthusiasm.

"We're not sure at the moment."

Suri frowned. "I don't know if it's related, but I overheard her say something to the cat-thing when they were holding me captive in the freaky light world. It didn't make any sense to me at the time, since everything was pretty crazy, but now I'm wondering if it might have something to do with your security problem."

Krieger stopped what he was doing immediately. "What did you hear?"

"Katherine asked the cat-beast about the 'infiltrations' and how they were coming along. The cat-woman said they were going well, and that their influence was spreading, to keep news about Echidna under the radar. No idea who or what Echidna is. I always thought they were cute, spiky creatures, but I'm guessing it's important, since Louella kept mentioning that name, too. Anyway, she wasn't specific about it, but she mentioned members of a cult and the use of mental spells. Does that make any sense to you?"

Do bears crap in the woods?

"It certainly does," Krieger replied nervously, glancing at me. "It confirms some of my suspicions, as well as Isadora and Remington's."

I nodded. "It means Katherine's cult is spreading. Like, really fast."

"If what Suri says is true, that means we can't trust anyone. Katherine could well have operatives everywhere, and we wouldn't know a single thing about it." He grimaced. "From here on out, we must take every display of apathy coming from the authorities as a sign that Katherine's Dark magic tricks are at play. She's pulled the wool over magical society's eyes. And let us just hope that this business with the security magicals is mere coincidence." I knew he didn't believe that.

"Can we go public with this?" I asked.

"Not without making more magicals fearful, which may drive them to join Katherine."

I threw my head back in exasperation. "So we just have to keep working on this and pretend like nothing is happening?"

"It's more that we have to keep a low profile. With this device, we can find Katherine and destroy her before she completes the final ritual. We have to focus on that and the things we can actually do. At this point in time, we can't expect the upper echelons to help us. Magical society, as a whole, may well have been compromised, and may unwittingly be assisting Katherine at this very moment." Krieger's knuckles had whitened around his screwdriver.

We'd barely gotten back into the swing of things, with tension thick in the air, when Isadora came running into the office. She had O'Halloran with her. Suri ducked down under the table, peering up at me with scared eyes. I shared her fear. Had Isadora lost her mind? What was she doing, bringing O'Halloran here, when she knew Suri was around?

Isadora shot me an apologetic look. "Sorry for bursting in here unannounced, but I was out in the hallway, speaking with O'Halloran, and I thought it was something you might want to hear, Krieger."

"Not sure why it'd be important to you, but Isadora insisted," O'Halloran added.

"Go on," Isadora urged. "Tell him what you told me."

O'Halloran shrugged. "I was just saying that, after we started work on getting the Bestiary contained, after the… uh, the glitch that happened…"

That blank look came into his eyes. "What was I saying? Oh, yeah, after the cult's attack and the fallout from that, Levi called me into his office and gave me this big box of pills. He said I had to hand them out to all of the security personnel to help protect us from this mind-control hex that Katherine liked to use. I've been picking up more from him, and taking them, ever since." He frowned at Krieger. "Ah, I see now. Is that why you brought me to Krieger? Because he had the mind-control hex on him?"

Krieger went white. "I'm free of it now."

I looked between Isadora and the doctor. Krieger had gone through hell to get rid of that hex. There was no way that a pill could stop something that complicated from getting through. I could see it on their faces, too—a dawning realization. There had to be something in those pills that had gotten the security magicals to do whatever Levi told them. It also had to be the thing that was blocking their memory of Echidna being snatched.

"Do you think we should go to the Mage Council and the coven directors and tell them about Echidna's disappearance?" Isadora was testing O'Halloran.

He shook his head. "The National Council and the president know what happened that day. Levi is handling it. Nobody else needs to know about it."

"Do you think that's normal, to keep something so important from the rest of the magical authority figures?" Isadora pressed. "And to keep the entire magical world in the dark about what's really going on?"

O'Halloran froze for a full minute. He stared into the distance like a robot. Krieger snapped his fingers right in front of O'Halloran's face, but got nothing. No response. Nada. He just blinked, like his brain had wandered right out of his ears. I didn't even know if he knew we were still in the room with him.

"Discretion is of paramount importance to stop the general populace from panicking," O'Halloran replied, coming back around. That was the least O'Halloran-like thing I'd ever heard him say. It sounded like a rehearsed line. And it definitely sounded like it had come from someone else. Someone who'd fed him that line.

Isadora nodded. "Understood."

"Was that all you wanted me for? Am I good to go now?" O'Halloran waited.

"Yes, thanks for that."

He smiled like nothing had happened. "Great, then I'll get going. Alton and Santana aren't going to get themselves out of prison, and I doubt they'll get lucky enough to broker a deal. Not unless Jacob here plans on going AWOL again."

"No plans to," I replied.

"Shame, we could use some leverage." With that, he left. And a sense of doom settled over the rest of us. Even Suri seemed reluctant to creep back out of her hiding spot.

Isadora shook her head slowly. "I wanted you two to see and hear that. It's exactly how Louella described it, though the post-blackout answers change from security magical to security magical. But they always have that robotic, rehearsed tone to them."

"What you're saying is, the magic is obvious," Krieger interjected. "And Levi is the one behind it."

"Do you think he's working with Katherine?" I couldn't believe I was saying it. But it wouldn't have been the craziest thing to happen around here.

Isadora plopped down on a stool. "I have no idea, to be honest. I don't know if this is happening because he's in cahoots with her, or if he's an unwitting participant in her spread of power. All I know is, I'm getting to the bottom of this. This can't be allowed to continue."

"There must be some kind of chemical magic in those pills," Krieger said. "Once I'm done putting this detector back together, I'll come up with something to counteract their effects. I'll look through every textbook I have until I find an antidote. For the time being, however, it might be best if we keep this to ourselves. We can't risk getting imprisoned."

Sit back and do nothing, again? Only, this time, I kind of agreed with him. Until we knew which higher-ups weren't brainwashed and we found a way of reversing the effects, we couldn't say a word. Krieger had been right—outside of the people in our group, we couldn't trust anyone.

TWENTY-SIX

Harley

Taking the piece of charmed chalk from Remington, I drew a shaky rectangle on the carved rock of his office, making sure it was big enough for us to walk through. It looked pretty silly, just a raggedy set of lines dragged across the uneven rock, but Remington had sworn this would work and I had no reason to doubt him. This had come straight from the encyclopedia of Odette, so it had to be good.

"*Aperi Si Ostium*," I said confidently.

The lines lit up with green light. The center of the rectangle rippled like a mirage, the solid rock fading away to reveal a transparent screen with a silver handle throbbing to the far right. Through the hazy screen, I could see Grand Central Station beyond. Taking a breath, I turned the handle and swung it outward, then stepped beyond the threshold.

Wade, Garrett, Finch, and I emerged into the empty silence of Grand Central Station. Once everyone was through, I turned and closed the rippling door behind us, the transparent screen disappearing immediately, taking Remington's office with it. There was no going back now.

Our shoes echoed across the huge space, while pigeons cooed from their nooks in the roof. The golden-edged clock on top of the information desk showed that it was close to midnight. A few weary travelers headed across the elegant floor, having come off the last train to pull into the station, but that was it.

I'd always liked bus stations and train stations late at night. They'd been my refuge a couple of times, after some terrible arguments with my foster families at the time. They could be scary, but I doubted Grand Central Station could ever be anything other than awe-inspiring, like wandering into a time warp of old New York.

We'd chosen this location to scout out the New York Coven first. The parts I'd seen of it had had a great view of Central Park, but judging from these layout plans, it had moved farther south. At least, the entrance had.

I glanced at the others. Finch and Garrett had shifted into faces I didn't recognize—a middle-aged businessman and a slick-looking twentysome-thing, respectively. Wade and I had been forced to use ordinary disguises. I had my hair stuffed into a black baseball cap and wore a heavy, black denim jacket with a fur collar, which I'd borrowed from Remington. The man had style, what could I say? Wade was pretty much himself, still dressed in a sharp suit, but with sunglasses covering his eyes. He'd gone for a more Clark Kent approach.

"You realize it's more suspicious to wear shades at night, right?" Garrett said.

Wade turned to Garrett. "They're special lenses that allow me to see traces of spells or hexes. A gift from my parents." He glanced up at the American flag hanging from the marble wall. "It'll help us gauge the concentration of residual and current spells wherever we end up. It's the closest thing we've got to an alarm system."

With Garrett looking cowed, we exited the station and turned right, walking a few blocks toward Rockefeller Center and Central Park beyond it. This way, we were far enough from the coven itself to avoid detection and were able to approach it with more caution. There was no telling how wide they'd placed their security.

"How long have you had those, anyway?" I nodded to Wade's shades, trying to keep things light. "They would've come in handy a couple times in the SDC."

His eyebrow arched over the dark shades. "My mom was cleaning out the attic and found them. She sent them a week or so ago. Do you think I'd have hidden something like this if I'd had them sooner?"

"I wasn't saying that."

He shrugged. "Sorry, then. It sounded like you were."

Geez, what is UP with him? Subtly, I fed my Empathy toward him. I wanted to make sure his head was in the game, not focused on some simmering anger he had over me and Finch.

"Could you not do that?" he snapped.

I physically recoiled. "Do what?"

"Come at me with your Empathy all the time. My emotions are private, Harley. Everyone's emotions are private. You can't just hack into us whenever you feel like it."

"I... I can't help it. I'm worried about you." I felt like a naughty schoolkid who'd been caught with her hands in the teacher's candy jar. But I also felt irritated. If he had a problem with it, why hadn't he brought it up before, instead of yelling at me in front of Finch and Garrett?

Wade rolled his eyes and said nothing, but I could feel a sudden rush of stress pulsing through him, more or less hitting the roof. I didn't dare glance at Finch and Garrett.

As Wade strode off in front with Garrett, I hung back. Finch did, too, and he seemed antsy to speak with me. We'd walked a couple of paces before he cast me a worried look and nudged me playfully in the shoulder. He could probably see how down I was about Wade's behavior, and how confused it was making me. Wade had always been shy and wary of my Empathy ability, but he'd never gone off on me like that before. If he hadn't been acting funny since we'd arrived in San Francisco, I'd have put it down to his stress, but now it was starting to feel personal. And that stung like a bitch. He was supposed to be bolstering me, not bringing me down.

"Trouble in paradise?" Finch asked.

"With Wade?"

He grinned. "Who else? You got a secret boyfriend we don't know about? Seems like you're having enough trouble with the one."

I shoved my hands into the deep pockets of the jacket. "I don't know what's going on, to be honest. He's been acting strange toward me for a while. He feels anxious all the time, and there's this bubbling anger beneath the surface, too. I tried to confront him about it, but he just launched into some rant about you."

"Me?"

"Yeah, he's not too happy with my forgiving streak. He thinks I'm being an idiot."

"Do *you* think you're being an idiot?" Finch sounded miffed.

I shrugged. "I think everyone deserves a second chance, and you've proven yourself to me, for the most part." I glanced at him. "I don't know what Katherine talked to you about in her office. I'm guessing she tried to get you back on her side, but you didn't bend. That counts for something, in my book."

He smiled sadly. "Do you want to know? I bet it's been bugging you, huh?"

"Do you want to tell me?"

"She said she could bring Adley back from the dead if I joined her again," he replied. I could hear the pain and loss in his voice. My jaw nearly fell off its hinges. I'd expected Katherine to use her wily ways, but that was beyond anything I could've imagined. It also brought back some unpleasant memories of the prune in the glass coffin—the botched resurrection of dear ol' Drake Shipton. Would Adley have come back like that, if Finch had accepted Katherine's offer?

"I'm so sorry, Finch. I had no idea."

He chuckled bitterly. "She'd have offered me the universe if she'd thought it could persuade me. She did, in a way." His voice caught in his throat, but he quickly cleared it. "But I couldn't accept. I kept thinking about how your view of me would change. How much I'd disappoint you, even though I'm pretty sure you'd have understood, if I'd said yes to that. Besides, she probably wouldn't have come back the same. I made my bed, now I've got to lie in it… without her."

"Oh, Finch…"

"So, now you know. I'm in this for real." He forced a Finchy grin onto his face, but his eyes glistened with tears. "If you ever doubt me again, just think of that. I'm not going to double-cross you, Harley. Not now, not ever."

This was so surreal. These heart-to-hearts with Finch would take some getting used to. I always expected witty jokes and snarky comments, never genuine honesty and him sharing his raw pain with me. And, honestly, I didn't know what to do to make him feel better. It was too sad, and I didn't have the right words. But it made me think—what would I do, if I was given an offer like that, and Wade's life was on the table? Could I have found the strength to say no, like Finch had done? I'd had a momentary lapse with my mom, where I'd wanted to lock her back up in that jar and keep her forever, just so I could be near her. If Katherine had offered to resurrect her, what would I have said? I didn't have the answer to that, and it terrified me.

"Is it definitely me he's pissed with?" Finch nodded to Wade up ahead, who hadn't even checked to make sure we were following.

I gave a wry laugh. "I've got no idea what runs through that head of his. He says it's you and your bad influence, but who knows? He had plenty of opportunities to talk to me about it before we set out on this mission, but he seemed fine before. It's only since we got to San Francisco that he started acting odd."

"Then stop relying on him," Finch said. The stern big brother approach took me by surprise.

"What?"

"Stop relying on him. If he's making this harder, just put him to the back of your mind and keep your focus on the mission," he replied, like it was really that simple. "Meanwhile, I'll make sure nothing stands in our way. We'll get through this."

I smiled. "See, those are the words I want to be hearing right now."

"Wade needs to remember what's at stake. It's bigger than his dislike of me. If there's something in that Grimoire that might save us, I'm ready to pull out all the stops. Nothing scares Katherine—you know that. But that Grimoire does. Majorly."

"I hope you're right." If we were doing this for nothing, I would sink to my knees and scream until there wasn't a scrap of air left in my lungs. I'd pinned everything on this mission, as our last-ditch attempt to prevent Katherine's ascension.

We headed down a few side streets, following the layout of the coven and its surrounding area. After fifteen minutes of traipsing through the shadowed landscape of New York at night, we reached the gates of an old local library. It wasn't nearly as pretty as the New York Public Library, with its fancy façade and stone lions, but it had an old-world charm to it. In fact, it almost looked like a miniature version of that famous landmark. It had the same neo-Roman pillars, with a set of pale steps leading up to the broken wooden door. Had it not been for the heavy chains on the gates and the doors, and the wooden planks covering the windows, and the graffiti scrawled across the masonry, I might've thought this place was somehow connected to its big sister, closer to Central Park.

"Is this it?" Garrett looked back at me. Wade kept his gaze forward, shrouded by his shades.

I took out the coven blueprints and checked them. "Yep, this is the spot."

"Seems like a strange place for a coven entrance," Wade observed.

"The first director created it." Finch folded his arms across his chest, smug with insider knowledge. "No one's been able to remove it since. It's one of the only parts of the coven that doesn't change regularly. Guess we've got that guy to thank for our only way in without getting caught."

Garrett frowned. "We're not out of the woods yet, Finch. There's extra security here, by the looks of it." He gestured to the heavy chains on the door. "Remington warned us there'd be something like this. And, since there aren't any guards, I'm guessing he was right. This place has to have the kind of magic around it that doesn't even need security magicals to stand watch over it. That means it's going to be potent stuff."

"Way to bring down my enthusiasm, Garrett." Finch shot him a grin that said otherwise.

We clambered over the fence and dropped down into the overgrown garden. Weeds swayed around us, as tall as me, the main path seething with a mass of vines and spongy moss that had reclaimed the flagstones beneath. Since Wade wasn't saying anything, I guessed there were no residual hexes in the garden itself. However, he paused as we reached the main entrance to the abandoned library, glancing down at the heavy chains.

"The magic's in the chains, not the door," he said. "They're covered in ancient runes. They're pretty much glowing right now."

I peered down at the chains, but I couldn't see any runes. "Does anyone know how to get through this kind of thing?"

Wade touched the chains, a silvery light shivering up his arm. He snatched it away, like a lit match had gotten too close to his fingertips. His brow furrowed as he took a step back.

"Everything okay?" Finch asked.

Wade nodded. "They gave me a message."

Finch snorted. "The chains did?"

"Yeah. The only way to get through here is to touch the chains and tell a truth that they demand—one that proves we've got good intentions. If we're honest, and our hearts are open and good, we'll be allowed in. If we lie, we'll be killed on the spot."

"You got all of *that* from a piece of metal?" Finch didn't sound convinced.

Garrett stepped in. "I've heard of this kind of thing before. The same kind of magic is on some of the vaults that the National Council uses. It's supposed to prevent criminals from getting inside."

"That did a great job in Reykjavik," Finch muttered.

"You'd know all about it, wouldn't you?" Wade shot back.

Finch lifted his hands in mock surrender. "Hey, I'm a changed man."

"So you say," Wade whispered under his breath.

"What do you know about it?" I turned to Garrett, ignoring the bickering between Wade and Finch. I was doing what Finch had told me to—keeping focused on the mission, and nothing else.

"It's ancient, powerful magic. Stuff that's not used very much anymore, which is what makes it so efficient. It's supposed to catch people out," he replied. "And it's our only way into the New York Coven undetected, so we better hope our hearts are good enough. Finch, you might end up having to sit this one out."

He shook his head. "No way. I can be as open and honest as the rest of you. I'll answer whatever I have to, and I'll do it truthfully."

Honestly, I was more worried about the goodness of my own heart. What if these chains didn't like what I had to say? What if my heart wasn't as pure as I thought it was? What if they asked me something that I *couldn't* answer? If that happened, I wouldn't be able to hide that from these chains. I almost wanted to laugh. There'd be a sick irony to all of this if I died before I'd even had the chance to get inside the New York Coven.

TWENTY-SEVEN

Jacob

I portaled into the dragon garden. Suri gasped as she staggered out beside me. I offered her a hand to keep her steady. She took it, which brought a smile to my face. I liked having her near. And I was glad I'd been given the chance to show her this place. It was an oasis in the SDC. Pretty and secluded. The perfect setting for our first date. Not that it was actually a date. I'd just said I wanted to show her a cool part of the coven.

"How did you do that?" she gasped, patting herself down as if to make sure she was in one piece.

I smiled. "It's Chaos."

"Yeah, but *how?*" She smiled shyly. "I saw this light coming out of your hands and then *bam!* A massive tear, and now this."

"It's… It's just Chaos. It works differently for different people. I manipulate it into making portals. Some people can read minds with it, some people can bring other people back from the dead with it. It varies."

"Now you're just messing with me, aren't you? There's no way you can bring people back from the dead."

I chuckled. "I can't, but I know people who can."

"No way!"

"Yes way."

"Man, this stuff keeps getting more and more awesome by the second.

How am I supposed to go back to an ordinary human life after hearing all of this? I'll never look at anything the same way again."

My heart jolted. I kept forgetting she couldn't stay here for good. In a few days, she wouldn't remember any of this. She'd go back to her life, and I'd go back to mine. And I hated it. I hated that it had to be that way. So what if a human found out about magicals? Suri was cool. Suri wouldn't tell anyone. Probably.

"Do you like it here?" I gestured to the garden. Anything to change the subject. I had to savor the moments I did have with her, before the others sent her back.

She walked up to the stone dragon that spewed water into a shell and ran her hands through the liquid. Even that seemed to excite her. She was like a happy bunny, bouncing all over the place. If I mentioned her leaving, I'd ruin that. So I wasn't going to. Instead, I was going to enjoy this moment. We'd taken a break from the device, which was now a bunch of pieces on the table in the infirmary. Krieger had gone to sleep for a few hours, and Isadora had gone on a scouting mission. We needed rest. This was the next best thing. A rest for my mind.

"It's cool. This whole place is cool," she replied. "I wish I could be like you, with these abilities, so I could stay. Seriously, this place is like nothing else—it doesn't even seem real. It's like a fantasy world, and all of you get to be these amazing characters, running around and doing crazy cool stuff, making magical sparks fly and things. All I get to do is watch my dinner spin around in a microwave, listen to a load of crap on TV, and bury myself under a bunch of schoolwork. Being here makes me realize how dull my human life really is."

"Hey, don't say that."

She shrugged. "Why not? It's true."

"Ordinary life isn't so bad, is it?"

"Compared to this? One hundred percent!" She looked back at me with her big eyes. "What other ability did you say you had?"

"Sensate, and a weak Earth ability." I stepped toward her and crouched low to the ground. Putting my palms over one of the flagstones, I sent my Chaos into the stone. A moment later, a small flower twisted up between the cracks. I'd tried to make a rose, but I wasn't too good at the Elemental stuff.

Still, it looked pretty—a yellow tulip. *That's cheesy, even for you.* I didn't care. I wanted to give her a gift. Even if it died in a couple of days. I plucked the tulip out of the stone and handed it to her.

"You made this?" She stared at me excitedly. "See, this is what I'm talking about. This is insane."

I nodded. "It's about all I can do with my Earth ability, though."

"I love it." She took the flower and turned it over in her hands. "It looks so real."

"That's because it is."

She smiled mischievously. "You know that yellow flowers mean friendship, right?"

"Do they?" My cheeks reddened. "I didn't know."

"Would you have made a different one if you had?" She was teasing me.

"I like yellow. But I can make you another one, if you want."

She chuckled. "No, I like this one. It's vibrant. It reminds me of the sunset."

"That's what I was going for."

"Isadora seems pretty cool," Suri said, as she walked toward the wall at the far side of the garden. It looked out on Balboa Park, and it was one of the nicest views in the SDC. A starry night glittered overhead, and a crescent moon peeked out of the darkness.

I nodded. "Yeah, she is."

"Is she related to you? I get some maternal vibes from her when she's around you."

I smiled. "No, we're not related, but she's been a mentor to me. She can do what I can, so we're sort of bonded in a way. I learned a lot of my skills from her, where the portal stuff is concerned. The rest I've been figuring out as I go along."

"That must be hard on you."

"I manage. That's the key trait of a foster kid—we make it work." I went to stand beside her, my arm brushing hers.

"Did you move around a lot when you were a kid?"

I stared out at the night sky. "Yeah, I guess so. I ended up with a new foster family every year or so."

"Did you always know you were a magical? Like, even back then?" she asked. "Or did the abilities appear one day? How does it work?"

"I always knew there was something weird about me. Abilities get a little temperamental when you're a kid, especially without anyone to guide you. But they were always there. We're born that way, not created."

She sighed. "Aww, I was hoping maybe I was just a late bloomer."

"Sorry." I dipped my head.

She turned back to the view. "How come none of the foster families stuck? You seem like a nice guy. I doubt you're the type who was getting into scrapes all the time."

The memories of that period of my life raced through my head. The arguments, the slamming doors, the nasty grins of the kids in the homes I lived in, and the million ways they tried to frame me and make me out to be a bad kid. The parents were never as bad. A few were just in it for the payouts, but the rest tried, at least, to fit me into their family. It never worked. I was too different. My abilities made me different.

"They just didn't," I replied. "It's hard to fit into a family unit when it's already established. I can only think of one place that I wanted to call home, but that didn't work out. Nothing to do with the family—there were just weird circumstances that meant I had to leave."

"So they were good to you?" She turned toward me, her eyes blinking.

"Yeah, they were the best. I miss them. But the people I met here are cool, too. They've made me feel at home. They're probably the best family I could ask for." I struggled to hold her gaze. "I wish you could meet Harley. I think you'd like her. She's been like a sister to me, albeit a tough one. But I wouldn't be here without her. Like, literally."

Suri frowned. "How come she's not here?"

"Long story." I leaned closer to her. "How about you? Did you manage to get in touch with your mom okay? I know the signal can be a bit shaky around here. It's the bubble—it affects technology sometimes. You just have to find a good spot."

A sad expression washed over her. "Yeah, I managed to send a text to my mom to tell her not to worry. I said I was spending a couple of days at a friend's house so I could study. It gets lonely in our house, and my mind gets distracted all the time. There's only so much trash TV you can watch before the silence gets deafening. Anyway, she gets it." She took out her phone and showed me her mom's reply. All it said was, "Okay." I got the feeling there was more to this than she was letting on.

"She just said, 'Okay'? Isn't she worried?"

Suri shrugged. "She's too busy to worry about me. I love her, but I could probably be gone for a month and she wouldn't notice. She'd only be upset about it when the refrigerator started to stink or the school called her or something. Not that they care too much, either. As long as my grades are good, and I make sure to throw in a mystery illness or a 'personal problem,' they don't bat an eyelid about absences. I've ducked out enough times to pick up extra shifts at the Science Center, and they've never called anyone. I always make sure my ass is covered."

"I can't believe she just said, 'Okay.' Are you sure you're fine with that?"

She leaned against the wall, propping her chin on her hands. "It doesn't matter anyway. I'm going to get out of here soon enough. San Diego isn't where I want to be, and she's not going to stop me from leaving." She glanced up at me. "I want to be a musician and head out to LA to try and get a record deal. College always seemed like my way out, but I don't think I'd be happy there, shelling out a fortune for a degree I don't even want. That's just a one-way ticket to a job I'll hate. It makes me feel lost, sometimes. Like, I love my music, but it's a tough industry to break into. And nobody's going to take a high school kid seriously. But I think I'll only be happy if I can be some-where, with my guitar, making music. I'll only be happy if I do something extraordinary with my life, you know?"

I tried to picture her with a guitar, singing something. I thought about asking her to sing, but I didn't want to put her on the spot. Still, it was refreshing to hear the problems of a normal kid. Someone who was worrying about her future, instead of everyone else's. That should've been me. It probably would've been, if the Ryder twins hadn't come for me at the Smiths' house.

"I envy you," I said.

She peered at me, curious. "You do? Why?"

"Because your problems are a million miles away from mine," I admitted. "I'm worrying about the end of the world, while you're worried about your hopes and dreams. I'd give everything to be able to do that instead. That's why I envy you. I didn't ask for this much stress, but I got it anyway. And now, I can't get out of it."

"Now I feel silly." She dropped her gaze. "Here I am, chatting on about being a musician, and you're dealing with super powerful witches with a god complex."

I put my hand on her forearm. "No, don't feel silly. I like hearing about it. It reminds me that there's a normal world out there. One you'll get to go back to, with no memory of this place or any of the bad stuff that's going on. I envy that, too."

She froze. "What do you mean? I'm not going to forget you or this place. No way."

"You have to. They're going to wipe your memory so you can't remember. It's the safest thing to do, for you and for magical society. At least, that's what the protocol says," I muttered bitterly. "I don't believe it, just for the record. I think they could trust you with everything you've seen and heard. But they won't listen."

Suri gripped the tulip tighter. "I don't want to forget. If I don't remember any of this, then that means I won't remember you. I don't want you to disappear, Jacob." She sounded torn. "My life was boring as hell until I met you. I went to school, I went to work, I came home. That was it. And then you came into my life. Sure, we hit things off with the weirdest of bangs, but still... I like you, Jacob. You risked your life for me. I can't think of anyone who would do that other than you. I don't want to have to forget."

"I don't want you to, either," I whispered.

She covered my hand with hers, on the top of the wall. "There's a lot of pressure on you right now, huh?" she said softly.

"Yeah... Sometimes I wish I could just leave it all. But I couldn't, even if I wanted to," I replied with a sigh. "I'm needed here. I have to see this thing through."

Suri nodded. "Who are you doing this for? What gets you out of bed in the morning and makes you keep going? I'd probably have lost my nerve by now."

"I do it all for me, for you, for Harley, for your mom and friends, for the people I care about, for the world you know and the world you don't." It hurt to say it. "This is bigger than all of us. Too many people are depending on me. If I don't keep going now, it'll all be over, and we'll all be screwed."

"I get it... but I'd be lying if I said I didn't feel sorry for you." Her words took me by surprise. "You're a kid, like me, after all." She moved toward me, and my breath exited the building. "I don't think you should have that much weight on your shoulders. You said you wanted to be an engineer—you should be allowed to work toward that, instead of worrying about the rest of the world. I guess there's a lot that I don't understand, but I can see why you're doing what you're doing. Even if I think it's unfair."

I froze as she looped her arms around my neck. She smelled so good. As she pulled me into a hug, I felt her hair brush against my cheek. It was intoxicating. I relaxed against her and put my arms around her waist. I'd never hugged someone like this. This was different than a normal hug, somehow.

She nuzzled into my shoulder, squeezing me tighter. "I wish things were different, for both of us."

"You've already made things better for me," I murmured back. My heart was pounding. My head was filled with her scent, her touch, her closeness. Here, with her, I could imagine a future. Maybe, when all this was over, I'd see her again and everything would be okay. She was like a link to normality. If I got to be back in her arms someday, maybe I'd be able to be normal again. Maybe she'd be a musician and I'd be an engineer. Maybe I'd listen to her play her songs in our dingy first apartment. Maybe I'd go to her gigs and get to say, "She's my girlfriend." Or, maybe we'd all be bending to the will of Eris. This was the great uncertainty of my life right now.

"We need to head back to the infirmary," I said, reluctantly pulling away. She gazed up into my eyes, and I gazed back. I could've gotten lost in those eyes. They were so big and bright and seemed to reflect the starlight above. "You can sleep in the quarantine room, but you'll have to be locked in for the night to make sure nobody stumbles in on you."

She lifted her hand to my cheek. "I can't stay with you?"

"Uh..."

She smiled and brushed my cheek with her thumb. "I'm teasing you. The quarantine room sounds fine with me. Beats spending a weekend on my own. Besides, I want to be here, near you."

"I'll try to let you stay here for as long as I can," I promised.

Suri nodded knowingly, then her expression became serious. "I'm rooting for you, Jacob. And I hope you get that glowing bitch, after what she tried to do to me. If she's planning on punishing people who won't follow her, just because she feels like it, then I hope you smash her into little pieces. Seriously, if there's anything I can help you with, to bring her down, you can count on me. Even if it's just to take your mind off everything, I'll be there."

I covered her hand with mine. "Thank you, but I'd rather just keep you safe for as long as I can while you're here, and make sure Naima isn't out there looking to use you as leverage against me. I showed my hand when I came to get you. Naima might use you again, now that I've shown her what lengths I'll go to, to save you."

"Naima?"

"Cat-woman."

"Ah." She nodded, smiling sadly. "I'm sorry I gave them something they could use against you. Not that it would've stopped me from speaking to you when I did. You deserved that rocket ship sticker for getting me away from those kids."

I resisted the urge to bring her hand to my lips. "It's not your fault. If it hadn't been you, it would've been someone else." And I dreaded to think who that might have been because, if it had been anyone but Suri, I might not have gone after them. Maybe that would have been easier. But I'd never been one for easy.

TWENTY-EIGHT

Jacob

Having made sure that Suri was settled in her new room, I found myself taking a walk in the coven hallways. Nobody was around. I liked it at this time of night. It was just about the only time that the SDC was peaceful, especially now. I hadn't had any direction in mind when I'd started walking, but I was surprised to find myself heading down the corridor to Levi's office. I normally didn't come to this part of the coven. With Suri's hug and her eyes and her perfume racing in my head, I hadn't even been looking where I was going.

I thought about turning back, but Levi's door was ajar. Soft voices floated out into the corridor.

I approached quietly. If Levi caught me listening in, he'd spew out his usual "off with their heads" rant. I stopped and pressed back against the wall. Light spilled out onto the floor, and the voices got louder. I could pick out Levi and Imogene pretty easily. And Remington. And a couple more I didn't recognize. It had to be the whole California Mage Council, out in force—and, by the sounds of it, jumping down Levi's throat.

"Did you really think you could get away with something like this?" Remington seemed to be leading the ass-chewing. "Did you honestly think we wouldn't find out that you'd been keeping us in the dark? Seriously, Levi, this is low, even for you."

"I had no choice," Levi replied. He sounded shaken. Evidently, he *had* expected to get away with it. Although, if the Council members were this peeved, that couldn't be good for us. If they were finally coming for Levi, then what would that mean for the SDC? I had no clue. I just knew Levi was in a heap of trouble. And he'd put the SDC in even more trouble because of his lies.

"You had a choice, Leonidas." Imogene sounded disappointed, like a stern mother. "You had every opportunity to tell us the truth, so that we could help you fix this, but you chose not to. Don't pretend that this is anything other than self-serving pride. You wanted to be the only one in the know. You wanted to be the one with the upper hand, and what has it brought you? Nothing but mayhem. Katherine has succeeded in the fourth ritual because you wanted to prove something. And, in doing so, you have only proven how incompetent you are. No, incompetent is too kind a word—you have only proven how much of a danger you are in this position."

"Was it that important to you, that you stood out as superior to Alton and the SDC's previous directors? Was it that important that you had to risk global safety?" Remington spat. "What did you possibly think you could do on your own, Levi?"

I couldn't understand his motivation, either. What did he still have to prove?

"I had to show how strong we were," Levi replied. "Do you know how people view this coven? Magicals laugh at it. It's the butt of their jokes. I wanted to change that by retrieving Echidna ourselves. We were almost ready to strike. I had everything in order. I was handling it."

Bullcrap. Katherine had been lounging around Lethe without a care in the world. She'd been able to launch a trap for me, without worrying about the SDC fighting back.

"Well, I hope you think it was worth it now." Remington's voice dripped with bitterness.

"Need I remind you, Leonidas, that you were never elected as director of this coven?" Imogene said. "You were installed here as a substitute until a suitable replacement for Alton could be found. This was never a permanent fixture, and yet you have behaved as if you are emperor over this establishment. As if the rules of magical society, and their safety, do not apply to you.

You have behaved in a cowardly manner and have only made matters worse for this coven. How could anyone trust the SDC now?"

As if things weren't bad enough for our reputation. If Imogene was doubting us, we were screwed. She'd always been an advocate for this place.

Remington grunted in agreement. "Not to mention our trust in you. Your influence and connections got you into the Council in the first place, not your experience in leading a coven. We looked past that because you've always been a logical and cautious Mage. Now, you've just ruined any respect we ever had for you."

"This is not a one-person race to the finish line, Leonidas. This is a group effort. It has to be, if we're to stand the slightest chance against Katherine," Imogene added. "Nevertheless, now that your misdeeds have been brought to our attention, we will alert the covens and other Mage Councils. I don't give a fig what the National Council and the president have said."

I supposed that was as close to the F-word as Imogene Whitehall dared to get, though the impact was the same, coming from her. She sounded mad. Really mad. And for her to say she didn't care what the National Council and the president said was huge.

"You can't—" Levi tried to argue, but his voice wavered. I wished I could've seen his face.

"Which brings me to some troubling rumors I've been hearing, regarding your security magicals." Imogene was delivering another blow. My heart was practically in my mouth.

"What rumors?" Levi shot back sourly.

"That you're somehow manipulating them into remaining quiet. I would've said that was beyond you, but now I don't believe anything is too underhanded for you."

"That's a barefaced lie. I haven't done anything to them."

This punk was really going to try and weasel his way out of this. Not that I was shocked. But he was picking the wrong people to lie to. The Mage Council was already sick of his crap, and he wasn't doing himself any favors by keeping up the ruse. We'd seen the truth from O'Halloran's behavior.

"Then what do you have to say about the pills you've been giving them?" Remington replied.

Yes, Isadora! She'd clearly gone to Remington and told him about them.

"The National Council gave them to me for the security magicals' protection." Levi sounded eerily calm. "They're supposed to protect them from that hex Katherine used on Krieger. There's nothing untoward about them. And, if there is, then you need to take that up with the National Council, not me."

"There'll be an investigation, you can count on that," Remington said. "And I'll take it as high up as I have to, until someone gives me an answer."

My man! I trusted Remington. He'd get to the bottom of what was in those pills.

I figured it was a good idea to get away from the office before people started leaving. What else could they have to say? They'd told Levi how things were going to be. He couldn't really do much to argue. And I really didn't want to get caught.

I snuck away and decided to head down to the cells. I had a sudden urge to speak with Alton about what I'd overheard. It still bothered me that he wasn't the one in charge anymore. He'd have dealt with all of this like a pro. And who knew where we might have been, if he hadn't stepped down?

One thing troubled me as I headed for the coven's underbelly. Even if the California Mage Council told the other covens everything, it wouldn't stop Katherine's influence from spreading. It wouldn't stop her from getting more powerful. I hoped Alton might be able to give me some advice on how to act on what I'd heard, even if that was just to keep my mouth shut.

I'd just slipped into a side corridor to portal myself into the cells below, when a shadow crossed the entrance. I looked up, startled. But it was only Louella. *Thank God.* I'd been expecting one of the Mage Council, or worse, ready to berate me for eavesdropping.

"Geez, you nearly gave me a heart attack," I said. "What gives, creeping up on people like that?"

She frowned. "What gives, being out and about at this hour?"

"I could say the same to you."

Her expression softened. "Touché."

"I went for a walk, and I happened to pass Levi's office. He was getting an earful from the California Mage Council."

Her eyes widened. "What?"

"They found out about Echidna, and they found out about the security magicals acting weird. They're going to tell the other coven directors and the Mage Councils what's been going on, and where we're at with Katherine. You should've heard Levi, man—he was dead scared. Imogene and Remington are one scary team, when they put their heads together."

"So, Levi knows they know…" Louella said. "Where are you headed?"

"I wanted to speak to Alton about it."

"I'd like to help, if I can."

I shrugged. "Sure, I could use the company."

She stepped forward but hesitated. "I'm sorry about before, with the Suri stuff. I know I probably came across a little… intense. My Telepathy is still wrecked, so I'm on edge most of the time, at the moment. I keep getting bad vibes from everyone, even you, but I guess I've gone a little harder on Suri. I still don't like her being here, but I don't want to fall out with you over it. You're one of the only people I actually feel close to here. I love the Rag Team, don't get me wrong, but I always feel like the kid in the room, if you know what I mean."

I nodded. "All too well."

"And you're one of the only people I actually trust." She looked shy. "After what happened to you in Lethe, I just… I didn't want you getting into any more trouble. I know I can't change her being here, but I'd like to protect you, or at least help you keep focus. I won't get in the way. I'm just aware that this is all taking a turn for the worse."

"Louella Devereaux, my personal bodyguard." I chuckled.

"I'm tougher than I look," she retorted, with a grin.

"I don't doubt it, but are things really that much worse than they were yesterday?"

She stared at me. "Of course they are. Now that we know something is really up with the security magicals, chances are Katherine has infiltrated the highest levels of the magical authorities with either an operative or some kind of magical influence. To be honest, it's like they're not even trying. That's ringing massive alarm bells in my head, and it should be ringing them in yours, too."

"You're probably right, but what can we do about it? These aren't people we can go up against."

"We keep on working, in secret. It's up to you, me, Isadora, Krieger, and the Rag Team, plus a handful of allies like Imogene and Remington, to stop Katherine."

"You don't think they might be compromised—Imogene and Remington?" I didn't think so, but I wanted to hear her thoughts. Louella always had a way of explaining things that made everything make sense.

She shook her head. "They're way too proactive to be under Katherine's influence. If they were somehow affected, then Imogene would know about Harley's mission, and Remington would be trying to stop Harley. Instead, he helped her. Katherine's subtle, for sure, but if she knew what Harley was up to, she'd be sending everyone in, all guns blazing, to stop her from achieving her goal."

"I just needed to hear that out loud."

She grinned. "Happy to help."

"We should probably get a move on and go see Alton." I pushed Chaos into my hands and tore open a portal. Together, we stepped through it and stepped back out in the cells below. Ducking into the shadows, I sent a quick text to Astrid to ask her to tweak the security cameras. My phone pinged a moment later: *Already on it. Raffe is there. No worries.* That woman never seemed to sleep.

We walked along the strip-lit corridor. Sure enough, Raffe sat outside Santana's cell. He looked up as we approached.

"Looks like we've got a crowd tonight," he said sleepily. Santana sat on the floor on the other side of the bars. She looked tired. Her shoulders were slumped, and she had dark circles under her eyes. It didn't seem right, her being locked up. We'd all been as involved as she had been in Harley's trip to the cult. Yet she was being punished way more than the rest of us. And it definitely had more to do with her relationship with Raffe than her actual "crime."

"Who is it?" Alton's hand appeared through the bars next door.

"Jacob and Louella," I replied. "And we've got some news." As quickly as I could, I recounted what I'd heard in Levi's office. Once I'd finished, nobody spoke for a while. I couldn't tell if that was a good thing or a bad thing.

"We were hoping you might be able to intervene, Alton," Louella added.

I nodded, struck by an idea. "Yeah, maybe I could get Isadora down here, and she could plead your case with the California Mage Council. Levi's just proven that he's totally unfit to be director. Not that he wasn't before. But now the Council knows just how dangerous he is in this role."

"It'd be negligence if they let him continue." Louella had a determined glint in her eye.

"Oh, this is just too good."

My head whipped around. It sounded like Raffe's voice, but different. Darker, with a funny echo to it. And his eyes were red, like two flashing rubies.

"Levi, Levi, Levi, what a mess you've gotten yourself into. Useless fool." Rage twisted up his face, until I barely recognized him as Raffe. I supposed he wasn't Raffe anymore. The djinn had the reins. "Strutting around like a peacock while putting the whole coven right in the jaws of danger. And yet he keeps Santana here, like a common criminal."

"Raffe?" I approached him like he was a rabid dog.

"My, my, it's going to be so delicious when I tear his head from his neck. I can almost hear the ripping tendons. Can't you?" Raffe's eyes flashed brighter. "I'll break that jaw in my hands so I never have to hear another whining word from his mouth. You'll be able to hear the crunch of it from here. Be ready for it. It'll be the sweetest sound you've ever had the privilege of hearing."

Realizing I had seconds to get a handle on this, I lunged forward and pinned Raffe against the cell bars. Santana jumped up and tried to grab him around the neck, while Louella ran to block the exit. *Please be tougher than you look.*

"Raffe? Raffe? Come back to me," Santana begged.

He tore away from Santana. I tried to put my full weight against him, but he was too freaking strong. In one swipe, he threw me away. I hit the far wall with a thud that blasted through my body. Even my bones were shaking. I slumped to the ground as Raffe sprinted down the hall in a blur. He tossed Louella to the side like a rag doll. She hit the wall twice as hard as I had. I could almost hear the crack of it. A terrifying omen of the sounds we might hear, soon enough.

I tried to call out to Louella, but darkness was slipping over my eyes.

"Raffe, NO!" Santana roared. He'd already vanished. And I was about to black out. "RAFFE!"

I knew nothing she could say would bring him back. He was too far gone. News of Levi had brought the monster out. And he wasn't going back in until he'd gotten what he wanted.

TWENTY-NINE

Harley

W ade and Garrett worked to put up a barrier around the front of the library, to shield what we were doing from humans who might walk by. It was late, but this was New York—the city that never slept. Already, we'd had a rowdy bunch of drunken guys rattling on the gates, but they'd soon gotten bored and wandered off.

"Anytime today," Finch said, leaning back against the steps.

"Nothing stopping you from giving us a hand," Wade replied tersely. Bronzed Chaos surged out of his hands, adding to the energy that flowed from Garrett's palms, their combined forces merging to make a barrier over the front façade. I'd been relegated to guard dog, standing in front of the steps while they worked so I could tell them when I couldn't see them anymore.

"Almost there." I didn't want them bickering again.

A few minutes later, the barrier was complete, shrouding the whole front of the library in a mirage that made it look like there was nobody standing at the top of the steps. I made my way back to them, slipping easily through the barrier. Finch followed, taking the steps two at a time.

"Who's going first?" He grinned like an idiot. "Russian roulette, New York Coven style. Who'll survive? Tune in next week to find out."

"Are you ever quiet?" Wade peered at him over his shades.

"Not unless I'm really, really bored."

"I'll go first." Garrett volunteered, looking like he wanted to stop an argument, too. He stepped toward the chains, taking a deep breath. I didn't need to be able to read his emotions to know he was crapping his pants right about now. As long as he was honest, he had nothing to worry about. At least, that was what I was trying to convince myself. *Honesty is the best policy, right?*

No sooner had he touched the chains than his body went stiff, like someone had rammed a plank of wood up his back. Two bright shards of silver shot out of the chains and plunged into his palms. The veins in his forearms pulsated with a dull, internal light. *Freaky.* Not only that, but his eyes had gone wide, his mouth gaping, but he wasn't moving or saying anything at all. He just stood there, paralyzed.

I stepped forward to make sure he was okay, only to stagger backward as a torrent of emotions crashed into me. Wade put out his arm to catch me, though he quickly dropped it once he knew I was steady enough. Meanwhile, wave after wave of emotions pummeled through my body—emotions that didn't belong to me. Intense sadness, desperation, a hint of happiness, and a peppering of frustration twisted together. It took me longer than it should've to realize that the emotions were coming from Garrett. *What the heck?* How was that even possible? I couldn't sense Shapeshifters' emotions, and I'd tried enough times. But these emotions were unmistakably Garrett's. He was wide open to me, like a freshly cracked nut.

"What's wrong?" Wade sounded genuinely concerned.

"I… I can feel him. I can feel what he's feeling."

Wade took off his shades and glanced at Garrett. "You can?"

"Yeah. I don't know how, though." What made it even weirder was the fact that I couldn't keep the emotions out. Usually, I could put up a filter, or a blockade, but not with Garrett. The emotions were hammering into me, relentlessly.

"It's the chains," Finch said. "Got to be. Chains of Truth, spiked with some deadly, ancient mojo. Those things will force everything out of anyone who touches them."

I shot him a look. "I thought you didn't know what these were."

"Let's just say I had my memory jogged. I'd just about managed to block Iceland out, and then these damn chains get shoved in my face again." He dropped his gaze. "Just to be clear, I wasn't part of the team who went to Reykjavik. But I was in the debrief. I heard about the chains there."

Remember what he gave up. It didn't exonerate him from everything he'd done during his time with the cult, but it meant I could let these little reminders slide more easily. Wade, on the other hand, was glaring at him like he'd just shot Elmo. Leaving them to their glowering match, I turned my attention back to Garrett. He was stuck there, frozen, being forced to answer whatever the chains wanted to know. We couldn't hear what was being asked, which was insanely infuriating. Then again, I'd just been schooled by Wade for prying into other people's business, so maybe it was better that I couldn't hear what was going on.

After a few minutes of him standing like a petrified statue, Garrett began to spasm. "I want to save the world!" he blurted out, his eyes finally blinking. He was going to need some eyedrops after this. He paused, then answered again, more mobility coming back into his body. "Because it's the only one I know. I don't belong anywhere else, dammit! I'm lost without these people!"

Well, I guess we know what the chains asked you. It was a sweet revelation, but I knew better than to say anything to Garrett about it. We were all going to have to go through this, and there was every chance that one of us might get asked something that they really didn't want anyone else to hear. I was still freaking out about what they were going to ask me.

Silence settled across the library porch as the chains unfurled like a bulky metal snake, releasing Garrett from their paralyzing grip. The library doors opened wide for him, creaking on their old hinges. Garrett stepped through and turned over his shoulder with a smile on his face.

"Looks like we're in," he said confidently.

Finch snorted. "Nope, you're in. We aren't. Not yet."

We got one last look at Garrett's shocked face before the library doors slammed shut, the chains slithering back into position like Medusa's latest haircut. They tightened around the door handles with a strain of metal, the lock slotting back into place. Garrett was stuck inside, beyond the wooden doors. I could see a glimpse of him through the cracks in the planks, but he didn't seem to know we could see him. He was pacing frantically, no doubt terrified that he'd be the only one to make it through. He wasn't the only one.

The mood had shifted considerably, a sense of foreboding settling across the three of us.

"Who's next?" I asked.

Wade sighed and stepped up to the chains without a word. Just like Garrett, the moment he put his hands on the chains, two bolts of silver light shot out and into his hands. He froze, his body paralyzed by the ancient magic pouring out of these things. I got closer, wondering if I might be able to hear his question if I was near enough. I guessed I hadn't learned anything about privacy, but this was Wade. I needed him to survive this.

His brow furrowed, as if he was in some kind of pain. Tiny thread veins splintered across his wide-open eyeballs as he stared at the chains, his face turning red from the pressure of whatever these chains were doing... or asking. It took everything I had not to pull him away from the door, terrified that he might die if I did. This was pure torment, to watch the man I loved suffer while not being able to do a damn thing about it.

Less than a minute later, his body started to shake. "Because I want to keep her safe!" he shouted. I waited for a second part that might cast some more light on the question he'd been asked, but it didn't come. Instead, the chains seemed satisfied. They unfurled once again, letting Wade go and opening the doors wide for him to enter. He paused on the threshold, fixing his gaze on me.

"I'll be waiting for you inside," he said. "But just know that the quicker you answer, the less it'll hurt. I'm guessing this pain is going to stay for a while, so make it as quick as you can." He shook out his arms like they'd seized up and stepped into the darkness beyond. The fact that he'd even looked at me gave me a boost of confidence. He was worried about me being in unnecessary pain. Maybe that meant his frosty attitude was thawing.

Finch rolled his eyes. "How bad can it be?"

He found out, a moment later, as he put his hands on the chains. The silver light that shot out of the metal was way brighter than it had been for Garrett and Wade. The glow of veins beneath his skin pulsated, slithering all the way up his arms and spreading across his chest, pooling at his heart like a city seen from space at night. Even through his T-shirt, I could see the outline of every vein. Instead of freezing, like the others had, he dropped to his knees and fought to tear his hands away from the chains.

"I'll stop! I'll stop!" he howled, finally managing to pull his hands back. He sank back onto his haunches, dragging breath into his lungs and wiping the beads of sweat from his forehead with the back of his arm. I waited until the silver light had faded before I stooped to help him up. The chains hadn't given him an easy ride, that much was clear.

"Are you okay?"

"Yeah, I'm just peachy. Feel like I got hit in the chest by a sumo wrestler, but otherwise I'm grand," he wheezed. "You go next. I need to catch my breath."

"What happened?" I was getting more nervous by the second. My heart was having palpitations, just thinking about everything that could go wrong. At least Finch wasn't dead, but what if he couldn't get through the doors? I'd deal with the rest of the mission on my own, if I had to, but it was nice to have someone to hype me up. Finch was surprisingly good at that, and he also had a knack for talking me down off a ledge when my mind was getting the better of me.

"I wasn't ready, that's all." He clutched at his heart. "They gave me a chance to think hard before I answered. I thought I could trick them. They could've killed me, but they decided to show a little mercy. They blamed Katherine's influence on my shortcomings, which is sort of affirming. Hey, it's what I've been telling everyone since Purgatory, so at least they agree."

"Did you try to lie?"

He wouldn't look me in the eye. "I tried to skirt around the question. I didn't lie. There's a nuance. Anyway, they want me to go away and sit on the naughty step, and then come back. But you'll be fine, as long as you're honest. If you don't have an answer, you back out. I doubt they'll cut you any slack if you try and trick them, so don't. Unfortunately, I don't think you get to play the Katherine card."

"Well then, here goes nothing."

With a shaky breath, I touched the chains. Immediately, the silver energy shot out, and a current surged through my veins so powerfully I almost screamed. It stung like a million electric shocks, sending my heartrate into overdrive. On instinct, I battled to try and pull my hands away, but they were glued fast to the chains. All I could do was hold on and try not to pass out from the jarring pain that exploded in my chest, my arms burning with the strain of whatever was searing through me.

All of a sudden, I wasn't standing on the top step of the library anymore. Everything melted away, leaving nothing but white light wherever I looked. At least I could move again, though I was pretty certain I wasn't in my physical body. This felt similar to astral projection, only I still had to endure every sharp pain the chains were inflicting. My lungs were already fighting for air, my whole body on fire.

I struggled to focus my blurry vision as three figures rose from the endless white light in front of me, clad in glittering robes that looked as though they were encrusted in thousands of diamonds. Their hoods were brought so low over their heads that I couldn't make out their faces. If they even had faces. Although they looked humanoid, they moved in an unsettling way that verged on the spiritual—floating, rather than standing.

"Who are you?" My voice echoed across the never-ending sea of white.

"We are agents of Chaos, embedded within the Chains of Truth." I had no clue which of them was doing the talking. The words seemed to resonate from all three of them at once, booming through my skull and making the pain worse.

"We are Truth."

"And Lies."

"And Ignorance."

Okay, where's the White Rabbit—I want a word. This was starting to feel like a page from *Alice in Wonderland*, in one of the drafts that never made it into the finished version. For very good reason. These beings, whatever they were, were scaring the bejeezus out of me. They held my life in their hands, and if I didn't give them what they wanted, they'd take it.

"What do you want from me?" I had to fight to speak now that my throat had decided to close up. My entire body was having a violent reaction to these agents of Chaos and their slithering chains, and I didn't know how much longer I could hold on.

"We have one question for you. If you answer with truth, you may pass. If you answer falsely, you will die. If you take too long to answer, your body will suffer grievously. You cannot fight the pain within you. It will break you before long, forcing you to answer or relinquish the possibility of entry.

These are your only choices." Again, I had no idea which one of the hovering trio had spoken. Not that it mattered. They'd made their point, and then some.

"What's the question?" I rasped, eager to get this over with before I spontaneously combusted.

"Our question is a simple one. Are you willing to sacrifice everything, and everyone you know, in order to kill Katherine Shipton?"

All my previous worries came rushing back in a dark wave. This question was definitely one that I hadn't wanted to be asked, because... well, because I didn't know if I could answer it truthfully. And that was almost definitely why they'd asked it. After all, good people didn't sacrifice others, did they? Or did they, for the right reasons? I didn't know. And, honestly, I didn't know if I had that in me.

The enormity of this question loomed over me, holding up a horrible mirror to make me face the depth of my determination.

Even with the pain building inside me like an inferno, I couldn't bring myself to answer. As I saw it, I had three options. I could tell the Truth. I could Lie. Or I could say I didn't know, which would slip soundly into the category of good old Ignorance. That wouldn't bring me any bliss here. Chaos was going to judge me, one way or another.

The problem was... how could I tell the truth, when I hadn't figured it out myself?

THIRTY

Harley

The trio of floating specters were waiting, and the pain was only getting worse. I could barely hold my astral self up, my knees shaking, sweat dripping down my back. My chest felt like it had a giant elephant sitting on it, crushing my ribs into my spine.

But I couldn't answer.

This was the wrong time to have a bout of introspection, but I couldn't help it—my life was on the line here, and I needed to make sure I answered right. I'd played out the last fight a thousand times, and it had always ended with only me and Katherine, face-to-face, locked in a final battle. Naturally, I'd assumed that my friends and loved ones would be safe, but now I wasn't so sure. What if, to reach that final moment, I had to give up everything in the most terrible way? What if I was the last woman standing, in that scenario, because everyone else was gone? What if I was the last wedge between Katherine and her goal, but that battle was taking place upon the sacrifices of my friends?

No matter how many times the questions repeated in my head, my thoughts always hovered a moment longer on the idea of whether or not I could actually bring myself to go to those lengths. And if I'd even have the strength left, if Katherine had taken everything from me before it reached that point. I had no qualms about the actual ending of Katherine. I'd killed a cultist before, in Marie Laveau's lily garden. It had been her life or mine, for the sake of my friends' safety, too. I'd done it because I'd had to, and I'd kill Katherine because I had to, even though that moment in the garden still haunted me, deep down. Sometimes, when I was asleep, I'd see her face and watch the light go out of her eyes again.

I wasn't like Katherine—killing wasn't something I was comfortable with. But I would do it again if it meant ridding the world of Katherine. I could find the courage and strength to do that, knowing what Katherine had done to countless people. She would never have hesitated. She would have me killed without a second thought. I'd give her the same courtesy. But that wasn't the question they were asking. They were asking if I could sacrifice everyone I cared about in order to end her. And I really didn't know if I could.

I crumpled to the ground as an agonizing jolt of pain crashed through me. I was riddled with questions, but I was running out of time to answer theirs. Burning spikes of white-hot pain snaked up my arms and across my chest. A creeping iciness shivered underneath the pain, making everything both numb and excruciating at once. I knew that was my body shutting down, trying to block out the pain.

"You have the chance to retreat, if you so desire." That had definitely come from Truth. "It seems as though you are struggling. Perhaps you are not ready to answer such a question."

I blinked to clear the black spots dancing in my vision. "Wait, you're helping me? Like you helped my brother just now?"

"No, we turned your brother away," Truth replied. "He was not yet prepared, and so we made the decision to grant him as much time as he required to contemplate matters. Many of his wrongdoings were a result of a desperate desire to gain his mother's approval. We do not punish the sins of the son for the sins of the mother. His soul is broken, but it is not evil in nature. We are able to see that. He is at liberty to try again or step away and never enter here. It is our purpose to ensure that a heart is pure, but we cannot do so until a person is ready to reveal their heart to us. You do not seem ready, either. We function on objectivity, and it does not seem fair to us that you should put yourself at such grave risk without being truly prepared for the... repercussions."

What repercussions? My mind was on fire. It could barely think straight, let alone try and figure out the riddle of these three sphinxes. Nobody had mentioned anything about repercussions—unless they were referring to the whole death thing.

"I don't understand," I gasped, my astral hands clutching at my astral chest in a vain attempt to stop my heart from blasting right out of my ribcage in a bid for freedom.

"We may have been stationed here to guard this entrance," Truth continued. "But we are not servants of the New York Coven. We bend to no mortal. We answer solely to Chaos. We know of Katherine and what she plans to do —her terrible deeds to gain dominance on a global, and ethereal, platform. In truth, this is no simple test of your good intentions. We are here to ensure that you and your friends are truly ready, because the battle ahead will be unlike anything you have ever encountered. And not all of you will survive it."

That made things a million times worse. If they hadn't said that, I might have confidently replied I was willing to give everything to kill Katherine, knowing there was a strong chance everyone would live, and their question was purely hypothetical. But now they'd said, explicitly, that not everyone was going to survive... Did that mean that some of my friends were going to die as sacrifices? Did that mean the responsibility for their deaths would be on my shoulders?

"I don't know... I don't know," I rasped, clutching my stomach as another jolt of pain shot through me.

"War is never without its sacrifices, Harley. Death is bound within its very essence. As a soldier of this imminent conflict, you must make peace with that, or you will never be strong enough to endure," Truth said.

Somehow, their words had cleared a path in my mind. It was as though my brain was taking over, answering the question that my heart couldn't. That seemed strange, since this was supposed to be a judgment of my heart, but I supposed the two were intrinsically connected. Despite the vast horror of the question, all my doubts simmered away, replacing my fear with bitter determination.

"I will give everything I have to, in order to kill Katherine." I took in a painful breath. "Without hesitation. No matter what may come."

Truth bowed their head. "Very well. You have answered, and we shall take our time to review your reply."

Before I knew what was going on, the spectral trio spat me back out into reality. I was on my knees in front of the library door with Finch peering at me in concern. The pain had subsided, but not by much. I could still feel my muscles burning, with a deep ache lingering in my chest.

The chains unfurled and the doors creaked open. I let loose a huge sigh of relief, though it was tinged with guilt. *I did it.* I'd passed their test, even though I'd admitted that I was willing to sacrifice whatever it took in order to kill Katherine. Even with that, they'd judged that my heart was pure. I had to take comfort from that, regardless of how sickened I felt.

Wade and Garrett stood waiting on the other side, both reaching out to help me as I dragged myself to my feet and staggered through. I had a moment to look back before the doors slammed shut behind me, leaving us on one side and Finch on the other. I could still see him through some cracks in the wood, but he wasn't paying attention to us. His eyes were fixed on the chains, which had slithered back into position around the handles. The clatter of the chains echoed through the dark hallway.

"We're here for you, Finch." I pressed closer to one of the cracks. "You can do this."

He glanced at me, then back at the chains, then back at me. No hint of his usual comedy timing. Instead, he looked petrified, like he wanted to do anything but touch those chains again.

"Hey, it's going to be okay. They're not the enemy, Finch. You're ready for this."

"What if I'm not?" He sounded torn. "What if I'll never be ready? Maybe you just got an easier question than me."

Blocking out the burning in my veins, I kept my gaze on him. "What was your question? Maybe we can help."

His expression darkened. "They asked me... They asked me, do I love my sister enough to sacrifice myself for her?" Bitterness lurked in his voice. *Is that what it would come to?* Was he the one I'd have to lose? "It's a toughie. They gave me a way out, because they thought I wasn't ready, or I wasn't sure of my answer. They were right. I'm not ready to answer something like that.

No offense. I know I said I was ready to pull out all the stops, but... maybe not that one."

He was playing the joker again, forcing a smile, but it came off twisted. I could tell he wasn't bitter at being made to decide something like that. It was his angst, and his confusion, seeping through and morphing into something he could deal with, something that wouldn't make him look vulnerable in front of me. That was pretty much his worst nightmare, having his tough guy façade hacked away, to leave the soft and gooey center that he claimed he didn't have.

Although, his question from the chains brought me some comfort, ridding me of some of the lingering guilt about my own answer. Sure, that eerie trio had asked me if *I* was willing to sacrifice everything to kill Katherine, but they hadn't taken one thing into account: the free will of everyone else. When all was said and done, it wasn't up to me if they sacrificed themselves. That would be their choice, and their decision, given freely, one way or another. There were no assurances that it wouldn't happen, or that I wouldn't try to stop it if it did. I wouldn't know the true will of my heart, and my determination, until I was faced with that situation.

I smiled through the narrow gap, feeling a little better. "No offense taken. It's okay if you can't answer that." He wouldn't look at me. "You don't owe me anything. I care about you, Finch, but we've only really known each other for a short time. We were brought together because we both want to nail Katherine to a post, not because we shared a life together as siblings. If you're not ready, or willing, to sacrifice yourself, I won't hold it against you. How could I?"

"If he's not coming, we need to move," Wade said brusquely.

Finch finally met my gaze, looking totally heartbroken. "Then I guess I'll be out here, waiting for you guys to get back." He smiled a small, sad smile that let me know he was thankful for my understanding. "Don't have too much fun without me. I'll be standing by the door with a big old plank of wood, to knock out anyone who might be chasing you."

He was trying to cover his disappointment with humor. Same old Finch. And yet, it stung that he wasn't coming with us.

But his behavior confused me. If he wasn't willing to sacrifice himself, all he had to do was tell the trio that, and they'd let him through. The fact that he was hesitating spoke volumes. I realized, with a sudden sadness, that he might actually be thinking a different way, and he just wasn't ready to voice it or make peace with it yet. Until he was, he couldn't touch the chains again. If he did, and he tried to bend the truth somehow, the chains would kill him on the spot.

"We'll be as quick as we can," I said.

"Yeah, if you could, preferably before my balls retreat back into my body. It's freezing out here."

Oh, Finch... Turning my back on him and hating myself for it, I took the first steps into the creeping shadows of the gloomy library. With Wade and Garrett following, it was time for stage two.

Stealing the Merlin Grimoire.

THIRTY-ONE

Jacob

I blinked slowly, and instantly regretted it. A bomb had gone off in my head, and it was in the middle of shooting up my back. I heard fuzzy voices coming from somewhere. But they sounded swampy. Like I was in deep water and they were far away, muffled.

"Jacob? Jacob, you have to wake up. Jacob, can you hear me?"

Alton? I struggled to open my lids. The lights were too bright, and everything looked wrong. It took a moment for my brain to catch up. I was lying on my side. My head on the cold floor. Staring across at two cells. Two blurry figures stood at the bars. Santana and Alton, almost side by side but separated by a thick wall.

"Jacob, *mi amigo?* Jacob, can you hear us?" That was definitely Santana. "Louella? Louella, *mi querida*, please wake up. Louella?"

I groaned, and their eyes snapped to me.

"Jacob? Oh, thank God." Alton gave a low sigh. "Are you okay?"

I couldn't move. I couldn't think. Everything hurt. I tried to shift to look for Louella through the painful light. But it only sent a fresh jolt of pain behind my eyeballs. Blurriness followed, and I figured it was best to lie still and let my body settle. I'd just closed my eyes again when I heard footsteps. They ran right toward me. When I fought to open my eyes again, there were two figures standing over me.

"Dude, what the hell happened?" Dylan peered down at me.

"Can you move? Does anything feel broken?" An angel stood beside him. She was talking to me.

Dylan knelt down. "Yo, Taty, I think he's out of it."

"This is bad. This is very, very bad." Tatyana glanced over her shoulder. "Try and rouse him, and I'll see to Louella. She doesn't look good, either."

"Hey, buddy, you alive in there?" Dylan nudged my shoulder as the angel walked off. I wanted her to come back. But I had Dylan instead. I let out a gasp of pain as he took me by the arms and lifted me up. He sat me against the wall. Everything ached, but things were slowly coming back. I remembered Raffe with his red eyes. And him throwing me against the wall. And him running off… somewhere.

"Where's Raffe?" I croaked.

"No idea. He was down here. We got an alert from Astrid that he'd Hulked out. Nobody can find him. But that was twenty minutes ago—you've been out for a while, man. You okay? Do you think you've busted anything?"

I shook my head slowly. "No, just sore." I looked at him through one half-closed eye. "You really don't know where Raffe is?"

"He's going to do something terrible." Santana's voice echoed from her cell. With her behind bars, there was nothing she could do to help. We couldn't let her or Alton out. Levi was the only one with the keys, and I didn't exactly have the energy to build a portal right now. "It's not Raffe we're dealing with anymore. Kadar's on the warpath. You need to stop him before he does something really bad. Something he can't take back."

Dylan nodded. "Astrid tracked him through the cameras for a while, but he was too quick for her. He's been knocking cameras out. Good arm on him. But that's why we've lost him."

Panic made me lurch forward as I tried to stand. "He's going to go after Levi. We have to find him." Dizziness hit me, and I sank back down.

"You're not going anywhere right now," Dylan said. "Take a breather, dude. You've just had your head cracked against a wall by a djinn. And Kadar hasn't gone for Levi. Astrid's watching the cameras by his office. No sign of Kadar anywhere. No security magicals running around. No alarm. Nada."

I looked up as two figures walked toward us. Tatyana had her arm around Louella's waist. Louella looked worse than I felt, but she managed a dopey smile. Her eyes weren't quite in focus, but at least she was on her feet. I needed to be, too. Remembering about Raffe had sobered me up a bit. I might not have liked Levi, but things would get really bad if Raffe did away with his dad. Not only for the SDC, but for Raffe himself. He wasn't in control right now. But he'd be the one who'd have to live with the consequences.

"Help me up," I said. Dylan put his arms out and lifted me up like a sack of wrenches. I held on to him for a minute while my knees steadied.

"We should get these two to the infirmary." He looked back at Tatyana. *Or Taty...* I envied him for being able to call her that. My heart was solely fixed on Suri, but Tatyana had been my first major crush. That hadn't changed overnight.

Tatyana nodded. "I agree."

"No, we can't do that," I blurted out. "We need to go after Raffe. We need to go to Levi's office and wait there all night if we have to. I can walk. I'm fine."

"Me, too," Louella added.

"If you insist. We can't waste time." Tatyana looked worried. Instead of making us go and see Krieger, she turned with Louella and headed up the hallway. Walking was slow, but it was probably the best option. I was in no state to use my portal powers. If I tried, we'd probably end up in freaking Poland or something.

To my massive embarrassment, Dylan scooped me up like a baby and set off after Tatyana. When he reached her, he took Louella and slung her over his shoulder. At least it'd be quicker this way, thanks to Dylan's Herculean abilities. But man, was it degrading. Dylan powered up the stairs, heading for Levi's office, with Tatyana sprinting after as fast as she could.

We came to a halt in the corridor to Levi's office. Dylan dove behind a towering bronze dragon. Tatyana squidged in beside us. And not a moment too soon. Up ahead, the rest of the California Mage Council members were pouring out of Levi's office, including Imogene. She looked majorly pissed off. Levi had come to the door, and she glowered back at him as she turned around, her arms stiff at her sides. She was about to have the last word, I could tell. She stopped, like a beautiful bull ready to charge at the weaselly matador. Her voice rang through the hallway, laced with polite but unveiled anger.

"You're to report to us at all times. Do I make myself clear? You will answer to the Mage Council, and a replacement will be sent as soon as possible."

Levi said nothing. With that final warning hanging in the air, Imogene strode away. Her heels clacked past our hiding spot, but she didn't see us. She likely had enough on her mind. The rest of the Mage Council filed past behind her, ducklings following their mother. Remington had his head down.

With the hallway now empty, we crept out of our hiding spot. Levi still stood in the doorway, but he wasn't looking in our direction. He was staring at the floor. Probably contemplating the giant mess he'd made and the things he was going to lose because of it. His freedom, for one. Imogene and the others would be watching his every move, from now on. *How do you like them apples, Levi?* The tables had been turned. The watcher had become the watched.

Dylan set us down so we could walk toward Levi together. I was ready to take my first shaky step when a dark shadow whizzed past from the opposite hallway. I saw black smoke and a blur, and that was it. Maybe a flash of red, but that could've been my mind seeing what it wanted to see. The blur slammed into Levi and knocked him into the room beyond. The door thudded shut behind them. And the rasp of a key turning echoed out. Raffe, or rather, Kadar, had locked them in.

"Man, that's not good. Not good at all." Dylan stared at the door.

You think? Levi was in so much trouble right now.

With all the energy I had left, I sprinted for the door. Dylan got there first and yanked on the handle. It wasn't just locked, it was charmed shut. Normally, he could've ripped the damn thing off its hinges if he'd wanted. But Kadar had done some djinn trickery on this door. Dylan kept trying, but it kept pushing him back. He kicked it and almost went flying up the corridor.

Tatyana stepped up, and a funny look came over her. Her eyes flashed white and her body lit up. She was clearly talking to some spirit about what she needed. I watched her intently, hoping she could sort this out. However, she blinked, and the light faded a moment later.

"There's nothing they can do," she said. "The spirits can't get past whatever he's done to the door."

"That djinn is one powerful son of a bitch." Dylan ran a hand through his hair. He didn't seem to like things that could counteract his Herculean ability. Helplessness wasn't his natural state. I smiled secretly to myself. Dylan couldn't do anything, but I could.

"Hang on." I gathered Chaos into my palms and swallowed the pain still hammering in my temples. This had to work. I just hoped we wouldn't end up halfway across the world. But this was a risk I had to take if we wanted to stop the djinn. There was no time to walk there; otherwise, we might be too late. My mind was still all over the place and my head was throbbing, but I forced myself to focus. With a powerful push, I tore open a portal. It crackled violently, the edges shaky, but it held. Hopefully, it would lead us right into Levi's office. I leapt through first, with the others following.

I stepped back out into Levi's office, but I almost ran right back into the portal at what I saw. Kadar had Levi pinned against the obnoxiously big desk, one hand wrapped around Levi's throat, the other gripping Levi's skull. By the looks of it, Kadar hadn't been lying. He was really going to crush Levi's head like a coconut and tear it right off his neck. From the sound Levi was making, it seemed like he was already starting with the coconut part. The howl was like nothing I'd ever heard. It was the sound of a man in the worst agony of his life. And it was getting louder, turning into a piercing, bloodcurdling scream.

Trickles of red ran down Levi's cheeks. I almost threw up as I realized the blood was coming out of his eyes. It was seeping out of him like tears. And his eyeballs were already a dark, stomach-churning scarlet, as the pressure built inside his skull, with nowhere to go.

"Stop!" Tatyana lifted her hands. Water spiraled out of the nearby jug on Levi's desk. It twisted through the air and slithered around Raffe's neck. She sent a pulse of spirit energy toward the water, the icy-cold essence of the spirits turning the ring of water to ice.

Dylan sprinted for the desk. The ring of ice was already melting against Raffe's searing red skin, but it had caused enough of a distraction to give

Dylan the shot he needed. He tackled Raffe to the ground and put himself between the djinn and Levi.

"Raffe, if you can hear me, you need to take control," Dylan said. Kadar kept coming at Dylan, darting around to try and get past him. But Dylan was fast, too. Kadar almost managed it, only for Dylan to snatch at his arm and swing him away. He hit the wall with a thud but got right back up again, his eyes flashing with fury.

"Step aside, Dylan. I could tear you to shreds, but I know Raffe would be upset to have your blood on his dainty hands." Kadar crouched, preparing to spring again. "I will put your head on a pike if you continue to annoy me, and I will wear your skin as a coat and make your pretty girlfriend watch. She is likely due an upgrade. And I'd be only too happy to oblige."

"Raffe, buddy, if you're in there, we really need you to get control!"

Kadar sprang through the air and swiped at his head. Dylan shoved Kadar right back. I watched with my jaw wide open.

Kadar crouched back down, his mouth twisted in a grimace. "Leonidas must be punished. He must be made to pay for the torment he laid at Raffe's door. I am doing your friend a favor—something he is not brave enough to do by himself. I am serving him in the most delicious way. He will never have to fear his father's oppression again, once he sees me lift this man's head from his shoulders and suck his brains through his eye sockets. Have you ever tasted fresh brains, Dylan? You look like you're a fan of protein. Or steroids."

"You're not killing him, Kadar." Tatyana stood beside Dylan, her eyes white. Her voice came out all weird and echoey. Little silvery spots danced in the air around her. If I'd thought she looked like an angel before…

The djinn paused at the sound of his name. He stared at her, seemingly surprised. Names held power. I guessed he hadn't expected his own to be used against him.

"You want to save him?" Kadar asked after a beat. "After everything he's done?" His voice intensified, the menace returning to his features. "Did you know he used to lock Raffe up in a cell when he was a child, denying him food so he could try and starve me out? He bought handcuffs and collars from charlatan peddlers who claimed they could destroy me without destroying Raffe. The pain that Raffe went through when Levi forced those restraints on him. I can still hear him screaming for mercy. But do you think Levi offered him any? No, he did not. So why should I? Raffe cried alone in his room when Levi turned around and said that he, an innocent child, was responsible for the death of his mother, and I was the only one to comfort him. You think you know what is best for him? You have not lived within him his entire life. I know Raffe better than any of you imposters. I know what he truly desires, and that is Levi's death. The ultimate freedom."

Damn. I'd known things were bad between Raffe and his dad, but I'd never expected that. That was the sort of stuff you heard on true crime podcasts. I already hated Levi. This made me hate him even more. But not enough to watch Kadar literally rip the man's head off.

Dylan flexed his muscles. "Still, that's not your call. You don't get to kill someone just because you want to."

"Oh, but I do." Kadar grinned. "Have you forgotten how Levi has treated that exquisite slice of Mexican caramel? How he threw her in a cell? He has put you all at risk, time and time again, and you would see him walk out of this room tonight? Perhaps it is your brains that require some rearranging. And I am only too happy to crack open every skull I have to, to avenge Raffe."

Louella and I snuck forward to protect Levi, while Kadar paced. He was getting more aggressive by the second, and Dylan was flagging. With every smoky dart, Dylan used every scrap of his strength to force Kadar back. And it was taking a lot out of him, even with his Herculean stuff. Dylan couldn't fight him forever.

"Follow my lead," I whispered to Louella.

She nodded.

I kept my hands down and gathered Chaos into them. With one big push, I created a portal right beside the desk. It made a huge mess of Levi's things, but that didn't matter. Kadar's head snapped up, but Dylan stood between him and me. With Louella's help, I dragged Levi off the desk and into the portal. I heard Kadar roar.

"Get him to Santana!" I yelled. The last thing I saw was Dylan slamming into him and white light surging at him from Tatyana as the portal snapped shut behind us. Santana was the only hope Raffe had. She was the only one who could subdue the beast.

THIRTY-TWO

Jacob

I portaled us right into the infirmary, giving a sleeping Krieger the fright of his life. He sat bolt upright, rubbing his eyes before leaping to his feet and running toward us. He really couldn't catch a break these days.

"What happened?" he gasped. Levi hung limply between Louella and me. His eyes had rolled back into his head, and there was blood pretty much everywhere. It was running out of his mouth, nose, eyes, and ears. I didn't need a doctor to tell me that it really didn't look good.

"The djinn," I replied. "He tried to kill Levi."

Krieger flipped into business mode. "Help him over to the bed."

Struggling under Levi's weight, Louella and I carried him to the closest bed and laid him down. We stepped back as Krieger took over, sprinting toward a cart that he then pulled up to the bedside. He took a vial and a syringe from one of the drawers and filled it halfway. The liquid glowed, letting me know this was no ordinary medicine. Squirting away the excess, Krieger pushed the needle into Levi's arm and pressed down on the plunger. A bright pulse shot up Levi's arm, following the path of his veins and flowing around his body.

"What was that?" Louella asked.

"A stabilizer," Krieger replied rapidly. He took out two more vials, one filled with a blood-red liquid, the other tinged with purple. I turned away as

232 • HARLEY MERLIN AND THE DETECTOR FIX

he injected the purple one directly into Levi's neck. As for the blood-red fluid, he tipped a large quantity of it onto some gauze and wrapped it tight around Levi's injuries—his throat, his skull, his temples. Bruises had formed beneath his skin, and I could still see the deep claw marks where Kadar had tried to gouge out chunks of him.

All the while, Levi lay still. He groaned from time to time, muttering the same thing over and over: "Don't let him out... Don't let him out..." But he gradually grew quiet and was out for the count. I didn't know if that was Kadar's doing or Krieger's. The glow from the first vial had faded slightly, but it had given his skin a waxy sheen. I thought it made him look worse, like he was close to death, but Krieger knew what he was doing. As for Levi's mutterings, I guessed he meant Raffe, but we'd have to wait and see how he was first, before we did any locking up. If he could get Kadar back under control, maybe we wouldn't need to.

"Is he going to make it?" I asked.

Krieger sighed. "You got him to me quickly, which should work in our favor. That stabilizer is only useful if I receive a patient within a short time of their injury. We'll have to wait and see just how deep the damage is. There's a great deal of blood pooling in certain areas of his skull, which is applying pressure to his brain, but that ointment I applied should work toward absorbing it out of his head. It's an organic magnet of sorts, designed to draw blood away from places it shouldn't be."

I frowned. I hadn't seen him do any tests. "How do you know where the blood is pooling?"

Krieger glanced at me. "I'm an Organa, Jacob. It's part of the reason I became a physician. You'll find that most magical physicians are gifted with healing or sensory abilities."

Louella smiled. "And that means he can sense trauma in organic matter."

"Like a human X-ray?" I asked.

Krieger shook his head. "Not quite. I can only get a sense of what's wrong. I can't actually see it. In that way, it's rather like your Sensate ability. There is no visual aspect."

"Well, you kept that one quiet, Krieger," I muttered.

"No, I simply choose not to mention it unless I'm asked," he replied. "My predecessor had the same ability, if the files are correct. It's very common in medical professionals like Adley and myself. You find Sanguines, Squelettes, Epiderms, and Healers in this profession, too."

"Who?" I stared at him in confusion.

He smiled wearily as he wrapped more bandages around Levi's wounds. "Sanguines have blood abilities, Squelettes have skeletal-based abilities, Epiderms can perform healing magic of the flesh, and Healers have a more generalized ability to fix people. Not all of them can use their Chaos on others, but some can, and most end up as physicians, for obvious reasons."

"When will we know if Levi's going to pull through?" Louella glanced down at him. She looked worried. Even he didn't deserve this.

Krieger shook his head. "Hours, days, weeks... it's hard to tell with head injuries. They're more fragile than others. One moment, it can seem as though everything is fine with someone who's suffered a head injury. The next, they're dead on the floor, having had an aneurysm that we couldn't pick up on."

We fell into silence as Krieger continued with what he was doing. He hurried back and forth, bringing machines that he hooked Levi up to. Soon, the only sound that filled the infirmary was the steady beep of Levi's heartrate, flashing on the monitor. Any moment, that line, which peaked and troughed, could go flat. And, no matter what Levi had done, I didn't want him to die.

I thought of Suri, still hiding in the quarantine room. She'd probably be wondering what the heck was going on, but I couldn't go to her now. I'd explain everything once things were more settled here. In fact, part of me hoped she was asleep or something, so she'd missed all of this chaos. She hadn't shown that much fear since being here, but hearing about an attack like this might change things. And I didn't want her to be scared.

I was about to say something to break the uncomfortable silence, when my phone went off. Picking it up, I saw Tatyana's name flashing on the screen. A short while ago, I'd have given anything to get a call from her. But I knew she wasn't calling just to chat. Swiping the answer button, I pressed the phone to my ear.

"Hello?"

"We've got the djinn, and we're taking him down to Santana," Tatyana said, sounding like she'd been breathing hard. "It took a very complex spell, but Dylan and I got him under control. We'll let you know more once Santana has seen to him."

I nodded. "Thanks for letting us know."

"How is Levi?"

"He's stable, for now. Krieger's still working on him, but he's alive. So… there's that." I looked at Levi's motionless body, taking comfort in the beep of his heartrate monitor.

"Okay, let me know if anything changes," Tatyana said.

"Yeah, I will."

"Talk soon."

I smiled, even though it was totally inappropriate. "Yeah, talk soon."

Putting the phone down, I heaved out a sigh of faint relief. Levi was safe. Raffe would soon be back with us. And, somehow, we'd completely averted disaster.

Half an hour had passed, and there'd been no change in Levi. Krieger had added another vial, to put him in a magical coma while his body recovered, and the other potions kept on with their work. Almost having your head caved in took some time to heal, apparently. I wasn't sure I'd ever get the memory out of my head—the blood trickling out of his eyes. *Yeesh.* Louella had gone to check on things with Raffe and Santana, though I got the feeling she just didn't want to be around this mess.

"The djinn didn't take kindly to Levi's actions, I see," Imogene said, sitting at Levi's bedside. Her empathy surprised me, for some reason. She didn't have to sit with him, after everything he'd done to the Mage Council, but she was. I'd called her right after Krieger had set to work on fixing Levi. I figured she needed to know.

Isadora nodded. "Yeah, he did quite the number on him." I'd called her, too, though she wasn't being quite as forgiving. "Raffe must've been in a heck of a state to let things get this bad."

"It's hard to associate the two of them, isn't it?" Imogene said softly. "Raffe is such a sweet, intelligent young man. It hardly seems fair that he should have to suffer for the behavior of something he has no control over."

Fear hit me. "Please don't do anything to Raffe." I'd told her everything that had happened in the office. But this was the first time I'd heard her actually mention Raffe. She'd been more concerned about Levi pulling through. "He's got Kadar under control, I swear he does. It's just that, what Levi did, it… it made him so angry. If Santana wasn't in a cell, it might not have gotten that far. She helps him control the djinn stuff. Right now, Raffe is back to being himself because he's downstairs with Santana and the others. And he feels awful. Like, sick to his stomach awful."

Imogene glanced at me with sad eyes. "I know you share a personal bond with Raffe, as we all do, in our own way, but I'm not sure it's a good idea to allow Raffe his freedom. I don't deny that he has a certain level of control, but… he attempted to murder his own father tonight. That can't be ignored."

"The djinn did. Not Raffe," I insisted.

"But the djinn is part of him, Jacob. And we can't gauge what the djinn will do, and that's the trouble. Raffe may feel as though he's in control of the situation, but he likely thought he was earlier, before all of this occurred, and you have the awful proof of how that has turned out."

Krieger slammed his fist into a medical cart, making me jump out of my skin. "I have had just about enough of all this tiptoeing around, walking on eggshells, always-by-the-book nonsense!" He'd clearly lost it, speaking to Imogene like that. Though, her expression hadn't changed. "I have been working like a maniac, trying to prepare the magical detector for use. Everyone in this room, and on the Rag Team, has been working tirelessly to stop Katherine. Meanwhile, Leonidas Levi has done nothing but hamper everybody's efforts and punish those who are actually taking action. All so he could satisfy some selfish longing to be the Großer Käse and make up for his shortcomings as a youth."

I had to sit on my hands. The tension in the room was unbearable. Even Isadora looked stunned. Imogene was just sitting there, looking at Krieger. Her expression was as calm and composed as ever, but that felt even scarier than if she'd flown off the handle at him.

At last, she spoke. "I can't argue with you, Dr. Krieger. I'm also weary of the secrecy and inaction, though I have only recently discovered how far the proverbial rabbit hole goes with Levi. It's frustrating beyond belief, to be out of the loop like this."

"I have had enough. Everyone has," Krieger replied. "Our community here is worthy of suitable leadership. We need a leader, not an incompetent oaf. And we need one soon."

Krieger's outburst was pretty awesome to see. He was usually the calm and clinical one.

Imogene sank back in her chair and sighed, taking her time to say anything. That was one of her unique traits—she always thoroughly pieced together what she was going to say, before she said it. I'd seen the same thing in Levi's hallway. She could've shot words at him in the doorway or the office, but she'd waited. She'd probably learned that acting rashly didn't get anyone anywhere.

After a brief, awkward silence, she nodded slowly. "You make an excellent point, Dr. Krieger. But, in all honesty, I don't have a solution for you. The Mage Council promised to oversee Levi's behavior from now on, until another director could be found, but I can see that's not going to be enough. Levi is not likely to wake up anytime soon, and I agree with you that he's no longer up to the task. The trouble is, it's not as though I have a book of potential prospects with indicators beside their names, telling me who is trustworthy and who has been compromised."

"Then do it yourself," Krieger shot back. "Put your money where your mouth is and take the directorship on your own shoulders."

She stared at him, and I did, too. "I don't think that's a good idea," Imogene said. "As it is, I am drowning in the work of the Mage Council and the bureaucracy surrounding everything. My days are already packed to the brim. I don't know that I could abandon all that in order to replace Levi. And I already have the LA Coven to contend with."

"Yeah, but you have a deputy there, right?" Isadora cut in. "You wouldn't have to worry about LA. You could just check in from time to time. It might even be beneficial to have the two covens more united. As for the Mage Council, they won't fall apart without you. Remington, or one of the others, can cover your work. I'm sure they'd understand, given the circumstances."

Imogene was starting to look uncomfortable. "I lack the objectivity that a coven director should have. I have some very close, personal relationships with individuals here, and I would hate to be accused of favoritism, or of striving to seize the directorship for myself. People will gossip. They'll think me an opportunist."

"Why does it matter what other people say?" Krieger replied. "The SDC is suffering right now. We need leadership. True leadership. And if you agree with that, then you should feel a duty toward us. A duty that leaves only one option: you stepping up to take over from Levi. Anything less is tantamount to willful neglect."

"That is hardly fair, Dr. Krieger." Imogene looked somewhere between outraged and resigned.

"I am tired of sugarcoating everything to make it palatable," he retorted. "You can't say that you agree we're in dire straits, and then leave us to deal with it ourselves. A coven without a director is like a ship without its captain. Who else is there to take over? You said it yourself, you don't have a book of trustworthy individuals. So, it has to be you."

"Perhaps Alton could be reinstated, instead?" Imogene said. I could almost see the stress pressing down on her shoulders, but I was on Krieger's side with this. If Imogene really wanted to help us, then she had to step into those shoes herself. I couldn't see another option now that Krieger had put this one in front of us. Glancing at Isadora, I could tell she felt the same.

"Well, that's against the rules, isn't it?" Isadora replied. "Because he resigned, he can't take up this directorship again, not without a tribunal. You know it would take months to get that underway, with everything else that's going on." She smiled reassuringly. "The people here really do deserve viable leadership, Imogene. They don't deserve to be tarred with the brush that Levi wanted to spread all over them. You could fix that. People would pay attention if you took over. And since when have you been afraid of hard work?"

Imogene dipped her head. "I am loathe to admit it, but I've been pushed almost to my limit of late. I didn't think I even had one of those." She gave a tight laugh. "And, if I'm being entirely honest, I wouldn't want to be a disappointment, if I can't make the time to put forth my best effort as interim director."

"That's okay," I replied. "Whatever you give is fine. A toad would do a better job than Levi."

"Are you saying I'm a toad, Jacob?" Imogene chuckled.

My cheeks burned. "No, not at all! I just mean, even if you put in only a shred of effort, you'd already be doing a better job than Levi has."

"You'll be thanked for this, Imogene," Krieger added. "I, for one, would be grateful. Although, I think I've already said everything I have to say about that."

"Yes, I feel like I'm back at school, being scolded by the principal." Imogene sighed nervously.

"Then, I hate to add to the tough love, but we're sort of director-less here," Isadora said. "We need an answer. If you say no, we'll have to come up with something else, and I don't know about everyone else, but I'm pretty much stumped for options."

Imogene squirmed in her seat. "I suppose…"

"Yes?" Isadora and Krieger chorused, leaning forward.

"I suppose, after everything you've all said, I could take over for Levi, as a temporary solution. I'm not promising that I can remain permanently, given my positions in the LA Coven and the Mage Council, but I can, at the very least, help for a short time. After all, I wouldn't want to be responsible for neglect." She offered a reluctant smile to Krieger, prompting him to chuckle sheepishly. "I'm certain that the Mage Council won't have any objections to it, as long as they know it's temporary. Although, naturally, I will have to discuss it with them before I can announce anything in an official capacity."

"You're really going to do it? You're really going to be the new director?" I stared at her in excitement. I knew we'd shanghaied her into this mess, but a reluctant director was better than no director. And Imogene would definitely give the SDC some clout. Krieger had asked for action, and she'd given it to him, albeit unwillingly. But she had my vote. Even now, she could have shifted the responsibility to someone else, but she wasn't going to do that. Plus, with Imogene in the director role, maybe I'd have a better chance of convincing her to let Suri stay. Levi would have given me a big, fat no, but Imogene wasn't as cold as him. She'd at least listen to what I had to say, instead of cutting me off without any hope.

Imogene nodded, looking tired. "If everyone is in agreement, then yes, I will. But I must repeat, this has to be a *temporary* measure."

"We understand." Isadora grinned. "And we're grateful."

"Well then, I should be instated by the morning, if I speak with the Mage Council now and they decide it is the best course of action."

Krieger beamed from ear to ear. "I know you're not yet officially our director, but I'd like to ask your permission to continue with the magical detector, given its importance in locating Katherine."

"Yes, of course," she replied. A hint of regret still lingered in her voice, as though she wished she hadn't been cornered like this. It faded a moment later, as a determination seemed to wash over her. "You were right when you said there have been far too many people sitting on the sidelines, hoping that someone else will resolve the matter. Please, continue with your work, and I will grant you all the resources you require. You need only ask. I suppose that's one good thing I can do in this position."

"Thank you," Krieger said, looking more cheerful than he had in weeks.

"And, as soon as my position has been officiated, I will see to it that Santana and Alton are released from their cells. If I'm to be accused of favoritism by the gossipmongers, I might as well play up to it." She smiled. "Plus, I could use Alton's assistance to keep my schedule from getting so stuffed that I don't have a second even to use the little girls' room."

Everyone chuckled. The thought of Imogene using the bathroom was a weird one for me. Then again, she was human, after all. She probably went to bed at night worrying over the same things as everyone else. She probably took her first sip of coffee in the morning and gave a satisfied sigh. She probably locked herself in her car, just to get a moment's peace. To be honest, I kind of felt bad that we'd forced her into this, but I was looking forward to seeing what she could do for the SDC.

"Do you think you could get Harley reinstated and get Levi's charges against her dropped?" Isadora asked, her voice catching in her throat.

Imogene furrowed her brow. "That may be beyond me. There's a lot of fear surrounding Harley. I don't share that sentiment, but it's prevalent in the general populace."

"Then, surely it's better that she's here, where she's under coven rules, than out there amongst them?" Krieger added.

"Perhaps." Imogene brushed her fingertips along the lapel of her jacket. A thoughtful tic. "I suppose I could try, using that line of logic. After all, she hasn't actually behaved criminally, and Levi shared very little information with the authorities. Plus, we have already established that the current authorities are not to be trusted."

"Does that mean you'll attempt it?" Isadora pressed. *Poor Imogene.* We were really piling up the tasks, and it wasn't even her first day yet.

She sighed uncertainly. "I will, Isadora, on your behalf. They might answer me with cries of 'Purgatory' or 'Avarice,' but I will do what I can to try and have her reinstated as a coven member. Beyond that, it may fall to you to bring her back here, if such a thing can be done." She paused. "But Harley isn't safe out there, wherever she may be. Katherine would give her left ventricle to harm her. At least here, we can reduce the possibility of that happening."

Isadora looked about ready to fall off her stool. "You'll really do that?"

"She has been wrongly condemned without a fair trial. Levi judged her without listening, and that cannot be allowed to stand," Imogene replied. "Although, as I've said, you will have to be the ones to find her if I can grant her amnesty. She has likely ceased to trust the word of directors, and your encouragement may have more sway."

"Yes, of course, we'll take responsibility for that," Isadora replied, border-line giddy.

"Do you know if she's safe?" Imogene asked, turning to me.

I shrugged. "She was when I left her, but I haven't heard from her since she made me portal myself back here."

"I imagine she didn't want to risk Levi discovering her. She told Jacob that it was safer for him not to know where she was, or what she was doing," Krieger added.

We were both lying, for Harley's sake. Imogene might have been about to take on the director role, but that didn't mean we could give her the chance to get in Harley's way. I didn't know what Harley was doing, exactly, but Harley had given me the impression that it was probably illegal. But it was to stop Katherine, and that was worth covering for. At least for now.

Once Harley was reinstated, we could tell Imogene everything. After all, it was better to ask for forgiveness instead of permission.

THIRTY-THREE

Harley

Things didn't improve much as we got deeper into the network of the New York Coven. We jogged through an endless labyrinth of dark and decaying hallways, which reeked of years of abandonment, and we slipped through secret wall hatches every time the blueprints dictated we had to. If we missed one, we doubled back, edging through the impenetrable gloom with only Wade's glowing Fire to cast some light on our surroundings.

As maps went, this one was hard to follow. We'd come out of the library itself a while back, not that anyone would have noticed. The endless corridors and passageways looked the same, drenched in an oily glaze that pulsated as if it were a living thing. I guessed this was the slow rotting of the interdimensional bubble that encompassed this forgotten part of the coven's makeup. After all, places like this needed care and upkeep—there were magicals whose sole duty it was to make repairs in any parts of the bubble that were ebbing away. Undoubtedly, New York wanted this part of the coven to disappear, but since they couldn't physically detach it, they had to wait for it to decay over time instead, like the secret tunnels that Finch had showed us. I just hoped we weren't nearing the time when it would all finally collapse.

I stopped in the middle of a narrow walkway, the oily walls so close they were almost brushing my shoulders. This whole place was shady and unnerving, but now my heart was thundering like a prize racehorse. I didn't know if it was some residual effect of the Truth Trio, or if it was something else entirely. I was still struggling to get rid of the dull ache that the chains had inflicted, but this didn't feel the same. This was pure, unadulterated fear.

"What's wrong?" Garrett put a tentative hand on my shoulder.

I gulped down breaths, trying my best to swallow the terror. "Can't you hear that?"

"What?"

Is it just my heart? Was that what I could hear? A series of thuds boomed through the corridor, confirming that it wasn't just my heartbeat. I almost lost my nerve as the sound hammered right past us, on the right-hand side.

"Man, I'm beat. You want to get some coffee?" An unfamiliar voice hissed through the oily walls, sounding both distant and close.

Other magicals were all around us. Those booming thuds were the sound of their boots on the ground. They were right beside us, and yet, here we were, hidden in the ancient underbelly of the coven. Just as Remington had hoped, the interdimensional bubble wasn't reacting to our intrusion, even though we were right in the midst of the coven itself.

"Why aren't alarms going off?" I whispered.

"The entrance we came through must work differently," Garrett replied. "The current directorship can't do anything about these hallways, so they've forgotten them. It's the perfect loophole, when it comes to protecting our asses."

I glanced at Wade, but he'd been silent the whole way through the labyrinth. He kept putting his shades on, then taking them off again. Right now, he didn't have them on, and his gaze was fixed on the hallway ahead. I could sense his urgency to move on, though he didn't say anything. All the while, that undercurrent of anger and frustration seeped out of him, way more frightening to me than the writhing walls that surrounded us. Was I losing him, without even realizing it?

Don't rely on him. Finch's words echoed in my head, switching my focus back to the mission at hand.

"Come on, before the coven does pick up on something." I pressed on down the narrow passage for a few more minutes, until that grip of terror seized my chest again, my heart beating harder than ever. *What the heck?* It was starting to hurt. Every hyperactive beat felt like a stab. I had to stop for a moment to catch my breath and wipe the cold sweat from my forehead.

"Why do you keep stopping?" Wade hissed, grabbing my hand. "Are you sick or something?"

"I just need a minute." I looked up at him with desperate eyes, but his expression didn't change. His hand felt cold and clammy in mine, to the point where I didn't want him touching me anymore.

"This isn't the time to have a rest, Harley. We need to keep moving."

I wrenched my hand away, my mind bubbling with frustration and confusion. "I'm taking a freaking breather, Wade. Just give. Me. A. Minute."

"You think you're the only one who's tired? We've been walking for ages. We're all tired. But you don't see us stopping every couple of minutes to rest. We don't have time for this." His eyes glinted with anger.

"My heart feels like it's about to explode, Wade. If I suddenly keel over in these hallways, you'll have more trouble on your hands than me having a tiny friggin' break." I didn't want to retaliate, but I couldn't help it. His sullen silence and snarky comments had brought me to the breaking point. I wasn't going to let him berate me when I felt like something was wrong inside me, even if I felt like crap, snapping at him like that.

Garrett stepped between us and turned to Wade. "Why does it matter if she takes a break?"

"We don't have time, that's why," he shot back. "If she wasn't up to the task, then she shouldn't have suggested we come here."

Wow... That one hit me like a knife to the gut.

Garrett frowned. "What the hell is wrong with you, man? Why are you acting like a colossal asshole? She clearly doesn't feel right. And yeah, we might be on a tight deadline, but a minute so she can catch her breath isn't going to kill us."

"You don't know that. And there's nothing wrong with me. I'm just aware that we've got a massive clock clanging over our heads, which Harley doesn't seem to get."

Ouch.

"You need to chill out, Wade. Seriously. I don't know what's up with you, but it needs to stop. We're supposed to be working together here. So just put up or shut up. Harley's dealing with a lot right now, and she doesn't need this crap, especially not from you." He glanced over his shoulder. "Are you okay? Do you know what's wrong?"

I shook my head. "No idea. My heart is racing so fast."

"Is it the chains?"

"I don't—" I stopped midsentence. My heart was thumping harder the farther into the network of passageways we got. *Could it be?* It was the only thing that made sense. This had to be the pull of my parents' Grimoire, getting stronger with every step I took toward it.

"What's up?" Garrett peered down at me.

"I'm not sure yet. Just let me test something." I carried on walking, with them following behind. Sure enough, my heart raced faster with every step. Reaching the end of the hallway, I felt a strange pull, leading me off to the right. A solid wall sat in front of me. At least, it looked solid at first glance. Taking a breath, I stepped right up to it, only to find that it was an optical illusion that parted the moment I walked through.

"How did you do that?" Garrett stared at me, with Wade standing impatiently to the side.

I smiled. "It's the Grimoire, leading me toward it. We don't need any tracking spells or gimmicks to find it. The closer I get to the book, the stronger the bond is getting. Remington was right. I'm linked to it, by blood, and it's calling out to me. I guess it can do that, now that I don't have the Suppressor anymore. My heart and my Chaos are open to it, and that bond is strong as heck."

Wade shook his head, the blueprint in his hands. "It's not reliable, and it's only a theory. I'd rather trust hard facts than some 'bond' you think you have. I know where the Grimoire is—it's obvious if you look at the blueprints. And it isn't this way."

He didn't stop to let us respond. Instead, he kept going down the open left-hand hallway without us, leaving Garrett and me to exchange a worried look. It was almost like Wade was working against us now. And, at the moment, he was walking in the opposite direction, putting even more distance between us, in both senses of the word.

"We'd better go after him before he falls down a hole or something," Garrett said.

I nodded and followed Garrett down the left-hand hallway, my heartrate slowing as we did. It was like a painful game of Marco Polo, and Polo was down the corridor we'd just walked away from. Garrett broke into a sprint to catch up with Wade, and I did my best to run after them, despite the ache in my bones.

"Wade! Wade, would you just stop?" Garrett barked. "You're going the wrong way."

"Who says I am? The blueprints don't lie, Garrett." He whirled around, narrowing his eyes.

"We should listen to Harley. She's got some link to this thing. If she says it's the other way, then I'd stake my money on the fact that it's the other way. Blueprints aren't always right." Garrett grabbed Wade's arm and tried to yank him back. "So, come on, stop being an ass."

Wade tore his arm away from Garrett. "Don't you dare touch me."

"Then stop acting like a child." He tried to grab for Wade again, but Wade lashed out at him, shoving him hard in the chest. Garrett staggered back in surprise, his expression quickly morphing into a mask of anger as he lunged back at Wade. He swiped a blow at Wade's jaw, grazing his chin as Wade leaned back. A second later, Wade threw a punch right at Garrett's nose, but he ducked back just in time to avoid any serious damage. After that, all I saw was a blur of fists and bodies as the two of them wrangled with each other.

They're going to kill each other.

I sent out a powerful wave of my reverse Empathy, feeding the tendrils of it right into their minds. Just like my childhood pal Peter Pan, I forced myself to think happy thoughts, even though they were going at one another like animals. I thought of the good times we'd all shared as part of the Rag Team. I thought of Astrid and the way she smiled at Garrett whenever he walked into a room, and I thought of the first time Wade had kissed me in the Luis Paoletti Room, splitting the thoughts and the emotions and pouring them into the right brains.

Garrett stumbled into the wall, bent double as he calmed down. His eyes had taken on a faraway look, a small smile on his lips as he sank into the emotions I'd pushed into him, spurred on by memories of Astrid. Wade, on the other hand, was having some kind of violent reaction to the reverse Empathy. He sank right down to his knees, holding his head in his hands, tears rolling down his face. I hadn't pushed any sadness into him, so I had no idea why he was acting like this. It was almost as if he was feeling the opposite of the emotions I'd put into his head.

This isn't right.

Curious, I switched up the emotions I was sending toward him and thought of something angry instead. I focused on the way he'd snapped at me before and powered the emotions I'd felt right into him. The anger and frustration and confusion. Immediately, his face changed, his mouth curving up into a loopy smile. A soft laugh rippled from his lips, his eyes twinkling as though he didn't have a care in the world.

Yep, there was definitely something strange going on with him. Something magical that was messing with his head.

Determined to keep him in a better place, I changed the emotions to a wave of enthusiasm. No sooner had it hit him than he sank into a dopey silence. Realizing that wouldn't do much good, I tried a small amount of panic. He blinked up at me, very calm and collected all of a sudden.

"What did you do?" Garrett asked, coming around from his bout of reverse Empathy.

"Stopped you guys from killing each other. Now, come on, help me with him."

Garrett took Wade by the arm and pulled him to his feet. He stood up obediently, his whole manner subdued, letting Garrett drag him back toward the right-hand corridor without a word. I glanced into Wade's eyes, holding his face to keep his head up.

"You're behaving really weird, Wade," I said. "Is everything okay? Do you feel odd? Do you feel like you might be under a spell or something?"

He stared back listlessly. "Nope, I'm fine. I feel fine. I'm just under a lot of pressure."

"Are you sure? Because you're acting like you're under a spell."

Garrett nodded. "She's got a point. This isn't like you."

"What would you know about it? You can't feel what I feel," Wade replied woozily. "I'm fine, honestly. I'm my usual self, just a bit on edge. I'm surprised you aren't the same, considering the situation we're in. I got a little aggravated, that's all."

"A *little* aggravated?" Garrett snorted.

"I shouldn't have swung at you, I admit it. I'm sorry. I'm just worn out and nervous, nothing else. No hexes. No spells. Just good old-fashioned stress and some annoyance that we've been put in this position. It'd be enough to make anyone feel weird." He folded his arms across his chest, swaying slightly.

"So, you *do* feel weird?" I pressed.

"I just feel tense, that's all," he answered. "Now, can we get on with this?"

Even if something was going on with Wade, we had no choice but to keep going, grab the Grimoire, and get the hell out of here. I could deal with this magical weirdness later. Krieger would know what to do, for sure. I could send Wade back to the SDC with Garrett, where they'd take care of him. But who'd done this to him?

One freaking guess...

I kept trying to convince myself that it might have been the Chains of Truth, mushing up his brain and switching everything around by accident. But that didn't make sense. His behavior had started changing way before that. Then again, it didn't make any sense that Katherine had done this to him, either. How would she have even gotten close enough?

Eris Island. My stomach sank. Katherine had captured Wade, and there'd been some time before he ended up in her office with Finch—plenty of time to plant something, if she'd wanted to. A ticking timebomb, to divide and conquer. And if she'd really done this, she'd gone right for the jugular, trying to put distance between me and him to screw with me.

"What did you do to zombie boy?" Garrett nodded to Wade, who was walking along in a daze.

"What I had to."

"Do you think he might be a security risk?"

I swallowed my own fears about that. "It doesn't matter. We can't fix him here. We need to keep moving for now." The Grimoire's pull was getting stronger with every step we took.

THIRTY-FOUR

Harley

W e passed through the eerie darkness of the right-hand tunnel, but it was getting harder to keep going. Whatever this beacon was, pulling me toward the Grimoire, the wrench of it was becoming unbearable. My heart couldn't take it, and neither could my lungs. Not that it was exactly a bad sensation, it just felt totally overwhelming. It was like the excitement of every Christmas, every birthday, every special event, thrown together in a shivering mass of nervous energy, bouncing around inside of me like an overzealous pinball in a machine. There was so much of it flowing through my veins that I could have cried, or collapsed in hysterics, or leapt the height of the Empire State Building.

After what seemed like a lifetime of trekking through this place, the tunnel finally ran out. My heart felt it before I saw it. It was like that lurch of seeing the guy you were crushing on walking into a room and making eye contact with you when you thought he had no idea who you were. The guy *I* was crushing on was still trailing along like a zombie, but my hold on the reverse Empathy was dwindling, thanks to the jacked-up joy going through me.

A door was tucked away in the darkness. I approached it cautiously, noticing faint lines carved into the thick, black metal. I got closer. A pentagram had been etched into the surface of the door. Those were par for the course in magical society, so I wasn't too surprised. The other thing etched into the door, however…

Slap bang in the middle of said five-pointed star was a handprint, barely noticeable unless it caught the right light.

"What's this for?" Garrett peered over my shoulder.

"I guess this is how we get in."

Wade frowned. "What do we have to do with it?" He'd been a little more like himself since the fight in the hallway, but I knew that relied on me keeping up my reverse Empathy. I fought to hold on to the tendrils of it, even now, with my heart about ready to jump out my throat.

"Put your hand on it, maybe?" Garrett tilted his head to get a better look. "Trouble is, we don't know what the risks are. What if it's the wrong hand? What if it has to fit exactly? What'll happen if we don't get it right?" This was like the Truth Troop all over again.

"My guess is death." Wade chuckled weirdly.

A soft drumming peppered the air, and I lifted my finger to my lips. "Hush for a second."

They fell silent. I glanced around, listening for the sound I'd just heard. Even with them quiet, it took me a while to pick it out again. A steady beat thudded out a familiar rhythm—the rhythm of a heartbeat. Only, it wasn't my heartbeat that I could hear. It seemed to be pounding from somewhere beyond the walls, Jumanji-style.

As I looked back at the door, the oily glaze of the walls surrounding it started to contract and relax, pulsing exactly the way a heart would. It moved to the beat of that sound.

"The coven knows you. It knows the scent of the Merlin bloodline…" A whisper hissed past my ear, making my head whip around so fast I almost gave myself whiplash. But there was nobody in the hallway but us. No spirits, no ghosts, just us. The Grimoire's pull was getting way stronger now, and I half suspected it was the very thing giving me these scary hallucinations.

"Everything okay?" Garrett eyed me. Could he not see and hear what I did? Apparently not. Otherwise, he'd have been freaking out, too.

I nodded slowly. "Just thinking."

"Well, could you hurry it along? No pressure or anything, but these tunnels are weirding me out. They definitely knew what they were doing when they built this network. Nobody would be mad enough to willingly come this way into the coven."

Nobody would be mad enough? It hit me. My father had been the New York Coven's director at one point. Of course he'd have known about these tunnels. With Katherine after him, it stood to reason that he might have charmed an escape route for himself. *And maybe the hand and pentagram are part of it.* It would definitely explain these crazy reactions I was having.

"Wade, can you put on your shades and tell me if there's a charm here?" I asked.

He slipped them on. "Yep. Right there, where the hand is."

Before they could stop me, I put my palm flat against the groove of the imprint. The moment my skin touched the metal, which felt oddly warm, a creepy red glow pooled out from my hand, filling the lines of the pentagram. They lit up a brighter ruby red, each point bursting with a tiny explosion that sent out a flurry of scarlet sparks.

The heat beneath my hand started to burn, but not in an unpleasant way. It was more like an icy tingle, spreading from the center of my palm out to each of my fingers. Five more of the tiny explosions bristled at my fingertips, with the ruby light sinking back down into my skin and running right up the length of my arm.

I wasn't sure what it was supposed to achieve. The door wasn't opening, and my hand was stuck in place.

The snaking line of red light tingled up the back of my neck and darted right into my brain. My head filled with a bombardment of memories. Not my memories, but the memories of my mom and dad—a hurricane of precious, intimate moments. There were so many of them, flashing through my head.

I saw my mom and dad at the altar, gazing into each other's eyes. She wore a white lace gown that pooled down a set of steps like a silky waterfall, while he looked sharp in a three-piece suit, a grin fixed on his face. I saw them sitting together on a bench in Central Park, my mom stealing a lick of my dad's ice cream. I saw them laughing at the terrible taxidermy in an exhibit in the Natural History Museum, my dad pulling a face to make himself look like the poor otter in the glass case beside him. My mom's laugh rippled through my head like the sweetest music. He caught her in his arms a moment later, kissing her, both of them smiling like loons. They looked so young and carefree and in love that it damn near broke my heart.

I saw them arguing in their apartment on Park Avenue, with my dad pointing at the dishwasher and asking why my mom had stuffed it so full. He said it had to be precise, or nothing would get clean, and she said he was being ridiculous. I watched her storm out, only for my dad to follow a couple minutes later, to hold her in his arms and brush the hair back from her face. I saw my mom crying on her bed, her knees tucked up to her chin, because her period had come again. "What if it never happens?" she'd asked, and my dad had gone to sit beside her, cuddling her close. "It'll happen when it's supposed to, and whoever she or he is, they'll be worth the wait," he'd replied.

I saw my mom get out of the car on some distant, dusty highway, walking with her hands shoved in her jeans' pockets. My dad drove after her, the car crawling at a snail's pace, for half a mile before she gave up and got back in. I had no idea what they'd argued about, but even in their stony silence, I could tell how much they loved each other. Then I saw her lying on their couch, her stomach swollen with me, with my dad sitting beside her, his feet up on the table. He was flipping through TV channels, one hand resting casually on my mom's leg. Nothing special was going on—it was just a snapshot of their life together as it had been before Katherine had stolen it away from them.

I couldn't hold on to every single image, but there'd been a lot of laughter, a lot of tears, a lot of bickering, and a lot of love. It was remarkable in its ordinariness, although there were the obvious magical elements eking through: the two of them forging spells together, and testing out their abilities, and training side by side, both before and after they were a couple. The surge swelled in my head, like a gigantic data dump right in the middle of my brain. I hoped it would stay there so I could make more sense of it later and go through the memories with the time, attention, and patience they deserved.

As the rapid slideshow came to an end, my hand broke away from the handprint, followed by the soft click of the door as it swung wide.

I turned toward Garrett and Wade, smiling so wide I thought my cheeks might fall off. That smile faded the moment I saw Wade. The Pentagram's surge had broken my reverse Empathy, and he was looking at me like he wanted to kill me.

Panicked, I struggled to regain control as Wade lunged for me. Garrett tried to yank Wade away, but Wade turned on him, launching a blast of powerful Fire right into his face. Garrett staggered back and let go of Wade, covering his eyes with his hands to get out the embers. Wade sprinted right for me, his hands outstretched, grasping for my throat. He snarled in my face as he tried to squeeze the life right out of me, the veins at his temples throbbing, like blue-tinged slugs embedded in his skin.

"Wade!" I croaked. His thumbs were pressing down on my windpipe, his fingertips burning with Fire, forging a coil of liquid heat around my throat.

He's going to murder me. He's actually going to kill me!

With my nails digging into his hands, I battled to peel his fingertips away from my throat. Gathering my Chaos into my palms, I sent out my own blast of Fire to singe his hands, but he barely flinched. I sent wave after wave, but it had no effect. He was too hellbent on killing me to feel pain, and I was holding back. I could've killed him with my own Chaos, if I'd wanted to, but I didn't have the strength to do it. And if I used my Earth ability, the tunnels might come crashing in on us.

All I could do was stare into his wild eyes and thrash and kick and forge Fire with every breath I had left. His weight was crushing me down into the floor, my windpipe buckling under the pressure of his thumbs as they dug deeper. The heat of the fiery coil was getting hotter, and I had visions of it cutting right through my neck.

Wade, NO! I couldn't speak. Instead, a gargling sound came out. My cheeks were hot and tight, my eyes bulging out of my head as he cut off my air supply. I thrashed and magicked harder, determined not to die like this, but I was running out of time. If my windpipe snapped, that would be it. Game over.

Shadows crept into my vision. This was it. I was about to die, feet away from the Grimoire—from finding something that could stop Katherine. She had somehow managed to get to Wade. She'd wanted me to suffer first, at the hands of the man I loved.

Mom died the same way. Katherine must've loved this particular form of cruel revenge.

I clung to consciousness long enough to hear a grunt and the sound of glass breaking. I could've sworn I'd heard Finch's voice, too, but that wasn't possible.

I guess this is goodnight, then.

That was my last thought.

THIRTY-FIVE

Harley

I awoke to find myself standing in the corner of a nursery room with sunflower-yellow walls and hand-painted motifs. They were taken from book illustrations. *Winnie the Pooh* crouched opposite, his paw dipped in a pot of "Hunny." *The Little Prince* swept his asteroid clean on the far wall, with his precious rose tucked under its glass case. The fox from the same story ran underneath, surrounded by stars and tiny, delicate flowers. *You become responsible, forever, for what you have tamed.*

Those words came back to me, though I couldn't remember reading the book. I just knew they were taken from its pages, somehow, like it was embedded in my brain. Like hymns and nursery rhymes popping right out of my mouth while I was shampooing my hair in the shower—songs I hadn't sung in years, yet I knew all the words.

Everything felt weirdly familiar. The stuffed animals scattered everywhere, the cuddly blankets spread over a bright blue beanbag with cartoon elephants imprinted on the fluffy fabric. Even the lamps, which were shaped like toadstools, rang a bell. *Have I been here before?* I didn't exactly hang around nurseries. And the only places I could remember from my childhood were the bare-walled, stark bedrooms of my foster homes and the orphanage, complete with the torn fragments of paint and adhesives, ripped away by the posters of previous kids.

But I couldn't swallow the feeling that I knew this nursery. It was like a nagging sensation at the back of my head, trying to push the memory to the front of my brain, from way back in the dusty caverns of my mind. A tip-of-my-tongue kind of thing.

It's my nursery. The realization exploded in my head. Or, rather, it would've been my nursery had my parents lived to raise me here. I could see the green landscape of Central Park outside the window, letting me know that I was in the same Park Avenue apartment where I'd seen my parents laughing and crying and squabbling over the right way to fill a dishwasher. The place where my mom had hoped for me and my dad had told her it would happen, when the time was right. Only, thanks to Katherine, the time had never been right. Man, I figured Wade must've done a number on me to send me flying back through time to a place that had never really existed.

It only got weirder as the door opened and a tiny person came strutting in, with the confidence only a kindergartener has. The red hair and sky-blue eyes were a dead giveaway. The kid was me. Well, not me, but a manifestation of me, the way I might've been.

This had to be the Grimoire messing with my head. It felt like a message sent from my parents. A lasting hope, maybe, left within the Grimoire for me to find, so I'd know what they'd wanted for me. It must've been activated the moment I touched the handprint, and all that info had been dumped into my brain. Whoever had made this—my mom or my dad—they'd gone to huge lengths to make it vivid. Frankly, it hurt. I hadn't lived this life, and that stung.

I pressed back against the wall as my little self walked right toward me. She giggled, wrinkling up her button nose, and sat cross-legged on the floor in front of me, rocking back and forth like she didn't have a care in the world.

"This is a message," she said with a grin. "It's a message to tell you that the Grimoire was made with Katherine in mind. Every spell your parents put in there was made to stop Katherine." She didn't speak like a kid, and she didn't speak like me, either. Her voice was distant and echoey, like it was being channeled from somewhere else entirely.

I frowned at the kid. "They did?"

She nodded, twisting a strand of hair around her stubby finger. "Your parents knew about Katherine's underhanded dealings, even before she used Sal Vínna on your father. They began working together on magic spells to make sure that, whatever happened, there'd be something in place to stop her or destroy her. Whichever comes first." She chuckled creepily, like an old doll in a vintage shop. "Of course, Mom and Dad never thought she'd get this far. Thanks to her, the Grimoire is being forced to react. Its Merlin blood is throbbing and reaching out to you. It's up to you, now, to do something about Katherine. Mom and Dad have given you the tools, but you need to use them."

Oh, the irony. I'd done nothing but try and do something to end Katherine since I came into the SDC, and it was sort of annoying to hear my shortcomings from the mouth of a mini-me. As if I didn't know what needed to be done.

Little Harley picked up a stuffed bunny and flapped its arms. "Everything has stepped up a notch now that Echidna is dead and Katherine has completed the fourth ritual. The whole realm of Chaos is contracting to prepare for the final showdown. Nobody, not even Chaos itself, expected Katherine to come so far. It is quaking in its particles." She giggled, flopping the bunny's ears. It was pretty disturbing to watch, considering the things coming out of her mouth. "Because of that, some rules no longer apply. Some charms that would previously have stopped you are no longer standing in the way of you getting what you need."

"What kind of charms?"

She shrugged. "Many of them. Most of the ones that would have created obstacles." She grinned up at me. "Did you really think that Chaos wouldn't at least try to do something to stop Katherine, without breaking the universal rules? Did you really think that Chaos was perfectly okay with Katherine becoming its Child?"

I frowned, thoroughly weirded out. "I guess not... but then, why isn't Chaos doing more? Why's it leaving it all up to me, if it's so freaking worried about Katherine joining its ranks? Wouldn't it be easier for Chaos to just swoop in and explode her, or something?"

"You've got a twisted mind, Harley. What have we become?" The kid pointed the bunny's paw right at me. "But at least you're asking the right questions. Some rules can't be broken. Others... well, there's some flexibility.

Which is why you're here, in the New York Coven, and not in Purgatory. Chaos has put the right people in your path so that you could evade a life-time prison sentence and find the Grimoire instead. It wanted you to find it. After all, if anyone can read and decipher those spells, it's you. Or, rather, us. Nobody else."

I didn't know whether to be flattered or appalled. It didn't seem fair that everything should be put on my shoulders like this—me, a nineteen-year-old girl who didn't even know she was a magical until a few months ago. *Man, has it only been a few months?* It felt way longer.

"But why me?" I was genuinely curious.

"It is your birthright. A final gift from the Primus Anglicus, in the world's time of need. You've heard the legends of Arthur, no doubt?"

"What, like Excalibur and stuff?"

The kid laughed. "As the myth goes, King Arthur always said he'd return when a great threat arose. Only, it wasn't King Arthur who said that when it really happened. It was Merlin. Your ancestor. The man you're named after."

I snorted. "That stuff didn't really happen, though."

"Didn't it?" The kid grinned, like she knew something I didn't. "Katherine makes mistakes because of you. She can't help it. She's drawn to you in a way she can't explain, which is why she's let you slip through her fingers so many times, when she's had the chance to kill you. You are a Merlin. You are here, in the world's time of need. You were sent, through the ages to this moment, because of your mom and dad. Chaos created you, through them, as a protector of worlds. Just as the Primus Anglicus were created to protect the world and implement the rules of secrecy that we abide by, even now. Forget all of the mythical business if it's too much, but the truth remains: it all boils down to the fact that you may very well be the only one who can stop Katherine."

Is that true? I didn't have time to find out.

"So get off your ass and wake the hell up!" the kid snapped, startling me. It wasn't the kind of language I'd expected from her, despite everything she'd just said. "And get that Grimoire before your boyfriend ruins everything!"

Just like that, I snapped right back into reality, to find Finch and Garrett a little way down the corridor, wrestling Wade to the ground. *Finch? How did he get in here?* I didn't know how much time had passed in my little trip down fake memory lane, or how much I'd missed, but I could see they were struggling to hold Wade down. He was writhing like a man possessed.

"Let go of me! I have to end her!" Wade roared, throwing punches wherever he could. *Wow... comforting.*

Energy sparked through my veins, my strength reignited by that weird-ass dream. Plus, I had a bevy of mental spells floating around in my head now, amongst all the memories and the sensation of being pulled in by the Grimoire. By putting my hand into that imprint, I'd received more than a nudge in the right direction—I'd received a whole freaking directory of magic, things I'd never even seen or heard of before, and all of it was right inside my pulsating brain.

I staggered to my feet. Wade's head whipped around, his eyes wide and wild. He was frothing at the mouth. The moment he set eyes on me, he was up on his feet, practically throwing Finch and Garrett off him. But I was quicker. Sprinting forward, I pressed my tingling palm to his forehead.

"*In somno pacis invenire. Et usque nunc. Transire sinebat,*" I whispered, the words coming to me automatically. It meant something along the lines of, "In sleep, find peace. Be still now. Let the demons pass." It was a Latin spell I didn't even know I knew, but my overcharged mind had picked well. Every gemstone of my Esprit lit up as I spoke, pulsing with the same white glow as the whorl of energy seeped into Wade's skull. He keeled over backward, stiff as a post, with Garrett catching him before he hit the deck.

Finch gave a low whistle. "Where'd you learn that one, Sis?"

"Let's just say a little birdie came to me in a dream," I replied. "Now, we need to hurry the heck up. There's no way someone didn't hear that racket, and we need to get the book and get out of here before the New York cavalry arrives."

"Did you have to knock him out?" Garrett complained. "He weighs a ton."

"Then stay here with him. We'll grab you both on our way back out," I replied.

Garrett shrugged. "Works for me."

He set Wade on the cold floor and sat beside him. Wade's eyes were closed and peaceful. It'd take me a while to erase the image of him looming over me with his hands pushing down hard on my windpipe. But I still loved him. This wasn't him—this was Katherine in action. The devil worked hard, but Katherine? She worked harder.

I leaned down and kissed him on the forehead, sweeping his sweat-soaked hair out of his face. It was a promise of forgiveness, if we could get him out of this mess. And if we couldn't… I wasn't going to think about that. I would get my Wade back, one way or another, even if I had to hold him in my reverse Empathy for the rest of my life.

Finch and I stepped through the doorway and into another corridor steeped in gloom. My heart began to race again, leading me toward the Grimoire. Not that there was anywhere else to go—this was a one-track road.

"What's the deal with Wonderboy?" Finch glanced at me as we walked together. "Why's he gone all Jack Nicholson in *The Shining*?"

I shrugged in frustration. "We don't know. I'm guessing he's been hexed or something. He's definitely not my Wade."

"People aren't possessions, Sis." He smiled at me. "But I'd say you're right. He wanted to rip your throat out. And, as much as I hate to be on loverboy's side, that's not him. He'd be more likely to tear my throat out than yours. But who'd have done that to him?"

I cast him a wry look. "Who do you think?"

"Ah, Mother dearest."

"Bingo. Anyway, we won't be able to fix him until we get out of here, so if it's okay with you, can we not talk about him?" I wasn't being unkind; I just needed to focus. "I'm compartmentalizing, like you taught me."

He nodded. "Bottle it up. Do what you've got to do."

"I will." I glanced at him curiously. "How come you're here, anyway? Not that I'm not glad to see you, since you stopped the whole throat-tearing thing."

He dropped his gaze. "A weird thing happened. I was sitting on the front steps, waiting for you all to come back, when I got this odd feeling—I could almost sense that you were in some kind of danger. I can't really explain it properly, but it was like the coven was somehow talking to me, like a sentient being. Creepy, I know. But it did. I knew I had to get to you before something bad happened. Spidey sense sort of vibes, and man, were they tingling." He looked back up. "Does that make sense?"

I nodded. "Total sense." If I hadn't dreamt of the mini-me, I might've thought he'd lost his mind. But now, I could make sense of what he was saying, however odd. The New York Coven was somehow embedded with Merlin blood. It reacted and connected to it on a molecular level. And Finch was Hiram's kid, too, after all...

"Good, because I thought I was going mad. Snaky chains are one thing. A whispering coven is another."

"Does that mean you—" Finch cut me off before I could finish.

"Yeah, it does." He fidgeted awkwardly. "I did the spooky polygraph again. If I hadn't, you'd be dead."

I frowned. "So that means you passed?"

He rolled his eyes. "All hail the genius. Yeah, I passed. Of course I did. I had to, if I wanted to save your ass from getting your windpipe snapped like a runway model's leg."

"Finch!"

He grinned. "What?"

"You can't say things like that."

"Looks like I just did." His eyes glinted with mischief and something else. A sadness that he was trying to hide. "Anyway, I found my answer, so you can get off my case about it. If I have to, I'll sacrifice myself for you. All the stops, remember?" His voice caught in his throat, unable to conceal his emotions any longer. His hands were shaking, too, though he quickly put them behind his back.

I didn't know what to say. What *could* I say to that? I didn't want anyone sacrificing themselves for me, but this was Katherine we were talking about —we had no idea what we might face in the days and weeks to come. I just hoped mini-me had been right and I could find the antidote for her evil inside the pages of my parents' Grimoire so I could stop her before a single one of my friends suffered at her hands.

"I know we got off to a nasty start, but... well, I've always wanted a brother or a sister. A family, really. Not the crazy, psycho kind." His voice was shaking, and even though I knew we should be running right now, I couldn't bring myself to interrupt him. Finch never got emotional, and I didn't know if I'd ever see this again. "Anyway, I'm just hoping that, if we get through all this, we can try to be real siblings. To sort of fill in the gaps that our parents left behind. That bathroom in Eris Island has a lot to answer for. Therapy central."

Before he could ruin it, I stepped forward and put my arms around him. He stiffened, as though he didn't know what to do. And then, with his shoulders relaxing, he embraced me and hugged me tight.

"Just don't let it go to your head," he mumbled into my shoulder. "If you weren't my sister, I wouldn't bother. We're stuck with each other, and that's that." Jerky Finch had come back in full swing, but at least I'd gotten a hug out of it.

Releasing him, I smiled and said nothing. Instead, I held his gaze, a silent agreement passing between us that we'd probably never talk about this again. Finch's ego wouldn't have been able to handle the teasing. He'd have crumbled like a stale cookie.

I skidded to a halt as we passed through a shimmering barrier masquerading as a wall and entered a large, empty hall. The transition between the corridor and the room beyond was so sudden it took my breath away. The vaulted ceilings and wooden paneling reminded me of being in a church. In the very center of the room stood a plinth. On top of that plinth, a glass case with a single book inside.

The Grimoire.

Finch slipped on Wade's sunglasses. "Yep, that thing's riddled, all right."

"Did you steal those from him?" I gaped at my brother.

"What? He wasn't using them."

I rolled my eyes. "What can you see?"

"Protection charms. Most of them deadly. The kind of stuff you'd expect from these uptight magicals."

They'd put extra spells on the book since the last time I'd visited it. *Great, that's just peachy.* However, there was something about this entire room that felt off.

"Feels weird in here, right?" Finch said.

"But is it good weird or bad weird?" I glanced around, the emptiness making me nervous. There should've been other things in here, other artifacts, but there weren't. Just the Grimoire, standing out like a sore thumb.

Finch shrugged. "Good, probably. This place was made by Daddio. It's filled with his magic."

My head whipped around at a scuffling outside the main door of the vaulted room. *Crap.* We needed to move fast. Someone had definitely heard the ruckus with Wade and had come to check on their most valuable artifact. Which meant we now had a matter of minutes to snatch the Grimoire and dart back out the way we'd come. I hoped Wade and Garrett were okay.

I lifted my finger to my lips and approached the Grimoire case. If I made the slightest sound, security would be on us like flies around a steaming pile of crap. My nerves jangled as I got closer, not only because I was about to take this thing, but because we were on borrowed time. The clock was running out.

As I reached the case, the Grimoire echoed inside my head: *"Just take me. Just take me."*

"Did you just say something?" Finch asked suddenly.

I shook my head. "That wasn't me. That was the Grimoire. You can hear it?"

He shrugged. "I guess I can. A remnant of Dadski, perhaps? A bit of my Merlin blood finally being useful?"

Just take me. Just take me. The Grimoire's voice was getting louder, urging me on.

Obeying, I put my hands on the glass box, yearning to touch the book inside. To my alarm, the glass crumbled beneath my fingertips, turning to glittering sand that spilled onto the floor with a quiet hiss. It seemed like no amount of protective magic could stop the Merlin bloodline, not right here in the pulsing heart of my dad's magical domain.

"No wonder Levi is so terrified of you," Finch said. "Or Katherine, for that matter."

Grinning like a maniac, my eyes like saucers, I reached for the Grimoire. I couldn't have stopped, even if I'd tried. Not that I wanted to. This was what we'd come here for, and I was going to take it, if it was the last thing I did.

As soon as I touched the soft binding, a surge of energy burst through me, splintering through every nerve ending like wildfire. I threw my head back to try and contain the overwhelming blast of power that shivered up into my brain, my body trembling under the weight of it.

Through the blinding burst, I felt the love of my parents swelling in my heart. And the promise of knowledge to come, within its pages. I also felt the sinking, dark dread of what might lie ahead if I walked down this inevitable path that was, supposedly, my birthright. After all, according to what mini-me had said, I wasn't even a person in my own right—I was merely a tool, to be used and manipulated by Chaos, for its own benefit.

Lastly, I was hit by the understanding that there would be a terrible fight to come. That image throbbed in my head, far longer than the other sensations. It hadn't been very clear—just a bright, hazy landscape that shifted in and out of focus, thanks to a powerful light burning my eyes, and the battle cries of unseen people all around me.

This is nowhere near over.

"Yo, Jean Grey, you might want to get your ass in gear!" Finch hissed, breaking me from my reverie.

I snapped out of it as the sound of keys getting pushed through locks scraped through the air. In a matter of seconds, the security personnel would infiltrate the room. I yanked the Grimoire into my arms, pulling it close to my chest. I turned tail and sprinted for the exit, ducking through it with Finch running behind me.

Protect us, please protect us. I sent the prayer out to the New York Coven, willing it to listen. If the security magicals got into the room, they'd surely find us in these tunnels. Unless they didn't have a way in?

We came back to the spot where Garrett was waiting with my still-unconscious boyfriend. Garrett and Finch grabbed Wade between them as we raced through the heavy metal door that my father had imprinted with his magic, the four of us barreling through the tunnels. In that moment, I really wished we'd brought Dylan along for the ride. He'd have thrown Wade over his shoulder like a sack of spuds, barely batting an eyelid. Instead, the guys had to drag said sack of spuds through the seemingly endless labyrinth, all the while hoping that the security magicals weren't giving chase.

As I glanced back over my shoulder, my eyes widened at the sight of the metal door shifting into a solid wall, the pentagram and the handprint fading into nothing but stone. A grin tugged at my lips. It was amazing, but true—the New York Coven was reacting against its own inhabitants for our sake. Somehow, as though it were actually a sentient being, it was helping us.

I ran on, ignoring the ache in my legs and the burn in my lungs, desperate to reach the exit. All the while, my focus remained on the Grimoire in my hands. Thanks to Jacob, Remington, and mini-me, we knew there was a big chance that this book held the key to defeating Katherine. Somewhere inside this thing, we would find what we were looking for. For that reason, we couldn't afford to get caught.

Plus, as selfish as it might've sounded by comparison, I needed to find a safe spot for Wade. Then, and only then, would I be able to figure out what was going on with him, before he tried to kill me again.

THIRTY-SIX

Jacob

The mood in the infirmary couldn't have been tenser. Mostly because of Raffe, who couldn't take his eyes off his dad. He'd been allowed up here on the provision that he wear Atomic Cuffs, though he didn't look very happy about it.

Levi hadn't woken up yet. He lay in the bed, in a coma, his throat and head wrapped in bandages. I tried not to think of an Egyptian mummy, but it was pretty hard, considering. Still, it looked like the djinn had abandoned ship. With Imogene in the room, Kadar likely didn't dare to raise his smoky head.

Isadora, Louella, Dylan, Tatyana, and Astrid were here, too. And Santana and Alton. Welcome additions, now that they'd been sprung from jail. All thanks to our reluctant new director. In the space of an hour, she'd done more of what she'd promised than Levi had done in months.

She'd spoken with the Mage Council as soon as we'd talked to her about taking over. They'd jumped at the chance to have someone useful in the role. Now, with her position official and above board, Imogene wasn't stopping—she was already on a roll. There was work to be done, and she was on it. A proper general to lead this army.

It should've been a positive moment, but I kept thinking about Suri. She was still in the quarantine room, a little too close for comfort, with all these folks standing around. I hoped she wouldn't make a noise. She knew better than that. Sure, she wanted to stay here, but I needed to find a better solution. A better way of keeping her here. She couldn't hide in there forever. But I didn't want her memory getting wiped, either. I was walking on major eggshells, here. But I was sure of one thing: I didn't want her to go.

Remington walked in. He looked crazy flustered but slightly relieved at seeing Imogene in charge. "Sorry it took me a while to get here," he said. "I wasn't expecting to get a call so late."

"Apologies if I disturbed you, Remington," Imogene replied. "I wouldn't have if it weren't important. We'll have something of a full house this evening."

A knock on the door distracted everyone's attention. *Who else is coming?*

Rita Bonnello, immaculately dressed and made up, even though it was insanely early in the morning, peered into the room. "Ah, excellent. You haven't started without me?"

"Not at all, Rita. Come in and take a seat. You're precisely on time." Imogene smiled at her. I'd never seen so much elegant beauty in one room. If Suri had been here, I wouldn't have been able to concentrate.

"I come bearing gifts," she said brightly. "Call it a congratulatory offering for your new position, Ms. Whitehall."

"Imogene, please. And I'm not sure there's any need for congratulations, though I appreciate the sentiment." Imogene gestured for Rita to take one of the empty stools. She did so and laid a wrapped item on the workbench. A medium-sized cylinder, by the looks of it. Everyone watched as she unwrapped it. Inside, there was a long tube. Gold twisted around the glass exterior, with two pointed ends that looked like arrows. Sparks darted inside, bouncing off the glass walls. A thin, bronze bar ran down the center of the cylinder. Energy thrummed along the metal, reminding me of the atrium in the Bestiary.

"It's the alchemical battery for the magic detector," Rita explained, glancing at Krieger. "I trust you've managed to reassemble the device?"

"Not at this present moment." Krieger had turned shy again. "But we're continuing to work on it. If the battery is all in order, I'll install it in the device once it's complete."

Rita smiled. "The battery is perfect. The detector must be, also."

"It will be, I assure you." I felt bad for Krieger. He'd been working relent-lessly on this detector, but it was one crazy puzzle to put back together. Still, I trusted him. He'd do it; he just needed a little more time. Rita seemed to understand that.

"That's good to hear," Imogene said. "In the meantime, can one of you send word to Harley that it's safe for her to return? I won't blame her if she doesn't want to, but let her know that the offer is open."

Isadora nodded. "I'll see to it." She cast me a knowing glance that let me know I was the one who'd have to do the honors. Harley only had her burner phone on her now, and I was the only one with the number.

"Good, then I'd like to begin assigning roles to you all, so we can make our move against Katherine. There has been far too much inaction, and it's my duty to try and remedy that, as best I can," Imogene went on. "You have all proven your worth and ingenuity, several times over, and I should like to utilize you to your full potential. Tatyana, Dylan, please assist Astrid in her computer searches for sightings and information regarding Katherine. Santana, I will need you to watch over Raffe. Raffe, I don't want to talk about you as though you aren't in the room. And so, it will be your duty to resolve matters with your djinn. I can't in good faith allow you to join the others yet. Is there a place you can go to, to contain the djinn?"

Raffe nodded sullenly. "Yeah, I've got a cage."

He does? Where? I'd never heard of him having a cage before.

"I hope that you understand why it's necessary." Imogene offered him a sympathetic look. "After what happened with Leonidas, your freedom to roam as you wish must be restricted."

He shrugged. "I get it."

"Rita, it would be best if you were to return to your usual duties, so as not to arouse suspicion. Isadora, Louella, please join me in my office. I have some sensitive work for both of you, but I can understand if you'd prefer to wait until you've rested. We've all had rather a lengthy day."

Isadora shook her head. "No, I'm good to speak with you now. I'm already awake, might as well keep going."

"Yeah, me too," Louella replied. I could tell she was excited. She was getting to work with the big dogs. That probably felt like a promotion.

"Excellent, that means I might be able to sleep easier tonight. Although, I may still have to ask Dr. Krieger here for some of his finest sleeping pills, after everything that has happened. I confess, I didn't expect to finish my day in charge of the SDC, but life does have a way of throwing curveballs." Imogene chuckled.

You can say that again.

"Speaking of you, Dr. Krieger, I'd like for you and Jacob to remain at your work here, so you can complete the magical detector," Imogene continued.

"Right now?" I replied. I was tiring, big time. No amount of coffee could fix this.

She smiled. "No, not right now. I simply mean that will be your task."

"Oh, right."

"If you succeed, you may well have created the magical development of the century, and that's no exaggeration. It will put the SDC on the map." She took an anxious breath. "With such a device available to us, we may stand a chance of finding Katherine. That must be our main goal. Beyond her, we can use it to simplify our means of encountering new magicals who don't have a single clue as to their true natures." Her eyes brightened. Clearly, this device had her stoked.

"We'll get it done, Director." I grinned up at her. She had a way of turning me goofy.

"Wonderful." She looked around the room. "Just to reiterate, if anyone should happen to hear anything from our own lost soul, Ms. Merlin, please do let her know that it's safe to return. I've made certain calls and have managed to clear Harley's name from the Most Wanted list. I'm continuing in my endeavors to negotiate temporary amnesty for Finch, though that will take more time to execute, given the actual crimes laid against him. It may prove impossible, when all is said and done."

"What can I do?" Remington folded his arms across his chest. He looked tired.

"I'll need you to resume your internal affairs investigation, in order to discover just how deep the cult's influence is running. We must find out if the upper echelons of magical society are under the same mind-altering manipulation as the security magicals in this coven. Or, indeed, something worse—if we have infiltrators to contend with." She paused, letting the seriousness of the situation sink in. "Your next task will be to question the National Council, to uncover what it is we are dealing with."

Remington nodded. "I'll schedule a meeting with them for the morning, back in San Francisco."

"Very good, then I think that's all I have to say. You provided Alton with excellent support during his tenure here, and I'm certain that you will do the same for me. Especially as you were the ones who put me in this position." She laughed softly. Krieger looked shamefaced.

"Does that mean we can go?" Raffe asked bluntly. He clearly hated being in the room with his dad. Especially since he was the one who'd put him in that bed.

Imogene nodded. "Of course. Isadora, Louella, would you join me?"

Everyone dispersed. Raffe and Santana left first, with Rita and Alton heading out after. Imogene, Isadora, and Louella went next. Tatyana and Dylan were about to head out with Astrid, but Remington quickly stood in Dylan's way.

"Do you have a minute?" Remington asked.

Dylan frowned. "We're pretty busy."

"It won't take long. There's just something I need to talk to you about."

He shrugged. "Sure, I guess. Tatyana, I'll follow you. Just let me know where you're going."

"Will do," Tatyana replied, casting Remington a weird look.

"Krieger, is there a private room we could use?" Remington asked. He seemed really nervous.

I shot up from my stool. "Uh, I think the triage room is free." I couldn't have them going into the quarantine room. Not with Suri in there.

Krieger stifled a discreet chuckle. "The triage room is definitely free. I'll make sure nobody disturbs you."

Thank you, Doc. Thank you!

With everyone else disappearing to the far corners of the coven, Krieger and I were the only ones left in his office. About ten minutes had passed, and we were setting back to work on the magical detector.

Somehow, I'd managed to get a second wind, no coffee needed. Besides, I couldn't have slept now if I'd wanted. My mind was wired. The battery lay on the desk. I couldn't stop looking at it. Once this device had been put back together, and we fitted that battery into it, we'd be onto something. This thing might actually work!

I was just about to screw one of the smaller panels back into place, when a loud shout made me drop the screwdriver. It clattered on the workbench. My head snapped toward the open office door. The shouts were coming from the room opposite. The triage room.

Setting down my tools, I crept toward the doorway and looked out. From the quarantine room a short distance away, another figure emerged. Suri.

I hurried over to her. "You shouldn't be out here."

"I heard shouting," she whispered.

I glanced back at the triage room. "Yeah, Dylan and Remington are going through something."

"What?" Her eyes widened.

"Are you kidding me? You knew how they died?" Dylan's voice boomed into the rest of the infirmary. *Ah, so they've gotten that far.* "You knew that, and you didn't think you should tell me?"

"I am telling you," Remington replied.

I looked down at Suri. "Long story short? Remington is Dylan's uncle." Harley had let that secret slip to me a while ago, and I'd sworn to keep it to myself.

Suri gasped. "Did he not know or something?"

"No, he didn't, but Remington's apparently getting around to telling him," I replied.

Awkward silence stretched across the room. It gave me a moment to think. It sucked that Dylan was finding this stuff out now. He'd probably thought he was on his own, for so long. And now, he was finding out he had a living uncle. That had to sting. He was a foster kid like me, after all. It hurt to see so many kids like him, with dead or crappy parents. Even Suri could relate to that.

I really wanted to stay awhile to see how their conversation turned out. I'd already gotten a reputation for eavesdropping. Why break the habit of a lifetime?

"Come with me," I whispered. There was a storage closet right next to the triage room. I slipped into it, and Suri came in after me. Realizing how tiny this space was, I instantly felt awkward. She was so close that I could hardly breathe. All I could smell was the scent of her perfume. Her eyes glittered in the pale light from the single bulb. We were surrounded by shelves full of medical supplies. It wasn't exactly romantic, but I was glad to be in here with her.

Suri blushed. "Why did you bring me in here?"

"Uh... I wanted to hear what they were saying." I wondered if she wanted a different answer. After all, if I'd leaned forward a little, I could've kissed her. I thought about it, but I wasn't brave enough. And this wasn't where I wanted to kiss her for the first time, surrounded by scalpels and bedpans.

"Oh." She sounded disappointed. *Dammit.*

Trying to cover the awkwardness, I pressed my ear to the separating wall so I could listen to the conversation next door. I touched my hand to the wall.

"*Exaudi Me,*" I murmured. It meant, "Let me hear." Isadora had taught it to me, to use if I ever got in trouble. The wall rippled, like soundwaves coming off a speaker. The voices got subtly louder. I felt a little bad, but I really wanted to hear what they were saying.

"So my mom died from complications after some surgery," Dylan snapped. "And my dad jumped off the damn Golden Gate Bridge, and you *knew* about it? You didn't think to mention that the first time we met?"

"I didn't know how to," Remington replied. "If I came to you and told you I was your uncle, you would've hated me. You would've wondered why I hadn't come to get you."

"Why didn't you?"

"I tried, Dylan. I tried to find you, but your dad didn't leave any sort of note to tell me where he'd taken you. He didn't leave any note at all. He just... jumped one afternoon. I hadn't spoken to him since your mom's funeral, because he'd been screening everyone's calls. I phoned people to get them to check up on him, but they just said he was sad. His wife had just died, of course he was sad." I heard Remington take a shaky breath. "If I'd known he was going to do something like that, I'd have gone to him right away. It's why I ended up in San Francisco. I wanted to stay close to the place he'd died."

"It couldn't have been that hard to find me."

"It was, I promise you. Nobody would tell me anything, and I couldn't break through all the bureaucratic red tape. It was like they wanted to keep you a secret. I traveled all over California trying to track you down, but I couldn't find you."

I almost reeled back at the sound of Dylan struggling with his emotions. Dylan was hard as nails. He didn't cry. But I could hear the lump in his throat as he continued.

"What surgery did my mom have?"

"Thyroid."

"And the complications?"

"Severe infection and a blockage in her airway." Remington sighed. "Does it matter? It'll only cause you more pain."

"I don't care. I want to know. Why didn't anyone keep an eye on my dad?"

"They did, but they just thought it was normal, understandable grief. Because of you, I don't think anyone ever thought he'd take his own life."

Nobody ever does. I'd seen enough suicides in the foster homes and orphanages to know that it could come out of nowhere. One day, someone was smiling and laughing, the next... they were hanging from the shower rail. And that was without the added pain of losing their wife.

"Why weren't *you* keeping an eye on him?" Dylan shot back. "You were his brother, right? Why did you leave him to deal with everything on his own?"

"I'm sorry, Dylan. I wish I'd done more. You have no idea how many years I've thought about that, and thought about everything I could've done to stop him from doing what he did. I should've done more, but I can't change what happened."

Suri touched my arm. "We should have brought popcorn." She was clearly trying to lighten the mood. I adored her for it.

"I sort of feel like I shouldn't be listening," I whispered back.

She nodded. "That's rough for Dylan. I don't know him at all, but from what you've told me about the foster system, if he'd had an uncle all this time, I guess that could've changed a lot of things. He's probably got every right to be upset."

"Yeah... it really could've changed a lot for him." If Remington had found him, Dylan wouldn't have had to spend the majority of his life in foster homes. That wasn't the kind of thing that someone could easily forgive.

The door slammed. I waited for the second set of footsteps to follow before peering out of the storage closet. Dylan stormed out of the infirmary, and Remington went after him. Clearly, the end of that conversation hadn't gone well. I glanced over at Krieger's office to find that he'd come to the door. I went over to him, with Suri at my side.

Krieger sighed. "It's sad to see them like this, given everything that's going on."

Suri smiled hopefully. "I think Dylan just needs a little time to come to terms with this. It can't be easy, can it?"

No. No, it can't. I looked at her and smiled back. Suri was the most empathetic person I'd ever met. The girl continued to amaze me.

Or maybe that was just because I was smitten with her.

THIRTY-SEVEN

Jacob

A few hours later, after finally getting some sleep, Isadora was back in the infirmary with Krieger and me. The magical detector was coming together nicely, but I'd been forced to take a nap on one of the spare hospital beds. I had no idea if Krieger had done the same. He still looked exhausted, but he was pushing through. A bit more refreshed, I cradled a cup of coffee in my hands and watched Isadora and Krieger work. We were supposed to be taking turns.

"Morning." Louella poked her head around the door. "I thought you could use some breakfast." She stepped in, carrying a tray from the Banquet Hall. It was loaded up with sandwiches and pastries.

"Did you manage to get some rest?" Isadora replied, looking up from a half-turned screw.

She nodded. "Yeah, I slept a bit. You?"

"Same."

"How about you, Jacob?" She glanced at me.

I shrugged. "I got a couple of hours."

"I brought some food for our human friend, too, if she's hungry." Louella brandished the tray. Was that a white flag of peace she was waving, in the shape of bacon rolls and cheese Danishes?

"Go, eat," Isadora urged. "We'll keep working and take a break when you get back." She cast me a knowing smile that made my cheeks get hot. It wouldn't exactly be a romantic breakfast if Louella was playing third wheel. Not that I minded her being there. She was my friend, after all. Even if we didn't entirely agree on Suri, that wasn't about to change.

"You sure?" Louella didn't seem overly eager.

"Of course. Go on, take a break," Isadora replied.

Together, we exited Krieger's office and went through to the quarantine room. I knocked first, so Suri wouldn't be startled.

"Come in," she said. Pushing open the door, I found her cross-legged on the floor, flipping through *A Brief History of Magicals*, which I'd snuck in for her. She was engrossed in it. She didn't even look up as we entered.

"Are you hungry?" I asked. She looked cute, sitting like that.

Finally, she lifted her gaze. "Starving!"

"I brought a mix of stuff. I didn't know what you might want," Louella said shyly.

She grinned. "I'm not picky. I'll literally eat anything."

Joining her on the floor, Louella set out a sort of picnic. Cheerfully, Suri put the book to one side and reached for a raspberry croissant, devouring it in a couple of bites. *Wow, she really was hungry.* I took a bacon sandwich and started to eat. My stomach was growling like crazy. I couldn't remember the last time I'd put something in my belly other than coffee.

"So, what did Imogene want to talk to you and Isadora about?" I asked, swallowing a bite. I couldn't stand the silence.

Louella brushed crumbs from her mouth. "She wanted us to protect Krieger and the detector at all costs. So, you know, no pressure." She gave a nervous laugh.

"Ah, I thought it might have something to do with Remington's mission."

She frowned. "The pills and the security magicals, you mean?"

"Yeah."

"That's going to be both their domains, I think, once Krieger's finished with the magical detector. Imogene is really enthusiastic about the device, which is cool to see." Louella took another bite of her Danish.

"That makes sense," I replied. "I kind of feel sorry for Krieger, though. He's got a lot on his plate."

"Too much, probably. He looks wrecked."

"He doesn't always look like that?" Suri chimed in. I was pleased to see her getting involved. It would've been way too awkward if it had just been me and Louella, talking like she wasn't here.

I shook my head. "No, he doesn't always look that tired."

"Poor guy," she murmured, reaching for another pastry.

"It's nice that we're actually making some progress, though." I toyed with my own food. "I think Imogene is really going to pack a punch here. Like, it seems like she actually gives a damn, which is refreshing."

Louella laughed. "Tell me about it."

"Who's Imogene?" Suri looked between us.

"She's the new coven director. She took over after the stuff that happened last night." I'd filled her in as best I could about the Raffe stuff, but I'd forgotten to mention the changeover of leadership.

Suri nodded. "Is she nice?"

"Yeah, way nicer than the old one," I replied.

"So, what do you plan to do next, Suri?" Louella cut in. She sounded like a protective mom. "Obviously, you can't stay here much longer, but if you leave, then it's protocol to wipe your memory of everything you've seen. I'm interested to hear what you've got to say about it."

Suri glanced at me with sad eyes. "For starters, I don't want to forget Jacob, and I don't want to forget anything that I've seen here. I wonder if you even realize the extent of the gifts you were all born with, or if you all just take it for granted. I'm not saying that to be harsh, but you have no idea what it's like to be ordinary, because you've never been ordinary. Even just being around you guys… it makes me feel like I could be more. By proxy, I guess." She paused.

"It's not all it's cracked up to be," Louella replied. "Sometimes things don't work. Sometimes you can't do something you want to. And there are magicals who end up being what we call Mediocre—magicals who don't have a lot of power. I guess that's a different type of ordinary. You're right, this is all we've ever known, but I doubt it'd do you any favors in the long run. You'd end up being envious or resentful, that's my guess."

Suri shook her head. "No way. Why would I be envious if I could be part of it? Here, with all of you? I mean, there must have been exceptions in the past. Didn't you say one of your friends was human? Couldn't I just stay here, like her, and help the way she does? A non-magical ally, so to speak."

Louella shook her head. "That's different. Astrid is Alton's daughter. She's related to a magical. As far as I know, you're not." She didn't sound mean, just logical. "I know you don't want to go, but it really would be best for everyone if you had your memory wiped and went back into the human world."

"Louella!" My voice held a warning. This wasn't the time to talk about this.

"I know I'm coming off like a bitch, but that's not what I'm trying to do. Really, it's not," she continued, focusing on Suri. "I just want you to be aware of the circumstances. Being here is putting you at risk. You're a nice person, but you're asking a lot of Jacob, too, by trying to stay. It's against our rules."

Suri sat back on her haunches. "That's not my intention, but you have to understand things from my perspective. Would you want to leave all of this? Would you want to be the person who gets her memory wiped after being let into this world? I don't know you too well, but I'm guessing you'd be fighting as hard as me to stay."

"Maybe, but that's beside the point." Louella sighed. "I get where you're coming from, I do. Not long ago, I was alone in the human world, not really knowing where I belonged. I didn't know about covens, and I only had a vague knowledge of how big the magical world was. But it's just not suitable for you to be here, with things the way they are."

"Because of Katherine, you mean?" Suri asked. "You don't need to worry about me. I can handle myself, and I'm not planning on getting in anyone's way. I just don't want to go back to being ordinary. And I don't want to have my memory wiped against my will."

She had a point. Wiping her memory without her consent was a bit of a moral gray area. Not that I was in support of her having her memory wiped. The trouble was, they were both making good points. With Katherine's threat and all of the steps we were trying to take to destroy her, this wasn't a good time for Suri to be here. But I knew that her being released into the human world with her memories intact wasn't a possibility. That was a big, glaring security risk, even if I knew she was trustworthy.

Louella nodded. "Katherine is one of the issues, yes. We've got a million other things going on, dangerous things, which you'd be better off away from. Like, as far away as possible." Louella sighed and glanced at me. "Jacob, it's not fair to Suri if you keep hiding her here, not when *you* know what the stakes are and what the dangers are. Right now, this is no place for a human. And if Imogene were to find out she was here, she'd be furious. Imogene may be way better than Levi, but she has to follow the rules. That's literally her job. And she won't take kindly to the added stress of dealing with a human."

"Why is everyone so afraid of a human?" Suri looked somewhere between angry and frustrated. "I've already said I'm not going to get in anyone's way. Surely, you can see how immoral this is? I'm guessing it's been done countless times before, wiping memories left, right, and center, without any issues at all. But I'm aware of what I stand to lose, and I'm not having it. There has to be a way I can stay."

"Believe me, it'd be more trouble than it's worth. I'm sorry you feel the way you do, but that's the truth—we have too much going on, as it is, to worry about keeping you safe, too," Louella replied.

I hated that she was bringing this up, but she was right. At a time like this, I couldn't afford to be selfish. But I didn't want Suri to have to go, and have to forget, either.

"After everything she's been through, Suri deserves a little leeway," I said after a moment. "I'll speak with Imogene about it. Come clean, completely. And I'll see what she has to say."

Louella gaped at me. "Are you insane?"

I shrugged. "I want to at least try."

Suri smiled at me, but it didn't reach her big eyes. "I really, really want to stay, but... don't get yourself in trouble for me, Jacob. If I have to go, then I have to go. I wouldn't want you breaking any rules because of me."

I flashed her a reassuring grin. "It's already too late for that. Might as well see if honesty is the best policy."

"I happen to agree." My head whipped around at the sound of Isadora's voice. She stepped into the doorway, having evidently been eavesdropping from behind the wall.

"With whom?" Louella replied.

"With both of you." Isadora smiled and leaned up against the doorframe. "I agree that Suri being here is a huge security risk, not only to us but to her, but I also think that Jacob should try and speak to Imogene about it. You never know."

My heart lurched. "Do you really think so?"

"All I ask is that you hold off on that for a few more days. Imogene already has her hands full after the mess with Levi, and she's dealing with enough as it is without having to worry about a human on the loose." She paused. "And you may have a better chance of persuading her when she's not so bogged down in other things."

"Thank you, Isadora," I gasped.

Suri nodded effusively. "That's all I've been asking for. A chance."

"Don't get me wrong, I'm not too happy with a human being here," Isadora continued. "But I understand your views, Suri, now that I've gotten to know you better. And I understand you, Jacob. Sometimes, exceptions aren't such a bad thing."

Words couldn't describe how grateful I was to Isadora. Not just for this, but for everything she had done for me. She knew me better than anyone, and she was my last tie to my parents. And the fact that she had my back, all the time, would never lose its novelty. I'd never had that before, not really. The Smiths had been supportive, but that hadn't lasted long. If Isadora had said she didn't think it was a good idea to talk to Imogene, I'd probably have backed off and done the hard thing of letting Suri go instead. She'd stopped that from happening, at least for now. And I was thankful for that. So thankful.

"Dr. Krieger?" Imogene's voice floated through the infirmary, prompting everyone to panic.

I jumped up, and so did Louella. "I'm so sorry," I whispered to Suri. "We'll be back."

"I've got breakfast and the hope of being allowed to stay," Suri replied. "I'm good."

With that, Louella and I hurried out of the quarantine room with Isadora, who locked the door behind her. Imogene had just stepped into Krieger's office, oblivious to our secret human. We waited for a couple of seconds before following our new director into the room where Krieger was hard at work, as usual.

"I hope you don't mind my intrusion, Dr. Krieger." Imogene turned as we entered. "However, I have an urgent matter that I must speak with you about. An old chemist friend of mine has recently been in touch regarding the pills that Levi has been giving to the security magicals of the SDC. I described them to him and sent a sample from some of the remaining boxes I discovered in Levi's old office."

"What did this friend of yours find?" Krieger perked up, interested.

"He mentioned something by the name of Delirium, though he didn't go into detail. I was hoping you might be able to cast more light upon it, given your background in medicine."

Krieger frowned. "Yes, I know of Delirium. It's derived from ancient herbalism, from what I remember, which means it's most likely dangerous and forbidden. People use it to forget traumatic moments from their lives, but I've never seen it manufactured on such a large scale, given the illegality and complexity of it."

"That's what I thought," Imogene replied. "I've asked Remington to verify this with the National Council, to see if he can garner a confession of some sort. At least then we could work toward freeing the security magicals from its grip. If we know the nature of the poison, we can discover the antidote."

"I'll look further into it once I've finished putting the magical detector back together," Krieger promised. "It shouldn't be too much longer now."

Imogene shook her head. "There is no need, Dr. Krieger. I just wanted to inform you, as I know you were interested. I already have people looking toward a cure, though it will take some time. I'll update you when I know more."

"Have you slept?" I asked, trying to be polite.

Imogene smiled. "I've had a lot to contend with, but I'm used to only sleeping a few hours a night."

"Do you want to get some coffee?" Isadora asked. "You could probably use a break, if you've been working through the night."

Imogene shook her head. "I'll rest later, and I'll likely drink a gallon of coffee before then. My office is well equipped. Levi seemed to have a penchant for fancy coffee machines, which is one benefit to his former directorship."

Isadora laughed. "That might be the only benefit."

"So, which poor devil did you wake up to ask about the pills?" Krieger asked.

"Fortunately, the friend I spoke to is currently on sabbatical in the Seoul Coven, so I wasn't waking him up in the middle of the night." She chuckled. "I can't say the same for the magical authorities that I called in pursuit of temporary amnesty for Finch, mind you. There's something rather satisfying about hearing the irritated wife of a judicial director yell for him to come to the phone at four o'clock in the morning."

I laughed. "I wish I could've been a fly on the wall for that."

"I can't picture Levi getting on the phone at four a.m. just to try and free a known criminal," Louella said.

"That was a little unusual for me, too," Imogene admitted. "I'm used to tracking down criminals, not trying to gain their freedom. I suppose it's keeping me on my toes." Her expression changed to one of concern.

Krieger sighed. "Speaking of Levi, I would ask that you all show a little leniency toward him when he finally wakes up."

I snorted. "That's a joke, right?"

"No, I honestly do mean it, as hard as that might be to believe," he replied. "I know I kept mentioning his incompetence when I urged you to do something, Imogene. But I'm becoming surer, with this new knowledge of Delirium, that his actions weren't entirely his doing. I know him quite well, and though he may not always be the most pleasant man to be around, I don't know if he's that foolish, either. He wouldn't have hushed all of the Echidna business up if someone else hadn't been pulling the proverbial strings."

"You mean Katherine?" Isadora frowned.

Imogene exhaled slowly. "I suppose it makes sense that, somehow, she got to him. Her influence is already widespread, so why not Leonidas, too? I know him much better than you, Dr. Krieger, so perhaps I'm simply seeking to give Leonidas the benefit of the doubt. But there is some sense of possibility in what you are saying. I just wouldn't be able to comprehend the idiocy of his behavior, otherwise."

"It's not that hard to understand," I retorted.

"There'll be evidence of foul play when he wakes up from his coma, if that's the case," Krieger went on. "I've put a series of spells on him precisely for that purpose. They're currently scanning every atom in his body for foreign magic. When he comes around, we'll know for sure whether it's something like Delirium, or if he really is just an idiot. Although it's possible he was intentionally working for Katherine."

Before Imogene could respond, the air rippled inside Krieger's office. Everybody froze. It was like watching a pool turned on its side, sort of like a portal, sort of not. The ripple spread out across the nearside wall, making it seem less solid. And then, somehow, a rectangular strip of the wall itself opened like a door.

Harley hurried out, followed by Finch and Garrett, who were dragging an unconscious Wade between them. Behind them, in the weird doorway, I could see the front of a rundown building with graffiti sprawled across it.

The door slammed shut behind Harley and the others, melding back into the wall until everything was solid again. Harley was panting hard, bent double. She held something in her arms—a book of some kind. A Grimoire.

"Harley?" Imogene gasped, her eyes wide. She'd turned pale. "Is that... the Merlin Grimoire?"

Harley nodded, still fighting for air.

"Are you okay? Are any of you injured?" She got up and hurried toward Harley.

Harley shook her head. "No, not injured."

Imogene looked seriously anxious. She put her hand on Harley's shoulder. "What on earth is going on here?"

Harley looked her dead in the eyes. "We need your help."

THIRTY-EIGHT

Jacob

I mogene looked tense. "How is it possible that you have the Merlin Grimoire? That's a dangerous item to have in your possession." She couldn't take her eyes off the book. I was just as dumbfounded—Harley would be in a whole heap of trouble if New York found out it was missing. I guessed the job of director was looking even less promising for Imogene now.

Harley paled. "We kind of snatched it from the New York Coven, but I'll get to all of that in a minute. Right now, I need help with Wade. Something really weird has happened to him. No idea what, but he's been acting strange toward me—violent, if I'm being totally honest." She rubbed her neck, which was red and splotchy. *What the hell did you do to her, Wade?* I narrowed my eyes at his limp figure.

Garrett nodded. "That's a pretty huge understatement, Harley. He tried to kill you."

Everyone in the room gasped, me included. But Finch—Finch looked like he really wanted to murder Wade. He couldn't take his eyes off him. It was probably a good thing Garrett had hold of Wade, too, or else there was no telling what might've happened.

Wade's eyes blinked open. The moment he saw Harley, he tried to lunge out of Garrett and Finch's grasp. His eyes were wide and mad, his mouth contorted in a snarl. Finch and Garrett did what they could, but Wade seemed to be crazy strong. Like, even stronger than he usually was.

"You!" he roared, yanking himself out of the hands that held him. Finch and Garrett tried to grab him again, but he twisted away from them. Before anyone could stop him, he leapt through the air, his hands outstretched to snatch at Harley. I watched, stunned. He really did look like he wanted her dead.

Imogene stepped forward, visibly concerned. She took a handful of stones out of the pocket of her white pantsuit and threw them at Wade. They skittered on the floor around him in no particular order or direction. A second later, bright red ropes shot up, crisscrossing over Wade and bringing him down to the ground with a thud. He writhed and strained underneath them, but the ropes had him trapped, like a Purge beast.

"Everyone, stand back," Imogene urged. "You're certainly right about him acting strangely, Harley. Isadora, Dr. Krieger, would you mind providing some backup?"

Isadora stepped up, with Krieger beside her. They both had their palms up. Even now, Wade wouldn't stop thrashing against the ropes. It was hard to even think that this was the same person we knew—our friend, and Harley's boyfriend.

Harley had turned away from the sight of Wade on the floor. There were tears in her eyes. I could tell she didn't want us to see how hurt she was. Garrett put a tentative hand on her shoulder, making the tears come faster. That friendly touch had broken the dam holding everything back.

"I just don't understand what's wrong with him," she murmured. "It came out of nowhere. He just started acting like an ass, but I figured he was stressed or something. And then he suddenly snapped and tried to... you know."

Everyone in the room looked scared and confused. This wasn't just anyone we were talking about. This was Wade. Stoic, solid Wade. I could tell we were all thinking the same thing: Katherine had to be involved in this somehow. It was the only explanation. But that came with its own set of fears. If Katherine had managed to get her claws into Wade, then that meant any one of us was fair game.

My gut churned with panic. My head filled up with worst-case scenarios, and a pain stabbed in my chest that was so intense it made me want to cry. Emotions bombarded my brain—sadness, confusion, frustration, and crushing hurt. They didn't feel like they belonged to me, but I was feeling them. Big time.

"Finch, can you do something to calm your sister down?" Imogene asked, her voice choked. "It would appear that her Empathy has gone into reverse, and I'm finding it rather hard to focus with all of her emotions spilling out."

Finch had tears running down his face. Louella was practically on the floor, bawling her eyes out, and Krieger and Isadora were hugging it out. Even Garrett had tears in his eyes, since Shapeshifters weren't immune to the reverse version of what Harley could do. He was trying to keep it together but failing miserably, just like the rest of us.

This is crazy. Harley was clearly in so much pain that it was causing this huge reaction in everyone in the room. Finch stepped forward and put his arm around Harley.

"It's going to be okay, Sis. Wonderboy is going to be fine. He didn't mean to almost crush your windpipe. We'll sort him out, and then you'll be slurping off each other's faces, same as before."

She nodded miserably. "I just don't understand what's wrong with him."

"We'll find out, don't worry," he replied.

I turned my attention back to our new director. Still battling tears from Harley's reverse Empathy, Imogene sank down to her knees in front of Wade, getting dangerously close to his thrashing arms. Resting her hand on his back, she began to whisper a few spells in Latin, moving her hands around him in a mesmerizing pattern. She was clearly trying to figure out what sort of voodoo was going on here. It had to be some kind of magic, because this *wasn't* Wade at all. It was like he'd been replaced by a demon version of himself.

"*Ipsum revelare. Occulta revelando. Videtur quod non possit revelare,*" she whispered. No sooner had she spoken the words than Wade's eyes lit up red. It gave me major Raffe flashbacks, but I didn't think it was possible that Wade could have a djinn inside him. They didn't just pop in unannounced.

"Get away from me!" Wade howled. "Get away from me!"

"I can feel something," Imogene murmured in response. "There's something controlling him."

"What? What is it?" Harley barked.

"Give me a moment, the spell is still doing its work." She closed her eyes as little pulses of red light rippled back into her palms.

"What did you find?" Harley pressed.

"I need another moment. Please, I have to concentrate," Imogene replied, her tone exasperated. Then her eyes flew wide.

Harley's eyes were practically bugging out of her head. "What is it?!"

"It's a hex, and, my goodness, it's an old one. An ancient Romany hex, if I'm not mistaken, used to turn love into hate at great speed—so quickly that the loved one doesn't even see it coming until it is too late." She glanced at Harley. "It's a miracle you were able to notice it before he got close enough to kill you. Good thing Finch and Garrett were there to help you, or there's no telling what may have happened."

Harley looked heartbroken. "My Empathy helped. I sensed something was off about him, but I just couldn't figure out what."

"You were lucky, Harley. If you hadn't been so perceptive... well, we don't need to discuss that right now. It's not something I care to think about," Imogene replied. "However, we still have a problem. Hexes such as these usually derive from a cursed object, as is common in Romany magic. That object may or may not be on Wade at this present moment."

"An object?" Harley looked puzzled. Wade wasn't really one for accessories. Fancy suits and vests, yeah. Hipster bracelets and necklaces, not so much. He was wearing a watch, though. I could see it glinting on his wrist. It looked super expensive.

"Is it his watch?" I piped up.

Imogene stooped and wafted her hands over his wrist. "No, it doesn't seem to be. Romany hexes have been known to function through proximity, too, so it may not be something that's actually on Wade."

"What about his Esprit? His ten rings?" I asked.

"An Esprit can't be hexed. It must be something else." She glanced at Isadora. "I'm going to take Harley to my office to speak with her in private. If my assumptions are correct, Wade should calm down once Harley is no longer in the room. If you temporarily remove the ropes, you should be able to search him for any hidden objects. Call for me if you find anything."

I didn't envy Isadora the task of giving Wade a pat down. He was still writhing beneath the red ropes, his eyes glinting with fury. Krieger would probably have to sedate him first.

Isadora nodded. "We'll get to the bottom of this."

"I hope so," Imogene replied. "If we can't find the cursed object, then there will be no way to remove the curse from Wade. Not without putting him through a great deal of suffering."

I raised my hand, though I wasn't exactly sure why. It seemed like the right thing to do. "What do you want us to do?"

"You should stay here and assist Isadora in her search. Garrett, please return to the LA Coven and report to me when you've been brought up to date. I need someone there, in my place, to keep an eye on things."

Garrett nodded. "You're worried about those kids?"

"Precisely. With Echidna now dead, the magical children in my care will be in even more danger. There's every chance that Katherine will attempt to take them for the final ritual. She can't be allowed to succeed." She cast Garrett a steely look.

"And how about little old me?" Finch flashed a mischievous grin, but I could tell he was really worried about Harley.

Imogene offered him a stern smile. "You shouldn't move an inch."

"Like this?" He took a step forward, chuckling to himself. Even I had to smirk at that. At least it defused some of the tension in the room. I was still dealing with some of the after-effects of Harley's reverse Empathy bombardment.

"You're not to leave this room," she replied coolly. "You may have gained your sister's favor, but that doesn't mean you've won *my* trust. You decided to evade Purgatory, and you got Harley into very deep trouble. So, until I can decide what to do with you, you'll remain here in the infirmary, out of sight."

Finch nodded sheepishly. "Just a joke, Imogene. You know, to lighten the mood a little?" He dropped his gaze. "Thanks for not making me leave. I'm not abandoning Harley now. Not for anything. So, cheers for not throwing me back in Purgatory, either. At least not right away."

"It's not that I don't want to, Finch. It's that you may prove to be more useful to me here, given your knowledge of our enemy." With that, she took Harley gently by the arm and led her out of the infirmary.

THIRTY-NINE

Harley

It was weird to see Imogene surrounded by Levi's things, but it was even weirder that she didn't look too out of place inside this Persian palace. She seemed at ease behind Levi's ostentatious desk, even though I was still trying to piece together what was going on here. Evidently, a lot had changed since we'd gone to New York, including a much-needed change-up of the SDC's leadership.

I sat opposite her, clutching the Grimoire to my chest. It was like the most dangerous, powerful security blanket in the world.

"As you've probably guessed, there have been one or two modifications since you disappeared from the SDC, including my instatement as the new director. As Levi has been compromised, it appeared to be the only viable solution, and your friends were quite adamant that I should put my money where my mouth is," Imogene began. She seemed to be having a hard time taking her eyes off the Grimoire, which was to be expected; this was probably going to be a gigantic thorn in her side.

I nodded, grateful to have something to take my mind off Wade. "Yeah, I guessed as much. Do I want to know what happened?"

"I'm sure your friends will bring you up to speed, but there's something more pressing I need to talk to you about. I didn't want to do it in the infirmary in case I lost my temper." She sighed heavily, visibly collecting herself.

"Do you realize the trouble you've caused by stealing that Grimoire? It's one of their most valuable items. There's not a single sliver of a chance they haven't noticed it's missing. And I can't even begin to imagine how long it's going to take me to fix this terrible mess."

"I had to do it, Imogene, but I promise you we were careful. Nobody saw us go in, and nobody saw us come out." She wouldn't convince me that I'd done the wrong thing, even if I *had* put her in a bind.

"And you believe that matters?" Imogene retorted. "You will be their main suspect, regardless of how careful you were. Leonidas spread the news of your fugitive status across the covens, and though I've been working around the clock to reduce the amount of damage to your reputation, I can't do much about their suspicions."

I shook my head. "They don't have any proof that I did it. You don't have anything to worry about."

"You don't understand, Harley. I spent the better part of last night speaking with every person of influence I could find, to ensure that your name was cleared and you could be reinstated as a full member of this coven. I managed to do that so you could return to the SDC, for your own safety, and so Katherine couldn't get her hands on you." She sank back in her chair. "And then you come to me with *that* book and a tale about robbing the New York Coven."

"But even if they think I did it, they've got no evidence. They've got no way of pinning it on me."

Imogene leveled her gaze at me. "As long as I don't breathe a word of this, you mean? Do you see the position you have placed me in, Harley? What am I supposed to do about that? Do I protect you and pray you have a reasonable excuse for doing something this absurd, or do I tell the truth, to defend the reputation of the SDC and ensure that no allegations of deceit can be laid against me? We have already had far too many liars in this coven. I wouldn't want to add my name to such a list. I have my own reputation to think about."

"I did it for our sake. There might be something in that Grimoire that can stop Katherine. You know me, Imogene. You know I wouldn't have done something like this without a good reason." I was starting to feel really small. This was like being shouted at by my mom, and it wasn't like I could argue her point. I *had* put her between a rock and a hard place, but I needed her to back me on this. I needed her to understand why I'd taken the Grimoire, but my mind was all over the place, with all this Wade stuff.

She sighed tensely. "While I'm sure that's true, I have a great deal to contemplate. However, there's a somewhat larger issue to contend with first: the curse on Wade. That's another reason I brought you here. I didn't want to alarm your friends in the infirmary. You see, I've already searched him for the cursed object, and it's not on him. I would have been able to discover it with the spell I performed."

"I don't understand." I just hoped she had a solution in mind. I had to know Wade would be okay, or I didn't know if I could bring myself to get to work on the Grimoire. My head would be too messed up to focus.

"What I'm saying is, the cursed object is not on *him*." She paused. "Do you remember me mentioning that it could work through proximity?"

I nodded. "Yeah."

"So, the hex may not be coming from Wade at all." She got up, her expression uncertain. "What if... Perhaps it could be... There is only one way to find out." She stopped beside me and moved her hands across me in counterclockwise circles. Her hands lit up with shimmering silver light tinged with sparks of bronze.

"What are you doing?" I tried not to flinch as the sparks rained down on my skin, tiny pulses rippling underneath.

"Checking something," she replied nervously. "*Ipsum revelare. Occulta revelando. Videtur quod non possit revelare.*" Imogene repeated the spell she'd used back in the infirmary, only, this time, I was the subject.

I was about to ask what she was checking for, when the pendant around my neck became scorching hot. I scrabbled for it, desperate to get it away from my bare skin, sucking air through my teeth at the sudden pain. It felt like molten lava had just been dropped directly onto my chest, right where Imogene's gift rested against me.

"That evil wretch!" Imogene bit out. With her eyes wide in panic, she snatched the pendant away from my neck and threw it into the air. Blinding bolts of light shot out of her palms, hitting the pendant head-on. The light seeped into the plated metal, and the gemstones that had brought me such comfort exploded outward, disintegrating the pendant in a storm of spiraling sparks. They sank to the ground in a snow-like flurry. I stared at the fragments as they melted away.

"Imogene...?"

Her chest heaved with the exertion of what she'd just done. To be honest, I still wasn't sure *what* she'd just done, exactly, but I knew I wasn't getting my pendant back anytime soon.

"I'm so sorry, Harley," she rasped, leaning against the back of her chair. "I didn't give you the pendant cursed, I swear it to you. I had nothing to do with this."

"What do you mean?"

"Someone must have hexed it." She frowned in thought. "Though, it would've had to have been someone who could get close to you. A cultist, perhaps? Or one of the security magicals under the influence of those pills?"

"No... Katherine did this." Her name dripped from my tongue, wrapped in venom. She must have hexed it, somehow, during our last encounter in Tartarus. I'd gotten close enough to her, for sure. She couldn't have hexed it during my time on Eris Island, because the pendant had been disguised as a different necklace, but there was every chance she'd managed to send her evil toward me while I was distracted by Erebus. I'd been wearing the pendant then, and Katherine had promised to hurt my friends first, to make me suffer. Maybe this was what she'd meant. Maybe she'd gone right for the jugular, affecting Wade first because she knew it would hurt me the most.

It made me think suddenly about the Chains of Truth. How had Wade managed to get past them with that hex on him when we'd gained entry into the New York Coven? He'd promised to defend my life, after all, and then gone ahead and tried to murder me.

Maybe because he'd been transferred to an astral plane, the hex hadn't gone with him? Or maybe the spectral trio only dealt with each individual's personal truths, soul-deep honesty rather than added spells and hexes that didn't affect their true nature.

Perhaps because I'd been the one wearing the pendant and he'd been far enough away from me, they hadn't noticed anything strange with Wade? It had only started to get really bad *after* our encounter with the chains, so maybe it had slipped under the radar, as it wasn't working at full capacity at that point.

Or maybe Katherine had orchestrated it so that the hex hid from powerful things and beings, like those that protected the hidden coven entrance, in case they tried to stop it?

Whatever the answer was, the chains hadn't prevented him from entering. And the latter speculation made the most sense to me. The only reason Imogene had been able to find the hex was because she'd been given a heads-up that there was something going on, which had allowed her to pinpoint the problem with a hex-searching spell.

"I should've known she would attempt something like this. Her influence is everywhere, like a virus." Imogene shook her head, her face twisting up in a grimace of anger. I wanted to delve further into her emotional turmoil, but she was wearing her blocker bracelet. Still, I didn't need my Empathy to read the fury on her face. It was a reflection of my own expression.

"You couldn't have known," I replied. "It was only a matter of time before she tried to get to me. *I* should have been warier. *I* should've been looking over my shoulder, checking everything."

"It's just proving impossible to get one step ahead of her. And every time she gets away with something, it riles me up even more." A muscle twitched in her jaw, her teeth gritted. "I thought it was simply Levi's pride that had led him to keep Echidna's theft a secret, but now I'm not so sure. Now, I'm growing ever more certain that his mind has been affected by Delirium, as have the minds of the security magicals."

"Delirium?" I hadn't heard of that before.

"Chemical-based magic that alters the mind, forged from ancient herbalism."

"You think that's what's affecting everyone?"

She nodded. "I'm looking into it as we speak."

"Are you about ready to knock Katherine's head off her shoulders, too?" I held her angry gaze.

She chuckled bitterly. "I reached that point a long while ago."

"Well then, it's good we've got a chance of stopping Katherine now, even if I took it in a slightly illegal way." I offered her a shy smile. Imogene was probably still pissed with me over stealing this book, but I was sure she'd soften up once I explained why in more detail. "We can put an end to her reign of terror, once and for all. End her influence and her power."

Imogene narrowed her eyes. "You mean the Grimoire?"

"Bingo."

"From what I've read of that book, it only has a handful of spells in it, and nothing capable of destroying someone like Katherine." She sounded doubtful, but I was about to give her a huge dose of hope. One hundred mils of it, stat.

I shook my head. "Those are only the pages that ordinary people can see."

"I'm sorry to sound ignorant, but I don't follow." Imogene looked puzzled.

"I really hate to toot my own horn, but I'm not exactly an 'ordinary person.' You know how it was meant to be super secured and everything?"

Imogene nodded. "I was just about to ask you about that. It should have been almost impossible for you to get close to it, with New York's heightened security measures."

"*Almost* impossible." I grinned at her. "I had the Merlin bloodline on my side. See, my dad had integrated some crazy stuff into the coven itself, and it showed me the way to the Grimoire. It took me through a secret entrance, older than the current coven, and directed me straight to it. Like, I could feel it, right here in my chest—an inner compass kind of deal. It led us to a door that my dad charmed. I put my palm on it, and the door opened. Even the case it was in, inside the main room, disintegrated right under my hands, like it wanted me to take it."

Imogene's eyes widened. "How peculiar."

"That's not the weirdest part," I replied. "As it turns out, I'm the only one who can actually read it and perform spells from it, even though it's not finished. I had a slight accident with it a while back, so I already knew I could read from it, but the magnetic pull of it only made me more sure of what I could do. Plus, there are supposed to be extra pages in this thing—hidden spells. I haven't had the chance to look yet, but I'm hopeful we'll find what we need inside here."

"I had heard the rumors," Imogene murmured, peering curiously at the book. "Can you show it to me? Maybe I can help you figure it out. I've studied a lot of Grimoires in my time, many of them written by magicals as powerful as your parents."

I laid the Grimoire on the table, figuring I needed all the help I could get. Even though this wasn't any ordinary Grimoire, there had to be similarities with other powerful Grimoires that Imogene might have seen. I flipped it open to the first page and glanced back over my shoulder as Imogene's eyes flitted across the words.

"What's that symbol at the top? Does it mean anything to you?" Imogene asked. "It looks vaguely familiar. A voodoo symbol, if I'm not mistaken. Although, it has been a long time since I've had to study their magic. I may be wrong."

"This one?" I reached out nervously and brushed my hand across an inky emblem in the top right-hand corner. It reminded me a lot of the Veve of Erzulie that had led us to Marie Laveau's lily garden. I hadn't noticed it the first time I'd looked through this book, but then I'd been a little preoccupied with *not* summoning Erebus and accidentally killing Santana. The page morphed immediately, revealing a palimpsest beneath the top leaf. As far as I could tell, it was just a jumble of words and drawings, making no sense whatsoever. The etchings swirled across the page, unreadable even to me. Then again, part of me didn't want to be able to read it in front of Imogene. I wanted to break this code by myself, when I had time to figure out how to decipher it.

"My goodness... I guess the rumors were true." Imogene stepped away from me. "And you are certain you can read from this? You've done so before?"

I nodded. "Yeah, it happened by accident, but I know I can do it again."

"Katherine has made several attempts to steal this and have it destroyed. If she discovers it has been taken, she will stop at nothing to find you and it, especially now that it's in the hands of someone who can actually read the spells." She looked on edge, which wasn't exactly what I'd wanted. I'd hoped to comfort her, not freak her out. "Just when I thought this couldn't get any worse. Dealing with New York *and* Katherine is not my idea of a good time, but at least you had a decent reason. I can't deny that."

"I'll look through this until I find something I can use against Katherine, and I'll guard it with my life," I promised. It wouldn't be long before news got out that the Grimoire was missing, which meant we were dealing with another ticking clock, right over my head in particular. I had to end Katherine before she could get to me. Even if I didn't sleep for the next week, I'd do it.

"The Merlins' Grimoire has always been something of a mystery for magical society, but I didn't fully understand until I laid eyes upon it, just now," Imogene said. "It's a lot of pressure on your shoulders, Harley, but you may be the only one who can help us now."

I grimaced. "I had a feeling you might say that."

"I understand why you had to steal this," she replied. "I'll keep your secret for as long as I'm able. New York won't be given the chance to accuse you. You have my word on that."

My heart soared with relief. "Thank you, Imogene."

"All of this will come right in the end." She cast me a nervous smile. "Now, go check on Wade. You'll likely find him greatly changed, now that the cursed object has been destroyed. And don't let Finch out of your sight. We're on thin enough ice as it is, and we have too much trouble to contend with already."

"You can count on me."

She sighed, placing her hand on my shoulder. "It is a big ask, even if you feel ready. I just hope you won't have to sacrifice too much to see this to fruition. I don't want to see you destroyed in the process of destroying Katherine."

I grinned and closed the book, holding it tight to my chest again. "Oh, believe me, she has no idea what's coming for her."

FORTY

Jacob

I sat opposite Suri in the quarantine room. She looked nervous, her knuckles white around a coffee cup. I couldn't blame her. She'd been stuck in here for ages while all kinds of crazy raged on next door.

"What happened in there?" she asked.

"Harley came back," I replied. "Her boyfriend, Wade, had gone a little mad. So, we had to deal with that. He seems to be feeling better now, though. Krieger has him connected up to a bunch of wires so they can make sure he's not going to go bonkers again."

"What do you mean, 'mad'?"

"He tried to kill Harley, but it was all just some hex. I guess they managed to find the cursed object, because he hasn't tried to kill her again since she came back from Imogene's office." I shrugged, still worried about Harley. She'd been hit hard by Wade's violent outburst. And just because he hadn't tried to lunge at her again didn't mean he was fully fixed.

Suri gasped. "He tried to *kill* her?"

"Yeah, but I'm sure they'll kiss and make up. It wasn't really Wade doing those things, so they'll probably work through it."

"That's awful," she said quietly. "To be attacked by someone you love? That's horrible. She must've been so scared."

I nodded. "She's tough, though. She'll pull through it."

"I wish I could meet her."

"Me, too. I'd introduce you, but I don't want to add to her stress right now." I glanced at her shyly. "And, anyway, I've been looking forward to spending some time alone with you. Even if it's just to get you up to speed on all the crazy stuff that goes on around here."

"So, this isn't unusual?" A small smile played upon her lips.

I shrugged. "Nope, not really. This is kind of a slow day, by SDC standards."

She laughed. "Are you trying to put me off this place, Jacob?"

"If you're still here, and you're not running for the hills, I'm guessing nothing could put you off." I grinned at her, watching her big eyes sparkle with mischief. This girl was truly remarkable. After everything she'd seen and heard, she should've been begging to leave, but she wasn't. She wasn't scared; she wasn't intimidated. She was just taking it all in stride. And that was way cool in my book.

"Not that I get much of a choice in the matter," Suri replied, her voice tinged with sadness. "They're going to wipe my memory, anyway, aren't they?"

I held her gaze. "I'm still trying to figure something out so I can make sure you walk out of here with all your memories intact. I'd go and speak to Imogene right now, but I don't know if she'd be up for any negotiating at the moment. She's mega stressed. Even more stressed now that Harley is back, and she's brought that book with her."

"Book?"

I shook my head. "Long story. Basically, she's stolen this powerful, magical spell book from a high-security coven, and everyone's crapping themselves over what might happen to her because of it. I'm guessing Imogene will lie for her, but she's a by-the-rules sort of magical. Which is another reason I'm not sure how to talk to her about you. I need to spin it right, which means I need a little more time. But I *will* speak to Imogene, I promise."

Suri smiled. "Take as long as you need. I don't mind hiding here for a while, as long as I get to stay." She traced her fingertip around the rim of her coffee cup. It looked like a nervous tic. "I meant what I said earlier, you know? About you and me. It's like you said, I would've run for the hills by now if I wasn't totally into this whole 'magical world' stuff and everything that comes with it. Plus, I feel like there's still a lot more about you that I want to get to know."

Oh my God... "Yeah, me too." I kept it cool, even though my heart was hammering.

"The last guy I crushed on was the captain of the high school football team, and he was an absolute scumbag. He ghosted me like nobody's business. Or maybe he zombied me—he kept coming back, out of nowhere, making me think he still liked me."

I tried not to get jealous. "I'm not too good with dating terms."

She chuckled. "Ghosting is disappearing completely. To zombie is to ghost someone and then keep coming back—you know, like they were dead, and they came back to life to make your life miserable? Romero-style."

"You're so cool," I blurted out. "You're probably the only girl I can think of who would drop Romero into conversation."

"*Dawn of the Dead* is a masterpiece. What can I say?" She narrowed her eyes. "The original, not the remake—naturally."

"Naturally." I grinned from ear to ear.

"Anyway, you're different from him in so many ways. You're sweet. I doubt you'd drop off the face of the earth, which is always nice to know," she said, smiling. "Plus, you're a friggin' wizard who can jump to anyplace you want to go, which is insanely cool. I can only imagine what kind of things you do for fun, and what places you go to. Paris? No problem. Hawaii? No sweat. Rio? Absolutely."

"I don't really do any of that," I admitted.

"You should! If I had your ability, I'd be zooming off to a different country every day." She smiled shyly at me. "Maybe, one day, when I know you a little better, you could show me somewhere outside America? I've never been anywhere."

My cheeks turned hot. "Yeah... that'd be cool."

"Well, if I get to keep my memories, that is. I won't remember any of this conversation if I get wiped."

"I really hope Imogene agrees to let you keep your memories."

"Me, too." She leaned forward on the edge of her bed, so close I could've kissed her. "Although, if I'm going to be staying here a while longer, I'll need some comic books or something, because I'm about to lose my damn mind in this room, with nothing to do. Unless you can think of something more fun to distract me?"

My throat constricted. "I'll get you whatever you need."

"Like this?" She leaned farther forward and placed a soft kiss on my cheek.

I froze. "Uh… maybe."

She sat back and grinned at me. "Maybe we'll stick to comic books for now."

"Or… I could do this." I cupped her face in my hands and leaned in. I'd never kissed anyone before. I wasn't even sure what I was doing, but I'd seen guys do this in movies. The hands-on-the-face thing. She smiled wide, right as I kissed her, and my lips pressed against her teeth. I pulled back in surprise as she collapsed in a fit of giggles.

Way to blow it, Jacob. Way to blow it.

"Sorry." I lowered my gaze.

"Why? Just try it again." She smiled. And I did just that.

FORTY-ONE

Harley

T he next morning, I awoke in the chair beside Wade's bed. My muscles were stiff, and my throat felt dry and raspy, but I was happy to see him looking so peaceful beneath the covers. Krieger had been watching over him, letting him sleep off the hex that had taken hold of his mind. Destroying the pendant had knocked Wade out completely and he'd been unconscious ever since. Now, the poor doctor was back in his office with Jacob, working tirelessly on the magical detector. Wires crisscrossed over Wade's body, making him look more like an android than a person, but he was hopefully back to being *my* Wade. My heart and my windpipe could rest easy knowing he wasn't going to try and crush either of them again.

"Ah, little Miss Stockholm Syndrome awakens." I turned to find Finch watching me from a nearby bed.

"Don't call me that, Finch."

He shrugged. "Did you know it takes the average victim nine times to walk away from their abuser?"

"It was the hex, not Wade!" I snapped back.

"Tell that to the bruises on your neck." He glowered at Wade's unconscious figure, cracking his knuckles.

"Well, now I know there's no way I'm leaving you alone in a room with him," I said. A flutter of panic rippled through me as I patted my body, checking for the satchel with the Grimoire inside. Santana had given it to me last night, after a brief reunion, and I hadn't taken it off since. I was going to keep this bag on me at all times, no matter what. If Katherine wanted this thing, she'd have to rip it from my cold, dead body.

With all this Wade business, I hadn't had the chance to look inside the Grimoire, though I was dying to after what I'd unearthed in front of Imogene. There had to be a way to read those swirling symbols, and I was going to figure it out. But only after Wade woke up and I knew he was okay. That might have seemed stupid, but my brain would continue to be mush until I knew he was back to his usual self.

Finch grinned. "Why not, Sis? You scared I'm going to do to him what he did to you?"

"It wasn't *him*, Finch!"

"You keep telling yourself that. You don't think that hex played on feelings he already had? You don't think he was really harboring some resentment toward you? Maybe he was just being honest, for once." Finch folded his arms across his chest. "I mean, come on, our dad fought an insanely powerful curse to keep you alive. Wade could've put some effort in. But he didn't. You don't find that odd?"

I shot him a warning look. "No, I don't. I think it took him by surprise, that's all." Finch was exploiting some of my biggest insecurities here, and he freaking knew it, but that didn't make what he was saying any easier to stomach. What if he was right? What if Wade *was* harboring some resentment toward me? He'd said as much even before he tried to squeeze the life out of me.

"You shouldn't rely on him, that's all I'm saying. I said it before, I'll say it until I'm blue in the face. Love makes people stupid. It doesn't cement loyalty. Only blood can do that."

"Have you tried telling that to your mom?" I shot back.

He chuckled. "Oof. Low blow, Sis."

"Or maybe you're just off your meds." I knew I'd gone too far, but I couldn't stuff the words back in my mouth. He scowled, a wounded look drifting across his face.

"Now that really was a low blow. Maybe you're the one who needs meds, if you can sit by his side and not hate him for what he did," Finch replied curtly. "I'll never get that image out of my head. If I hadn't come running when I did and smashed him over the head, he'd have killed you. No question about it. I'd suggest you remember that."

I sighed wearily. "I'm sorry, Finch. I didn't mean to say that. I'm under a lot of pressure, but that's no excuse." I dropped my gaze, reaching for Wade's hand. "See how you'd feel if the man you loved had tried to hurt you."

"Sorry, Sis, I don't swing that way." A small smile turned up the corners of his lips, letting me know I was forgiven. Finch could hold a grudge like nobody's business, but he was also pretty good at picking his battles. I guessed I was off the hook this time, after everything I'd been through. "Anyway, where are the rest of the Muppet Babies? I haven't seen any of them this morning, and I've been watching you like a creepy weirdo for at least an hour."

I chuckled. "Comforting to know."

"You fallen out with them, or something?"

I shrugged. "Santana seemed fine when I spoke with her yesterday."

"Seems, madam? I know not seems."

"Eh?"

He rolled his eyes. "It's Shakespeare, you philistine."

"I'm sure everything's peachy. They're probably steering clear so Wade and I can patch things up when he wakes up. They're good like that." I let the hint dangle in my voice, but Finch didn't take it.

"See, that's why you need me around. I'm not leaving your side for anything. I've even got a puke bucket ready for when the beast does wake up." He kicked a genuine bucket that he'd managed to find somewhere, probably just so he could make that joke.

"You really haven't seen anyone this morning?" That hurt me a little bit, though I'd never admit it to Finch.

He grinned. "I may have been exaggerating slightly. I saw Isadora and Louella earlier, but they're on some menial assignments for Captain Whitehall around the coven. They said the rest of the Muppet Babies were doing similar stuff. Not Raffe, though—that liability is on probation. No need to guess why."

He nodded toward the other occupant of the ward. Levi. He was still out cold, which was probably for the best. He wouldn't take kindly to finding out he'd been usurped while he slept, and then there was the whole deal with his son almost murdering him to come to terms with.

"Poor Raffe," I murmured. Raffe was no more responsible for what he'd done than Wade was, but I knew he'd be beating himself up about letting his djinn get the better of him.

Finch snorted. "You've got a warped idea of empathy. He almost squished Levi's head like a watermelon. Not that that would've been such a bad thing."

"See, this is why nobody trusts you. You can't go around saying stuff like that."

"I can to you." He smiled shyly, before turning back to kicking his bucket in a really irritating way.

A sense of order seemed to be coming back to the SDC, emerging from the ashes of Levi's dictatorship. Imogene hadn't seemed too thrilled about becoming the new director, but at least she wasn't resisting the need to jump into action. The fact that she was still working on temporary amnesty for Finch was comforting, too, even if she didn't personally trust him. And it was good to see Alton back in a position of usefulness. He seemed happier when he had something to do… and wasn't behind bars. At least, that had been the vibe I'd gotten from him last night, when I'd bumped into him on my way back to the infirmary.

After Levi's colossal screw-up, the upper echelons of magical society now knew about Echidna and Katherine's advancement to the final ritual, and they'd all gone straight into high alert. Garrett was dealing with the magical children to make sure they stayed safe, and everyone finally appeared to have a useful purpose, instead of being kicked to the sidelines. However, one question remained—how many of the higher-ups would actually do something about it, and how many of them were under the cult's stealthy influence? Only time would tell, but any inaction would be one heck of an indicator as to who was being manipulated and whose minds were still free of Katherine's grasp.

"Ooh, battle stations." Finch smirked and gestured toward Wade.

"What?" I glanced down in time to see Wade stir beneath the covers. He groaned softly, his eyes blinking awake. He looked around in confusion for a moment before he set his gaze on me. I braced myself and held the satchel close to my side, terrified that it hadn't worked, that Wade would lunge at me again with that wild look in his eyes. Instead, he smiled sadly.

"Harley," he croaked.

I squeezed his hand. "I'm here."

"Yeah, he can see that," Finch muttered. I shot him daggers, and he held up his hands in mock surrender. He wasn't going to ruin this for me, and if he dared to try, I'd kick him out of this infirmary so fast it'd make his head spin.

Wade smiled up at me. "We've got a guard dog, huh?"

"Unfortunately," I replied.

"What happened?" He struggled to sit up, clamping his free hand to his temple. "I don't remember much."

Finch snorted. "Convenient."

I ignored him and held Wade's hand tighter. As he looked at me with confused eyes, I relayed everything that had gone on since we'd decided to go to New York to steal the Grimoire. I left nothing out, no matter how much it hurt me to tell him what he'd done. Not that it was all bad—I had the good news of Imogene taking over to soften the rest of it, although that came with the revelation that Raffe had nearly caved Levi's skull in. He looked horrified, his face growing pale as I recounted the story of our journey through the underbelly of the New York Coven and his brutal attack on me. I finished by telling him about the Romany hex, in the hopes it'd make him feel less awful.

"So, it wasn't your fault," I said. "Katherine had managed to hex my pendant, probably when I got too close in Tartarus, and it twisted your mind so that up was down, and left was right, and love was hate. You didn't mean to hurt me, I know that. You couldn't control what she'd done to you through that pendant." Another mole or cultist might have hexed the pendant, but the only people I'd been around since being reunited with Wade were Finch, Jacob, Garrett, and Kenzie. Remington, too, but the first hint of the weirdness had started before our meeting in San Francisco. That left Tartarus and Katherine as the only option.

Wade turned to look at Finch. "Thank you for stopping me."

"What?" Finch's eyes widened in surprise.

"Thank you for standing in the way. If anything had happened to Harley,

I'd never have been able to forgive myself. I might have a doozy of a headache from whatever you hit me with, but I've got you to thank for keeping her alive."

He shrugged petulantly. "Someone had to."

"Nevertheless, I'm grateful to you."

He smirked. "Does that mean you owe me?"

Wade frowned. "I wouldn't go that far."

"Can't blame a guy for trying."

With that, Wade turned back to me. "I'm so sorry, Harley. You must have been terrified of me. I'm so sorry if I scared you, or made you think that I didn't love you, or made you think that I actually wanted to hurt you." Tears glittered in his deep-green eyes. "You have to know that I'd never do that. I'd rather die a thousand times over than hurt you."

I nodded. "I know."

"Do you? You're looking at me like you don't even know me." He dropped his chin to his chest.

Leaning over, I cupped his face in my hands and forced him to look back into my eyes. "I do know you. I know you weren't responsible for what happened. I'm not scared of you, Wade. You'd have to do a lot more than try to kill me to make me scared of you. I'm not scared of Katherine, and she's tried a handful of times." I grinned at him, trying to coax a smile onto his face.

"Yeah, and she *really* meant it," Finch interjected. "No hex necessary."

I rolled my eyes. "Ignore the idiot in the room."

"That's not a nice thing to say to a guy who's just come out of a hex," Finch said snarkily. "Sorry about her, Wade. For an Empath, she's got a surprising lack of actual empathy."

Wade chuckled. "Has Krieger got any drugs to knock him out so I can apologize to you properly?"

"I could always ask." I gazed into his eyes, happy to see some light coming back into them.

"I really am sorry, Harley. I can't even begin to describe how sorry I am." He turned sad again. "I'm almost glad I don't have any memory of it, because I don't know how I'd deal with that. I love you, Harley. I love you so much. And I promise, as of this moment, that I will never do anything to hurt you again. I'll be on the lookout for Katherine's spells, and I'll never let her get a hold of me again."

I brushed my thumb across his cheek. "I'm just glad you've come back to me. I love you so much, Wade. I thought I'd lost you back there, and I didn't know if it could ever be fixed. You've got no idea how happy it makes me just to be able to sit here, right now, and look at you, and know you're my Wade again."

"I'll always be yours, Harley."

I leaned closer as he lifted his chin, his lips meeting mine in a tender graze that sent bolts of electricity through my veins. I held his face tighter, sinking deeper into his kiss, and his own hands slid around my waist, pulling me up onto the edge of the bed. Suddenly, his hands were in my hair as he kissed me with the passion of a man who'd been separated from his lover for far too long. I kissed him back with equal desperation, reveling in the rough brush of his stubbled jaw, enjoying the rough and the smooth together. The rest of the world, and all my multitude of worries, fell away as I disappeared into his kiss and his touch. He was definitely my Wade again, and I was grateful beyond all sense for that.

"Can we keep it PG-13, kids?" Finch's voice shattered the delicious moment, and I could've punched him in the face. "I'm not sure this is sanitary. We're in an infirmary, for Pete's sake. Think of the germs!"

I pulled away from Wade, the two of us grinning like idiots. "I might go and find those drugs now, to knock him out."

"Finch, get out." Wade shot a warning look at him.

Finch rolled his eyes. He got up and stalked out of the room in sullen silence. I felt kind of bad for him, but I wasn't going to argue, seeing as Wade and I hadn't had a moment alone in… well, forever.

As soon as Finch had gone, Wade scooped me up into his arms and pulled me into his lap. His mouth was on mine before I even knew what was happening, his hands trailing a delicious line up my spine as he held me close. I kissed him feverishly, my hands in his hair, my body flush against his as we disappeared into each other. I thought about all the times I'd wanted to tear off his expensive shirts, but I lacked the courage to tear away his hospital gown now, with Finch on the other side of the infirmary door. Nevertheless, I pressed my palms to his chest, feeling the rapid beat of his heart as we sank deeper into the kiss, his tongue caressing mine and his teeth gently grazing my bottom lip, making me shiver with excitement.

I felt his strength as he flipped me over and laid me down on the bed, smiling at me. He leaned back in, kissing me harder. My hands smoothed along the taut muscle of his abdomen. His hand came to rest on my thigh, squeezing it gently, as his mouth caught mine. I pulled him down, letting his emotions flow into me, feeling the vibrant pulse of his love and desire for me. I was desperate for his touch, but now wasn't the time or the place. And that sucked massively.

"I missed you," he murmured against my neck, as he planted kisses along the curve of it.

I hugged him tightly to me. "Not as much as I missed you."

"I'm sorry for everything, Harley. I'm sorry that I hurt you." He pulled back and traced the outlines of my bruises, before leaning back in to kiss them. "I won't hurt you again, I promise. I'll protect myself from hexes from now on. I'll be vigilant."

"Is this your idea of sexy talk?" I chuckled against his shoulder.

He pulled away again. "I mean it, Harley. I feel terrible about what happened. I don't want to be a liability to you—I don't ever want to put you in that position again."

I kissed him on the nose. "You aren't a liability to me, Wade. You're literally one of my greatest strengths. I wouldn't even be here if it wasn't for your stubbornness, and that's no exaggeration. You're everything to me. You're the person who keeps me going when I feel like everything is hopeless. Just thinking about you saved me when I thought my affinities were going to tear me apart. I love you, Wade. And that love is what keeps me fighting, because if we don't survive Katherine, I'll never get to know how deep and how far that love can go. And I want to. I really, really want to."

"I feel the same way," Wade whispered, his voice thick with emotion. "I love you so much that it hurts sometimes. I love you so much that I don't know what I'd do without you. I—"

"Yo, you want to hurry it up in there?" Finch's voice barked through the door. "Hate to be a killjoy, but there's no sexy time allotted in the schedule. And I don't think you'd be too happy if Katherine won because you two couldn't keep your paws off each other."

I collapsed in a fit of giggles, and Wade did, too. It was so nice to hear him laugh again. I'd forgotten how much I missed his laugh, and his smile, and the way he was when he wasn't up to his eyeballs in stress. I didn't know when we'd get the chance to be alone again, just him and me with no outside pressures, but I'd savor this moment until we had that opportunity again. After all, if we couldn't have this, then what the heck were we fighting for?

"Are you decent?" The door opened and Finch stepped back in, his hand covering his eyes. Cue me and Wade scrambling to make it look like we hadn't been smooching each other's faces off in his hospital bed. Wade shot me a cheeky grin as I readjusted any clothes that were askew and waited for Finch to take his hand away from his face.

Wade chuckled. "What are you doing here, anyway? I would've thought Imogene would've sent you packing to Purgatory by now, Finch."

"Nice use of alliteration," Finch replied. "But no, I'm still hanging around like a bad smell. Imogene's given me temporary amnesty, so long as I stay within the SDC and I don't leave Harley's side. So, you've got her to blame for me ruining the romance. Ugh, now you've got me doing it."

"At least we managed to get the Grimoire," Wade said, his fingertips stroking the dappled bruising and faint singe-marks on my throat. I could tell he hated looking at the marks he'd made. "Which means we've got work to do."

I nodded. "You can say that again."

"Which means we've got work to do," Finch parroted.

"We need to figure out what's in the Grimoire," I replied, trying to shut Finch out. "Specifically, how to find the hidden pages inside it. I think I might have found one when I was in Imogene's office, but it was all jumbled and weird. I couldn't read it, but that doesn't mean I can't."

Finch frowned. "Whoa, you didn't tell me that."

I shrugged. "I didn't think it was important yet. It's just comforting to know there are actually secret spells in there, but we still need to find a way to discover all of them, and then decipher the code that my parents put on them. That first page might have been a fluke, you never know."

"Let's hope it wasn't," Wade replied.

Finch grinned. "Well then, it's a good thing I've kept to Imogene's rules, or you'd be stumped. I know a decent spot in the coven where we can open the

Grimoire and look through it for as long as we need. It'll be isolated enough that this chump and I can save your ass if you don't handle the magic well."

"That's a good point. We don't know how you might react to the spells, especially now that your Suppressor is gone," Wade added. "Plus, you haven't exactly reacted well in the past."

"Not cool, Wade. You should never bring up a lady's shortcomings." Finch tutted.

"Just so you know, Finch, if I accidentally summon Erebus again, it's your name that's going into the ring." I shot him a look, and he smirked.

"You wouldn't do that to me, Sis. You like me too much."

Ugh, he's going to be insufferable. I smiled.

As Finch reluctantly helped Wade out of his bed and put him in something other than a somewhat risqué gown, I took a moment to tell Jacob and Krieger where we were going. Although, I couldn't help but steal a glance at Wade's peachy backside as he turned to put proper clothes on. *Like two Christmas hams, and just as delicious.*

"Keep your burner phones on," Krieger urged, while I tried not to blush, hoping the doctor hadn't noticed where I'd been staring.

I nodded. "For sure. How's the detector coming along?"

Jacob groaned. "It's never-ending."

"That's not exactly true," Krieger interjected. "We're getting there."

"Who's your friend?" I spotted a strange girl crouched under Krieger's workbench. She was definitely hiding from me—there were no two ways about it.

"Oh... she's a... she's a friend of mine," Jacob replied stiffly.

"A human friend, called Suri. Jacob saved her from Lethe. She's staying here, at my request, until we can be sure that a memory wipe will hold." Krieger looked shifty, and now I knew why. He was covering for Jacob, out of some misplaced sense of kindness. It only took a little hint of Empathy to feel their emotions pulsing outward; Jacob and Suri were both besotted with each other. That worried me, though I couldn't say anything about it right now. I mean, she was adorable and everything, but this couldn't possibly end well for Jacob. He'd have been better off letting Krieger wipe her mind there and then and letting her go. This world wasn't the right place for humans, and he was already scarred for life after what had happened to the

Smiths. What if something like that happened to Suri because he cared about her?

Speaking of which, a thought hit me—it was probably better for the Smiths if their memories were wiped, too. They'd seen way too much and knew way too much, which was putting them at risk. Ever since that huge memory dump I'd gotten back in the New York tunnels, I'd been having a few changes of heart over certain things. It wasn't that I'd become colder, simply more logical and less emotional about matters. It was almost like I was seeing things through my parents' eyes, making me understand why some difficult choices had to be made. Including Suri's memory wipe.

However, that could wait. The Grimoire couldn't.

FORTY-TWO

Harley

Finch's "decent spot" turned out to be an abandoned classroom in a very old part of the coven that I'd never been to. It looked pretty similar to the classrooms in the newer part of the coven, though it had a dirty chalkboard standing front and center, and the vaulted ceiling, complete with a Neo-Classical frieze of winged gods, didn't quite fit with the current aesthetic. It looked more like something I would've expected to see in New York. And some of the walls had taken on patches of that same oily glaze I'd seen back in New York—a tell-tale sign that this part of the coven had been left to decay, since it was apparently too much hassle to just sever it completely.

"Geez, Finch. Is there anything you don't know about the SDC?" I glanced at him, expecting to see a smug expression. Instead, he looked sad, like he had the weight of the world on his shoulders.

He trailed his fingertips across the desks. "I used to come here with Adley."

"Ah..." What was I supposed to say to that after everything he'd told me? He'd given her up for us, and that decision was probably going to haunt him for the rest of his life. Especially here, in the room where he'd snuck off with her.

"How did you even find this place?" Wade marveled at the room.

Finch forced a smile onto his face. "You know how it is, when you've just got to have a moment alone with your woman. You'll always find what you need. What can I say? The SDC delivered."

I removed the Grimoire from my satchel and laid it out on a desk, sitting down in front of it. With the book unopened in front of me, I felt the enormity of what I was about to do and all the weight of responsibility that came with it. Like Imogene had said, I might well have been the final hope in stopping Katherine dead in her tracks. No person alive could know that and not feel terrified about messing it up.

"Well then, here goes nothing," I murmured. Finch and Wade were standing off to one side, ready to intervene if everything went awry.

Slowly, I reached out to touch the cover, my body buzzing with the Chaos spilling out from inside. I let my fingertips move across the black pearl and the white pearl, and the indented vines that had been inlaid in silver and gold. *Guide me through this, okay?* I didn't know if my mom and dad could hear me, but at least touching this book brought me close to them. They'd created everything inside it, and I was about to try and find the hidden spells that they'd put there for me to discover.

My nerves jangled as I opened the cover and looked at the first page. Finally, I had the chance to look through it, with no pressure or fear of being caught in the act. Finding nothing of interest on the first page, I flipped through the fully written leaves until I found that secret symbol again. It was tucked away in the corner of a spell called "The Binding of Souls." Reading through it, it seemed to be a more romantic kind of magic, rather than the kind that bound souls to the earth, the way that Katherine had done with my mom. I wondered if my mom and dad had performed this to bind their souls together. If they had, then perhaps they really had been able to reunite in the afterlife, whatever that might be.

As I touched the Veve of Erzulie design, the whispers grew louder and more intense inside my head. This hadn't happened in the office with Imogene, making me realize that the Grimoire had chosen this moment, when I was more or less alone with it, to whisper its secrets again. "The blood is strong. The blood is clear. The blood will bring clarity." Those three sentences pounded between my temples, repeating in an endless cycle.

Is that how I read this? The hidden spell had appeared, but it was no clearer to me. The strange symbols and words swirled around the page, just as they'd done before, moving beneath the fully written page. I fixated on the symbols, trying to go into some kind of *Beautiful Mind* mode, where the words and symbols would somehow come together to give me the answer. They didn't, but that didn't stop me from staring at the page, begging it to become clear.

Across the room, Finch and Wade were busy putting up protection spells, more for their sake and the coven's than mine. If I accidentally caused the interdimensional bubble to crack, they needed to make sure that all angles were covered. Returning my attention to the book, I delved deeper into the symbols, trying to make sense of them. The trouble was, they seemed to be from a mishmash of cultures—voodoo glyphs, with some random bits of Cyrillic, Hangul, and Arabic thrown in, just to baffle me even more. And that was just the stuff I vaguely recognized.

You need to help me... I couldn't do this alone. I needed my mom and dad now, more than ever. Only, they weren't here—I just had these pages as a reminder that they were gone, and they were never coming back. My sadness flowed outward, spilling right into the pages and spreading across the jumbled ink.

"I can't feel her moving. How can I concentrate on this when she's not moving?" A very clear voice echoed in my head. A soft, feminine voice that I recognized as keenly as my own. My mom was talking to me, transcending time and space to enter my brain.

"You don't feel that?" That was my dad, his voice a rich baritone that boomed into the core of my chest.

"Don't tease me, Hiram. I can't feel anything. I should be able to by now, shouldn't I?" My mom sounded worried.

"There! Didn't you feel the peanut kick?" There was a pause.

"I... I think I felt it that time!" My mom sounded deliriously happy. I could hear them laughing together, all her worries disappearing in a split second of joy.

Peanut? Was that what they'd called me? The voices shifted, the room they were in sounding more echoey.

"Nope, I don't see it," Hiram said.

"There! That's her head, and that's her cute little butt, and those are her legs," my mom replied, chuckling.

"You sure she isn't a he? That looks like a—"

"She's going to be our daughter, Hiram," my mom interjected. "We're going to have a little girl."

"If you say so."

"You're not happy?" My mom sounded sad.

"I couldn't be happier, love. I'm just being silly." He paused. "I can't wait to meet her. Our little peanut."

The voices shifted location again, their surroundings making them sound more muffled, almost like I was hearing them underwater.

"We should write one that locks your sister deep in the earth, like she's one of the Titans." My dad chuckled, but my mom didn't sound too impressed. I realized, in that moment, that I was hearing clips of their conversations, from when they'd written the spells into the book. Although, I hadn't seen one that involved trapping Katherine inside the earth. I could've used something like that.

"It's not funny, Hiram. She's dropped off the face of the earth. Nobody's heard from her in months."

"That's probably because you tried to invite her to the wedding. You should be happy she didn't show up. She'd have waltzed in like freaking Maleficent and cursed everyone. You know what she's like."

"Yeah, I do know… That's what worries me." My mom seemed to be the more logical of the two, and it hurt to know that she'd been concerned about her sister. If she'd acted on those concerns earlier, I wondered how things might have turned out. Would I be with them right now, in the land of the living? Or would Katherine have killed them anyway, and me too?

The voices shifted again.

"What are we supposed to do, Hiram?" My mom sounded like she was in tears.

"Don't worry, Hester. Katherine isn't going to risk getting thrown in Purgatory. And even if she does try something, we've got these spells to protect ourselves and the peanut. Nothing's going to happen to us."

"What if she comes for us? You saw her face at Christmas. She wanted to kill us all then, I'm sure of it. She's gone mad, Hiram, and I don't think there's anything I can do for her this time."

"You've wasted enough time on her, sweetheart. We just need to make sure we can fight her if she does anything stupid." He paused. "I'll always be here for you. Always. I'm not leaving your side. And if she wants to hurt you because of something I've done, then she'll have to go through me."

"I love you." That damn near broke me in two. The dramatic irony was unbearable. Kathcrine did go through Hiram, and she murdered my mom by using him. What hurt the most was how earnest he sounded. He genuinely meant what he was saying, but he hadn't realized that Katherine would use his greatest weakness against him—my mom.

"Not as much as I love you," he replied softly.

The voices shifted again, the clips getting shorter. At first, I'd thought this insight was pretty amazing, but now it was borderline torture. I had to listen to my parents' last moments, more or less, and that wasn't easy to stomach.

"No matter what happens, we have to protect her," my mom said.

"We will, love. We will. Katherine isn't getting her," my dad replied.

"Do you promise?"

"With all my heart."

My mom's voice disappeared altogether, leaving only my dad's. He was talking rapidly, like he was running out of time. He seemed to be putting one more spell into the Grimoire, going solo, and that meant one thing. By this point, my mom's death warrant had likely already been signed, and my dad was doing everything he could to keep the promise he'd made to her, to protect me.

"It's too late for us," my dad murmured. "It's too late for us, but there's still hope. I'm going to kill my wife tonight, and there's nothing I can do to stop it. But I can stop her. I can stop Katherine. I have to." His voice broke, as though he was crying. "This spell will put an end to her, once and for all. And though I won't live to see it, I hope that my daughter might be saved. Let her be saved. Let her know that she was loved. I love you, Hester." He choked on his words, whispering them as he spoke with a shaky voice. "I love you, peanut. I'm sorry. I hope this can make it better, in some small way. Forgive me. Please, forgive me for what I'm about to do."

I wrenched away from the Grimoire, realizing I'd been almost nose-to-paper with it. Where there'd been nothing but a jumble of symbols, now there was an actual spell. The inky etchings had spread out, forming coherent sentences that filled the page in a hasty scrawl. There was just one major problem: the spell was written in an ancient language that I couldn't read.

I kept looking at it, feeling rattled by the dangerous buzz that shivered off the unfamiliar text. This wasn't a simple spell—this was dark and menacing, and very, very important. I didn't know why it was important, but it was just a sense I got. It *felt* important. My dad had been crying and whispering as he wrote the spell, to the point where I could see splashes on the ink. This was the last entry in the Grimoire. The very last thing he wrote before he gave in to the Sal Vínna curse and killed my mom. And it was on one of the hidden pages.

But what does it mean? I wasn't leaving this room until I figured it out. My parents had left this for me, and I wouldn't let them down. Not now. Not after they'd sacrificed themselves so that I might find this and end Katherine for good.

FORTY-THREE

Jacob

I stared at the magical detector.

After so many hours of work, it was almost finished. A few more screws, and this thing would be complete again. We had an audience, too. Krieger, Louella, and Isadora were standing around the workbench. The latter two had come back to the infirmary as soon as Krieger called Isadora to tell her we were close to finishing it. And, where Isadora went, so did Louella. They'd become a double act lately. I didn't mind. Louella needed good people around her, and Isadora was the best.

Raffe, Santana, Tatyana, Dylan, and Astrid had also come to watch the grand unveiling. So it was more or less a full house. No Suri—she'd been sent back to the quarantine room, since this was top-secret info. There was no Harley, no Wade, no Finch, and no Garrett either, but they were here in spirit. *Actually, come to think of it, where are they?* I'd sent a couple of texts and received pretty vague replies. Garrett was back in LA, so he was accounted for. But the other three? I tried not to let it worry me. Harley was a big girl. Whatever she was up to, she could handle herself. Besides, Imogene had probably given her something to do, same as everyone else. The rest of the Rag Team were shirking right now, but it was for a good cause.

"Could you pass me that piece, Jacob?" Krieger gestured to a small bronze panel. I nodded and handed it to him while the rest of the team stared in excitement.

"Is this thing really going to work?" Dylan asked.

"We'll find out soon enough," I replied. *It better, after the work we've put in.*

"I'm sure the two of them have been doing a great job." Tatyana shoved Dylan lightly in the shoulder, making him pull her in for a squeeze. I had to fight the urge to get between them. Instead, I focused on Suri. She was in the nearby room. Why would I need to crush on Tatyana when I had her to crush on?

Santana smirked. "I'm just waiting for Katherine freaking Shipton to pop up on that thing so we can snag her once and for all."

"Because that keeps working out so well for us," Raffe said. He looked sick, barely able to prop himself up on the workbench.

"Hey, don't talk like that. We're going to get this bitch." Santana put her hand on Raffe's shoulder. He instantly relaxed, leaning his head against her.

Astrid nodded. "I've got good feelings about this detector."

I passed Krieger the last panel, letting him fix it into place. He'd made some modifications to fit the new alchemical battery. As soon as that was fitted, we just needed to add the battery, and the device would be good to go. Provided we'd put everything back together right and didn't accidentally cause the kind of explosion that would bring the whole coven down. *No pressure...*

"This could be exactly what we've been looking for," Astrid added. "Especially since Smartie's had no luck with the CCTV and news channels."

Louella sighed. "This is pretty much our last chance of finding her, isn't it?"

"It'll work." Isadora smiled at me reassuringly. "They've been working for ages on this device. There's no way it's not going to work."

What did I say about no pressure?

"I think it's time, Jacob." Krieger picked up the gold-and-glass tube that held Rita's battery. I wanted to swear, I was so nervous, but Isadora would've yelled at me. She'd always told me that "manners maketh the man," and I didn't think that stretched to swear words. No matter how necessary.

"Now?" I gulped.

"It'll work," Louella said quietly. Everyone nodded in agreement, though I could've cut the tension in the room with a knife.

"It's a shame Suri can't be here. She'd love to see this stuff." I realized I'd spoken out loud, and now everyone was staring at me.

Astrid smiled at me encouragingly. "You know, it's actually kind of nice to have another non-magical around the place." I knew Astrid had been having some emotional issues after she'd died and been brought back to life, so it was odd to hear her speak so kindly. I appreciated it, though. That smile had even seemed genuine, and she didn't smile very often anymore.

"Shame it won't last," Raffe muttered. "You know the rules. I doubt even Imogene could bend that one."

My heart sank.

"Speaking of which, does Imogene know about our human friend yet?" Santana glanced at me.

I shook my head. "I'm going to tell her once we know the device works. I'm going to ask her to reconsider wiping Suri's mind." Everyone gaped at me, like I'd just said I wanted to lop off the Easter Bunny's head.

"Are you insane?" Dylan stifled a laugh.

I shrugged. "Maybe."

"I think it's a good idea," Astrid chimed in. "Does it really matter by now if Suri gets to keep her memories? She hasn't run off. She's not scared of us. What difference does it make, if just one human gets to know about the magical world?"

"It sets a dangerous precedent," Louella said. *Seriously?* I'd thought we were over this.

"We can talk about this later." Krieger cleared his throat. "We have more pressing matters to attend to. Namely, if we can actually get this device to work. If we can't, then Astrid is right: it won't matter if one human knows about the magical world, because there will be no world for it to matter in."

I nodded slowly. "Sorry, Krieger."

"Well then, now that everyone's attention is back to the task at hand, shall we try this?" Krieger's hands were shaking as he brought the battery to the magical detector. Carefully, he slotted it into the space he'd made. Everyone held their breath, me included.

An orange light shot through the center of the battery, and I could've sworn every member of the Rag Team gasped. Two glowing sparks erupted from either end of the tube. And then... they fizzled out, the orange light dimming back down to just dull metal.

"Something must be wrong," Isadora murmured.

Krieger cast her a disappointed look. "You don't say." Exasperated, he fiddled with the battery, but the same thing kept happening. It lit up, and then fizzled out. The rest of the present Rag Team looked disappointed, too. No, it was more than that—they looked crushed. We needed this so much right now, and any sort of hiccup felt like a massive blow to our collective confidence. We needed it to work, or it was game over. We'd never find Katherine.

"I was so sure it would work," Louella said. "And then it goes and snuffs out like a damp squib."

Santana chuckled. "Damp squib? Where did you pick that up?"

"I've become a bit of an anglophile, watching old British movies to help me relax," Louella replied.

"Hey, whatever floats your boat." Santana flashed her a grin. "It's telenovelas for me. Call me cliché, but I love those things."

"I've been reading a lot of Dostoyevsky," Tatyana added thoughtfully. "There's nothing like a bit of *Crime and Punishment* to—"

"What's that?" Louella jabbed her finger at the back of the magical detector, cutting Tatyana off.

Krieger frowned. "What's what?"

"There's something stuck at the bottom there." Louella got closer, pointing out what she'd seen. "It's underneath that strip of wires. It's like a fragment of metal or something."

"Jacob, could you?" Krieger looked at me desperately. His hands were shaking. Getting the fragment out needed steady hands and a delicate touch to avoid accidentally tearing out any of the wires.

"What is it?" Astrid leaned in.

Krieger sighed. "I think it might be a piece of the lead suppressor that I'd put in to compensate for the Chaos. One of them cracked when we were dismantling the device—this must be a fragment from where it broke. I can't believe I didn't see it."

"It's not your fault," Isadora replied. "You've been working around the clock to fix this. I'm surprised you're even standing."

"So am I," Krieger admitted. He really had put everything into getting this device going, and I felt for him. He was at breaking point right now. If this device didn't work, he'd crumble completely. His heart and soul and blood and sweat were in this thing, as gross as that might've sounded.

I took his place and tried to reach into the device, careful to avoid nudging the wires, but my hands were shaky and sweaty, too. Every time I thought I had it, it slipped out of my clammy grasp. I couldn't risk being more forceful, in case I knocked something else out.

"Here, let me." Louella sidled up to me and took up a pair of tweezers. With hands as steady as concrete, she reached into the device and whipped the lead piece right out. As soon as she did, a small golden connector clicked into the hole underneath—the one the lead piece had been hiding. She staggered back as the battery fired into life, sending a jolt of sparking energy right through the detector. Only, Louella's hand was still in the device. Her body shuddered, like she was getting the worst electric shock of her life, the current searing through the tweezers and into her skin.

"Louella!" Isadora lunged forward just as the fingers that had been holding the tweezers exploded in a burst of black dust and spatters of blood. The tweezers didn't fare much better. They just crumbled in her hands, like iron filings.

Louella stumbled into the counter behind her, hissing as she clutched her injured hand to her chest. Blood smeared across her T-shirt, right across the eyes of Hello Kitty. She always said she wore those T-shirts ironically, but I wasn't so sure. I glanced at Raffe in time to see his eyes roll back into his head. Santana darted toward him and caught him before he fell, her arms wrapped around him as she urged him back into consciousness. He was breathing heavily, his skin tinged with the faintest flush of red. There was something about the blood, in Raffe's weakened state, that had clearly gotten the djinn going.

"It's okay, I've got you. Stay with me," Santana whispered, holding him closer. I glanced at Louella, who was wincing as she held onto the spot where her fingers had been. She could grow them back, I was guessing, but that didn't mean it wasn't painful. She was dealing with it like a pro, though.

"I'm fine, by the way," Louella announced, with a half-smile. "Nothing major. No need for panic stations. No need for anyone to swoop in and scoop *me* into their arms."

Dylan snorted, shooting a wry glance at Raffe, who was blinking back into normality. Tatyana smacked him over the back of his head, prompting Santana to offer her a grateful smile.

"Ow!" he yelped.

"Oh come on, you're a Herculean. That didn't hurt." Tatyana kissed the spot where she'd smacked him regardless.

"Raffe's been through a lot. Leave him alone or you'll have me to deal with," Santana muttered, half-joking. "Are you sure you're okay, Louella?"

She nodded. "Dealing with it. I'll be fine in a minute."

"Hey, in my defense, I don't normally go white at the sight of blood," Raffe replied with a weak laugh.

"Well, I think it's romantic," Tatyana said. "It shows Santana cares."

"I care!" Dylan protested.

"Don't worry, I'm happy with the cuddle I'm getting." Raffe laughed.

"It's working!" Krieger shrieked. "It's working! I'm *so* sorry about your fingers, Louella, but the device is actually working!"

Louella shrugged and turned to run her bloodied hand under the faucet. "Do you think this is the first finger I've lost? It's fine, I just need to adjust to the pain until it grows back."

"The coven's lizard strikes again," Dylan joked.

"Eh, Regen, if you don't mind," Louella corrected. "Or gecko, or something cute, but not lizard."

"Hello? I just said the device is working!" Krieger yelped. "Why is nobody reacting?"

"Huh?" I stared at the magical detector. The rest of the Rag Team did the same. With Louella's fingers being singed off, we'd been sort of distracted. Sure enough, it really looked like it was working. The battery had lit up a fiery orange again, sending its energy through the circuits and into the orb of Chaos at the center of the newly shrunken device. My strand of Chaos spiraled like a tornado, reacting to the energy. It sputtered and sparked, before settling into a steady rhythm.

The revamped device was no bigger than a Chinese takeout box, and the whole thing was whirring smoothly. The circuits were holding. The circuits were freaking holding! Had Rita been in the room, I would've thrown myself at her feet and kissed her pricey shoes. As long as Suri hadn't been in the room, too.

"What do we do next?" I looked to Krieger.

"We test it!" He was grinning like an idiot. The relief he was feeling must've been huge.

"How?"

Krieger chuckled. "Point this part at someone." He gestured to a small arrow on the top of the device. "Come on, try it."

Nervously, I approached the device. I turned it by its protective panels and aimed it at Krieger. At first, nothing happened. Looking more anxious, he stepped in and toyed with some of the dials. As soon as he stepped away, the Chaos orb sparked with a bronze glow. The next minute, his image appeared as a hologram, alongside a list of information.

Name: Wolfgang Krieger

Affinity: Dark

Abilities: Organa, Fire

The detector had done it. It could literally read anyone's strand of Chaos and recognize them, forming an image and a list from what it detected. Unlike Astrid's beloved Smartie, it didn't have to hack into any kind of database. Instead, it drew its information straight from Chaos itself.

"That's friggin' incredible!" Santana gasped.

"It works even better than I could have imagined." Krieger beamed from ear to ear.

Curious, I turned the device and pointed it at Astrid. A very faint image came up. And, instead of a big list, it simply flashed with the words—*Human. Astrid Hepler.* I guessed it was fainter because she hardly had any Chaos inside her. Just the usual, dimmed sparks that humans had.

Astrid smiled sadly. "That sucks. I was hoping it might find some secret magical-ness that I didn't know about. I guess I should've known it would be there in black and white."

"Sorry," I mumbled, turning it away.

"But how can you use it to find Katherine?" Tatyana asked.

Krieger smiled. "I broaden the calibrations, extending it as far as I want to. See?" He leaned forward eagerly and turned the device into the empty space between Isadora and Raffe. He turned a few of the dials, prompting the Chaos orb to light up even brighter. A name flashed up, accompanied by a picture. I didn't recognize the guy, but he looked middle-aged, with jowly cheeks and a worn-out expression.

Name: Harold Milliner

Affinity: Light

Abilities: Earth, Air

"It found the janitor!" Dylan whooped. "My man!"

"How about this?" Krieger turned the dials again. Another image flashed up. This time, it was a younger woman with long blonde hair and blue eyes.

Name: Alice Fowler

Affinity: Dark

Abilities: Telekinesis, Water

Louella nearly choked. "Alice Fowler is a magical?"

"You know her?" I glanced her way.

"She works in the archives! I never knew she was a coven member! Sneaky girl—she never mentioned anything to me. I just thought she was a human. I'll have to have some words about this."

Krieger chuckled. "You see, I just have to tell the device how far I need it to search. At the moment, it's scanning the Fleet Science Center and its surrounding area. I can ask it to specifically search for a magical, too, which is how we'll search for Katherine Shipton. However, that's going to take a while longer to calibrate, if I'm to use that rag that Finch left me. Blood is a tricky thing to blend with technology, especially blood that isn't fresh— organic and mechanic rarely like to mix."

"Lots of knob twisting?" Santana asked.

"Exactly. A lot of knob twisting. And perhaps the need for another alchemical addition from Ms. Bonnello. This device is extremely sensitive."

This thing is a total gamechanger.

If it could really do what Krieger said it could, then we now had a way of finding Katherine. An actual way. Sure, we didn't know what we'd do, exactly, when we found Katherine—but Harley had that book now. She'd find something in there that could finally put us a step ahead of that psycho. It was obvious that we couldn't keep doing the same things we'd been doing. We'd failed before, time and time again. This time, we needed new weapons. And we couldn't make our move until we had them.

FORTY-FOUR

Jacob

I found out where Harley was, and it worried me. Wade had been to see us and debriefed us on what she was doing. He'd told us everything and had been antsy to get back to her. But a whole day had passed, and she still hadn't come out of the room where she was delving into the Grimoire.

To try and make it easier on her, the Rag Team had taken turns bringing the three of them food and water. Not that Harley seemed to be eating or drinking anything. She was just stuck in a weird black bubble in the corner of the room. At least, she had been whenever it'd been my turn to deliver stuff.

It seemed like they'd be there for ages still. Wade had assured me that she was taking breaks, but I didn't know whether to believe him. Then again, he had her best interests at heart... right? He didn't have the hex on him anymore, so it wasn't like he was trying to slowly kill her. *He better not be, anyway.* Apparently, she got immersed in it way too easily, and it was tough to bring her back out.

Right now, however, I was sitting across from Imogene in her office. Isadora was with me. Krieger was still in the infirmary, tinkering away with the device and adding safety features. I wished I was with him. I liked Imogene, but I hated meetings like this. They always felt ominous, like I was about to get yelled at. Major high school flashbacks.

Imogene had done a good job mixing the office up a bit. The Persian palace had gone. In its place was a room with sleek white walls and a white desk. Everything was white, pretty much, aside from a few bits of color. A blue striped chair. A blue set of drawers. A fancy gold lamp. A few gold things on the desk. It looked like something out of a magazine. So did Imogene, to be fair, even though she looked like she'd had a tough night, her face paler than normal.

"I expect you're wondering why I asked you here," she began, at last, in a quiet voice. "The truth is... How do I even say this? The truth is... I have some news, and it's not good." A tear slipped down her cheek, and she went silent. I shared a shocked look with Isadora.

"Imogene?" Isadora said. "Imogene, what's happened?"

She shook her head. "The magical children that were rescued have been taken. My deputy director is dead. The LA Coven has been forced into lockdown." Her expression looked hollowed, like all the grief had been scooped out of her, leaving her with nothing left to feel. "I wasn't there to protect them, and now they've been taken. Marjorie, Micah... They're missing, and I suspect Katherine is responsible." Her eyes narrowed. "We had every security measure in place, but she is everywhere, and yet nowhere, moving like smoke through solid walls and endless defenses."

"Oh my God..." Isadora gasped. I couldn't even speak. This was terrible, and that was putting it mildly. I felt like throwing up.

Imogene wiped away another tear that managed to sneak out of her eye. I could tell she was trying her hardest to stay professional. "Now Katherine is moving on to the next and last ritual. That's her purpose in stealing these children, I'm certain of it. And I cannot even begin to comprehend what she'll do to them..."

"Did anyone put trackers on the children?" Isadora asked.

Imogene grimaced. "They did, but the trackers have gone dark. Katherine must have removed them, somehow, knowing we would use them."

"How can we stop her?" I asked quietly.

"I don't know, as of yet, but if she's seeking out rare magicals, Louella might be a target again." Imogene fixed her steely gaze on me and Isadora. "As such, Louella must be confined to the infirmary. She must stay with you both, at all times."

"Of course, Imogene," Isadora replied, while I gave a nervous nod. Louella was one of my best friends. If her life was at stake, then that made things way more personal.

Imogene sank back in her chair. "Thank you, both of you. I trust that you'll keep this a secret. I'll tell those who need to know when the timing is somewhat better." She sighed. "I'll inform Harley later tonight, and we'll send out security teams to retrieve the children. We cannot lose hope."

I didn't feel too sure. If Katherine had those kids, she'd do everything in her power to keep them hidden. She'd done it before; she'd do it again. But at least Imogene was doing something. If Levi had been in charge of this, it would've been a total car crash.

"Was there something else?" Isadora prompted.

Imogene nodded. "Yes, thank you for reminding me."

"Is it better news?" I added.

"Sadly not," Imogene replied bitterly. "Remington has met with the National Council. Not a single person is willing to give him a sample of those pills. In fact, they have entirely denied giving any such pulls to Levi, to begin with. And, with Levi still unconscious, we have no means to verify that with him. Hopefully, once Levi awakens, we will be able to discover more, especially with the use of Dr. Krieger's medical interventions."

Isadora pulled a sour face. "So you're saying we've hit a dead end?"

"It would appear so, but Remington has assured me that he'll continue to investigate." She paused. "However, that means the danger remains. Very few people within the magical leadership of the covens, worldwide, can be trusted. Naturally, you'll understand why we can't declare our suspicions publicly."

I smiled nervously. "Then our best bet is to find Katherine and destroy her before she ascends." We had the magical detector, and Harley was working away at the Grimoire. We had everything in place—we just needed it all to come together.

Rattled by everything Imogene had said, we immediately brought Louella to the infirmary. We told her about the stolen kids and the danger she was now in, and she immediately agreed to our version of witness protection. That was good. I wasn't going to let anything happen to her, no matter what. She might have been funny about Suri, but she was my friend. She'd always had my back. Now, it was my turn to return the favor. If Katherine wanted to come after Louella, she'd have to go through me and my portals. I'd keep jumping for the rest of my life if it kept Louella safe.

In addition to looking after Louella and Suri, the most useful way I could spend my time was making sure the magical detector was working, with Krieger's modifications.

"We should do a test run in the Banquet Hall," I said. "To help iron out the kinks."

Krieger nodded. "That sounds very sensible. It needs to be tested in a larger area, with more magicals around. I keep trying to make specific choices, but it can't seem to lock on to the person I want to find. There's too much interference from other magicals, so testing it in a larger crowd may prove useful."

"I'll come with you, Jacob," Isadora insisted. "Krieger, will you watch out for Louella while we're gone? You should probably make sure Suri stays in her room, too."

"Of course, though I'm rather sad I won't get to see the device in action out there." He smiled at Isadora.

She smiled back. "We'll come back with all the results, don't worry. And if there are any glitches, we'll just bring it back so you can keep calibrating it."

"Yes, it's a very sensitive contraption. More sensitive than I anticipated. It is by no means perfect, given that it's the first of its kind."

And I helped build it. That would never stop being awesome.

We hid away in the corner of the Banquet Hall. Setting the device on the table, I concealed it behind a book that I'd set up. Old detective movie style, only no eye-holes to peep out of. Isadora sat next to me as we prepared to test the device on the people in the room. There were still quite a lot of people around, even though it wasn't a set mealtime.

"How are you feeling after what happened in Lethe?" Isadora glanced at me as I twisted one of the dials. It was supposed to tighten the field of detection. "I know we haven't had much chance to talk about it, but it's bound to have affected you. You saw your dad, after all. That can't have been easy. How are you coping with everything?"

I shrugged. "I'm trying not to think about it."

"You should, though. It's not healthy to bottle things up."

I chuckled. "I suppose I'm just waiting for it to lose its fizz before I deal with it."

"Seriously, Jacob. How are you feeling?"

I kept my focus on the dials. "I honestly don't know. I don't think I'm ready to process it."

"I imagine Suri is a good distraction." She smiled.

"Yeah... she is." It was true. I hadn't thought about my dad much with Suri around. And I hadn't really thought about what had happened in Lethe. My only concern was for Suri and keeping her here. That way, I'd never have to think about all the hard stuff that I didn't want to think about. I could just think about Suri and keep things light and fluffy. No tough emotions necessary. Only the good stuff.

"You like her a lot, huh?"

I nodded awkwardly. "Yeah, I kind of do."

"Kind of?"

I rolled my eyes. "Fine, I really do."

"She seems to like you, too." Isadora nudged me playfully.

"Come on, you're making me feel weird."

"Why? Because I'm interested in who you're dating?"

I gaped at her. "We're not... We're not dating." My heart sank. "Besides, I couldn't date her even if I wanted to. You've heard what everyone's been saying. They think Suri should get her memory wiped, even though she doesn't know anything she shouldn't. I doubt I'll be able to change anyone's mind. Rules, remember?"

She laughed. "Rules are made to be broken. Especially coven rules."

"Oh yeah, I forgot how much you hate these things." I smiled at her sadly. "But it doesn't change the facts, does it? Unless..."

"Unless?"

I turned back to the dial. "Unless you can help me with Suri."

"In what way?"

"Well, Imogene might say that Suri doesn't have to have her memory wiped, and she might let her go without doing anything, if you were to give me a little adult backup." I could feel my cheeks getting hot. "I really want to see her again, Iz, but I know I can't keep hiding her here for much longer. It's clearly not safe, and I don't want her to be in danger again."

Isadora sighed. "I'd love to help you, Jacob, but if you don't want her to be in danger, then there's one very simple solution. I don't like it any more than you do, since it's a stupid coven rule, but it might put her out of harm's way. The less she knows, the safer she is."

"You don't really believe that." It wasn't a question. "I'd be careful about it, I promise. I'd make sure she didn't say anything, and I really don't think she would, anyway. She likes us. She likes it here. Why would she risk that?"

"Humans often do foolish things without meaning to."

"What, so someone else's stupidity means I can't have a chance?" I turned to her. "I really like her, Iz. She's kind, and sweet, and smart. She wants to learn about magicals, she doesn't want to expose us. And, honestly, neither of us have had normal lives. She's always on her own, and I... well, I've never had anything normal. I'm not bringing out the violins here, but I want to have something normal, just once. And I can, if you help me. I can have that, with someone who knows what I am and doesn't care."

Isadora sighed. "Damn, did you pick the wrong time to fall for a girl."

I managed a grin. "Tell me about it."

"You're right, though—she does seem like a nice girl. Everyone's taken to her, even if they won't say so. Plus, I think she's even managing to chip away at Louella, which deserves a medal in and of itself." Isadora put her hand on my shoulder. "I already agreed to help you, so what are you worrying about? You know I've got your back."

I fiddled with the knob, just for the sake of keeping my hands busy. "Well, first off, that Imogene will say no. And, secondly, I was worried that you might have changed your mind, after hearing about the missing kids and stuff. You said so yourself, it's safer if Suri is away from here. Wiping her memory is the simple solution. I guess I wondered if you were starting to have doubts."

"Maybe I'm more cautious, and maybe wiping her memory is the simplest solution, but I promised to help you. That hasn't changed." She gave my shoulder a squeeze. "But I do think you should wait another day or two to speak to Imogene. Her circumstances *have* changed. She's crushed over the magical kids being taken, so she's not going to be in a very generous mood, especially not if it means putting someone at risk. Wait a while, until the dust settles, and then go to her."

I stopped what I was doing. "I get it. I'll wait. Plus, it's not like I'm asking Imogene to let Suri stay here, you know? Even if Suri's mom doesn't seem to care about her, she should be back at home, away from the coven. That way, there's less danger. Now that Levi isn't tracking my every move, I could go see her whenever I want, using portals. No evil cultist would be able to follow me there. I'd get Santana to ward Suri's house, too, and—"

"One thing at a time, Jacob," Isadora said softly. "And, right now, we've got much bigger fish to fry. Suri can wait another day while we test this baby and I come up with a strategy for convincing Imogene not to wipe your girlfriend's mind."

I grinned. "She's not my girlfriend."

"Sure, and my name isn't Isadora Merlin."

FORTY-FIVE

Harley

As it turned out, reading a Grimoire wasn't like riding a bike or reading a regular book. This wasn't the kind of thing that came naturally to anyone—well, not to me. I'd discovered the first hidden page, with that dark and ancient spell written on it, but no matter how many times I'd tried to read it out, nothing had happened. To be honest, I wasn't completely sure it wasn't just gibberish, made to look pretty. Perhaps my ability to read unfinished Grimoires only extended to the Latin or English kind of spells. I really hoped not; otherwise, my dad's last ever spell was going to be a total bust.

After that colossal, exasperating failure, I'd decided to delve deeper into the book, and it had already taken up about two days of my life, give or take a few very short breaks. After all, I knew that there couldn't just be the one hidden page. I figured that first one had been a sort of marker, to let me know that there were definitely more in here—I just needed to find them.

Saying that, searching this book on such a deep level was proving to be incredibly intense. I kept unearthing symbols hidden in the corners and in the actual text of some of the fully visible spells, spending hours trying to decipher what it all meant, my eyes swimming by the end of it. Only that first secret spell had turned into actual words, even though I couldn't read them. The rest were playing hard to get, just inky smudges and multicultural marks across the near-liquid pages, their purpose evading me.

It was almost hypnotic, the way they swirled and drifted, dragging me into a strange trance that was tricky to get out of again. If it hadn't been for Wade and Finch yanking at my shoulders until I snapped out of it, these pages would have consumed me by now. I'd be a listless, blathering idiot, yapping on about inky symbols I couldn't figure out.

Totally at my wit's end, I flipped back through the book to the "hidden things" spell. I didn't know how much more staring at pages that didn't freaking do anything I could take. I sat up straighter in my chair at a sudden thought.

If it finds hidden things, maybe it'll find the hidden pages, too.

Nothing in this book seemed to be easy, aside from the spell that had summoned Erebus. It didn't seem fair that a spell so chaotic could have been so simple, while these other ones were super complicated. And, right now, this spell to find hidden things was battering my brain.

In life and death, there is unity beyond measure,
It can be found in the bond that will go on forever.
Through time and space, a pattern appears,
The kind to allay uncertain fears.
A triad unwavering, against all odds,
One that may challenge even the most vengeful of gods.
Through history and legend, power has grown in threes,
And with that, we may find the path to appease.
Light and Dark survives with Gray between,
The bridge that joins, as yet unseen.
To make eyes that see what others cannot,
One must make the sacrifice to remember what they forgot.
Fragments lost from long ago,
Must be put back together before the truth may show.
Pieces of the essence of life,
Must come together to end future strife.
Whether in despair or Euphoria, these slivers must be found,
Unearthed beneath the debris that covers common ground.
A union of three points, made in blood,
Each line united for the greater good.
Father, Child, and Ghost we know,

But Time and Death cannot interrupt the flow,
Of souls combined, in shared pain,
And so this ends this brief refrain.
But one thing more is known above all,
If what is hidden is found, the mighty shall fall.

I stared at it blankly. *What the heck is that supposed to mean?* I'd never had either of my parents down as poets, but this was a lyrical work of complete frustration. I kept reading it, in the hopes that it would somehow make sense. There was a lot of talk of threes and triads, but what did that mean? And fragments? Fragments of what, exactly?

One thing was for sure, I wasn't supposed to do this on my own. It seemed to be suggesting I work in a trio of some kind, but with whom? It couldn't be Wade or my friends, because the spell seemed to be alluding to some blood bond. As far as I could tell, there were only three possible variations of this blood triangle—Me, Finch, and Isadora. Me, Finch, and Katherine. *No chance.* Or me, my mom, and my dad, which seemed even more unlikely than the second one. They were dead and gone. Perhaps they'd written this thinking they'd make it out alive, but surely... surely, they'd have put in a failsafe of some kind?

My brain is going to fall out of my head. This "hidden things" spell held the secret to the rest of the book, I was sure it did, but there were secrets upon secrets within that secret.

"Why don't you take a break?" I looked up to find Wade standing close by. I had no idea how long he'd been there watching me, but his brow was furrowed in concern. "You need to be careful with the Grimoire, Harley. It'll suck you right in if you're not careful."

I sighed. "Or suck my brain right out."

"Come on, why don't you put it to one side for a little while." He held out his hand to me, and I took it reluctantly. Feeling the weight of forty-eight hours with very minimal sleep, I dragged my feet as he led me over to one of the other chairs. I sank down, grateful to be away from the book and to take some of the weight off my mind. Even the natural pull of it was exhausting, though I hadn't realized it until I'd stepped away for a moment.

"It's driving me insane, Wade," I murmured, reaching for a water bottle and downing the contents. "I keep finding things, but then I can't read them.

And there are all these swimming images, but there's nothing I can do to figure them out. I thought it'd be easy. I thought I'd just have to look at it and find the hidden pages, and the spells would trip off my tongue, simple as you like." I put my forehead to the desk. "Why did they have to make it so friggin' hard!"

Wade smiled and knelt beside me, his hand on my thigh. "Listen, if anyone can read this damn thing, it's you. Chaos literally made you so you could do it. I know it feels impossible right now, but you'll crack it."

I bumped my head against the desk a couple times. "It feels like I'm getting nowhere, and we're not exactly drowning in time. I thought the 'hidden things' spell might work, but it's just some poem that makes zero sense. It's a total mindf—sorry, I promised myself I wouldn't swear."

He chuckled. "It's testing you."

"Well, I wish it wouldn't. I don't have time for some worthiness exam. If what everyone is saying is true, that I'm some custom-made Chaos magical, then it shouldn't be this difficult."

"I've seen you blast through every challenge, Harley. I've seen you kick and scream and lie and fight for what's right, sticking to your guns no matter what." Wade shook his head. "I've seen you literally break open a massive hole in the earth out of sheer determination to fight Katherine. I've seen you go into Echidna's box on your own to get what you wanted. You'll pull through this one, too, and when you do, we'll get Katherine."

He lifted his hand to my face and brushed away a bit of dust, before bringing my head down and kissing my forehead. I knew he loved me, right then, because I probably stank and my forehead was drenched in sweat, but he kissed me anyway. Soft, and sweet, and lingering.

"I should probably get back to it," I said, looking him in the eyes.

He nodded. "If you're sure."

"I have to keep at it until I get some answers."

"Okay then, but if you need another break, just say the word. I've got the Rag Team on speed-dial for anything you want or need."

I smiled. "Can they get me an idiot's guide to reading the most complicated Grimoire in the world?"

"Afraid not."

"I had to ask." I let him walk me back to my seat and watched him return to his guard position before settling into the open book again. Cracking my knuckles and turning my neck from side to side, I read the spell again, going over it line by line.

I'd just reached "Fragments lost from long ago," when the world began to spin, my vision filled with the inky marks of the spell. They pooled out across my eyeballs and turned everything black, my heart racing like crazy. I tried to blink the darkness away, but it made no difference. Not only that, but I could feel cold tendrils snaking through my body, tugging me down into an uncertain oblivion.

I woke with a start to find myself back in that could've-been nursery, staring into the eerie black eyes of Winnie-the-Pooh. I staggered back, almost running into the equally creepy figure of the mini-me. She was sitting on the fluffy rug, cross-legged, staring up at me with a smile. *So, my dad left me more than one message, huh?*

"You're trying too hard," alternative me said.

I glared at her. "Oh really? You try making any sense out of that book."

She giggled. "You should take it easy. It's a powerful Grimoire you're working with. You shouldn't rush the process." I'd forgotten how weird the disconnect was between the way mini-me looked and the way she sounded. Like someone had thrown an adult voice-box into the throat of a kid, except when she giggled.

"What are you talking about, not 'rushing' the process? Do you know how much time I've got to solve this? Not a lot, let me tell you!"

She laughed again. "Time may be running out, but time is a mortal construct. Your perceived lack of it won't make the Grimoire reveal its secrets any faster. Chaos is not absolute in its values. Sometimes, it shifts—it changes its mind. It flows differently."

"So you're telling me that Chaos is one big hippie?"

Mini-me's eyes grew stern. "You're not listening to me, Harley. Unless you learn to tune in to the current of Chaos, unless you learn to ride the wave of it, instead of drowning as the tide changes, you won't succeed. But, if you *can* learn to do that, and you stop stubbornly fighting it, you will have everything at your fingertips. If you can reach the true end of this Grimoire in one piece, with a complete understanding of all its secrets, Katherine won't stand a chance against you. That is the way it has been designed."

"You don't get it, do you? Time might be a mortal construct, but Katherine is about to finish the rituals, and she's going to do it soon. And when she does that, Chaos can kiss its ass goodbye. Then, it might wish it'd been a bit fairer with that particular mortal construct and me."

Mini-me grinned. "When did a challenge ever stop a Merlin? When did time running out ever make a Merlin give up? You should be less concerned about time and more concerned about Katherine trying to stop you reading from the Grimoire. She already knows you have it."

I shook my head. "She can't know. New York would never let it slip; they'd be too embarrassed."

"She knows, Harley. Trust me when I say that she does. The good news is, she can't touch it. She can't get too close. The Grimoire decides whom it allows near, but that may only protect you for so long."

I stared at the mini-me in horror. "Then that just means I've got even less time."

"Time, time, time—is that all you ever talk about? That is the least of your problems. You should be doing this alone. Katherine will kill anyone you love, just to break you down until you beg her to put you out of your misery. Attachments make you weak. Wade. Finch. Isadora. Jacob. All of them… they're all in danger now, because you made this choice to take the Grimoire. Katherine is terrified of it. It's why she used that curse on Hiram, and it's why she wanted all the Merlins dead. She knew what your mother and father were up to, and she wanted to put an end to it before it could be used against her."

"Then stop yapping and help me!" I snapped. Who was she to get all high and mighty? And if she'd been put here by my dad, who was *he* to get all high and mighty, when he could just freaking help me! It was hoop after hoop after hoop, and I was getting sick of jumping.

"I am," mini-me said bluntly. "If you figure out the 'hidden things' spell and use it to reveal the hidden pages, you will gain access to some truly powerful and dangerous magic. A great deal of it has previously been untested, but the strength of it remains. They are theories that our parents turned into spells, without trying them out first."

"Seems a bit reckless, even for them," I muttered.

"Not reckless—inspired. Chaos spoke to them. It told them what to write down, and they did its bidding."

My jaw dropped. "What?"

"I believe you heard me."

Chaos itself had directed my parents to write this magic? How was that even possible? I just stared at mini-me, completely speechless. However, it seemed like she was already pretty much in my head. She started talking again before I had the chance to ask questions.

"That is the very core of Katherine's fear—that Chaos somehow foresaw all of this happening and has taken measures to ensure she can be beaten to the final punch. She is terrified that Chaos did this, without breaking the ritual rules. And she is petrified of defeat."

I smiled, my mind flooding with fear and excitement and confusion. If all of this was true, then what sort of magic did Chaos get my parents to secretly write down? I couldn't wait to find out. Literally. We didn't have a second to waste.

FORTY-SIX

Jacob

I stepped into the infirmary with Isadora, the magical detector clasped to my chest, and froze. We'd come back to tell Krieger how perfectly the device had worked. Only, he wasn't here. Neither was Louella, which was worrying. All my enthusiasm disappeared in an instant as I saw the two figures who *were* here. Imogene Whitehall. And Suri.

Oh crap...

Suri looked scared and pale. She was shaking on her stool, like a wet dog. A cute one, though. Meanwhile, Imogene was standing close by with her arms folded across her chest.

"Would someone care to explain to me why there's a human in the coven? She doesn't seem to want to talk, but I'm assuming you know something about this. And could you explain yourself quickly, if you don't mind? As you know, I have a list as long as my arm to contend with." Imogene leveled her gaze at me. Yeah, she was pissed. Mega pissed.

"It was Katherine," I blurted out. "Katherine took Suri, and I went after her into one of the otherworlds. I saved her, and I brought her back here. She was too scared to go back into the human world, and Krieger didn't think a memory wipe would hold. And I like her, and she's not scared anymore, and she doesn't want to get her memory wiped, and—"

Suri leaned forward. "Don't blame Jacob, Imogene. I asked to stay. I wanted to be here, around him and the other magicals. Please, don't punish him!" She was tearing up now, her voice cracking as she spoke.

Isadora moved closer, trying to get between Suri and Imogene. "Imogene, perhaps we could go to your office to discuss this? Suri is clearly distressed, and Jacob was only doing what he thought was best. They're kids, they didn't mean any harm. And besides, he was going to come and talk to you about it, but I told him to wait because of everything else you've got going on."

"Don't punish Isadora, either!" Suri begged. "She was only helping us because I asked her to. I don't have anything to go home to. I just wanted to be around you all because everyone was so welcoming. I won't say a word about the covens, I promise."

I was about to add to what Suri was saying, when I noticed the magical detector flashing. The golden arrow was pointing right at Imogene, her hologram flashing up. Only, it didn't have her name and her image. Instead, it showed a very different face, and a *very* different name.

Name: Katherine Shipton

Affinity: Dark

Abilities: Telekinesis, Shapeshifting, Healing, Fire, Air, Water

"What is it, Jacob?" Isadora asked, looking over my shoulder. "Is the detector acting up?"

"I—I don't know." I shuddered at the sight of Katherine's face spinning around in vivid Technicolor. The more powerful the Chaos signature, the clearer the image. But this didn't make any sense. Had I broken it, somehow?

"It looks like the detector is picking up on Katherine, somewhere in the vicinity of the coven," Isadora said.

Imogene paled. "Is that so?"

As the device whirred back to life, I pointed the arrow at Imogene. Katherine's image flashed up again, with her name and abilities. Every Chaos signature was unique and recorded in the coven system. No fake identity could lie to Chaos... or this detector.

Realization sucker-punched me in the gut.

"Isadora, she's Katherine!" I yelled. "Get away from her! Suri, get away from her! Imogene is Katherine!"

"What?" Imogene stared at me with widened eyes. "That is nonsense. It's a glitch. A problem with the magical detector. If we speak with Dr. Krieger, I'm sure he will know of a way to fix it."

Isadora looked between me and Imogene in confusion.

"Seriously, Iz! Look at the detector! It's her. Don't believe a word she says!" I shouted. If Katherine realized the jig was up, she'd do everything she could to get out of here. And she'd take the evidence with her. "RUN!" I lifted my palms to forge a portal, but Imogene flicked her wrist, sending out a jolt of Telekinesis that had me flying back against the wall before I could create one.

"This is all a terrible misunderstanding." She stepped forward. Isadora put herself between that lying cow and Suri, urging Suri backward, away from Imogene.

"Yeah, I think it might be," she said coldly. "The detector doesn't lie, Katherine."

Imogene's face changed. "I suppose I couldn't keep up the ruse forever. This Shift was starting to bore me, running around, kissing everyone's ass all the time. It makes me sick to my stomach, to think of all the pandering I've done." She shuddered, a cold smile on her lips.

"You bitch!" Isadora lunged at Imogene, her palms up. Before she could land a blow with her fist or her Chaos—whichever came first—Isadora's eyes flew open in surprise. At first, I didn't understand what had happened. Isadora turned slowly, revealing Suri behind her. Her fingers were wrapped around something metal that glinted in the infirmary lights. A medical-grade scalpel, the blade embedded in Isadora's side. With a look of terror and panic on her face, Suri dragged the blade across Isadora's stomach.

"Suri?" I whispered the name. I was too shocked to say it louder.

"Suri?" Isadora echoed. She looked confused and hurt, staring down at the gash in her abdomen. Blood poured, thick and almost black, staining Isadora's shirt. She sank to her knees, clutching the wound. She looked back at me with shock. Her mouth moved slowly. But no sound came out.

"Iz, NO!" I howled. I rushed forward, wanting to stem the blood, wanting to do *something*. But Imogene stepped forward, standing in my way. *Not Imogene... Katherine.* I tried to get past her, but she shoved me back with a blast of Telekinesis. I crashed into the far wall, hitting my head with a crack.

"Thank you, Suri," she purred.

Shaking off the blurry haze, I leapt to my feet and paused. I stared right at Suri, who was looking back at me. Her hands were shaking on the blade. Her eyes flickered between me and Isadora. She looked pale, like she might throw up at any moment.

"What are you doing?" I spat, my eyes filling with tears. "Why did you do that?"

"I... I had to," she whimpered, pushing her hair out of her face. It left a streak of Isadora's blood across her cheek. Red and vivid, and sickening.

"Iz?" I gazed at her. She was frantically gripping her stomach, though the blood continued to spill out of her. "Iz, talk to me." I just wanted her to tell me she was going to be okay. Realizing I had to do something, I sprinted at Katherine again. With another flick of her wrist, she sent me right back against the wall. I wasn't going to stop. I would keep getting up until I got to Isadora. I wanted to build a portal to get us all out of here, but Katherine wasn't going to let that happen. Every time I lifted my hands, she just kept slamming me backward with her Telekinesis.

"It's like watching a hamster in a wheel." Katherine chuckled. "Tell me, how long are you going to keep this up? What could you possibly do to save her? No, really, I'm intrigued. What can a kid do that not even a skilled surgeon could?"

I shrugged off my last crash against the wall and stood my ground. "Kill you."

She roared with laughter. "Good one. You're funny."

I ran full-pelt at her. I wasn't ready to give up on Isadora. She'd come through a lot. She could pull through a wound like that. All I had to do was get her and portal her to Krieger, and he'd be able to help her. Speaking of which, I had no idea where the doctor was, but I could worry about that later.

Katherine stepped toward me, as if to meet the force of my sprint. I half expected another scalpel to appear and slice me up, or something worse. Instead, she just tapped me on the forehead. My body went rigid, just as it had back in Lethe. *NO! No, you can't do this to me!*

"Nerds really are annoying." She sneered. "You're like a newborn Bambi, stumbling about on your little twig legs. Tell me, how is it that geeks can work their way around a device, no problem, but ask them to speak to a girl?

Not a hope in hell. Not unless the girl wants something in return. Am I right, Suri? Who am I kidding? Of course I'm right." She flashed me a wink that made my blood boil.

Suri? I couldn't speak, but I wanted to. She just stared at me from across the workbench, shivering even though it wasn't cold. Her big eyes were even bigger. And they looked scared. Scared and sick, as the blood trickled down her hand. I wanted to know why she'd done this. And I wanted to know what part she had to play in this. She didn't exactly look like a willing sidekick.

My eyes drifted back toward Isadora, who was bleeding out onto the floor. She wasn't on her knees anymore. Instead, she was crumpled in a fetal position, her arms still wrapped around her stomach. I couldn't see her breathing. And her face was so pale it was almost blue.

No... please, no.

"Still, I suppose I underestimated you and Herr Krieger. Everyone always underestimates the Germans, don't they? I should've known he'd get the damn thing to work. Not that it'll do any of you any good. This baby is mine. And it will do *me* a lot of good." Katherine took the device right out of my hands and put it on the workbench, admiring her image. "Aren't I a stunner? Holograms are usually like passport photos—nobody looks good in them. But it looks like Chaos did me a favor on this one."

Katherine had been playing the long game, all this time. This was how she'd infiltrated everywhere, and everything, without anyone realizing. Her act as Imogene had given her access to every upper echelon. Nobody doubted Imogene. She was an angel amongst magicals. Only now, as it turned out, she'd been the devil all along.

FORTY-SEVEN

Jacob

I strained to speak, but Katherine's curse had me frozen. Suri kept looking at me, her hands stained with Isadora's blood. Shaking her head, she lifted the scalpel. Like she was seeing it properly for the first time. Covering her mouth with her non-bloodied hand, she sprinted to the sink and lurched over it, vomiting into the basin. She dumped the scalpel in alongside it while she heaved. A moment later, she ran the faucets. Washing away the puke first, she turned to her hands. Frantically, she washed the blood from her skin and from the weapon, before turning over her shoulder.

"It wasn't personal, Jacob," she said, her voice scratchy.

Really? It feels pretty personal. I narrowed my eyes at her to let her know exactly what I was thinking.

She turned away sharply. "I'm not happy about what I had to do, I didn't think I'd have to… Anyway, it was the only way. And I kind of still like you. You probably don't believe me, but I became quite fond of you. I've always liked nerds."

No, you're damn right. I don't believe a word coming out of your mouth. Tears trickled down my cheeks. I hoped they showed just how hurt I was. No, not hurt… destroyed. She'd stabbed Isadora. Her blood was still flowing. What else was I supposed to think about that? I *couldn't* think. Not with Isadora on the floor, in pain, facing her own death. All alone, with nobody helping her.

"Because they did your homework? Pretty girls like you can get a guy to do just about anything." Katherine smirked at me. "It's why she was the perfect honeytrap." It was still unsettling to see her as Imogene, now that I knew the truth, though she'd dropped the elegance a little bit. Her voice was rougher, her tone coarser. More Katherine-like.

Suri gripped the edge of the sink. "I hate that word. Honeytrap. It's used for old pervs whose bored wives want them caught in the act."

Katherine laughed. "She's feisty, right? I bet you just loved that about her. Smart, sassy, spunky, and cute as heck. Naima chose well."

"I'm not cute!" Suri fired back, shaking violently.

"Oh, but you are. I've never seen anyone stab someone so cutely in all my life. It was adorable, the way you crept up on her like a little imp." Katherine smiled. "Now, go on, why don't you tell him what you've done? I'm dying to see his little face as you break his heart. There's nothing more satisfying than watching a guy's heart break, right in front of your eyes. I saw it happen to your dad, Jacob, and I saw it happen to Harley's dad. And Alton. Man, I must have a thing for dads."

I wanted to wrench her head off her neck. I wanted to plunge my hand into her chest and rip out her heart. I wanted to pummel her until I smashed the Imogene right off her stupid face.

"Gross." Suri shot a nasty look at Katherine.

"I like your spirit, Suri, but you'd better watch that sass before I go after *your* dad," Katherine replied coolly. "The ones with the wandering eyes are always the easiest, and when I put on my little black party dress, those eyes *do* wander. Now, *tell him.*"

Suri dropped her gaze. "The whole abduction thing... it was just a ruse to get me in here."

You look at me when you're telling me why you've betrayed me. You tell me why to my face!

As if sensing my thoughts, she lifted her gaze again. "I needed to be close enough to you so I could... so I could mess with you while the device was being completed."

"Because..." Katherine prompted, smirking.

"Because Katherine knew you'd try and save me, and she knew you'd try and keep me here, especially if I asked. She needed to know when the device was ready so she could come in and take it." Her face twisted up in a sad grimace. Tears brimmed in her eyes.

Don't you dare cry. Don't you dare! She could have changed this anytime she'd wanted to. She could have told us what was going on, and we'd have protected her. Instead, she'd gone ahead with it all and signed Isadora's death warrant.

"Only, you and Isadora weren't supposed to come back so quickly," she whimpered. "And you definitely weren't supposed to come back with the device still on. So… we had to improvise."

"Which is hugely irritating, by the way," Katherine added. "I plan these things out so carefully, and then—*boom!*—all that work gone, in an instant. Lethe, for example. Isadora wasn't supposed to show up out of the blue and save the day, but there she was, exploding out of a portal. Although, her portal days are definitely behind her now." She smirked. "But, thanks to her, I lost valuable persuasion time. And here she is, having ruined my plans again, and now there's blood on the floor, which is going to take a lot more work to cover up. You know, for all the people I've killed, I'm still not a big fan of the stuff. Apparently, that's why surgeons make the best murderers—they don't even flinch. And they definitely don't make this much mess."

I'd forgotten how much you love the sound of your own voice.

"I was improvising," Suri protested shakily.

"Yes, and now I have to fix it for you." Katherine gestured at me.

Why? I tried to force the word out, but it pushed through my closed lips as a grunt. As if I was trying to cry for help from the inside of a locked box.

"I think he's trying to ask you why." Katherine laughed. "So, come on, hurry up and give him an answer. Put the poor boy out of his misery. He probably thinks it was something he did."

Suri nodded slowly. "I did it because Katherine promised me magic, once she ascends. I wanted to be more than just a human. Although, I wasn't expecting to have to do all of this to get it."

"Don't tell me you're having second thoughts." Katherine gave a look of mock horror.

"I didn't think I'd have to kill someone, Eris! I didn't want to. But she lunged at you and… I reacted." Suri looked genuinely freaked out, her bravado fading rapidly each time she looked at the pool of blood on the floor. I couldn't look, either.

"Aww, bless her, she was trying to protect me." Katherine sneered. "Oh, and if it makes you feel any better, you didn't kill anyone."

"What?" Suri gasped. It mirrored my own thoughts. *Isadora isn't dead?*

Katherine rolled her eyes. "Isadora is still alive. Can't you tell the difference? Honestly, you just can't get good minions these days. Not even human ones."

Suri looked relieved. "She's still alive?"

"Of course she is. Dead people don't tend to breathe, now, do they?"

"Then do something! Save her!" Suri begged. She was clearly having a change of heart. I'd seen the change in her shaking hands and her horrified face. But I knew that borderline admitting it was the biggest mistake Suri had made so far. Katherine hated weakness. And she hated turncoats even more.

Katherine rolled her eyes. "Do you see what I have to put up with?" She walked to the sink and took up the scalpel. "It's interesting, isn't it, how a blade like this can be used to kill, but it can also be used to save? In the hands of the right person, it can be more than a tool. It can be like poetry in bloody motion, cutting out bad organs to replace them with shiny new ones. In the hands of a layman, however, it can sputter someone's life out in an instant. No poetry. Just brutal execution. If used properly, of course. The wielder has to know where to strike."

"Katherine, you have to save Isadora," Suri pleaded. "She's useful, remember? She doesn't need to die. You can just take her away or something."

"I could, couldn't I?" Katherine smiled. "Thank you for the helpful suggestion."

Suri, you're in trouble! I struggled to get the words out. Instead, there were only panicked grunts. She'd wounded Isadora, but I wanted her to answer for that properly. I didn't want Katherine to take that chance. Suri looked at me in confusion, then back at Katherine, who had taken another step toward her. Realizing she was in danger, she backed away from the oncoming predator. With every step Suri took back, Katherine took one forward. Until there was nowhere left for Suri to go. Her back hit the wall with a gentle thud. Katherine kept coming.

"Now, place your bets. Do *I* know where the right place to strike is?" Katherine leered. *Suri, RUN!* The grunts kept coming out of my mouth, but Suri's focus was completely on Katherine.

"Eris, please." Suri put out her hands, as if that would be enough to stop what was going to happen. "I did what you wanted. I helped you. You've got the detector because of me."

"That's very presumptuous of you. Are you taking the credit for my schemes now?"

Suri shook her head. "No, no, of course not. I just meant, I'm useful to you. Please, show me mercy. I won't mess up again. I won't disagree with you again."

Katherine chuckled. "You *were* useful, Suri." I watched in horror as she lifted the scalpel and pushed through Suri's weak arms. As Suri tried to cover herself with her hands, Katherine jabbed the blade straight into Suri's heart. She looked so shocked it broke my heart. She just kept staring at Katherine, blinking slowly as the life left her eyes.

She staggered forward to grasp at Katherine, but she just sidestepped with a sigh. Suri slumped to the ground in a heap.

NO! Please, NO!

She'd wanted to change her mind. She'd wanted to save Isadora. And now... now she was dead.

"Humans are so deliciously expendable, aren't they? And they never see it coming." Katherine chuckled darkly. "She was a devious little minx, for sure, but not exactly magical material. And I really can't have anyone flaking on me at the last minute. I hate that so much. A word of wisdom to you, Jakey: true ambition requires a lack of moral compass."

"And you'd know all about that," Isadora rasped. My heart jolted as she dragged herself into a sitting position against the cabinet, smearing blood as she did. I'd been sure she was dead.

Katherine smiled. "You flatter me."

"Your ego shouldn't be so... big." Isadora grinned, even though she was clearly in pain. "Hands down, you've got to be number one on the list of crazy ex-girlfriends."

"Shut your mouth, before I shut it for you!" Katherine snapped.

"You're going to do that anyway," Isadora said. "But you had to go and be a real psychopath, didn't you? And all because he loved Hester instead of you. Can you blame my brother?"

Katherine glared at her. "You think this is for him? You think this is revenge?"

"Isn't it?"

"This has always been my plan. Mine and my great-grandfather's. Hiram has nothing to do with it—he was an obstacle, that's all."

Isadora snorted. "Doesn't matter what you say, though, does it? You'll go down in history as the psycho ex who wanted to take over the world, just to get back at the guy who didn't love her. People feel sorry for you, Katherine." Her lips had gone blue, but she was powering through.

Don't do this, Iz. If you do this, she'll kill you. Just like she'd killed Suri.

"You're trying to antagonize me, but it won't work." Katherine smiled.

Isadora laughed, though her face twisted in pain. "When Harley rewrites history, that's all anyone will remember. A jealous, heartbroken, pathetic woman who could never quite get what she wanted."

Please, Iz. Stop riling her up. Beg for your life if you have to! Show her how useful you are. Please...

Katherine knelt in front of Isadora. "Harley isn't going to get the chance."

"Now that I've got you down on my level, let me tell you." Isadora leaned closer. "That's where you're wrong. You've gotten cocky, and it's made you stupid. No matter what you do—even if you complete the final ritual—Harley's still going to end your miserable life, one way or another."

Katherine smirked. "Remind me, how many times has she failed?"

"Has she really failed, though?" Isadora held Katherine's gaze. "She managed to get your son on her side. I'd chalk that up as a win. He'd do anything for her. And, you know what, he's a good kid without you around."

"He's weak," Katherine hissed. "He'll only let her down, too." Finch was clearly a touchy subject for Katherine, even now. I had to give Isadora props for pushing all the right buttons—Finch, Hiram, Harley.

Isadora shrugged. "Maybe, or maybe he'll be the one to wring the life out of you with his bare hands. Wouldn't that be a divine sense of ironic justice?"

"Are you quite finished?" Katherine sighed.

"Not quite." Isadora's hands shot out and grabbed Katherine by the collar of Imogene's expensive suit. It took her by surprise. "You might think you're headed for the grand prize, but the Merlin kids aren't to be messed with. They'll finish you off, Katherine, and you won't see it coming. And it'll be wonderful!"

"I'm bored of you now." Katherine wrenched herself away and booted Isadora back against the cabinet.

Isadora grinned. "I'll see you in hell, then, shall I?"

"You'll be waiting a long time." She whirled around and brought the scalpel down into Isadora's heart, ending her the same way she'd ended Suri. I couldn't look away.

As Isadora went still, Katherine turned to me. She walked straight over, with Isadora's blood still dripping from her hands, and tapped me on the forehead. My body remained stiff, but my head instantly relaxed. With it, all my pain and grief erupted. Tears welled in my eyes as I stared at Isadora and Suri. Both of them gone. My heart felt like it might shatter. Evidently, she wanted to hear my suffering. She liked that.

"You monster," I whispered through gritted teeth. "You monster!" The tears fell, and I sank to the ground. My legs couldn't hold me up anymore. I just kept staring at Isadora. The woman who'd taught me so much about my abilities. The woman who'd been more of a mother to me than anyone I'd ever met. Her blood was still pooling across the floor.

And Suri... I'd never know how much was her own free will, and how much was Katherine's influence. She looked like she'd been wavering. Clearly, Katherine had gotten to her the same way she had everyone else. Playing on her pain, offering her the world. That didn't release her from the responsibility of what she'd done, but I wanted her to answer for it properly. I didn't want her to be dead over this. I wanted to see her sorry, instead of lifeless. But, right now, I just wanted to crawl up to Isadora and hold her and tell her *I* was sorry. But my limbs were like lead. I couldn't move out of sheer pain.

"You're probably wondering if it's your turn."

My head shook as I sobbed. She was right—I was terrified that this was my time, too. I didn't want to die. And Katherine had my life in her hands. I wanted to get out of here and warn everyone else. I wanted to make it so Isadora and Suri hadn't lost their lives in vain. Almost as much as I wanted to bring them back, somehow.

If I could just get to Alton, he could bring Isadora and Suri back.

Katherine leaned down and whispered in my ear. "You don't need to fear me. It gets so dull when people are scared of me all the time. Although, some have reason to be. Not you. You're valuable, Jacob, and I'd be happy to have you on my side. You never know, you might like me if you get to know me a little better."

"Go to hell!" I tried to bark, my voice cracking.

"I know you're sad now, but you'll see that they're better off. They wouldn't have fit into my world."

I glowered at her through blurry eyes. "Your world? You won't get to see it. You can't hold me here forever, and as soon as I'm free, I'm going to portal out of here and tell everyone what you've done. I'm going to tell them who you really are, so you can watch your dreams go up in smoke."

"*Sit corporis manent. May spiritum vestrum, non auferetur tibi. Sit habitas dimittere me ad vos,*" she whispered.

Nothing happened. "What did you do?" I was still frozen, but I didn't feel any different.

Katherine smirked. "Come on now, Jacob, did you really think I'd just let you pop out of here? I happen to be very good at forward-thinking, though you all keep expecting me to make silly mistakes. I suppose that's your biggest mistake, thinking I'll somehow slip up." She smiled. "Call it a failsafe, to keep you where I can see you."

"Why?" My hands balled into angry fists.

"Why Suri? Or why the nix on your portal power?" She chuckled. "Oh, that's right, you already know the Suri part. That little spell lends itself to what I call 'Controlled Portaling.' I'm planning to use it on all future Portal Openers in my service. That's if I decide to go to the trouble of making any new ones."

I shook my head. "You really are a psychopath."

"People are throwing that word around a little too casually for my liking. I prefer 'driven.'" She looked at me with that smug expression on her face. "Isadora obviously didn't make the cut for my Portal Opening needs, since most of her is on the floor, but you've still got potential. Once I'm a Child of Chaos, I'll make more to keep you company and to do all the menial stuff. Why do something yourself, when you can get others to do it for you, am I right? They'll be loyal, naturally. Unlike her."

I wanted to crumple into a ball and never get up. Everything I'd tried to do had been for nothing. I couldn't save Isadora. I couldn't save Suri. And I couldn't get the news out that Imogene was Katherine. She had me cornered, and I had nowhere to run. Katherine had planned everything, to the smallest detail. And now...

Imogene had seen Harley with the Grimoire, which meant Katherine had seen. Harley was in trouble, and she didn't even know. Everyone was in trouble. And they'd end up in the same state as Isadora if I didn't do something. But what could I do?

Katherine grabbed the magical detector off the workbench and turned it over in her hands. Smiling, she waved her hands over the device. A waterfall of crimson energy cascaded from her palms and enveloped the whole thing. And then, with a tug of her fist, the detector disappeared. It vanished into thin air, literally. But where did it go? Had she put it into some interdimensional hiding place? Or was it still there, floating, and I just couldn't see it?

Whatever she'd done, she had the detector now. And I knew why. There were two reasons I could think of. First, that she'd use it to find rare magicals to add to her collection. Second, that she'd use it as a quick route to get to the people who were the biggest threats to her reign.

"You won't be needing that anymore. Sorry to steal all your hard work—kind of feels like taking the credit for another kid's science project, but hey, that's character building. If it helps, I'm grateful that you did all the legwork," she said cheerfully. "Now, I've got you here, and I don't plan on letting you run off to flap your mouth at all your little friends. And you will serve my purpose in the future. You don't really have a choice, but I'm sure you'll come around to my way of thinking when all those friends of yours are dead."

I remembered my promise to Louella. The promise I'd made to Imogene. "Where is she?"

"Who?"

"Louella?"

Katherine laughed. "I sent her and the German away to research those influence pills. They won't find much in the Luis Paoletti archive, but I love a wild goose chase."

"So you *are* the one responsible for those pills?"

"Who else?" She gave a weird sort of ta-da movement. "I've got people all over the high and mighty echelons of the magical world. Those pills are spreading and vanishing faster than wildfire. Nobody can trace them. I arranged it that way. You should always cover your ass, Jacob—always."

I was speechless with grief and horror. She'd literally thought of everything.

"The magical world won't stand a chance when I ascend. I'm just *that* good." She cast me a sideways glance. "You have to admit, I did a good job with Imogene. I could walk into the president's office right now and hang her from the rafters, and nobody would suspect me. They'd all bow and scrape as I sent them after an attacker that didn't exist. I can do just about anything as Imogene 'Holier Than Thou' Whitehall. And you have no idea how much work I've put into her, having to keep up the ruse every time one of you ratbags came running with your petty problems. Ugh, the simpering. It makes me want to hurl just thinking about it. She's got a decent wardrobe, though."

"You're insane." I wanted to punch her so hard it'd make her head spin.

"The good thing about Imogene is I get to see and hear everything, but the bad thing is I can't act straightaway. If I'd arrived and that detector had suddenly gone missing, you'd all have gotten on your suspicious high horses. And if I hadn't let you finish it, I'd have been out of a detector."

"Where's the real Imogene?" I had to wonder how long Katherine had been pretending. When had she switched with the real one?

She snickered. "Kid, you've never even met the real Imogene. None of your band of do-gooders have. I've been playing that part for *years*, putting everything in painstaking place for so long, so I could move unseen, with nobody suspecting a damn thing. Now *that* is dedication. I'm pretty proud of it, to be frank. It takes a lot to pretend to be someone so disgustingly sweet. My teeth are starting to rot."

I couldn't wrap my head around it. "But Harley told me she read your emotions once. That couldn't have been you."

"A simple trick, Jakey. Easy when you know how."

"They'll figure you out," I hissed.

"No… no, I don't think they will. That's the beauty of the work I've put into Imogene—I ensured that she appeared infallible. A saint amongst ordinary folk. Everyone trusts her. I made it that way." She smiled and retrieved the scalpel. I watched in disgust as she dragged the blade along her forearm, and across her cheek. Blood trickled across her skin. I knew she had healing powers, but she could clearly pick and choose when she wanted to use them. She shuddered in sick delight and tossed the scalpel to the ground. "Now, Imogene still has work to do. But it requires patience. I'm good at that, as you may have guessed. That doesn't make it any less infuriating, though. I'd love to do a bit of swooping in and getting what I want right away, but I must wait."

I knew what she was getting at.

"You see, now Harley has that Grimoire." Her eyes darkened. "I'll be honest, I really didn't see that coming. A rarity for me. I'd call it refreshing if it wasn't so annoying. She's a devious little bitch, isn't she? And I definitely didn't think she could read from it and perform the spells. Although, I suppose it makes sense now. Summoning Erebus, for example—that had Hiram and Hester written all over it. I should've smelled that Merlin stench when we were in Tartarus."

"She's going to kill you, Katherine." Venom dripped from every word.

Katherine threw back her head and laughed. "I've got a heads-up on it now, which is handy. But I thought this whole Grimoire business was done with, since nobody could get at it or read it. Clearly, it's not, so more work for me. And I'm just *thrilled* about that."

"You've got no idea what you're dealing with."

"Oh, you're so very wrong, Jacob. It's sweet, really, to see how naïve you are. Knowledge is power. Now that I know what Harley can do, I can stop her before she does it. Although, I'm interested to see what's in there. Who wouldn't be? There might even be some tidbits I can use for myself. I just need to get past the Grimoire's defenses first; let it loosen up a little and unravel a bit, to the point where it stops blocking me out. A very annoying little addition by the Merlins. Nevertheless, once Harley unlocks its secrets, it'll be fair game. I'll just get her to do the hard work for me and read out a couple of those delicious spells on my behalf. The threat of a loved one dying if she doesn't can be a very potent persuader." She clapped her hands together. "So, Jakey, change of plans. You're going to be useful later, but I can't have you blabbing about this, not while I'm busy making Harley fail… again. And she's going to be so crushed. I can't wait." Before I could react, Katherine smacked me on the back of the head. *"Usque ad vos enim misit stare,"* she said. I winced, waiting for something to happen, but felt no discernible change in my body.

I wanted to lunge at her, but that same unseen force held me back. Still, she saw my head jerk forward and the snarl of my teeth.

She tutted. "Shame on you, Jacob. You should know better than to want to hit a woman. Now, you're going to sit here like a good little dog, where I can keep an eye on you. When the time is right, you'll come to me. You won't be able to stand the grief, and you'll beg me to take it away. And I will, Jacob… I will."

"Why not kill me now?" I rasped.

"Kill you?" She grinned. "Why would I want to do a thing like that when I can watch you crumble instead? I could've just taken you sooner, if I'd wanted to, but I needed you for the magical detector. How else am I supposed to find the abilities I need for my future domain? Chaos doesn't just come out of one's ass, Jake. It has to exist to be used. Don't they teach you anything about energy in school?"

"Screw you!"

She clutched her chest. "Ooh, you wounded me with that one, Jakey. Although, I'm more offended that you cut me off while I was monologuing. A villain should always get her soliloquies in where she can. Anyway, I need to make sure I have all the good stuff, when the time comes. Can't make more Portal Openers if I don't have a template to work from." She snapped her fingers suddenly, making me flinch. She chuckled. "What, did you think a bunny was going to appear? Nothing so fluffy, I'm afraid. I'm just dealing with surveillance. Wiping it, to be exact. Wouldn't want any pesky recordings of what happened here, now, would we?"

I didn't know if it was the click of her fingers or what, hitting me like a hypnotist, but I found myself falling to the ground. My mind turned blank. I was slowly fading out. Just as my eyelids slid closed, I saw Katherine launch into her best performance yet. She turned back into Imogene Whitehall a split second before Astrid walked in.

"Katherine was here!" Imogene gasped, her eyes wide in panic, clutching her side like she'd been injured. "Katherine was here! I tried to stop her... I tried to stop her, but she was too strong!"

Damn... Even I'd have believed her, if I didn't know the truth.

"Jacob? Jacob, are you okay?" Astrid sank down beside me, but I couldn't speak.

Everything faded away to a living nightmare. My friends were in trouble, and I couldn't do a single thing to help them. They were right in the middle of the lion's den, and they didn't even know.

FORTY-EIGHT

Harley

I stared at the mini-me with about a thousand questions racing in my
mind. I wanted to ask her what she knew about my parents and
Katherine and how all this Grimoire stuff had come about, but I didn't know
how much time I had. So I had to keep things simple and hope I got the
answers that I wanted from this irritating, vague little imp.

"What's in there? What's in the Grimoire that Katherine is so terrified
of?"

Mini-me smiled. "You'll have to find that out for yourself once you
understand everything within its cryptic pages."

"Cryptic is putting it lightly," I muttered.

"Your parents designed it to be complicated, for the sake of keeping out
unwanted eyes and to ensure that you were thoroughly tested. It is a trial, in
and of itself. It will prove whether you have the means necessary to take
Katherine on. It is not a simple case of power here; it's about opening one's
soul and mind and truly giving everything to fight her. It will take more than
strength to defeat Katherine, but you already knew that."

Was mini-me taking a swipe at me? I knew we'd failed a bunch of times,
but that reminder wasn't exactly useful right now. I was about to ask what
she meant by that, when the could've-been nursery disappeared. I was back

to reality, sitting in the same dusty chair with the Grimoire in front of me. Only, Wade and Finch were shaking me violently by the shoulders, and the room definitely wasn't in the same state I'd left it in when I'd been zapped into the weird dreamworld. The abandoned classroom was collapsing at the seams, fragments crumbling away in big, oily blocks that burst into a silvery dust. Cracks splintered across the floor, spreading wider into gaping crevasses that gave way to black oblivion. It was like the Bestiary incident all over again, only this seemed to be the speeding up of the coven's natural decay.

Is this because of me? I didn't have time to ask, as Wade grabbed me by the arm and yanked me toward the door, with Finch chasing after us.

"Wait! The Grimoire!" I darted back and snatched it off the desk, with the room falling apart around us. Sprinting like heck for the door, the three of us dove into the hallway beyond, just as the room came tumbling down. The door slammed shut behind us automatically. A bronze shimmer rippled up the doorway and turned it into a solid wall, as if the classroom had never actually been there. The Bestiary appeared to have compensated for the decayed room, cutting it right off and repairing the gap, now that it had fallen away of its own accord.

"That was way too close!" Finch rolled onto his back, panting heavily. "You picked a crappy time to go all cuckoo on us, Sis. It was like trying to wake the dead."

"You should've called for Alton," I replied, smiling. I knew I didn't have much to be glad about, but my last meeting with the creepy, alternative me had given me a few more answers to figuring the Grimoire out. Vague ones, for sure, but it was something, and until I'd gotten sucked into the Grimoire, I'd been clutching at straws. Plus, thanks to mini-me, I knew it was only a matter of time before I cracked the code in this book. After all, my parents would never have set me up to fail...

Finch had opened his mouth to make some other wisecrack, most likely, when footsteps made us turn. They were approaching fast, like someone was running. O'Halloran skidded around the corner, his face white.

"O'Halloran? What is it?" Wade jumped to his feet, with me and Finch following suit.

"You need to come to the infirmary." His voice was shaking uncontrollably, which was a terrifying thing to see in a man normally so composed. "Something's happened… something terrible."

FORTY-NINE

Harley

I sprinted into the infirmary, with Finch and Wade flanking me.

O'Halloran had gone to speak with the rest of the security magicals and hadn't told us what had happened; he'd just told us to get to the infirmary, ASAP. There hadn't been time for more explanation, but I could tell something awful had happened the moment we stepped into the room.

Blood pooled out from under Krieger's closed office door, and scarlet footsteps led all the way across the infirmary to one of the empty beds. Only, it wasn't empty. Imogene was sitting on top of it, propped up with pillows, blood streaming from a gash in her cheek and on her forearm, staining her cream suit crimson. She looked like she'd been crying. Krieger sat on the bed beside her, preparing a syringe with something clear inside. I watched as he slid the needle into her arm, administering whatever was inside the canister.

"Krieger?" I could barely force the word out.

"I'm just giving Imogene a mild sedative," Krieger replied solemnly. He'd been crying, too, which threw me completely. "She's been through a lot, and she needs to rest."

Louella and Astrid were sitting on the bed opposite, Astrid's arm around the younger girl, who was shaking like a leaf, her hands covering her face as a wrenching sob tore out of her throat.

What's going on here?

The rest of the Rag Team members were standing around the main section of the ward, grouped together in a frieze of despair. Garrett stood close to Astrid, his hand resting on the rail of the bed, his chin dropped to his chest. Tatyana was wrapped up in Dylan's arms, her face splotchy and her eyes rimmed with red. She buried her face in his chest when she saw me. Dylan had tears in his eyes, too, but he was clearly trying to keep up a ruse of strength for Tatyana. Santana had her head on Raffe's shoulder, her face contorted in an expression of intense pain, both of them holding each other as they wept. Alton was facing the wall with his arms folded across his chest, not wanting to show how much pain he was in, but I could feel it flowing off him in heartbreaking waves. I could feel it from all of them. Even Tobe, who stood guard in front of Krieger's office door, his golden eyes glittering, his feathers shaking as though he was struggling to hold it together.

"Can someone tell me what's going on?" My voice cracked, my gaze continually drawn to the blood spilling out from under the office door. There was so much of it, and there were two people missing—Isadora and Jacob. My stomach sank. *Where are they?* I spotted Jacob lying flat on the bed behind Astrid and Louella, but that left one person unaccounted for.

Krieger made to stand, but he sank back down onto the edge of Imogene's bed, his head sagging as his body began to shake. Nobody seemed to be able to speak, making my panic hit the roof. Every time they looked at me, it seemed to make things worse, rendering them all silent with a grief I didn't yet understand.

In the end, Tobe was the one who stepped forward, taking my hands in his massive paws. "Isadora is gone, Harley... Katherine was here, masquerading as Rita Bonnello. Imogene saw her and tried to stop her, but Katherine murdered your aunt in cold blood and appears to have done something to Jacob. From what Imogene has said, we believe it's because Jacob pointed the detector at Rita, revealing her to be Katherine. He is currently in a magical coma, and not even Dr. Krieger knows how to awaken him. He has tried, but he is weary in body and soul." He held my hands tighter, urging the warmth of his fur into my trembling fingers. "Suri is also dead. Katherine murdered her as well. And the magical detector has been taken. It will take a great deal of time to rebuild, if we wish to replicate it."

I couldn't breathe. I kept trying to get my lungs to work, but they'd turned to two blocks of ice in my chest. My heart felt like it had actually stopped, though everything seemed surreal and impossible. Was I in another one of my dad's visions? Was he just trying to show me what might happen if I didn't find the secrets of the Grimoire? I hoped so, with all my heart. Never in all my life had I wished for a nightmare to get me out of an equally horrifying reality.

Alton turned toward me. "We don't have the time to build another one, even if we wanted to, and we certainly can't extract Jacob's Chaos without his permission. It won't work unless given willingly, due to Chaos rules." He moved closer. "The upper echelons of the magical society are under the cult's influence, without a doubt—some of them, or more of them, or all of them. We're not sure as of yet. But it is enough that we can't go public with what has happened here, for the same reasons as before—mass panic and potential absconders to Katherine's side. There are new reasons now, however. These influenced individuals might come after us with a vengeance. Both matters will only make your job harder, Harley."

Why was he talking about the magical detector and the influenced authorities? Why was he focusing on that, when I'd just been told my aunt was dead and Jacob was out cold and Suri had been killed, too? Did I not get a moment to let this sink in, without having to think about the rest of the freaking world? It was borderline cruel, even if this was his warped way of dealing with what had happened. Not that I could say anything about it—my throat had sealed shut, my brain fogging over, my hands shaking as they gripped Tobe's comforting paws so hard my nails were digging into him.

"We've got no choice but to play up to our public roles, with Imogene, Remington, and the rest of our handful of trusted allies to help us defeat Katherine. And we must be careful what we discuss in front of O'Halloran and the rest of the security magicals. We know they're almost certainly under the cult's influence, so they can't be trusted. At least until we can figure out how to stop Katherine's influence." Alton was all business, and I hated him for it. Tobe had just delivered a knife to my heart, and now Alton was battering me with punch after punch after punch of bad news. I wanted to scream at him. I wanted to lunge at him and tell him to care, but I couldn't even move.

Tobe looked into my eyes, a tear falling onto his furry cheek. Without a word, he drew me into his arms and pulled me to his broad chest, his embrace a vain attempt to stop me from falling to pieces. I turned over my shoulder to look at Wade and Finch, but they were just as frozen as I was. This didn't seem real at all. *Please, please, please, let this be a nightmare. Please, let me wake up. Please!*

"And Katherine has taken the children that we saved before. She snatched them from the LA Coven while Imogene was away, unable to prevent it." Alton delivered the killer blow, and I fell apart. *Micah, Marjorie... I'm sorry, I'm so sorry. Isadora... I'm so sorry. Suri, Jacob...* I had no words. I just broke. I sagged in Tobe's arms and let him set me on the ground as a bestial scream shattered my throat. It wrenched out of me, making my ribs ache and my throat scrape, my whole body shaking violently as another and another followed, tears flowing down my cheeks in hot, angry, devastated streams.

Katherine had warned me. She'd freaking warned me. Through blurry eyes, I stared at the blood pooling under Krieger's door and knew it belonged to Isadora. Hunching over, a roar of pure, unadulterated grief thundering out of me, I let my fury and grief take over. I let it come, because what else could I do?

Isadora had been my last real link to my dad, the only person who knew him better than anyone, and she'd been everything to me. She'd been a friend, a mentor, an aunt, and someone who'd given me so much hope when I'd thought everything was lost. And now she was gone, she was really gone, and that made no sense to me at all.

"Bring them back," I rasped.

Alton shook his head. "I can't, Harley. I already tried to resurrect them when I arrived, but their bodies have been tampered with. I can't sense their spirits at all. They've been chased away—it can happen in tragic, shocking circumstances such as this. The spirit is almost catapulted from the body, unable to be retrieved."

"Bring them back... please, Alton, please bring them back."

"Harley... I can't. I did all I could, but they were already gone." His voice caught in his throat, his eyes filling with tears. Now I understood why he'd talked about everything else instead. Alton blamed himself for not being able to bring Isadora back, for being too late to do more. His guilt had disconnected him from his grief, because he had to be strong. My anger toward him faded away, replaced with a bittersweet gratitude that he'd tried.

I felt hands on my shoulders and whirled around to find Wade kneeling behind me. If he hugged me now, I'd disintegrate into a million fragments of Chaos and grief.

"I'm so sorry, Harley," he whispered as he put his arms around me. I thought about fighting him, for the sake of my sanity, but I couldn't. I sank back into his chest and let him hold me, feeling him take the weight of me as I leaned into him. His arms tightened around me, and I shattered completely. How many more would I have to lose before I ended Katherine? Would I have to lose Wade, too?

"She's gone, Wade," I murmured, finding some semblance of my voice. If Alton couldn't bring my aunt back, then she really was dead. "She's gone, and it's all my fault. Katherine warned me. She warned me, and I didn't listen, and now Isadora is dead."

"This isn't on you. My God, this isn't on you." Wade held me closer. "Don't even think that for a second."

"This is Katherine, not you," a familiar voice said. I blinked the tears from my eyes to find Finch kneeling in front of me. He put out a tentative hand and held mine. "This is her evil. She killed Isadora out of spite, and because she always wanted to. It's not your fault, and it never will be. She's a heartless, vicious, cruel bitch. You're good, and kind, and sweet, and she hates that, because she hates what she can't understand. She wants to break you, but you can't let her. You can't, Harley."

Louella sucked in a breath, distracting me from my overwhelming pain. She was leaning over Jacob, touching his face in a tender way. "It's coming back," she murmured.

"What is?" Astrid replied.

"My Telepath abilities." Louella put both her palms to Jacob's temples. "I can feel him in there. He's alive. I can't hear anything clear, but he's definitely in there!"

Nobody jumped for joy, but it was a fragile hope that there might be a way to wake him up. It felt like putting a bandage over someone who'd been blown in half. However, it seemed to stir Imogene from her sedated doziness. I realized she must have been the one to find Isadora and Suri dead in

Krieger's office, with Jacob out cold. The haunted look in her eyes was a tell-tale sign, and I knew it sounded sick and twisted, but I envied her for being the one to find them. If there'd been a sliver of life left in my aunt, I would have given everything to speak to her, one last time.

"What is he saying?" Imogene croaked. "Is he saying anything? Oh, please tell me he'll live through this."

Louella shook her head. "I can only feel him. There's nothing clear. I'm sorry."

"Don't be sorry. You're doing all you can." She reached her hand across the covers of her bed.

"Thank you, Imogene," Louella murmured. "I wish I could do more, but Kenneth broke my brain. I've been working on my Telepathy, but it's like I can't get control of it anymore."

"I will do all I can to help once I recover from this." Imogene sank back into the pillows, tears running down her face. She looked as broken as I felt.

"We all will." Santana pulled away from Raffe and crossed the infirmary toward me. "We're all going to be here for you, Harley, so you can bring this *pendeja* down. Whatever you need, whenever you need it. We'll be here for Jacob, too. He's one of us. And so are you."

I couldn't even look at her. If I did, I'd shatter all over again. I wanted her words to bring me strength, but I didn't have the capacity for that right now. My only thoughts were of Isadora and Suri and Jacob, and the terrible things that Katherine had done to them. She'd used Rita's form to get in here, and they wouldn't have suspected a thing until it was too late. Until the detector had revealed the truth. I guessed I shouldn't have been too surprised. She could drift in and out of places like a ghost, given her Shapeshifting ability, disappearing again without a trace.

"You're not alone in this, Harley." Tatyana joined Santana beside me. "We're not going to let you do this alone."

"If I could punch my way through that Grimoire for you, I would." Dylan smiled as he put his arm around Tatyana's waist.

"I know we can't read the Grimoire for you, but we'll do the rest—just tell us what you need from us, and we'll be on it. No matter what time, or how weird," Raffe added, letting Santana lean against him.

"Me and Smartie are at your beck and call." Astrid gazed at me with her empty eyes, but I could tell she was trying to show emotion, with what little spirit she had left.

Louella nodded. "And I'll ransack every library I have to, to find a way to bring Jacob back and to make things easier for you in any way I can."

"And I'll... I'll be here for you, Harley." Garrett looked awkward and sad, like he wasn't quite sure what to say.

Finch squeezed my hands. "None of us are going anywhere. See, look around you—you've got a tribe. And what does Katherine have? Nothing but a puffed-up ego. She has to force people to back her. You've got us because we want to be here. Because we're rooting for you, every step of the way."

"We love you, Harley," Wade murmured against my ear. "We love you, and we're with you until the end. We'll figure out another way to find Katherine, while you keep on studying that book and find those pages, just the way your mom and dad wanted you to. They're here, too, even if you can't see them."

Alton approached, looking tired. "I really am sorry I couldn't get here sooner, and that I couldn't do more." He paused. "I won't let it happen again. I'll be here for you."

"And you have me, Harley," Imogene rasped. "You've come too far to turn back now, though I know it will be hard to persevere, after all you've lost. I'm sorry, Harley. So very, very sorry that I couldn't stop Katherine."

Imogene's words lingered in my head as I looked at the people around me. I wouldn't let Katherine get her claws into any more of them. I would keep Isadora's memory alive. The worst thing I could do would be to let her death be in vain. I would use that grief and direct it all into uncovering the secrets of the Grimoire. My parents' message had been clear: if I could get through the Grimoire in its entirety, I'd have the power to stop Katherine for good. And I couldn't wait to watch her burn for everything she'd done and everything she'd taken from me.

I might have been broken, but I wasn't dead yet. As long as my heart was still beating, and I still had the Grimoire, I had hope. And that was more powerful than anything in this world.

Ready for more?

Dear Reader,

Thank you for reading *Harley Merlin and the Detector Fix!* See the details for Harley's next book, ***Harley Merlin and the Challenge of Chaos***, at the end of the book, after the following announcement:

On April 29th, 2019, I will be releasing my first ever contemporary romance novel, called ***A Love that Endures***. Keep turning the pages for a special sneak preview!

Chapter 1: David

EMBANKMENT, LONDON

From the shadows of a stone underpass, a man stepped out into a yellowing pool of old-fashioned lamplight, a round wooden clock clutched in both hands. Before him stretched a dark swathe of cardboard, dim torchlight, and hunched figures—a small colony of makeshift homes perched by the river. It was where the invisibles of Waterloo lived. The residents of the city that the brisk traders, excited tourists, and gallery-goers didn't want to see.

David's clothes were as worn-down as those of the rest of the homeless, his hair and thick beard just as unkempt, his name unknown to most. Few Londoners ever stopped to look at him. But if they had, they might have paused for a moment—taken aback by his unusually upright posture. By the stark handsomeness of his face, an angular, arrogant jawline and Roman nose, and his youth, at odds with the rest of his shabby appearance. By the long, elegant fingers, better suited to the keys of a piano than riffling through waste bins.

Eventually, though, the observer would have turned away. The most marked similarity between David and the rest of his kind was all too obvious: the same haunted and defeated look that shadowed his face.

A roll of thunder echoed overhead, and David kept moving. He approached the colony, his eyes fixed on the far corner, where a group of four was huddled in front of a low wall.

"Whoa. It's...Clock Man?" One of the group—a wiry, plastic-swaddled male—rose from where he'd been crouched, his pale, grime-streaked face stretching into a broad grin.

"Shut up," David muttered, heading for the short wall.

"Where did you find that?" the man asked as David passed. "And isn't it for me?" His ginger eyebrows rose in offense.

"Not tonight, Charles," David replied, ignoring the first question. "Didn't you hear the thunder?" He placed the large, old clock on the ground and leaned over the brick wall, where he had hidden the materials for his own shelter.

Charles groaned. "Don't care, mate. When it's this bloody cold, it'll be worth burning even if we only get five minutes from it."

"Don't be daft," a coarse female voice reprimanded. "That thing'll last us a few hours. We're not risking ruining it in the rain! Here, hand it to me, David, love—I'll keep it with me. My box is always dry."

"I'll bet it is..." Charles replied.

"Oh shut it."

David sighed as he turned back around, his arms loaded with materials. "Help yourself, then, Tina," he addressed the thirty-something-year-old woman. He nodded at the clock before proceeding toward the patch of empty ground next to Giles's shelter.

"Long day, eh?" the older man asked as David passed his tent.

David paused to look the ex-businessman in the eyes. "Yeah," he replied simply.

The lines of Giles' tired face deepened as he chuckled—then some more as he rasped out a heavy cough.

David managed to return a faint smile. "You'd better get inside, old man. You've still got that fleece blanket, right?"

Giles nodded slowly. "Yeah. Don't worry about me."

David nodded and continued on his way. He had to get set up before the rain started.

"Hey—wait, Tina!" Charles called out behind him. "Hand me that thing for a sec. It looks antique."

"Says the man who was about to burn it on sight," Tina snapped.

Letting the bickering of his neighbors fade into the background, David arranged his collection of plastics and cardboard and got to work on his pop-up home. He set up as quickly as he could in a race against the blackening sky, then pushed open the plastic flap leading to his shelter's dark, musty interior and crawled inside.

He fumbled in his pocket for his rusty light, switched it on, and began to organize himself for the night. He pushed his boots and coat to one end of the shelter while gathering some newspapers he had collected and smoothing them out over his coarse woolen blanket. They would provide extra warmth during the night, as well as help to absorb any water that seeped through the ceiling. He was almost done laying them out when rain began to batter the roof. The newspaper right in front of him crumpled, then began to stain under an onslaught of drops.

But the tent roof had held fast. This was not the rain. This water was spilling from his own eyes.

For they'd caught a glimpse of a bold line of text. A headline that drove the cold already inhabiting his limbs straight to his heart.

Barely breathing, he clutched the sheet of paper and shook it straight with one hand, his other illuminating the text with his light.

"Princess in London for Grand Engagement at Palace" the headline blared.

The princess in question was Princess Katerina De Courtes, touted by the media to be one of the most beautiful and eligible bachelorettes in the world. "A modern day Grace Kelly," no less.

And at the sight of her picture, every memory David had fought to forget over the past five years came crashing back into him, ripping the breath from his lungs and crushing his windpipe.

The shock. The pain. The grief. The anger. The disgrace.

The injustice.

Each one a searing bolt of emotion, hot-wired to his chest.

Flashes of scenes lit up his mind like an unstoppable movie, forcing him to relive every second of it all.

He tore his eyes away from the paper, gasping for breath.

"You okay, David?" the muffled voice of Giles called from his left.

David swallowed hard, realizing his tears had been accompanied by sounds. Too loud sounds. He quickly cleared his throat. "Fine," he grated out.

Pushing the newspaper and the light to one corner, he swiped roughly at his eyes with the back of his sleeve and slowly leaned back in the gloom.

What would he have told his friend, anyway, even if he had wanted to talk?

For who would have believed it...that an invisible like him could have ever held the heart of a princess?

Chapter 2: Katy

Five years earlier.

Katerina stared at the letter, her heart in her throat. Her eyes zoned in on the closing sentences.

"Think about it, Katy. Please. I know I've been an absolute jerk but I am so, SO sorry for everything, and I'm paying for it now with each day we're apart. I'm thinking about you all the time, remembering when you stayed with me here in our chalet. I'm missing you, gorgeous, so very much...From Russia with love, Alexei."

She scoffed in disgust, then finally tossed the letter aside and slid off the kitchen stool. The heady scent of fresh cupcakes filled the room, but her stomach was roiling.

How dare the selfish prick contact her again! How *dare* he. After all he'd done. After all the hell he'd put her through. She always knew the guy had a pair of balls large enough for two, but she had never thought that he would stoop to *this*.

"Has the rage-baking session been helping any?" her cousin Cassie murmured, eyeing Katy closely from where she was perched across the table, frosting cupcakes.

Katy stopped by the counter and leaned against it. Exhaling heavily, she glanced over at the short, blonde-haired girl.

"He's already trying to convince me to get back together with him," she replied, struggling to keep her voice even. "Wants me to meet him in Paris over the winter break. We've barely started sophomore year, for crying out loud! He must think I'm completely stupid—or an utter narcissist. Like a bunch of smarmy declarations that I'm the center of his universe could erase the fact that he wasted three *years* of my life."

Cassie smiled. "I'll take that as a no, then..."

Katy dropped her head into her hands, giving another sigh. Usually, rage-filled baking with Cassie was the ultimate stress reliever. When her dad was being completely unreasonable and wouldn't let her garden because the hobby was "beneath her"? They'd rage-baked coconut macaroons. When her mom snidely told her she ought to try starving herself once a week? They'd rage-baked a decadent chocolate cake slathered in ganache. When Alexei's letter had arrived, Katy had immediately proposed making red velvet cupcakes with cream cheese frosting.

But today, none of it was helping. Not even the bonus multicolored sprinkles Cassie had discovered in a drawer.

Alexei had been her first boyfriend, and they'd been together for over three years. They'd explored the world together. Shared times that, even now, she would struggle to forget. Bonded in ways she'd thought had made them unbreakable. She had never felt so swept up by anyone in her life, and she had been so sure that he felt the same about her too.

Then, last summer, she had caught him behind the sauna with his pants down, screwing the family housemaid.

Not a good look, man!

It had shaken her world to the core, given how unequivocally—and stupidly—she had trusted him. It was the reason she had moved to America and enrolled at Harvard in the first place: to escape his lying, cheating ways and move on with her life.

Yet here he was, less than six months later, trying to lure her right back into it all—with a cheesy letter no less—even when he *knew* she wanted nothing more than to forget his face.

The thought alone was enough to throw her into a dark, sugar-craving mood.

Katy grabbed the letter and tore it to shreds over the trash can, then strode toward Cassie and started helping her with the frosting.

"What I don't get is how he even knows you're *here*," Cassie remarked, licking at a smudge of cream cheese on her wrist. "Maybe he hacked your phone's location somehow."

Katy shook her head, more irritation bubbling to the surface. "I don't think so," she said. "I mean, I blocked his number, so he couldn't have done it through a phone or text conversation."

Not even the paparazzi—or any of the girls who shared Cassie and Katy's house—knew Katy's true identity as the famed Princess of Lorria. Although the country was the smallest in Europe, it was still influential, and Katy had to be cautious.

Katy groaned, realization suddenly dawning. "I'll bet you anything my parents had a hand in it."

Of course they would have. It should have been the first thing she thought of. They hadn't been pleased to find out he'd cheated on her, of course, but that hadn't stopped them from asking her to give him a second chance. They had always believed that Alexei, being from a powerful Russian family, would be an ideal match in marriage.

Ugh. The nerve of them, too.

"Hey, don't squish that cupcake so hard," Cassie chided. "You're making it crumble in two!"

Katy loosened her grip begrudgingly and proceeded to frost, while Cassie made her way over to the sink.

After washing her hands, she pulled up a stool and sat down, glancing at Katy tentatively.

"What?" Katy mumbled, catching her cousin's eye.

Cassie's gaze wandered across the table toward the envelope the letter had come in—along with a small box, which Katy had almost forgotten about with all the frantic baking.

"You planning to open that thing or what?" Cassie asked.

Katy stared at the box for a moment, narrowing her eyes as she considered the question. Then she blew out a sigh and dropped the cupcake, wiping her hands on her apron. "I guess," she grumbled, slinking around the table toward it.

As she picked it up and opened it, her frown turned into a grimace. She immediately regretted opening it at all.

Inside lay a bracelet encrusted with sapphires and diamonds, alongside another damned piece of paper with Alexei's handwriting on it. This one was much shorter, though no less vexatious.

"Diamonds for my diamond."

Hurt and anger washed over her. She'd told him repeatedly when they were dating that expensive jewelry meant nothing to her, and yet here he went again, trying to win her back with that very thing. He didn't know her at all. Or, more like, didn't care to know her.

"We'll give it to charity," Katy spat, dropping the bracelet back into its packaging and pushing the box away with such force it skidded across the table.

Cassie lunged forward and grabbed it before it could reach the edge, and Katy paused from her tirade as she noticed the expression on her cousin's face.

Cassie gazed down at the box longingly. "You should've just let Alexei keep buying you expensive gifts," she murmured. "After all's said and done, you were lucky to have a guy who cared about you enough to try and woo you."

Katy immediately sensed the note of bitterness in her cousin's voice, and her heart ached for Cassie. She realized then how insensitive she was probably being, dragging out this whole ex-boyfriend subject over an entire evening. After all, Cassie had been just as unlucky in the love department. Much more so, in fact. Katy knew her cousin's scars ran far deeper than her own.

She moved over to the smaller girl and took her by the shoulders, squeezing gently and giving her a reassuring smile. "Don't worry, Cass. You'll capture the attention of a good man someday. There are guys out there much better than the likes of Alexei…or that douchebag, Jason."

Cassie's hazel-brown eyes warmed at that, and though a tinge of bitterness still lingered there, the overriding emotion was hope, which was the effect Katy had been hoping to have.

A creak sounded, and the two girls whirled toward the kitchen door to see a curvy brunette stride in. It was Michelle, one of the few upperclassmen who shared their building.

"And what are we chatting about in here?" she asked. Her eyes widened as they passed over the rows of cupcakes. "Good grief, don't let me near those. I feel like I've gained two pounds just looking!" She moved over to the sink for a glass of water.

Cassie sighed. "We're talking about men."

Michelle turned back around to lean against the counter with her glass, arching a manicured eyebrow. "Oh. Men. Well…you'll both want to start flaunting your natural attributes more if you want to be attracting one of *those*." At this, she flashed Katy a wry grin.

The blood rose to Katy's cheeks. "I would rather not attract a guy for the wrong reasons," she replied, feeling suddenly flustered. She turned away from the older girl and reclaimed her seat around the table.

Michelle's grin widened. "Oh, I'm all for that, hon. But the way you dress, it's like you're actively trying to *repel* them." She took another sip from her water, then giggled, placing a hand in front of her mouth to stop it from spurting out.

"You in particular, Katy. I mean, girl, you know I say this with love, but that turtleneck thing the other night, at Jessica's party…seriously? You'll never earn your "Mrs." degree going around dressed like that. If that was the first time I'd met you, I'd say you were a huge prude!"

Ouch. That hurt Katy more than she would like to admit. Her gaze shot to her lap and she bit down hard on her lower lip to keep it still.

Michelle, an overly talkative girl in general (per Katy's tastes) and the oldest in the house, had a penchant for generously distributing unwanted advice. But she wasn't the malicious type and didn't really deserve a snappy response.

Still, it *hurt*.

Yes, that particular dress Katy had worn to Jessica's had been a rather poor choice, in hindsight. But old habits die hard. Katy had spent her entire childhood and adolescence wrapped in traditional Lorellian clothing—as was expected of a member of the royal family—and for females, that boiled down to ankle-length dresses with high necklines.

She and Cassie had gone on numerous shopping sprees to try to shake the conditioning since arriving in America, and while Cassie seemed to be embracing normal-people's fashion fairly well, Katy still found herself subconsciously gravitating toward the most modest pieces. It was a work in progress.

But as for being a "prude"...she swallowed hard at that.

Truth be told, a little voice at the back of her head had accused her of being just that, on more than one occasion, over the past few years. It went back to another long-held tradition of Lorellian royalty: no lovemaking until marriage.

Which was the whole reason Alexei had cheated on her.

"Anyway," Michelle went on, breezing past the girls as she headed back toward the door, "I wanted to let you know there's a party on tonight at the Wolf Club. All the girls in this house are invited." She turned once she reached the frame and winked at them. "I hear there are some real hotties in that house, so probably not one to miss. And if you want some wardrobe advice, just come to my room and I'll fix you up."

With that, she padded out of the kitchen, leaving the girls staring after her.

"Oh my God. We've got to go, Katy!" Cassie exclaimed after a split second. "Who knows who we'll meet at the Wolfs'? I've heard so much gossip about their parties. It'll be the perfect distraction!"

Katy's stomach churned. Meeting a houseful of horny drunk guys really wasn't what she had planned for the evening. She'd been thinking more pajamas, Netflix, and an hour-long bubble bath.

She looked between Cassie and the door...then shoved a whole cupcake into her mouth.

Chapter 3: David

Harvard would be the death of him.

David rubbed at the swollen lump on his middle finger, formed by too many hours of holding a ballpoint, and looked back down at the spread of books scattered across his desk. It was late, and his brain was starting to feel less like an organ and more like a sack of Jell-O packed between his ears, but he wasn't nearly prepared enough for his impending exams.

He blew out a slow breath and slouched back over his copy of *American Politics Through the Twentieth Century*, willing his eyes to cooperate. Just a couple more hours, and he'd allow himself to hit the pillow. Just a couple. More. Hours…

A pair of heavy hands clamped down on his shoulders. He jerked upright, but his chair tipped backwards, slamming him onto the floor with a painful thud. Before he could glimpse his attacker's face, a second set of hands pulled him upright and came around his head with a blindfold.

"What the—" He brought his hands up to bat it away, but then the hands grabbed his arms, pressed a knee sharply between his shoulder blades, and wrestled his wrists together behind his back. Another heavy grip joined his ankles; he felt the scrape of rope against his flesh there, too.

"Are you ready for your true test of character?" a familiar voice boomed down from above in a tone so stupidly deep David would have laughed were he not so pissed off.

"Get the hell off me, Seb!" David snapped, realizing his housemates were hog-tying him. He tried to lash out and break away from the rope-tiers, but although he was a large guy, two (or three?) against one was foul play, especially when they had the advantage of surprise.

"Woohoo, we got the Brit!" another familiar voice announced. David felt the rope tighten into a painful knot around his ankles.

"Not funny, Max," Seb shot back, finishing the bind around David's wrists.

"Hey, David knows I didn't mean it like—"

"Just shut the hell up. We gotta get him outta here."

"No." David grunted, writhing like a snake as the guys hoisted him into the air. But their grip held, and they lugged him across the dorm room. He heard his door clicking shut, and then the two boys were out in the hallway, breaking into a jog that jolted him uncomfortably from side to side.

"Guys," David said through gritted teeth. "I *seriously* do not have time for this."

"Everyone who joins the Wolf Club has time for this," Max snorted.

The ride grew suddenly bumpier as they descended a flight of stairs. Then there was the whine of a door, and chill evening air surrounded him. His skin prickled with alarm. Where were they going?

Metal doors creaked open, and a moment later, David landed on a hard, metallic surface. Then the doors slammed shut, and he was engulfed by silence. Or, almost silence. He could hear someone else's ragged breathing just opposite him, a couple feet away.

"Who's there?" he asked, trying to shift into a more comfortable, upright position.

"David? Is that you?"

David grimaced as he recognized the slight Iranian accent. They'd gotten Zeke, too.

"Unfortunately, yes," David muttered to his roommate. "Where did they find you?"

"In the middle of the parking lot!" Zeke exhaled in frustration. "I was trying to get a better signal calling home."

The engine roared to life beneath them, and the vehicle jolted forward, sending them both skidding toward the front of the trunk. It was all David could do to avoid smashing his head against the wall. Judging by Zeke's groan, he hadn't been so lucky.

"You blindfolded too?" David managed, shifting himself back upright.

"Yes!" Zeke said. "God. I am an ignoramus. What the hell was I thinking when I joined this club?"

David sighed. Zeke was right. They really only had themselves to blame. The Wolf Club was an unsanctioned social club, and even though hazing was supposed to be banned, everyone knew it still happened. They had both heard some absurd rumors regarding its rituals, but David had just assumed they were only that—rumors—especially because they'd made it so far without anything happening.

"Clearly, we're both a bit thick," he said, wincing as he tried, and failed, to loosen his binds. He guessed they must have been biding their time, perhaps to make it all the more unpredictable. "What happened to your phone, Zeke? Do you still have it?"

"No." He huffed. "They snatched it, right in the middle of a conversation with my grandmother! She's going to have a heart attack, I tell you. Bloody *morons*."

A smile twitched at David's lips in spite of everything. His influence on Zeke's vocabulary was quite noticeable already, and they'd only been roommates for a couple months. David secretly hoped Zeke would be calling guys blokes by the time they parted ways.

"Well, I'm sure they'll give the phone back." David cleared his throat. "After they've done...whatever it is they're going to do."

"And what do you think that is?" Zeke's voice wavered a touch. "Make us rob a grocery store? Drop us in a lake? Bury us underground?"

"Umm...I have no idea. But hopefully none of those," David replied.

At this point, he was down to hoping that the rumors were grossly exaggerated. That they'd just have to run a few laps around a field or something. Maybe butt naked. He wasn't exactly an *au naturel* kind of guy, but even that would be better than doing something illegal.

Uncomfortable silence fell between the two men while David's mind continued to mull over what could possibly lie in store for them. He shoved himself up against the wall separating them from the front compartment of the vehicle, hoping to catch snippets of conversation. But try as he might, either the guys were being quiet or the engine was simply too loud, because he was still clueless when the van pulled to an abrupt stop what felt like ten minutes later.

The engine quieted, and the back doors swung open. Hands grabbed David by the ankles and dragged him out. Then he was being carried again, the sound of twigs cracking and leaves crunching underfoot. They must be in some kind of forest.

"Oi—watch what your hands are gripping, man!" Zeke yelled from several feet behind.

"Sorry, bro," one of the boys replied, sniggering. "It's dark."

"The sooner your initiation is over, the sooner you'll be back to base." Seb's voice rose up from somewhere on David's left. "If you survive it, of course…"

"What do you say, boys? Give these cubs the chant?" Max added.

Jeers erupted from around David and quickly transformed into a bizarre chorus of words he couldn't understand. Apparently, the whole club had been waiting on them out here. The chant sounded like Latin, though the intonation was guttural and downright tribal—effectively turning the creepiness dial up a notch. David had to wonder if they were going to roast them on a spit or something.

The group began to slow, then came to a halt. David was lowered onto coarse grass. Hands on his wrists and ankles loosened the bindings and slipped them off. David immediately reached up to remove his blindfold.

As he pushed himself upright, his eyes struggled to adjust to the darkness. He could hear a chorus of hurried footfalls disappearing into the distance. The guys had scampered already, leaving him with nothing but pale shafts of moonlight to guide his way.

"Zeke?" David called tentatively, rising to unsteady feet. "You here?"

He heard stumbling to his right and turned to see the dazed silhouette of his five-foot-seven friend staggering into the small clearing.

"Yes," Zeke sniped, swiping at his brow.

David navigated a fallen tree trunk and moved closer. Whatever lay in store for them next—finding their way home, presumably—he figured it was wise to stay close to each other in the gloom.

He'd almost reached his friend's side when something hit the small of his back. He whirled to see a large white ball at his feet.

"Ow." Zeke jumped as an identical ball caught him in the shoulder, flying at him from the opposite direction.

As David stooped down to pick his up, he realized it was less of a ball and more of a bundle. There was a white shirt and a pair of white pants rolled up tightly together. He unraveled them and furrowed his brow. Both were at least a size too small.

"I'm not sure how much more nonsense I can take this evening," Zeke grumbled, unravelling his own bundle. "What are we supposed to—"

"Put them on." Max's voice suddenly crackled through the forest, amplified by some kind of loudspeaker. "And leave your old clothes in a pile on the ground. You'll have no more need for them tonight."

David spun in the direction of the command, disoriented. So, the others were still in the forest. *Where?* At least two of them couldn't be far away, to have aimed the clothes with such accuracy. As David squinted, trying to make out their forms lurking among the trees, Max added ominously, "I also suggest that you be quick. The gauntlet will begin in three minutes."

There was a sound of loud static, and his voice cut out.

"Gauntlet?" Zeke whispered, his voice suddenly tense. "What is that?"

"I don't know," David replied, wetting his lips. "But I think we should get these on."

Clutching the bundles, they separated, each moving behind a tree. David slipped off his trousers, still feeling paranoid about who was standing where, who might be watching. Tugging on the smaller pair over his boxers, he managed to get them up to his waist—though they looked ridiculous, the hems coming up several inches short around his ankles—then tore off his shirt and replaced it with the white one. Thankfully, it was made from slightly stretchy material, though he still felt like the Michelin Man.

Conscious that their allotted three minutes must nearly be up, he ducked out from behind the tree to reunite with Zeke, who had also changed—into clothes that were clearly several sizes too big.

David grimaced. Whoever had thrown the bundles had bollocksed it up.

Before he could suggest switching clothes, something whooshed past his ear and splattered against the tree beside him. He turned to see a dark splotch.

Then a barrage of tiny balls started shooting at them from all directions.

"Oh, no," Zeke said. "No, no, no—"

David launched forward, grabbing Zeke by the arm and pulling him into motion. Paintball wasn't something he knew much about by any stretch of the imagination, but he understood enough to know that people wore protective gear for a reason. He didn't feel like discovering what it felt like to get hit.

"Son of a—" Zeke staggered and swerved off course, coughing and wheezing. One quick glance over his shoulder told David he'd been caught in the ribs. The boy was on his knees, clutching at his sides.

David slipped an arm beneath Zeke's shoulder and hauled him back up. "We've got to keep moving." He poured on the speed, dragging Zeke across the undergrowth as the boy struggled to recover from the hit.

Then he heard the groan of stitching around his crotch and winced. *Maybe tonight was going to be* au naturel *after all.*

Or close to it.

He tried to do a better job of zigging and zagging through the forest, despite his physical constraints, to make them less easy targets as Zeke recovered. But they were outnumbered, and their stark white clothes didn't help.

Several rapid heartbeats later, pain exploded in his right shoulder as a paint-ball found its mark, though he didn't have time to pause and catch his bearings like Zeke had. He could hear footsteps approaching swiftly, and flickers of light started to break through the brush around them. Their attackers were gaining on them, and the closer they got, the harder the hits were going to land.

"Are you okay, David?" Zeke huffed. He was on his own two feet now, darting along a couple yards away and clutching at his pants to keep them up.

David merely grunted, not having the breath to respond, and ducked beneath a thick branch, just as another ball came whizzing past his head. He was hit by a second ball two seconds later, and then by a third. He cursed, realizing his shirt was half soaked already. He was going to be black and blue by the time this was over.

And he was going to have a flaming wedgie.

"How *long* is this going to go on for?!" Zeke cried out, wincing as another bullet caught him in the leg.

No response came back from the men behind them, other than a round of snickering.

Until we somehow get out of here, David thought.

He tried to stay focused on his breathing, rather than the discomfort radiating from his lower half (though he couldn't help but think bitterly now that the outfit switch had been intentional). He had no idea how much farther they'd have to run; so he had to remain steady. David squinted, trying to see what was up ahead, whether there was any end in sight, or at least any sign of the trees thinning.

Then his foot hit an unearthed root, and he almost tripped headfirst into a large pit. He caught his balance just in time and was about to continue darting ahead after Zeke when an idea struck him.

"Zeke, stop!" he hissed.

His friend halted and whirled around, and David immediately dropped into the hole, waving at Zeke to do the same. Zeke was quick to catch on and rushed back, leaping into the hole with David and hunkering down.

David pressed a finger to his lips, trying to quiet his own heavy breathing. Their attackers were still a dozen feet or so behind and might not have been able to catch where David and Zeke had suddenly vanished to. If they could just lure a couple, or even one, this way…

"Where did they go?" David heard one of the boys shout as the sound of crackling twigs grew closer.

There was a brief pause before Max replied, "Spread out a bit. They might've ducked behind a bush or something."

David pushed his back harder against the damp soil as two sets of footsteps grew closer to their hole. He exchanged a glance with Zeke in the gloom, and they both nodded wordlessly, forming a silent understanding.

They tucked their legs and feet as close as they could to their chests and waited until the footsteps reached the pit's edge.

They had the element of surprise, but only a split-second window to take advantage of it.

David nudged Zeke in the arm. They sprang up as one, reaching for the two visible pairs of ankles and yanking them forward. The men and their weapons tumbled to the ground. They yelped and scrambled to sit up, but, leaping out from the pit, David and Zeke lunged for their weapons and managed to snatch them up first, pointing them straight at their former attackers. Dressed in black protective gear and masks with goggles, they weren't exactly easy to identify, but it didn't matter at this point. David was ready to make them pay.

"Breathe a word, and we'll fire," David whispered tersely, tightening his grip around the gun. He cast a quick glance around to check if the others had noticed them go down, but it sounded like they were still trudging on through the woods, unaware of the boys' takeover. David and Zeke had the opening they needed.

Keeping the gun poised threateningly, David backed away around the hole, motioning for Zeke to follow, then broke into a run.

The second the guns were turned away, the boys behind them shouted for their cohorts. An explosion of paintballs came hurtling toward them, but now they could fire back. And fire they did.

Before long, the offending projectiles had reduced significantly as the other boys were forced to duck and dart for cover, allowing David and Zeke to better focus on gaining ground.

"Is it just me, or does it look like the trees are getting thinner?" Zeke panted after a long minute, gazing around wildly as he struggled to hike up his pants with one hand.

"I think you're right," David breathed back. It was becoming easier to run, with less low-hanging branches and fat trunks to dodge. He realized he could also hear the low zooming of vehicles. "Keep going," he said with renewed strength in his voice. "We're almost out."

A couple minutes and a few more rogue paintballs later, they were out of the trees and standing on the edge of a busy, brightly-lit road. David came to a halt, his chest heaving. He looked back into the forest, concerned the guys were going to follow them out and keep firing. But the trees behind them remained still. Their attackers seemed to have retreated.

"Guess we passed the test," David said, gingerly running a hand through his sticky hair. He glanced down at his trousers and was surprised to see they had survived the run. Mostly. Now he only hoped he hadn't permanently injured himself.

"And thank God for that." Zeke gasped, reaching his side and bending over, hands on his knees.

When he straightened, David finally got a proper look at his friend. Zeke's short, black beard had turned fluorescent pink, courtesy of a ball that had exploded on his upper chest, and the rest of his face had been splattered a sickly green. His bowl-cut hair had tinges of both colors and was sticking up at all angles.

"You look good," David said.

Zeke scoffed. "Oh. You are funny, David. For the record, I am sure I look just as good as you."

"Don't give me the details," David muttered, sliding a hand beneath his trousers to adjust his underwear.

Then the memory of his upcoming exam came slamming into him like a sledgehammer. He had to get home—now.

Looking left and right along the road, David realized he didn't have a clue where they were. He hadn't spent much time off-campus since he'd arrived in Cambridge, and he certainly didn't recognize this area.

He cast another glance over his shoulder at the forest, half tempted to venture back in to try to negotiate a ride with the boys if they hadn't buggered off already. But the risk of getting them all riled up and trigger-happy again didn't sit well, so he discarded the idea.

"We need to go that way," Zeke suddenly said.

David turned to face him, surprised at the confident tone. "How do you..." His voice trailed off as he followed Zeke's gaze to the other side of the road.

Signboard. Genius.

"Okay. Let's get moving."

David started striding forward but halted again after three steps. He looked down at Zeke, who had stalled alongside him, and they shared a glance.

"We should change first," David said.

Zeke nodded sullenly.

They moved back to the forest border and ducked behind a row of bushes, where they stripped to their underwear and exchanged clothes. As sodden and sticky as Zeke's were, they were infinitely more comfortable in size, and David emerged from the bushes a happier man.

Happier—but not exactly *happy*.

"Any guesses how long it'll take to walk?" David asked, his voice tight, as they resumed their brisk pace along the sidewalk.

Zeke let out a long breath, looking equally, if not more, stressed. "Um. I-I don't know." He dug a hand into his disheveled hair. "I think I have passed this area on a bus before, but walking…perhaps an hour."

David increased his pace. "I need to be back in half an hour—or less if we can manage it." He'd been pressed for time even before his housemates had snatched him. It killed him to think how much this was setting him back.

"You're not the only one who needs to get back," Zeke replied, his voice suddenly pitchy. "All this socializing is going to mess up my midterms. And if that happens, I swear, my parents will literally *disown* me." He cursed, his breath becoming sharp and uneven. "You have no idea how hard they worked to get me here. All the after-school tuition. Practically their life savings—" His voice choked up, and David turned to stare at his friend in surprise.

He'd known Zeke was under a lot of pressure. The guy had a large and highly ambitious family back home—and he often griped about the lofty expectations they had of him. David was used to his mood swings, too, and his habit of looking mournful and depressed almost every time he sat down to work.

But he'd never seen Zeke looking quite this…flustered. Judging from the glisten at the corners of his eyes and the slight tremor of his lower lip, he was close to *tears*.

David reached out to grip his shoulder. "Hey, man. It's okay. You'll pull through this. We both will."

Zeke bit down hard on his lip, his eyes fixing stoically ahead, and David tried to think of what more he could say—or even if he should say more, at this point.

David wasn't exactly in the same boat as Zeke, performance-wise. Because he had no family pressure. No family at all, actually…

He'd been adopted by a middle-aged British-Israeli couple when he was only a month old and raised by them until his late teens. His mother had passed away after a stroke when David was seventeen, and his father had died of lung cancer a couple of years later.

And he didn't know who his birth parents were, because it had been a closed adoption. The only thing his adoptive parents knew was that he'd been born in Boston, where they had been living at the time. They'd brought David back to London when he was two, and England had been his home for the rest of his childhood and adolescence.

That was one of the reasons David had worked so hard to get a scholarship at Harvard. He'd wanted to get back to America. He'd planned to take economics as his major, anyway, and he had never been one to settle for second best when a bit more effort would get him to first. His adoptive father had always encouraged him to push for greatness, and David had worked hard to make him proud. But more than that, now that the parents who'd raised him were gone, the UK no longer held enough for him.

Once he got a better handle on his classes, David wanted to try to pick up his birth parents' trail. He was profoundly grateful for the parents who'd raised him and the incredible start to life they'd given him, but now, he just… wanted to know who he was.

His mother had always said he was probably Jewish, but he knew it had been out of affection, that she didn't have any solid reason for assuming it. He'd been brought up in an ethnic Jewish background, but was that his culture? Who was David Rosen, actually?

He wanted to understand. He wanted to know whose ocean-blue eyes he had. Why his skin was a pale shade of olive. Why his hair was a dark mocha brown, and where he got his height from—his mother, his father, both? At six feet, he'd towered over Mr. and Mrs. Rosen. Did he share any personality traits with his birth parents? Or was every little part that made him *him* solely a product of his environment?

Why had his parents given him away? Had they ever wanted him, or had he been a burden from the start?

As uncomfortable as the answers might be, they were his story. His truth, which he'd been deprived of for the past twenty-one-years.

More than anything, he wanted to finally stop feeling secretly jealous of people like Zeke, who knew exactly where they came from and whose blood ran so clearly through their veins. And he wanted to fill the hole that had been growing steadily larger since he lost both his adoptive parents. They'd grounded him with a sense of belonging as a child, and while he'd never felt a true sense of identity, they'd loved him fiercely, and that had been enough.

But now they were gone, and he felt like a bit of a drifter, honestly. He'd lost that grounding, and he wanted...needed...to find it again. Without knowing his roots, the people who had brought him into this world, he struggled to make sense of his place in it. A part of him would always be restless, forever wondering. Never feeling quite *full*.

David rarely bothered to bring the subject up with anyone and kept things simple by sticking with the identity he'd inherited from his adoptive parents. It was hard to explain his conflicting feelings to someone who'd grown up surrounded by their birth family, knowing exactly who they were.

Well, that, and he worried he'd sound melodramatic...

"Maybe I'll just drop out," Zeke said after a long stretch of silence, his voice low and still a touch uneven. "It might be less painful for everyone than staying on and making a spectacle of myself..."

David cast a glance at his friend, whose hands had clenched into balls of tension, and sighed. "Come on, Zeke. You're not doing *that* badly. Like I said, we'll both bitch about the stress, but we'll get through it. Besides, you've got to stick around for Primal Scream. Nur would never forgive you if you don't."

Zeke slanted him a coy look. "Shut up. She doesn't like me."

David grinned at the rising flush in Zeke's cheeks, glad that *this* tactic seemed to be working. "How are you so sure of that?" he wondered aloud. "I saw her checking you out yesterday when we were in the lunch line."

Zeke groaned. "Oh, stop it. She was probably looking at somebody else."

David shrugged. "Alright. If you insist. I'm just saying, there's stuff to hang on for. Good times to come."

Zeke went quiet, once more turning his gaze to the road ahead, and after examining him for a couple more seconds, David took the opportunity to do the same. They'd made fairly good progress, and they were already back in familiar territory—which made it easier to travel faster.

Fifteen minutes of speed-walking later, and they were only a block away from home.

As they reached the end of their road, Zeke cleared his throat, and David looked over at him again. His expression wasn't quite as ashen as before, to David's relief, and when he caught David's eye, a smile slowly unfurled on his lips, brightening his round face.

"Anyway," he mumbled, "if I *do* stay, and I *do* pass, I won't be waiting for Primal Scream to show my naked ass. I'll go streaking around the dorm rooms—through the whole bloody house!"

David let out a surprised laugh. "Sounds brilliant. Just remind me to check into a hotel."

Zeke chuckled. "Now come on—my whole family is probably already on the phone to Interpol or something." He picked up his pace to a jog, and David smirked, glad the guy's spirits seemed to have cheered.

Though he couldn't fully shake how upset Zeke had seemed, and made a mental note to try to keep an eye on him.

For now, David ran to catch up, and the two boys sprinted the rest of the way, egged on by the promise of a warm shower.

When they reached their destination, however, David's face fell.

Music was blaring from within the house, florescent strobes pulsing through the windows, and the lawn was packed with people holding red Solo cups.

So much for a quiet night of recovery...

It was a struggle even to reach the front door, and when they did step through, it was even more crowded inside.

Unfortunately, it wasn't crowded enough to evade the notice of Max, who was hovering at the edge of the hallway, a pretty redheaded girl hanging from one arm.

"Yo!" he roared above the deafening beat. "The cubs made it back!"

He rushed over to David and Zeke, quickly joined by Sebastien and four other housemates whom David suspected had been involved in the kidnapping. They swarmed around, slapping the two boys on the back.

"Congratulations, man!" Max yelled into David's ear. "You survived the initiation."

"Yeah," David said dryly, trying to shrug Max off, as well as all the other hands that were pounding his bruised skin. Though he supposed he did feel a bit good about himself for surviving the ordeal. If he hadn't had so much on his plate, he might even have been in the mood to celebrate. But as it stood...

"Now I'd like to take a shower," he finished firmly.

"And get back to *studying*," Zeke said irritably, ducking out from beneath Sebastien.

"Whoa, what? *Studying?*" Seb gaped. "There's no way you're studying with this party goin' on!"

Without so much as a warning, Max dropped to his knees and rammed his shoulders into David's legs, throwing him off balance. He was caught by three sets of hands behind him, lifting him horizontally into the air. They rushed him across the hallway and barged into the heaving living room. Before David could fight his way back to the ground, he was hoisted onto a screaming crowd and surfing across a sea of hands.

David groaned. Now, he was going to have to escape *this* forest.

Ready to continue David and Katy's story? Visit www.bellaforrest.net for more information.

The next Harley Merlin book

Dear Reader,

Harley Merlin 8: *Harley Merlin and the Challenge of Chaos* releases on **May 13th, 2019**, and you might just get a peek inside the head of the Queen…(as we lead up to Book 9, which will provide resolution to this gripping conflict between Katherine and Harley!)

Visit: www.bellaforrest.net for details.

I can hardly wait to share this one with you!

Love,

Bella x

P.S. Sign up to my VIP email list and you'll be the first to know when my next book releases: **www.morebellaforrest.com**

(Your email will be kept 100% private and you can unsubscribe at any time.)

P.P.S. Feel free to come say hi on **Twitter** @ashadeofvampire; **Facebook** www.facebook.com/BellaForrestAuthor; or **Instagram** @ashade-ofvampire

Read more by Bella Forrest

HARLEY MERLIN

Harley Merlin and the Secret Coven (Book 1)

Harley Merlin and the Mystery Twins (Book 2)

Harley Merlin and the Stolen Magicals (Book 3)

Harley Merlin and the First Ritual (Book 4)

Harley Merlin and the Broken Spell (Book 5)

Harley Merlin and the Cult of Eris (Book 6)

Harley Merlin and the Detector Fix (Book 7)

Harley Merlin and the Challenge of Chaos (Book 8)

A LOVE THAT ENDURES

(New! Contemporary romance)

A Love that Endures

THE GENDER GAME

(Action-adventure/romance. Completed series.)

The Gender Game (Book 1)

The Gender Secret (Book 2)

The Gender Lie (Book 3)

The Gender War (Book 4)

The Gender Fall (Book 5)

The Gender Plan (Book 6)

The Gender End (Book 7)

THE GIRL WHO DARED TO THINK

(Action-adventure/romance. Completed series.)

The Girl Who Dared to Think (Book 1)

The Girl Who Dared to Stand (Book 2)

The Girl Who Dared to Descend (Book 3)

The Girl Who Dared to Rise (Book 4)

The Girl Who Dared to Lead (Book 5)

The Girl Who Dared to Endure (Book 6)

The Girl Who Dared to Fight (Book 7)

THE CHILD THIEF

(Action-adventure/romance.)

The Child Thief (Book 1)

Deep Shadows (Book 2)

Thin Lines (Book 3)

Little Lies (Book 4)

Ghost Towns (Book 5)

Zero Hour (Book 6)

HOTBLOODS

(Supernatural adventure/romance. Completed series.)

Hotbloods (Book 1)

Coldbloods (Book 2)

Renegades (Book 3)

Venturers (Book 4)

Traitors (Book 5)

Allies (Book 6)

Invaders (Book 7)

Stargazers (Book 8)

A SHADE OF VAMPIRE SERIES

(Supernatural romance/adventure)

Series 1: Derek & Sofia's story

A Shade of Vampire (Book 1)

A Shade of Blood (Book 2)

A Castle of Sand (Book 3)

A Shadow of Light (Book 4)

A Blaze of Sun (Book 5)

A Gate of Night (Book 6)

A Break of Day (Book 7)

Series 2: Rose & Caleb's story

A Shade of Novak (Book 8)

A Bond of Blood (Book 9)

A Spell of Time (Book 10)

A Chase of Prey (Book 11)

A Shade of Doubt (Book 12)

A Turn of Tides (Book 13)

A Dawn of Strength (Book 14)

A Fall of Secrets (Book 15)

An End of Night (Book 16)

Series 3: The Shade continues with a new hero...

A Wind of Change (Book 17)

A Trail of Echoes (Book 18)

A Soldier of Shadows (Book 19)

A Hero of Realms (Book 20)

A Vial of Life (Book 21)

A Fork of Paths (Book 22)

A Flight of Souls (Book 23)

A Bridge of Stars (Book 24)

Series 4: A Clan of Novaks

A Clan of Novaks (Book 25)

A World of New (Book 26)

A Web of Lies (Book 27)

A Touch of Truth (Book 28)

An Hour of Need (Book 29)

A Game of Risk (Book 30)

A Twist of Fates (Book 31)

A Day of Glory (Book 32)

Series 5: A Dawn of Guardians

A Dawn of Guardians (Book 33)

A Sword of Chance (Book 34)

A Race of Trials (Book 35)

A King of Shadow (Book 36)

An Empire of Stones (Book 37)

A Power of Old (Book 38)

A Rip of Realms (Book 39)

A Throne of Fire (Book 40)

A Tide of War (Book 41)

Series 6: A Gift of Three

A Gift of Three (Book 42)

A House of Mysteries (Book 43)

A Tangle of Hearts (Book 44)

A Meet of Tribes (Book 45)

A Ride of Peril (Book 46)

A Passage of Threats (Book 47)

A Tip of Balance (Book 48)

A Shield of Glass (Book 49)

A Clash of Storms (Book 50)

Series 7: A Call of Vampires

A Call of Vampires (Book 51)

A Valley of Darkness (Book 52)

A Hunt of Fiends (Book 53)

A Den of Tricks (Book 54)

A City of Lies (Book 55)

A League of Exiles (Book 56)

A Charge of Allies (Book 57)

A Snare of Vengeance (Book 58)

A Battle of Souls (Book 59)

Series 8: A Voyage of Founders

A Voyage of Founders (Book 60)

A Land of Perfects (Book 61)

A Citadel of Captives (Book 62)

A Jungle of Rogues (Book 63)

A Camp of Savages (Book 64)

A Plague of Deceit (Book 65)

An Edge of Malice (Book 66)

A Dome of Blood (Book 67)

A Purge of Nature (Book 68)

Season 9: A Birth of Fire

A Birth of Fire (Book 69)

A Breed of Elements (Book 70)

A Sacrifice of Flames (Book 71)

A Conspiracy of Realms (Book 72)

A Search for Death (Book 73)

A Piece of Scythe (Book 74)

A Blade of Thieron (Book 75)

For an updated list of Bella's books, please visit her website: www.bellaforrest.net

Join Bella's VIP email list and she'll send you an email reminder as soon as her next book is out. Tap here to sign up: www.morebellaforrest.com

CPSIA information can be obtained
at www.ICGtesting.com
Printed in the USA
LVHW010523261219
641679LV00004B/119